Kate Hardy always ⬚⬚⬚⬚⬚⬚⬚⬚⬚⬚⬚⬚⬚⬚⬚⬚⬚⬚⬚ ⬚⬚e went to school. She ⬚⬚⬚⬚⬚⬚⬚⬚⬚⬚⬚⬚⬚⬚⬚⬚⬚ ⬚⬚en she was twelve and decided this was what she wanted to do. When she isn't writing Kate enjoys reading, cinema, ballroom dancing and the gym. You can contact her via her website: www.katehardy.com

Fiona McArthur is an Australian midwife who lives in the country and loves to dream. Writing Medical Romance gives Fiona the scope to write about all the wonderful aspects of romance, adventure, medicine and the midwifery she feels so passionate about. When not writing, Fiona's either at home on the farm with her husband or off to meet new people, see new places and have wonderful adventures. Drop in and say hi at Fiona's website www.fionamcarthurauthor.com

Emily Forbes is an award winning medical romance author for Mills & Boon. She has written twenty-eight books and in 2013 won the Australian Romantic Book of the Year for her novel *Sydney Harbour Hospital: Bella's Wishlist*. Get in touch with Emily at emilyforbes@internode.on.net, via her website http://www.emily-forbesauthor.com/, her Author Page on Facebook or chat with Medical Romance authors at http://loveisthebestmedicine.wordpress.com/

THE MIDWIFE'S
PREGNANCY MIRACLE

KATE HARDY

For Scarlet, Susanne and Tina—really enjoyed working with you all on our quartet!

PROLOGUE

Hallowe'en

ALMOST AS IF someone had called his name, Oliver Darrington found himself turning round and looking at the doorway.

Ella O'Brien, one of the junior midwives from his department, was standing there. Despite the fact that she was wearing a mask that covered half her face—because tonight was the annual Hallowe'en Masquerade Ball, the glitziest fundraiser in the Royal Cheltenham Hospital's social calendar—he recognised her instantly.

Desire shimmered at the bottom of his spine and he dragged in a breath. He really needed to get a grip. Ella was his colleague. His friend. He'd been attracted to her since the very first moment she'd walked into Teddy's, the centre for birth and babies at the Royal Cheltenham Hospital. Her striking red hair, worn tied back in a scrunchie, had snagged his attention. Then he'd noticed her clear green eyes and the soft curve of her mouth. He'd wanted her immediately, though he'd held himself back. Since the fallout from dating Justine, Oliver didn't do serious relationships; plus he hadn't wanted to risk making things awkward on the ward between them, so he'd managed to keep things strictly professional between himself and Ella.

Though several times when they'd worked together, his hand had brushed against hers and it had felt as if he'd been galvanised. And sometimes he'd caught her eye and wondered, did she ever feel that same secret pull?

Though he'd dismissed it: Ella O'Brien was one of the most grounded and independent women he'd ever met. He knew she was dedicated to her career and she wasn't the type to let herself be distracted by a fling—which was all he could offer. Besides, over the last eighteen months, he'd discovered that he liked Ella: she was easy to work with, being both sharply intelligent and yet able to empathise with the mums on the unit. He didn't want to risk spoiling that.

But tonight...

Tonight was the first time he'd ever seen her all dressed up, and it threw him. At work, Ella wore uniform or scrubs, and on team nights out she'd always dressed casually in jeans and a T-shirt. Oliver couldn't quite square the no-nonsense midwife he was used to with the woman in the navy satin prom dress. Her dress had a sweetheart neckline and was drawn in sharply at the waist to highlight her curves before flaring out again to the knee, and she was wearing high heels which made her legs look incredibly long. She looked utterly gorgeous. Right at that moment, Oliver really wanted to pull her into his arms and kiss her until they were both dizzy.

'Stop being so shallow, Darrington,' he chided himself.

And then he realised that Ella had hesitated in the doorway; she was clearly scanning the room, trying to work out where the rest of the team was. For just a moment, she looked vulnerable—which was odd for someone who was always so confident and cheerful at work. And that look of uncertainty made him go straight to her rescue.

'Good evening, Ella. You look lovely,' he said as he joined her in the doorway.

Her fair Irish skin turned a delicate shade of pink. 'Thank you, Oliver. But you're not supposed to recognise me with a mask on, are you?'

'Your hair's a tiny bit of a giveaway.' That glorious dark red. And tonight it was in a sophisticated updo, with a few loose, soft curls framing her face, making him want to release the pins and let it fall like silk onto her shoulders... Oh, for pity's sake. Now was definitely not the time to start fantasising about her. He forced himself to concentrate. 'So how did you recognise me?' he asked.

'Your voice is pretty distinctive.'

As was hers, with that soft Irish accent. 'Fair cop,' he said easily. 'The rest of the team from Teddy's is over there.' He gestured in the direction of their table. 'Come and have a glass of champagne.'

Even though Oliver was a good six inches taller than she was, Ella noticed that he kept his stride short to match hers as they skirted round the edge of the dance floor. She was really grateful; the last thing she wanted to do was to make a fool of herself by walking too fast and tripping over in her unfamiliar high heels. Especially here, at such a glamorous do. Right now, she felt seriously out of her depth. She'd never really been much of a one for parties and balls; at university, she'd missed out on most of the big events, because she'd been concentrating so hard on her studies. It had been such a struggle to get to university in the first place, she hadn't wanted to jeopardise her career by partying when she should've been studying. And it was one of the reasons why she was still a virgin at the age of twenty-six: she'd concentrated on her studies rather than on serious relationships. Part of her felt ridiculously self-conscious about it; in this day and age, it was so old-fashioned to still be a virgin. Yet, at the same time, she felt that sex ought to mean something. She didn't want to have a one-night stand with someone just for the sake of it.

Last year, she'd been on duty so she hadn't been able to make it to the famous Royal Cheltenham Masquerade Ball; this year, she was off duty so she didn't have a good excuse to avoid it. But either Oliver hadn't noticed that she was a bit flustered, or he was too sensitive to make an issue of it. He simply chatted to her as they crossed the dance floor to join the rest of the team.

Ella, you look lovely.

Typical Oliver: charming and kind. It was one of the skills that made him popular to work with on the ward, because he always managed to make their mums-to-be feel more at ease and stop worrying. Just as he was clearly trying to put her at her ease now.

Ella had worked with the consultant for the last eighteen months; although she'd been instantly attracted to him, she'd been very careful not to act on that attraction. Although there had been moments when they'd accidentally touched at work and it had made her feel as if her heart was doing a backward flip, and sometimes she'd caught his eye in an unguarded moment and wondered if he felt that same pull, she hadn't acted on it because Oliver Darrington was way, way out of her league. According to the hospital grapevine, the string of women he dated all looked like models or had aristocratic connections; no way would he be interested in a junior midwife who came from a very ordinary family in County Kerry. So she'd kept things strictly professional between them at work, not even confessing to her best friend Annabelle how much she liked Oliver.

And she'd be strictly professional tonight, too.

Which was a real effort, given how gorgeous Oliver looked right now. He usually wore a suit to work, but she'd never seen him wearing evening dress before. He reminded her of Henry Cavill in his *The Man from U.N.C.L.E.* role: tall and handsome, debonair even, with his dark hair perfectly groomed. Except Oliver's eyes were grey rather than blue, and his mouth was even more beautiful than the actor's…

Get a grip, Ella O'Brien, she told herself, and she managed to smile and say the kind of things everyone expected to hear when she and Oliver joined the rest of the team.

The warmth of their welcome dispelled the remainder of her nerves, and she found herself chatting easily.

'Dance with me?' Oliver asked.

This was the stuff dreams were made of: waltzing around a posh ballroom with Oliver Darrington.

Except Ella couldn't dance. She'd always been horribly clumsy. The only thing that she was worse at than dancing was spelling, thanks to her dyslexia. And she'd spent so many years as a child believing that she was stupid and slow and hopeless at everything that she didn't trust herself not to make a mess of dancing with Oliver.

'I should warn you that I have two left feet,' she said. 'And I've never danced to this sort of music.' She gestured to the jazz trio on the stage. 'I've only ever watched *Strictly Come Dancing* on the telly. So on your head—or toes—be it, if you *really* want me to dance with you. But now's your chance to escape with all your toes unbruised.'

'You won't bruise my toes.' He smiled. 'Just follow my lead and it'll be fine.'

Was it really going to be that easy? Ella didn't share his confidence. At all.

But then Oliver led her onto the dance floor and they actually started dancing together.

It felt like floating on air. The way he guided her meant that she was moving in the right direction and her feet were always in the right place. And she'd never, ever experienced anything so magical. It was even better than she'd dreamed. Right at that second she felt like a fairy-tale princess in her swishy-skirted dress, dancing with the handsome prince. And she loved every moment of it. Being in his arms felt so right—as if this was where she'd always belonged. It made her feel warm and safe and cherished; yet, at the same time, there was the slow, sensual burn of attraction, dangerous and exciting.

Oliver danced with her for three songs in a row; and she was greedy enough to want to dance with him all night. Except this was the hospital's charity ball and Oliver was a consultant. He should be mixing, like the rest of the senior staff.

'Shouldn't you be—well—dancing with someone else?' Ella asked, feeling guilty both for being selfish and for wanting Oliver all to herself.

His eyes glittered behind his mask. 'No. It's up to me to decide who I dance with—and I want to dance with you.'

Her heart skipped a beat. Was Oliver telling her that he'd noticed her, the way she'd noticed him over the last few months? That for him, too, this had been building up for a long time? Or was she misreading him and hoping for too much?

'Though would you rather be dancing with someone else?' he asked.

'No, no—not at all.' Though she rather thought that Oliver might have spoiled her for dancing with anyone else, ever again. Not that she was going to admit that to him.

'Good.' He kept her in his arms, and Ella's pulse went up a notch as they moved round the dance floor.

* * *

Oliver knew he shouldn't be doing this. He'd meant to dance with Ella once, to be polite and friendly, then keep his distance.

The problem was, he really liked the feel of her in his arms. Which again was ridiculous, because Oliver didn't do proper relationships. Not since Justine. He was well aware that the hospital grapevine had labelled him a heartbreaker, a playboy who had an endless string of one-night stands. There was a grain of truth in the rumours, because he never got involved with anyone for the long term; but he really wasn't a heartbreaker and he was picky about who he slept with. He always made sure that every woman he dated knew the score right from the start: that it was just for fun, just for now and not for always. He definitely didn't leave a trail of broken hearts behind him, because that would be unkind and unfair.

But there was something about Ella that drew him. A simplicity of heart, maybe?

Which was precisely why he ought to make an excuse and get her to dance with someone else. Put some space between them until his common sense came back. He didn't want to mess up their working relationship. Even though right now he really, really wanted to dance her into a quiet corridor and kiss her until they were both dizzy.

Then he became aware that she was speaking and shook himself. 'Sorry, Ella. I was wool-gathering. What did you say?'

She gave him the sweetest, sweetest smile—one that made his heart feel as if it had just turned over. 'Nothing important.'

'I guess I ought to stop monopolising you and let you dance with someone else,' he said.

* * *

Which was Oliver being nice and taking the blame for her social mistakes, Ella thought. 'Yes,' she agreed. She kept the bright smile pinned on her face as they went back to join the rest of the team. Then Charlie Warren, one of the other doctors from Teddy's, asked her to dance. Although Charlie was usually quite reserved, his offer was genuine enough, so she accepted.

'So are you enjoying the ball, Ella, or here under sufferance like me?' Charlie asked.

'I'm enjoying myself.' In fact, much more than she'd expected to. Though she had a nasty feeling that Oliver was the main reason for that. 'I'm sorry you're not.'

'I never do, really,' Charlie began, then grimaced when she trod on his toes.

'Sorry,' she said instantly. 'I'm afraid I have two left feet.'

'I thought all Irish people were supposed to be natural dancers? I guess you have *Riverdance* to blame for that.' It was an attempt at humour, as he was obviously trying to make polite conversation, but for as long as Ella had known Charlie, he'd always been distant with everyone at work. Quite the lone wolf.

'Sadly, that gene bypassed me,' she said. 'I'm more Flatfeet than Flatley.'

'I think my toes have already worked that one out for themselves but, even though we're no Fred Astaire and Ginger Rogers, you look lovely tonight, Ella.'

'Thank you,' she said smiling. 'I think you look more like James Bond than Fred Astaire anyway.'

'You're very sweet, Ella.' He gave her a shy half-smile. 'And you've made an otherwise dull evening much nicer.'

Ella found herself going through a similar routine

with the colleagues she danced with from the Emergency Department.

'You know, we're going to have to set up a special broken toe department in the unit, just for the men you've danced with tonight,' Mike Wetherby teased.

'So I'd be better off sticking to delivering babies than dancing, hmm?' she teased back, knowing that he meant no harm by the comment.

'You can dance with me any time you like, Ella O'Brien,' Mike said. 'As long as I have fair warning so I can put on my steel-toe-capped boots first.'

She just laughed. 'In steel-toe-capped boots, you'd be clomping around the dance floor as badly as me.'

'Then we'd be the perfect match.'

'Yeah, yeah.'

And then Oliver rested his hand on Ella's shoulder. 'The next dance is mine, I believe.'

The warmth of his fingers against her bare skin sent a shaft of pure desire through her. She reminded herself crossly that this was a charity ball and Oliver had danced with at least half a dozen other women. He'd treated them in just the same way that he'd treated her, with courtesy and gallantry, so she was kidding herself and setting herself up for disappointment if she thought that his behaviour towards her tonight was anything more than that of a colleague. And she wasn't going to embarrass herself by throwing herself at him and being turned down.

Was it wishful thinking or did the lights actually dim slightly as they moved onto the dance floor?

Oliver drew her closer, and she shivered.

'Cold?' he asked.

'No, I'm fine,' she said, not wanting him to guess that her reaction had been something so very different.

He pulled back slightly and looked her in the eye. For

a second, Ella could've sworn that the same deep, intense yearning she felt was reflected in his eyes. But that had to be imagination or wishful thinking. Of course he didn't feel like that about her. Why would he?

She stared at his mouth, wondering for a crazy second what it would be like if Oliver kissed her. It must be that second glass of champagne affecting her, she thought, vowing to stick to water for the rest of the evening.

But dancing with Oliver was headier than any amount of champagne. And she noticed that, although she'd been clumsy with her other partners, with Oliver she didn't seem to put a foot wrong. Dancing with him made her feel as if someone had put a spell on her—but a nice spell, one that made her feel good.

And when he drew her closer still, she rested her head on his shoulder and closed her eyes. Just for these few moments, she could believe that she and Oliver were together. Just the two of them, dancing cheek to cheek, with nobody else in the room. Just them and the night and the music…

At the end of the evening, Oliver said casually, 'I think you're on my way home, Ella. Can I give you a lift?'

The sensible thing to do would be to smile politely and say thanks, but she'd be fine—though she hadn't remembered to book a taxi, and there was bound to be an enormous queue so she'd have to wait for ages in the cold. It was a twenty-minute drive from here to her flat. She could manage that without making a fool of herself and throwing herself at Oliver, couldn't she?

'Thank you. That's very kind of you,' she said. 'It'll save me having to wait ages for a taxi.'

'Pleasure,' he said. 'Shall we go?'

She walked with him to his car. It was icy outside, and the thin wrap she'd brought did nothing to protect her from the cold.

'Here,' he said, shrugging out of his jacket and sliding it across her shoulders.

'But you'll be cold,' she protested.

'Not as cold as you,' he said.

Typical Oliver: gallant and charming. But she appreciated the warmth of his jacket, and tried not to think about the fact that it had been warmed by Oliver's body heat.

Just as she'd half expected, his car was sleek and low-slung. When he opened the door for her, Ella nearly tripped getting in and was cross with herself for being so stupid and clumsy.

'Ella, relax. There aren't any strings. This is just a lift home,' he said.

More was the pity, she thought, and was even crosser with herself for being such an idiot.

'Sorry. Too much champagne,' she fibbed.

When she fumbled with the seat belt, he sorted it out for her. Her skin tingled where his fingers brushed against her.

Stop it, she told herself. He doesn't think of you in *that* way. And you're too busy at work to get involved with anyone—especially a colleague who apparently never dates anyone more than twice. Keep it professional.

'What's your postcode?' he asked.

She told him and he put it into the sat nav. Then he switched on the stereo and soft classical music flooded the car. 'Do you mind this?' he asked. 'I can change it, if you like.'

'No, it's lovely. I like piano music,' she said. 'We have a piano at home.'

'You play?'

'No, Mam does. I meant home in Ireland, not here,' she said. 'Mam's a music teacher. She plays the piano at school in assembly and in the Christmas Nativity plays for the little ones.'

'Did you ever think about being a teacher?' he asked.

'No.' Everyone had thought that little Ella O'Brien was very sweet but not very bright, and would never get through her exams. Until the new biology teacher had started at her school when Ella was fifteen, worked out that Ella was dyslexic rather than stupid, and batted her corner for her. 'I always wanted to be a midwife, like my Aunty Bridget.' Everyone had thought that Ella was being a dreamer when she'd said what she wanted to do, but she'd put in the effort and worked so hard that she'd managed to get through her exams with good enough grades to get a place in London to train as a midwife. 'It's so special, sharing those first few minutes of a new life coming into the world.' She paused. 'What about you? Did you always want to be a doctor?'

'Yes.' Though there was something slightly shuttered in Oliver's voice, and Ella wondered if he'd had the same kind of struggle she'd had about her choice of career. Although her parents supported her now, they'd worried throughout the whole of her degree and her training as a midwife, even though her tutors knew about her dyslexia and were really supportive. Her parents had told her all the time that she ought to give it up and come home to Ireland—particularly when she'd had her operation for a ruptured ovarian cyst and fallen behind in her studies. Thankfully Ella had been stubborn about it, and her parents had eventually come to terms with the fact that she was staying in England. She tried to make it home for a visit every couple of months, as well as video-calling them at least once a week through her laptop. And nowadays she knew her parents were more proud of her than worried about her.

Oliver didn't elaborate on his comment, and she felt too awkward to ask anything more. Particularly as she was so physically aware of him sitting next to her.

Well, she was just going to have to be sensible about this. But, when he pulled up on the road outside her flat, her mouth clearly wasn't with the programme, because she found herself saying, 'Thank you for the lift. Would you like to come in for a coffee?'

This was where Oliver knew that he was supposed to say no. Where he was supposed to wish Ella goodnight, wait until she was safely indoors and then drive away. But he discovered that his mouth wasn't working in partnership with his common sense, because he found himself saying yes and following her into her flat.

Her tiny flat was on the ground floor in one of the pretty Regency squares in Cheltenham.

'Come and sit down.' She ushered him into the living room. 'Black, one sugar, isn't it?'

'Yes. Thanks.'

'I'll be two seconds,' she said, and disappeared off to what he presumed was her kitchen.

He glanced around the room. There was enough space for a small sofa, a bookcase full of midwifery texts, and a very compact desk where there were more textbooks and a laptop. It looked as if Ella spent a lot of time outside work studying.

There was a framed photograph on the mantelpiece of her at graduation with two people who looked enough like her to be her parents, plus several others of a large group of people in a garden. Clearly she was at some family party or other, and everyone seemed to radiate love and happiness. Oliver felt a momentary pang. His own family wasn't like that, though perhaps part of that was his own fault for distancing himself from them. He could hardly be close to his brother while avoiding his parents, though; and when he saw his parents he was always on the receiving end of their disappointment.

Sometimes he thought that most parents would've been proud of their son for sticking through fourteen years of training and qualifying as an obstetrician. But the Darringtons had had rather different expectations for their son...

He really ought to make his excuses and leave. Ella was the last person he should get involved with. Apart from the fact that she was obviously much closer to her family than he was to his, she was his colleague and he didn't want things to get messy at work. Nothing could happen between them.

But when he went into her small kitchen to tell her that he needed to go, she turned round and smiled at him and all his common sense fled. Her beautiful green eyes held him spellbound. And right at that moment he felt the strongest connection to her. Her mouth looked warm and sweet and soft, and he really wanted to kiss her. When his gaze flicked up to her eyes again, he realised that she was doing exactly the same: looking at his mouth. So was she, too, wondering...?

Instead of saying goodnight, he stepped forward and brushed his mouth very lightly against hers—just as he'd wanted to do all evening. Not just all evening, if he was honest with himself: he'd wanted to kiss her for weeks and weeks and weeks.

Every nerve-end in his lips tingled, so he couldn't stop himself doing it again.

And this time she kissed him back.

'Ella,' he said when he broke the kiss. 'I've wanted to do that for months.'

'Me, too,' she whispered.

So she'd noticed him in the same way?

His common sense made a last-ditch bid to extract him. 'We shouldn't do this.'

'I know—we work together and we ought to be sensible,' she agreed.

'Exactly,' he said, relieved that he hadn't quite ruined their working relationship by giving in to that mad urge to kiss her. They could still salvage a professional friendship after tonight.

But then she rested her hand against his cheek. Her touch was light and gentle, and he found himself twisting his head to kiss her palm.

Her beautiful green eyes darkened.

Then the kissing started all over again, this time in earnest, and Oliver forgot all his good intentions. He loosened her hair, the way he'd wanted to do all evening, and let it tumble down to her shoulders.

Her eyes widened. 'Oliver!'

'I know.' He kissed her again. 'But I can't help this—I really want you, Ella. I have done since the first time I met you.'

'Me, too,' she said.

His whole body tingled with desire. She wanted him as much as he wanted her?

'So what are we going to do about this?' she asked.

'Right now, I can't think straight,' he admitted. 'I just want to make love with you.'

For a moment, he thought she was going to back away. But then she inclined her head very slightly and took his hand to lead him to her bedroom.

'Are you sure about this?' he asked softly as she switched the bedside light on.

'I'm sure,' she said, her voice low and husky.

He kissed her, and it made his head spin. Hardly able to believe this was happening, he slid the zip down at the back of her dress. Seconds later, he stroked the material away from her shoulders and it fell to the floor.

She undid his bow tie, then unbuttoned his shirt with shaking fingers, smoothed the material off his shoulders and let it fall to the floor next to her dress.

He unsnapped her bra. 'You're beautiful. All curves.'

She gave him a shy smile. 'You're beautiful, too. All muscles.'

And suddenly the faint awkwardness was gone—there was just Ella, kissing her, and feeling the warmth of her skin against his.

Oliver wasn't sure which of them finished undressing whom, but the next thing he knew he was kneeling between her thighs and her hair was spread over the pillows, just as he'd imagined it.

And then he stopped. 'Protection. I don't have a condom.'

'You don't need one,' she said, flushing slightly.

So she was on the Pill? Part of him remembered Justine's treachery and the repercussions. But he knew that Ella wasn't like Justine. The woman he'd got to know over the last eighteen months was open and honest. She wasn't going to cheat on him with someone else, get pregnant, and then try to make him believe that the baby was his. He knew that without having to ask.

'Oliver?' She looked worried, now. 'I don't sleep around. I'm not…' The colour in her cheeks deepened. 'You know.'

'I know.' He stroked her face. 'And the rumours about me aren't true. I don't have sex with every single woman I date.' He shouldn't be having sex with Ella, either; but right now her skin was warm against his, this had been a long time coming, and he wanted to do this more than he'd wanted to do anything in years.

'I know,' she said, and kissed him.

That kiss made him relax with her, and he slowed the pace down, wanting to explore her. He kissed and stroked his way down her body, starting with a dip beneath her collarbones and paying attention to exactly what made her sigh with pleasure, from the curve of her inner elbow to the soft undersides of her breasts, then starting with the hollows of her anklebones and feathering his way upwards until she was making tiny, involuntary noises and clutching at his shoulders.

'Now?' he asked softly.

'Now.' Her voice was raspy and husky with desire. Which was exactly what he'd wanted.

As he eased into her, he felt her tense.

'OK?' he asked.

She nodded. 'I just never thought it would be like…'

Her words slammed into his brain and he realised the implication of what she'd just said.

Ella was a virgin. And he'd just taken her virginity.

Oh, hell. But it was too late now. He couldn't reverse what he'd done. All he could do was try to make this as good for her as he could.

'Oliver?' And now she looked panicky. As if she thought she'd done something wrong.

It wasn't her. He was the one in the wrong. He should've thought. Should've checked. Should've walked away, instead of giving in to that desperate need to be close to her.

'You're beautiful,' he said, staying perfectly still so her body would have the time and space to get used to him, and kissed her. Because then he wouldn't have to talk and make a mess of things.

Slowly, she relaxed again, and kissed him back. And he paid close attention, finding out what made her whimper with desire, taking it slowly until he finally felt her body rippling round his and it tipped him into his own climax.

He held her close. 'Ella. I feel so guilty about this.'

'Don't. You didn't do anything wrong.' She stroked his face.

'But you were a—'

'Virgin. I know.' She bit her lip. 'Which is so stupid in this day and age. It makes me feel… Well, who on earth is still a virgin at the age of twenty-six?' She grimaced.

He knew the answer to that. 'A woman who's waiting for the right person.'

'There's no guarantee that Mr Right will ever come along.'

Or Ms Right. She had a point.

And right now she was clearly embarrassed by the situation, because her fair skin was flushed.

'I'm not judging you,' he said awkwardly. 'Ella, you're lovely.'

The 'but' was a mile high in flashing neon letters, and she obviously saw that straight away. 'But you don't do relationships,' she said. 'I know.'

'I'm sorry. I should go.' He dragged in a breath. 'But at the same time I don't want to leave you. I don't want to leave it messy like this.'

'I'm not expecting anything from you, Oliver.'

But he'd seen the flicker of disappointment in her eyes before she'd managed to hide it. She'd just given him her virginity. To simply walk away from her immediately after that would make him feel like a real lowlife.

Plus he didn't actually want to go. Having Ella in his arms felt so *right*.

'Can I stay for a bit and just—well, hold you?' he asked.

'Why?'

One answer slammed into his head, but he wasn't ready to consider that. He took a deep breath. 'Because I feel horrible. I can't just get up and leave you. I just took your virginity, Ella.'

'That isn't an issue.'

He rather thought it was. 'I feel bad about it.'

'Don't. It was my choice.' She paused. 'But you don't want a relationship with me.'

Trust Ella to hit the nail on the head instead of avoiding the issue. His no-nonsense colleague was back. 'It's not *you*. It's anyone.' He raked a hand through his hair. 'I've got an interview for the Assistant Head of Obstetrics job next week. If I get the post, then all my attention's going to be on my new job. It's the wrong time for me to get involved with anyone.'

'And I'm not your type anyway.'

Actually, she was exactly his type, warm and sweet and lovely; though his family wouldn't agree with him. His brother would be fine, but his parents would see her as the girl from a very different background—an unsuitable background. Not that anyone at work knew about his family. He'd been careful to keep his background very quiet. The fact that his father had a title had absolutely nothing to do with Oliver's ability to do his job, and he wanted people to judge him for himself, not for whose son he was.

He took her hand. 'Ella. I like you a lot. I respect you. And I've been attracted to you ever since the first time I met you. What happened tonight... I think it's been a long time coming.'

'It has.'

So she felt that weird, almost elemental pull, too?

'But we're not going to repeat it.'

He couldn't tell a thing from her expression or from the tone of her voice. Everything was neutral. 'It's not you, Ella. It's me.' The last thing he wanted was for her to take the blame. He knew the whole thing was his fault. He should've kept himself under his usual control.

'As far as everyone else is concerned, you gave me a lift home from the ball—as your colleague—and you stayed for a cup of coffee,' she said. 'And that's it.'

'Thank you.' She really was letting him off the hook— and it was a lot more than he deserved.

'If you, um, need the bathroom, it's next door. The towels are clean. Help yourself to anything you need.'

'Thanks.' He pulled on his underpants and padded to the bathroom.

When he returned from his shower, with the towel still wrapped round his waist, she'd changed into a pair of pyjamas. Totally unsexy striped flannel pyjamas that buttoned right up to the neck.

And how bad was it that he wanted to unbutton them and slide the material off her skin again? To kiss every centimetre of skin he uncovered and lose himself in her warmth?

Then again, those pyjamas were also a statement. She was dressed—and he was wearing only her bath towel. 'Do you want me to go?' he asked.

'I think it would be best,' she said.

He knew she was right, and that leaving would be the sensible thing to do, but he still felt bad. As if he should've stayed a bit longer, and at least held her until she fell asleep. Going now felt as if he was deserting her.

'I'm sorry,' he said.

'I'm not.' She lifted her chin. 'We did nothing to be ashamed of.'

He had. He'd taken her virginity without a second thought. But if he pressed the issue, he had a feeling she'd take it the wrong way and think he was ashamed about sleeping with her—that she was the problem, not him. Which wasn't true.

'Uh-huh,' he said awkwardly. Normally he was good with words, but tonight that ability had completely deserted him. 'Ella—we've worked together well for eighteen months. I don't want that to change.'

'It won't. Nobody at the hospital needs to know anything about what just happened.'

She didn't meet his eye, he noticed. So that comment about not being ashamed had obviously been sheer bravado.

'I'm not a good bet when it comes to relationships, Ella,' he said softly. Though he didn't want to tell her why. How stupid was he not to have realised that Justine had been seeing someone else, and that he was her golden ticket to the good life for her and the baby that wasn't his? He knew that Ella wasn't a gold-digger, the way Justine had been; but he still couldn't face taking a risk with a relationship again. Making another mistake. Having his heart trampled on again. So it was better to stay exactly as he was, where everyone knew the score and that all his relationships were just for fun.

Not a good bet when it comes to relationships.

Neither am I, Ella thought ruefully.

What did she have to offer anyone? Thanks to the endometriosis that had dogged her for years and caused the ovarian cyst to grow and rupture, Ella couldn't have children. It was one of the reasons why she'd avoided relationships; what was the point of starting anything when you knew you were taking someone's future choices away? Who would want a wife who couldn't give him a family? She'd seen first-hand from her own best friend's experience how the pressure of infertility could cause even the strongest marriage to crack.

So she knew she was better off as she was. She'd come to terms with the situation over the last few years; now she had the chance to concentrate on her job and prove that she was better than her grades at university suggested—that she was worthy of her job. And her job would be enough for her.

'I don't want a relationship with you, Oliver,' she said. It wasn't strictly true, but she wasn't stupid enough to long for something she knew she couldn't have. 'Except a working one.'

The relief in his expression was so dazzling, it almost blinded her.

Well, she could be just as bright and chirpy. She wasn't going to let him see how much his relief had hurt her. 'Shall I make you a cup of tea while you're getting dressed?'

'No, it's fine, thank you. I'd probably better go.'

'I'll, um, let you get changed,' she said, and headed for the kitchen to give him some space.

The two mugs of instant coffee—never made—sat accusingly in front of the kettle. She tipped the coffee granules in the bin, rinsed out the mugs and made herself a strong cup of tea. Mam's solution to everything, she thought wryly. Though she had a feeling that it would take an awful lot more than a cup of tea to sort this out.

She'd just have to pretend that tonight had never happened. And hopefully things wouldn't be awkward between Oliver and her at work.

CHAPTER ONE

Saturday 3rd December

'EXCUSE ME, PLEASE. I'll be back in a second.' Ella held her breath and made a dash for the door. This was hardly professional behaviour, but it would be better than throwing up in front of the poor mum-to-be and her partner.

She made it to the staff toilet with seconds to spare. And then, weirdly, as she leaned over the bowl, she stopped feeling sick.

Huh?

If she was coming down with the sickness bug that was sweeping its way through the hospital and leaving all the departments short-staffed, she should've been throwing up right now. Big time. But the queasiness that had left her feeling hot and sweaty in the consulting room seemed to have vanished.

She frowned. The last thing she'd been aware of was how strong the dad-to-be's aftershave had been.

Sensitive to smells and feeling sick...

Had any other woman listed those symptoms, Ella would've suspected early pregnancy. But she knew that she couldn't possibly be pregnant. Her doctor had given her the bad news more than five years ago, after her ovarian cyst had ruptured. Between the cyst and the endometriosis that had dogged Ella and caused her to fall behind in her studies, her Fallopian tubes were in a bad way and she'd been told she'd never have children of her own.

How ironic that she'd specialised in midwifery. Cuddles with a baby she'd just delivered, or with a friend's or cousin's child, were all she would ever have. But after a lot of heartache and tears she'd come to terms with the situation. She loved her job. Trying to find a Mr Right who wouldn't mind that she couldn't ever give him a baby of his own— well, that was just being greedy and expecting too much.

She splashed water on her face, took a deep breath and returned to the consulting room to finish the antenatal appointment with her parents-to-be.

But when exactly the same thing happened at her next antenatal appointment, Ella began to wonder quite what was going on.

She and Oliver hadn't used protection, the night of the Hallowe'en masked ball. But she'd thought it wouldn't matter.

Of course she wasn't pregnant. She couldn't be.

As for the fact that her bra felt a bit too tight and her breasts felt slightly sore… That was purely psychological. Her imagination was simply running riot and coming up with other pregnancy symptoms. There was no way this could be a miracle baby. No way at all.

But, now she thought about it, her period was late. A quick mental count told her that it was two and a half weeks late. She hadn't had time to notice because they'd been so short-staffed and busy in the department lately. Actually, that was probably the reason why her period was late in the first place; she'd been rushed off her feet and working crazy hours, so it wasn't surprising that her menstrual cycle was protesting.

'Ella O'Brien, you're being a numpty,' she told herself

crossly. 'Of course you're not pregnant.' All the same, during her break she took one of the pregnancy test kits from the cupboard. Just to prove to herself once and for all that she was being ridiculous, and then she could get on with the rest of her life.

She peed on the stick, then waited.

A blue line appeared in the first window, to show that the test was working properly.

And then, to her shock, a blue line appeared in the second window.

But—but—this couldn't be happening. It *couldn't*. How could she possibly be pregnant?

She sat there staring at the test, in turmoil, emotions whirling through her.

The test result was clear: she was expecting a baby. The one thing she'd been told would never happen, by specialists she'd trusted absolutely. From what they'd said, the odds were so stacked against her falling pregnant, she'd have more chances of winning a huge prize on the lottery.

Though in some ways this felt better than winning the lottery. A baby. The gift she'd never dreamed she'd ever be able to have, except from the sidelines. Although she'd smiled and been genuinely pleased whenever one of her cousins or one of her friends had announced she was pregnant, a tiny part of Ella had mourned the fact she'd never know the joy of being a mum. And now she was actually going to be a mum. Have a baby of her own. For a moment, sheer joy flooded through her. Despite almost impossible odds, she was going to have a baby. A Christmas miracle.

But then panic took over. What about her career? She'd already lost a lot of ground during her studies, thanks to the combination of her dyslexia and the pain of the endometriosis. Some days, the pain had been so debilitating that she hadn't been able to sit through lectures, and she'd had to borrow notes from friends instead of recording the lectures, and struggled as the words danced across the page. Even when her doctor had finally found some medication to help deal with the pain, things hadn't got much better, because then she'd had the ruptured cyst...

She'd worried that if her tutors knew the truth about her illness, they'd make her drop the course. They knew about her dyslexia and they'd already given her so much help, letting her record lectures so she could listen to them and absorb the knowledge that way. She couldn't possibly ask for yet more help. It'd be greedy and selfish. Ella almost gave in to her parents' suggestion to forget all about being a midwife and go home to Ireland. But then she'd had a work placement and she'd loved working on the ward so much. It had made her more determined to follow her dream of being a midwife, so she'd struggled on and scraped through her exams.

And she was always aware that she should've done better as a student, that her grades had let her down. It drove her to work harder on the ward, to prove to everyone round her that she was better than her exam results said she was. All the way through her medical career, she'd asked to use computer software to dictate notes rather than rely on her terrible handwriting, she'd used coloured lenses in her glasses so she could manage with bright paper or a screen, and she'd asked colleagues to proofread her notes—because she'd never, ever put a patient at risk by not double-checking that everything in the notes was absolutely correct. And, even though people weren't supposed to discriminate against you at work if you had a medical condition, Ella had always felt the need to work extra hard, just to prove that her dyslexia wouldn't make any difference to her ability to do her job.

But going on maternity leave in six months' time would

have a huge impact on her career. She'd lose experience and study time. And what would happen when her maternity leave had ended? Juggling work and still managing to spend a decent amount of time with the baby, as a single parent, was going to be tricky. Arranging childcare to fit round her shifts would be tricky, too.

Though she wasn't the baby's only parent.

And that was something else that worried her.

There was only one man who could be the father, because she'd only ever slept with Oliver.

Once.

How, how, *how* had she managed to get pregnant? Then again, how many times had a young mum-to-be cried on her shoulder that it had been the first time she'd had sex and she'd been so sure you couldn't get pregnant if it was your first time?

But, that night, Ella had told Oliver it was safe not to use a condom. Her doctors had been so sure that she couldn't have children—that her Fallopian tubes were so badly damaged that she probably wouldn't be able to have children even with the help of IVF—that she really *had* believed it was safe not to use a condom.

And now here she was: single, and pregnant with Oliver's baby after a one-night stand. How on earth was she going to tell him about the baby?

She had absolutely no idea what Oliver would say or how he'd react to the news. Since the night of the ball, things between them had cooled considerably. She wasn't sure which of the two of them was the more embarrassed about what had happened. He'd really reacted badly once he'd realised that she'd been a virgin. Working together had been awkward, and both of them had made excuses to avoid work social events where the other might be there.

Things had cooled even more when it turned out that

Oliver had got the job as Assistant Head of Obstetrics. Although he wasn't directly Ella's boss, he was very much her senior. The last thing she wanted was for him—or anyone else at Teddy's—to think that she'd slept with him in an attempt to boost her career. She'd never do anything like that.

At least Oliver wasn't dating anyone else, as far as she knew, so that was one less complication to worry about. But how did you tell someone that you were expecting his baby, when you weren't even in a relationship with him and you had no idea how he'd react?

She couldn't even begin to frame the right words.

She knew she wasn't going to get a happy-ever-after, where Oliver went down on one knee with a hand clutched to his chest, declared his undying love for her and asked her to marry him. Though she wasn't naive enough to expect that. And if he did ask her, she certainly wasn't going to marry a man who didn't love her, just for the baby's sake. That wouldn't be fair to any of them.

But Ella did want Oliver to be involved with the baby. She'd had a really happy childhood. She'd been an only child, but her parents had both come from big families and she'd had plenty of cousins around, so it had been almost as good as having siblings. She wanted that for her baby, too: that feeling of being loved and wanted, of being part of a family. And, even though she wasn't expecting Oliver to resurrect anything more than a distant kind of friendship with her, she hoped that he would at least be there for their child as the baby grew up. It would be a terrible shame for either of them to miss out on any of that.

But what if Oliver didn't want anything to do with the baby at all? What if he expected her to have a termination?

Then she'd have to rethink her situation at the Royal Cheltenham. Seriously. She already knew that she absolutely didn't want a termination. Though working with

Oliver in any way, shape or form would be impossible if he expected her to take that option. She'd have to leave the hospital and find a job somewhere else.

Even though she loved her job here at Teddy's, Ella knew she would need some support with the baby. Even if Oliver didn't expect her to have a termination, if he didn't want to be involved with the baby, then she'd have no choice but to go home to Ireland. Although her parents would be shocked and a bit disappointed in her at first, she knew they loved her and wanted the best for her. And she knew how much they'd wanted to be grandparents, even though they'd assured her that of course they weren't bothered by her infertility. They'd be on her side and help her with the baby, and maybe she could work part-time as a midwife in Limerick. Have the best of both worlds.

She cupped her hands protectively around her abdomen. 'Right at this moment, I have no idea how this is going to work out, baby,' she said softly. 'But one thing I do know: I definitely want you. I never dreamed I'd be lucky enough to have you, and I'm so glad I am. You're the best thing that's ever happened to me—and I'm going to try my hardest to be the best mum to you I can.'

She splashed water on her face, wrapped the test kit in a plastic bag and stored it in her pocket, then returned to the ward.

'Are you all right, Ella?' Annabelle, her best friend and the head neonatal nurse on the ward, asked.

'I'm fine,' Ella fibbed. 'You haven't seen Oliver anywhere, have you?'

'I think he's in a meeting. Is it urgent, or can one of the other doctors fill in for him?'

It wasn't urgent exactly—her pregnancy wouldn't show for a few weeks yet—but absolutely nobody else could fill in for him on this. Not that she could tell Annabelle without telling her the rest of it. And, given the reasons why Annabelle's marriage to Max had collapsed, Ella wanted to choose her words carefully so she didn't rip open her best friend's old scars. Particularly as Max was now working at Teddy's, easing in to a role as Sienna's maternity cover. Annabelle had opened her heart to Ella about the situation, the previous day, and Ella just couldn't say anything that might hurt her best friend.

'It'll wait,' Ella said, trying to keep her voice light.

And it was probably for the best that Oliver wasn't available right now. It would give her some space and time to think about how she was going to tell him the news.

The afternoon was also filled with antenatal appointments; one mum in particular was really worried.

'So this baby's in the same position that her brother was in?' Sara Reynolds asked.

'Back to back—yes,' Ella confirmed.

'So that means another long labour followed by an emergency section?' Sara grimaced. 'I know I agreed to a trial of labour, but I'm so scared my scar might come open halfway through and I'll be rushed into the operating theatre. And the idea of being in labour for two days again and then being stuck in bed for a week, feeling as bad as I did last time, when Jack's so lively...' She shook her head. 'I can't do it. I can't, Ella.'

'It's not going to be like that,' Ella reassured her. 'We'll keep a really close eye on you, and we're not going to let you struggle. Though you're right about a back-to-back labour taking longer, and this little one's been very happily settled in that position for the last three appointments.'

'You don't think she'll move round?'

'At this stage, no. I'll go and have a word with your consultant,' Ella said, 'but I'm pretty sure he'll agree with me in the circumstances that we should be able to offer you an elective section.'

'But if I have a section, doesn't that mean I'll be stuck in bed for a week and I won't be able to drive for a month?' Sara looked worried. 'And I need the car to get Jack to nursery. It's four miles away and there isn't a bus.'

'Last time,' Ella said gently, 'you'd had a two-day labour before the section. It's not surprising that it took it out of you. This time round, you won't have to go through that first, so it'll be easier and you'll be a lot more mobile. Nowadays we say you can drive when you feel ready, though if you can give it three weeks to let yourself heal that would be good. Maybe one of your family or friends nearby can help with the nursery run?'

Sara bit her lip. 'My cousin said she'd come and help.'

'Well, that's great.' Ella smiled at her and squeezed her hand. 'Give me five minutes and I'll have a chat with your consultant.'

Who *would* have to be Oliver, she saw with dismay as she looked at Sara's notes on the computer screen.

Provided she didn't let herself think about the situation she hadn't had a chance to discuss with him, she should be able to deal with this. Her patient had to come first.

Thankfully, Oliver was out of his meeting. Ella could see him sitting at his computer, typing away and looking slightly grim. Working on notes following his meeting, maybe? Hopefully he wouldn't mind the interruption. She rapped on his open door. 'You look busy, but please can I interrupt you for three minutes on behalf of one of my mums, given that you're her consultant and you need to be the one to sign off on the decisions?'

'Sure.'

He didn't smile at her, but that was OK. This was work. She ran through the brief. 'The mum is Sara Reynolds, thirty-six weeks, second baby. Last time round, the baby was back-to-back and she had a two-day labour followed by an emergency section. This baby's been in the same position for the last three appointments, and I don't think she's going to move now. Sara originally agreed to a trial of labour, but she's really worried that she'll end up with another long labour, and she'll have to have another emergency section that'll leave her unable to function for weeks. Given the baby's position and that Sara's got a really lively toddler to cope with as well, I really think she'd be better off having a planned section.'

'Let me look at her notes so I can bring myself up to speed with exactly what happened last time,' Oliver said.

'OK.' And please don't let him be long, Ella thought. She was starting to pick up the smell from his coffee cup and it was making her stomach roil.

But clearly his computer system was on a go-slow when it came to retrieving the patient's notes, and it got to the point where she couldn't bear the smell of coffee any more.

'Excuse me a moment,' she said, and fled to the toilet. Thankfully it was queasiness again rather than actually being sick, and she splashed water onto her face until she felt able to cope again.

When she got back to Oliver's office, he'd clearly had time to review Sara's notes.

'Are you all right?' he asked.

'Yes. I just felt a bit…' No, now really wasn't the time for her to tell him that it was morning sickness. She stopped. 'I'm fine.'

'If you're going down with that sickness bug, I want you off the ward right now before you pass it on to anyone else,' he said. 'Go home, Ella.'

'It's not that.' She didn't want to tell him the real reason right now. It wasn't the time or the place, and she still didn't have the right words to explain the situation to him. 'So do you have an answer for Sara?'

'Yes. I agree with you, so I've marked on her notes that I'm happy for her to have an elective section. I'll get it booked in with Theatre. Do you want me to come and have a word with her?'

'No, it's fine.' Especially as that coffee was making her feel queasy again and she didn't want to have to dash off to the toilets again and risk him working out what was really going on. 'Thanks. I'd better get back to my patient. Catch you later.'

Ella was acting really oddly, Oliver thought. Rushing out of his office like that. Yet she'd been adamant that she wasn't going down with the sickness bug that was sweeping through the hospital.

So what was the problem?

Things had been awkward between them ever since the night of the masked ball. The night when he'd taken her virginity. He still felt guilty about it; and as a result he'd probably been even more cool with her than she was being with him.

He really ought to have a chat with her and try to get things back on an even keel between them. Especially as he was the Assistant Head of Obstetrics now. There was absolutely no way they could get involved with each other; although he wasn't directly her boss, he was her senior. Though it would be nice to salvage some kind of working relationship, so they were at least on semi-friendly terms in the department. He *liked* Ella. He missed the easiness between them.

As for anything more… Well, he'd told her the truth. He wasn't a good bet when it came to relationships. Even though Ella was the one woman he thought might actually tempt him to try, it just couldn't happen. It would all go wrong and wreck their working relationship for good.

He knew she'd be writing up her notes after her appointments, so he quickly typed out a message on the hospital's internal email system.

We need to have a chat. Come and see me when you're done today.

Before he hit 'send', he added 'please', so she'd know he wasn't being cold and snooty with her. And hopefully they could sort things out.

We need to have a chat. Come and see me when you're done today, please.

Oh, help. That sounded very formal and very ominous, Ella thought as she read the email at the end of her shift. Why did Oliver want to see her?

She hadn't put a foot wrong in her job ever since she'd moved from London to Teddy's eighteen months ago. But, now Oliver was Assistant Head of Obstetrics, he was bound to have read everyone's file, to help him get a handle on the team and see where anyone might need more training. If he'd read her file, then he'd know that she'd only just scraped through her exams at university. Was this why he wanted to see her? Did this mean he was going to expect her to prove herself all over again?

Great. Just the thing to start off a Saturday evening. Not.

Dreading what he was going to say, she went to Oliver's office. 'You wanted to see me?'

He looked up from his desk. 'Yes. Close the door, please.'

Now that was *really* worrying. Was he about to tell her

that he was reorganising the team and there wasn't a space for her? She couldn't think why else he would reverse his usual open-door policy.

Adrenalin slid down her spine, and she did as he'd asked.

'We need to talk,' he said, gesturing to the chair opposite his.

'Right.' She sat down.

'Coffee?'

Even the thought of it made her gag. She tried really hard to stop the reflex, using the trick her dentist had taught her last time she'd had to have an X-ray by making a fist of her left hand, squeezing her thumb with her fingers. Except it didn't help and she still found herself gagging.

'Are you all right, Ella?' Oliver asked.

'Mmm,' she fibbed. 'Maybe some water would help.'

He narrowed his eyes at her. 'What aren't you telling me?'

Oh, help. She wasn't ready for this conversation. At all. And it made it worse that every time she looked at him, she remembered what it felt like to be in his arms. What it felt like to kiss him. What it felt like when his bare skin was sliding against hers…

And this wasn't the time and the place for remembering that, either. 'Why did you want to see me?' she asked instead of answering his question. 'Am I losing my job?'

'Losing your job?' Oliver looked surprised. 'Of course not. Why would you think that?'

'Your note was pretty ominous.'

He frowned. 'It was meant to be polite.'

'And you just asked me to close the door…'

'I'm not sacking you, Ella, and this isn't a disciplinary meeting, if that's what you're thinking.' He raked a hand through his hair. 'Things are a bit strained between us and I wanted to clear the air, that's all. Look, let me grab you some water or some coffee, and we can—' He stopped abruptly. 'Ella, you've gone green. Are you quite sure you're not going down with the sickness bug?'

'I'm sure.'

'Then what's wrong?'

She couldn't see her way out of this. She was going to have to tell him at some point, so it might as well be now. And she'd had all afternoon to think about how to tell him and still hadn't come up with the right words. Maybe short and to the point would be the best option. 'I'm pregnant,' she said miserably.

Pregnant?

Oliver's head spun and he actually had to shake his head physically to clear it.

Pregnant.

He'd been here before. With Justine. Except the baby hadn't been his, because Justine had lied to him all along. He knew Ella was nothing like Justine; but the past still haunted him.

The last time those words had been said to him, he'd been just as shocked. The baby hadn't been planned and he'd still been studying for his specialist exams. He hadn't been ready for the extra responsibility of parenthood, but of course he'd done the right thing and stood by Justine. It was his duty.

And then, when Justine had finally told him the truth, he'd been let off the hook. Except by then he'd started to think of himself as a dad. Having that taken away from him had hurt even more than Justine's betrayal. He'd been shocked by how isolated and lost he'd felt—and he'd sworn that never again would he let himself get emotionally involved or in a position where someone could hurt him like that.

Now here he was again, hearing a woman tell him that she was expecting his baby. Even though Ella came from a completely different background, and he'd worked with her for long enough to trust her on a lot of levels—the situation brought back all the hurt and mistrust.

'How pregnant?' he asked carefully.

'My last period was the middle of October. I'm nearly three weeks late.'

'Seven weeks, then,' he said, calculating rapidly. They'd had unprotected sex on the night of the Hallowe'en ball. That would've been two weeks after the start of her last period, from what she'd just said. Which meant they'd had sex right in the middle of her cycle: the most fertile time.

And she'd been a virgin—something that made him feel guilty and protective of her at the same time. And which put all kind of inappropriate memories in his head: the way her voice had gone all husky with arousal, the way her pupils had gone wide and dark with desire, the way it had felt when he'd finally eased into her...

Oh, for pity's sake. He couldn't think of that now. She'd just told him she was pregnant.

Of course it was his baby. There was no question that it was anyone else's baby. Everyone knew that Ella was completely devoted to her job—come to think of it, she hadn't dated anyone since he'd known her.

Except for that one snatched evening with him. And he'd been the only man who'd ever shared her bed like that—with the ultimate closeness. Which made it special, because Ella wasn't the sort to sleep around.

She looked anxious. 'So you believe me?'

'That you're pregnant? Or that it's mine? Obviously the dates tally. And, given the situation, it's pretty obvious that the baby's mine.' He looked at her. 'I assume you've done a test, to be this sure about it?'

She nodded. 'Today.'

'And you didn't suspect anything before today?'

She frowned. 'No.'

'Even though your period was late?'

'I put that down to stress,' she said. 'You know it's been crazy round here, with so many people off sick, plus Sienna's going off on maternity leave really soon and it'll take Max a while to settle in properly. We're all rushed off our feet.'

'So what made you decide to do a test today?' Then he remembered how she'd run out of his office, admitting afterwards that she'd felt a bit sick. He'd assumed she was going down with the bug. But it hadn't been that at all. 'You started getting morning sickness,' he said, answering his own question.

She nodded. 'I can't bear the smell of strong aftershave and coffee. That's what made me...' She swallowed hard, obviously feeling queasy at just the thought of the scents.

He grabbed one of the bottles of water he kept in his desk drawer and pushed it across the desk at her. 'Here.'

'Thank you.' She unscrewed the cap and took a sip of water. 'Oliver, I didn't mean this to happen. I wasn't trying to trap you, or try to sleep my way up the ladder or anything like that. It wasn't planned.'

'Too right it wasn't planned,' he said grimly. He wasn't angry with her, but he was furious with himself. Why hadn't he taken proper responsibility when it came to precautions? More to the point, why had he made love with her in the first place, when he'd managed to keep his hands to himself and his libido under control for the last eighteen months? Why had he given into temptation that night, let the single glass of champagne he'd drunk go completely to his head and wipe out his inhibitions enough to let him kiss her and take her to bed?

Though he really wasn't prepared to answer those questions right now.

Instead, to cover up his guilt and confusion, he snapped at her. 'So what was it? The Pill didn't work?'

She flinched. 'I'm not on the Pill.'

What? He could hardly believe what he was hearing. 'You led me to believe you were.' So, in a way, she'd been as devious as Justine. Clearly his judgement was incredibly poor when it came to relationships.

'I didn't say I was on the Pill.'

'You hinted at it.' He remembered it very clearly. 'You said I didn't need a condom. Why would you say that unless you were taking the Pill?'

'Well, that lets you very nicely off the hook, doesn't it? Because it's all my fault. That's fine. I accept the entire blame for the situation.' She screwed the cap back on the water bottle. 'Don't worry, Mr Darrington, I'm not expecting anything from you. I just thought you had the right to know about the baby.' She stood up. 'I'm officially off duty right now, so I'm going home.'

'Wait. Ella.' He blew out a breath. 'You've just told me you're expecting my baby. At least give me time to process the news. And what do you mean, you're not expecting anything from me? As the baby's father, of course I'll support you financially.' Just as he'd supported Justine when he'd thought that she was pregnant with his baby. A Darrington always did the right thing.

'I don't want your money.'

'Tough. Because I have no intention of letting you go through this unsupported and on your own.' He stared at her. One thing he was very sure about: this time he wasn't going to have fatherhood snatched away from him. This time he was exercising his rights, and he was going to have *choices*. 'It's my baby, too, Ella. So that means I get a say. In *everything*.'

'I never had you pegged as an overbearing bully,' she said, 'but you're behaving like one right now. I'm telling you about the baby purely out of courtesy, and I know you're not interested in being with me so I don't expect anything from you. And now, if you'll excuse me, I've already told you I'm off duty and I want to go home. Good-night.'

This time, she walked out.

By the time Oliver had gathered his thoughts enough to think of going after her, Ella was nowhere to be seen.

Great.

If he ran after her now, everybody would notice. The last thing either of them needed right now was to have the hospital speculating about their relationship—or, worse still, actually guessing that Ella was pregnant with his baby.

He needed time to think about this. To get used to the idea. To work out exactly what he was going to do.

So much for thinking that he and Ella could smooth over what had happened that night and try to repair their working relationship. Her bombshell had just changed everything. And right at that moment he didn't have a clue what to do next, or even what to think. She hadn't even told him why she hadn't been on the Pill, and he needed to get to the bottom of that. His head was spinning.

He'd finish all the admin here and then go for a run to clear his head. And then, maybe, he'd be able to work out the best way forward. For all three of them.

The run cleared his head a bit. But then the reality slammed home. He was going to be a father.

Oliver took a deep breath. He'd been here before, but this time he had no doubts at all. The baby was his, and so was the responsibility. OK, so she'd told him he didn't need to use protection, and that had turned out not to be true—but it took two to make a baby. Plus Ella's family lived hundreds of miles away in Ireland; although her best friend lived in Cheltenham, it basically meant that Ella was on her own. She and the baby needed him to step up to the plate and be responsible.

He could start by making sure that she was taking folic acid and eating properly. Which was hard in the early stages, when you had morning sickness and couldn't face the smell or taste of certain foods. He now knew the smell of coffee was a trigger for her, so he needed to find something that was bland, yet nutritious and tempting at the same time. Decaffeinated tea might be easier for her than coffee; he knew she usually drank tea at work. And maybe some fresh strawberries, pasteurised yoghurt and granola.

He dropped in to the supermarket on his way home, trying to ignore the piped Christmassy music and the stacks of Christmas chocolates and goodies displayed throughout the shop. Right now it didn't feel much like Christmas. It felt as if the world had been shaken upside down and he wasn't quite sure what day it was. Though he rather thought he might need some kind of Christmas miracle right now.

He concentrated on picking out things he thought might tempt Ella to eat, and added a box of vitamins specially formulated for pregnant women. Then he came to the large stand of flowers by the tills. Did Ella even like flowers? He didn't have a clue. He knew some women hated cut flowers, preferring to let them bloom in a garden or on an indoor plant. And there was the scent issue. Something as strong as lilies might set off her morning sickness.

But it would be a gesture. A start. A way of showing her that he wanted to be on the same side. Maybe something not over-the-top and showy, like the large bouquets sprinkled with artificial snow and glitter. Something a little smaller and bright and cheerful with no scent, like the bunch of sunny yellow gerbera. Although he didn't have a vase at home, he could stick them in a large glass of water overnight so they'd still look nice in the morning. Hopefully Ella would like them.

Then maybe tomorrow they could talk sensibly about their options. Hopefully Ella would tell him what she really wanted. She'd said that she was only telling him about the baby out of courtesy, but did she really mean that? Did she want him to be part of the baby's life—part of *her* life? Or did she really mean to do what their colleague Sienna seemed to be doing, and go it alone?

And what did he want?

Since Justine's betrayal, Oliver had major trust issues when it came to relationships. He didn't date seriously. He hadn't even wanted a proper relationship, thinking that the risks of getting hurt again were too high. But the fact that Ella was expecting his baby changed that. He knew he definitely wanted to be a part of his child's life.

And Ella? He'd fought against his attraction towards her for months, keeping it strictly professional between them at work. Then, the night of the charity ball, he'd danced with her; it had felt so right to hold her in his arms. To kiss her, when he'd driven her home. To make love with her, losing himself inside her.

If he was honest with himself, he wanted to do it again. And more. He wanted to wake up with her curled in his arms. Being with Ella had made him feel that the world was full of sunshine. That snatched evening was the first time he'd felt really connected with anyone for years. He could actually see them as a family: Ella nursing the baby at the kitchen table, chatting to him about his day when he got home from work. Going to the park, with himself pushing the pram and Ella by his side—maybe with a little dog, too. Reading a bedtime story to the baby together and doing all the voices between them.

They could give their baby the kind of childhood he hadn't had. One filled with warmth and love.

But then reality slammed in. Did she feel the same way about him? Did she want to make a family with him, or did she just want financial support, the way Justine had? OK, so she didn't know who his parents were, and she'd said earlier that she didn't want his money—but was it true?

Had it meant anything to her, giving him her virginity? Or had it all just been a nuisance to her, an embarrassment, something she wanted to get rid of and he'd happened to be in a convenient place to do her a favour? And why had she been so adamant that they didn't need contraception—especially as it now turned out that she hadn't been on the Pill?

He didn't have a clue. In normal circumstances, that would be a difficult conversation to have. With pregnancy hormones clouding the issue, it was going to be even harder.

Tomorrow.

He'd sleep on it and hope that the right words would lodge themselves in his head by tomorrow.

CHAPTER TWO

ON SUNDAY MORNING, Oliver drove over to the pretty little square where Ella's flat was and rang her doorbell.

She opened the door wearing pyjamas, sleepy-eyed and with her hair all mussed. 'I'm sorry. I didn't mean to wake you,' he said.

'It's almost half-past nine, so it's my bad,' she said wryly. 'What do you want?'

He held up the recyclable shopping bag. 'I brought breakfast. I thought maybe we could talk.'

'Breakfast?'

'And these.' He handed her the gerbera. 'I hope you like them.'

Unexpectedly, her beautiful green eyes filled with tears. 'Oliver, they're gorgeous. I love yellow flowers. Thank you. Though you really didn't have to do that.'

'I wanted to,' he admitted. And right now, seeing her all warm and sleepy, he really wanted to take her in his arms and hold her close and tell her that he'd protect her from the world.

Except he wasn't sure how she'd react, and he knew he needed to take this slowly and carefully until he had a better idea of what was going on in her head. He wasn't going to end up in the same place he'd been after Justine, where he'd been in love with her but she hadn't loved him back.

'Come in. I'll put the kettle on.' She ushered him through to her living room. 'I'll go and have a quick shower and get dressed, and then I'll put those lovely flowers in water.'

'You don't have to change on my behalf.'

She gave him a speaking glance. 'I can't be sitting here at my kitchen table in pyjamas, with you all dressed up like a magazine model.'

'Apart from the fact that I'm not all dressed up, I don't mind if you stay in your pyjamas.'

'Well, *I* do.'

He really didn't want to sit around doing nothing. It wasn't his style. He'd always preferred keeping busy. 'Shall I make breakfast, then, while you're showering?'

He could see that she was torn between insisting that it was her flat so it was her job to make breakfast, and letting him do something. 'All right,' she said finally. 'I normally eat in the kitchen, if that's all right with you.'

'OK. I'll see you when you're ready.'

By the time Ella had showered and changed into jeans and a cute Christmassy sweater with a reindeer in a bow tie on the front, Oliver had laid two places at the tiny bistro table in her kitchen and had arranged everything on the table: freshly squeezed orange juice, granola, yoghurt and a bowl of hulled and washed strawberries. It looked amazing. And she couldn't remember the last time anyone apart from her parents had made this kind of fuss over her. Right now she felt cherished—special—and it was a good feeling.

'No coffee,' he said.

'Thanks. I really can't bear the smell of it.'

'And that's why I held off on the croissants. Just in case they affected you, too.' He gestured to the teapot. 'The tea's decaf—I thought it might be easier for you to manage.'

'That's so sweet.' He'd made all this effort just for her, and her heart melted. 'This all looks so nice. Thank you.'

'I had to guess because I didn't really know what kind of thing you like for breakfast.'

She blushed. 'You didn't stay for breakfast when... Well, you know.'

'Uh-huh.'

Right at that moment, he looked just as embarrassed and awkward as she felt. She'd been stupid to bring up the issue.

'I just wanted to do something nice for you,' he said.

'And I appreciate it,' she said meaning it.

He poured her a mug of tea. 'No sugar, right?'

She loved the fact that he'd actually noticed how she took her tea. 'Right.'

'So how are you feeling?' he asked.

'Mostly fine. Just as long as I avoid strong smells.' She smiled. 'And that should get better in about six weeks, or so I always tell my mums.'

'It's usually better by the second trimester,' he agreed.

'I thought Sienna was teasing me when she told me that tin cans actually smell when you're pregnant,' Ella said, 'but she's right. They do.' She shuddered, and took a sip of the orange juice. 'This is lovely. Thank you so much. I feel totally spoiled.'

'It's the least I could do.' Again, Oliver could imagine having breakfast with Ella on Sunday mornings. A lazy breakfast, with toast and tea and the Sunday papers, and then taking the baby out together for a late-morning walk in the park... It shocked him to discover how much he actually wanted that.

A real relationship.

With Ella and their baby.

Thankfully she hadn't noticed him mooning about, because she asked, 'So is everything OK with you?'

'Yes.'

'And you're settling in well to your new job?'

'Just about,' he said, smiling back at her. Maybe this was going to work out. They could at least make polite conversation. And they'd been friends before the masked ball. They respected each other as colleagues. He really believed they could salvage something from this now.

He kept the conversation going until they'd finished breakfast and he started clearing the table; then he noticed that there was still something left in the bag he'd brought with him. 'Oh, I meant to give you this earlier.' He took the box of vitamins from the bag and handed them to her.

She frowned. 'What's this?'

'Folic acid—obviously now you know about the baby, you need to start taking it.'

'Uh-huh.' Her face shuttered. 'Did it occur to you that I might already have bought a pregnancy vitamin supplement with folic acid?'

'I—' He stared at her. No. He hadn't given it a second thought.

'Oliver, I'm a midwife. It'd be a bit stupid of me to ignore my years of training about the best way for pregnant women to look after themselves and their babies, wouldn't it?'

She sounded really put out, though he couldn't for the life of him understand why. All he'd done was buy her some vitamins. 'I was just trying to help. To look after you.'

'To take over, more like,' she said.

'But—'

'Do you think I'm suffering from "pregnancy brain" and I'm completely flaky?' she asked. She shook her head, narrowing her eyes at him. 'And, for your information, "pregnancy brain" is a total myth. I came across a piece on the news the other day that said actually women's brains are sharper when they're pregnant.'

What? Where was all this coming from? He didn't understand. 'Ella, I didn't accuse you of anything of the sort.'

'No, but you bought me folic acid without even thinking that I might already have some. There's a huge difference between asking me if you can pick something up for me, and just presenting me with it as if I'm too stupid to have thought of it for myself.'

'You're overreacting.'

'Am I?' She folded her arms. 'If this is how it's going to be for the next seven and a half months, with you looking over my shoulder all the time and making decisions for me without even bothering to discuss things with me first...' Again, she shook her head. 'That's really overbearing and that's not what I want, Oliver. Actually, right now I think I'd like you to leave and give me some space.'

He stared at her in disbelief. 'All I want to do is to protect you and the baby, and provide for you. How's that being overbearing?'

Could he really not see it? Ella wondered. 'It's overbearing because you're not discussing anything with me. You've made the decision already and you're expecting me to just shut up and go along with it.' She'd been there before: when everyone thought that little Ella wasn't bright enough to train as a midwife. She hated the way Oliver seemed to be falling into those same attitudes and thinking he knew what was best for her. She'd had years of feeling undermined and useless, and she wasn't going to let it happen again. 'And if you *dare* say that's just pregnancy hormones making me grumpy, I'll... I'll...' She was too angry to think of what she'd do next. So much for thinking he wanted to cherish her. What an idiot she was, letting herself fall a little more in love with a control freak who wanted to boss her around.

'Ella, this is—'

'I need some space. Thank you for the flowers and breakfast, because that was very nice of you, but I'd really like you to leave now. Please.'

'What about the washing up?'

'I think I might just about be capable of sorting that out for myself.' She stood up and gestured to the doorway. 'Would you give me some space, please?'

Maybe making a tactical retreat would be the best thing to do right now, Oliver thought. 'All right.'

He wasn't sure whether her reaction had made him more hurt or angry. He'd tried to do the right thing, but Ella was being totally unreasonable. He'd never called her intelligence into question. Why on earth would she think he had?

Despite her protests, he was pretty sure that pregnancy hormones were affecting her mood.

He'd try to talk to her again later and hope that she'd be in a better frame of mind. More receptive.

Going to the gym and pounding the treadmill didn't help. Neither did going to his office and spending a couple of hours catching up on paperwork.

Was he really being overbearing and making decisions without asking her? Oliver wondered.

A simple box of vitamins really shouldn't cause this much trouble.

Justine had been more than happy for him to make a fuss of her and buy things for her while she was pregnant. Then again, she'd had her reasons. But Ella was seriously independent. Brave enough to travel to London at the age of eighteen to study midwifery, so far from her family home in Ireland that she wouldn't be able to just pop home for the weekend like most of the other students could. And she'd be brave enough to bring up this baby on her own.

Except she didn't have to.

He wanted to be there. For her and for the baby.

He didn't want to tell her about Justine—not just yet—but he could try to build a bridge. Try to see things from Ella's point of view.

It didn't take him long to drive back to her flat.

This time, when she answered the doorbell, she didn't smile.

'Hear me out?' he asked. 'Please?'

She said nothing, but at least she didn't slam the door in his face. 'I was going to get you flowers as an apology, but I already bought you flowers this morning and I don't want you to think I'm going over the top—especially as you already think I'm being overbearing. I had no idea what to get you. I don't know what you like, so I just...' Oliver hated feeling so clueless and awkward. Normally he was in charge and he knew everything would go smoothly. This was way out of his comfort zone.

'It doesn't matter. I don't need you to buy me things.'

Another difference between Ella and the women he usually dated: they expected presents. Expensive presents.

'The most important thing is that I'm sorry for being bossy. I don't mean to be and I'll try not to be. But,' he said, 'old habits die hard, and I can't promise that I won't mess up in the future.'

Her face softened, then, as if she understood the jumble of thoughts filling his head, and she stepped back from the doorway. 'Come in and I'll make some tea—and, for the record, I'm perfectly capable of filling a kettle with water and boiling it.'

'I know,' he said. He'd got the message that Ella liked her independence. 'But is there anything I can do to help?'

'Just sit down and let me do it myself.'

He waited on the sofa in the living room, feeling more and more antsy as the seconds passed.

Finally, she came in with two mugs of tea.

'Thank you,' he said, accepting one of the mugs.

She inclined her head in acknowledgement and sat down at her desk rather than next to him on the sofa. Making a point, he supposed.

'It must be difficult for you, being in this situation,' she said.

That was an understatement. She didn't know anything about the memories it was bringing back, and right at the moment it wasn't something he wanted to share. 'It's not exactly a picnic for you, either,' he said, trying to see it from her point of view. 'All I need to do is to get my head round this properly.' *All*. He was struggling enough with that. 'But it's worse for you because you get all the morning sickness and what have you as well.'

'Thanks for reminding me,' she said dryly.

'Ella, I want to be there for you and the baby.'

'I understand that. But it doesn't give you the right to push me around.'

He hadn't been trying to push her around, but he didn't want to argue. Now was probably not the right time to ask difficult questions about the contraception issue, either. He wanted to get their relationship on a less rocky footing, first. Instead, he asked carefully, 'So have you thought about what kind of care you want, and whether you want to book in at Teddy's or if you'd rather go somewhere else?'

'I know all the staff at Teddy's and I know I'll get the best care there, so it makes sense to book in to our department,' she said. 'Though it does mean everyone's going to know. And at a really early stage.'

'Is that a problem?'

She looked thoughtful. 'I guess not—I mean, everyone's been great about Sienna. After the initial gossip, wondering who the baby's father is.'

'Would you prefer people not to know I'm the baby's father?'

'I don't want people thinking I slept with you to get an advantage at work.'

He smiled. 'Ella, nobody would ever think that of you. You work hard enough for two people as it is.' He paused. 'What about a scan?'

'I already know I'm about seven weeks.'

'Which is about the right time for a dating scan—not that I disbelieve you on the dates, just…'

She nodded. 'Though it'll mean people will know now, not later on.'

'Yes, and they'll cut you a bit of slack—this is the stage where you're likely to feel really tired and need a break.'

'I'll still be part of the team, and being pregnant doesn't alter that.'

Why was she being so difficult about this? 'I'm not saying that you're not part of the team—just that maybe you could cut back a bit on your shifts for a while.'

Her face darkened. 'No.'

'Ella—'

'I said before, please don't push me around. You're not my keeper, Oliver.'

'I know. I'm just trying to do what's best for you.'

'Because I'm not bright enough to know what's best for me?'

'No, of course not.' He didn't get why she was being so prickly. 'Ella, is there something you're not telling me?'

'How do you mean?'

'You and me—we've always got on well. Until—well.' He didn't want to embarrass her by putting it into words.

But she clearly wanted to face it head-on. 'Until we slept together.'

'I feel guilty about that. You're not the sort who does one-night stands—and I took your virginity.'

'Which isn't an issue.'

'It is for me.'

She looked confused. 'Why?'

'Because it makes me feel dishonourable.'

She scoffed. 'Oh, get over yourself, Oliver. What are you, the Lord of the Manor?'

Not far off it. But he needed to get back on reasonable terms with her before he dropped that particular bombshell. 'I'm sorry. I did warn you I'd mess up on the control freakery stuff.'

'I guess. And maybe I need to cut you some slack, too—but how would you feel if I suggested you cut back on your shifts, just because you'll have a baby in seven months' time?'

He nodded. 'I get it.'

She rubbed her stomach reflectively. 'So is there a new girlfriend who might not be very happy to hear the news?'

'No, there isn't.' And the question stung. 'Do you really think I'm that shallow?'

'No, but you never seem to date anyone for long.'

'Strictly speaking, I didn't actually date you,' he pointed out. 'We both got carried away, that night.'

'I guess.' She paused. 'So why do you avoid proper relationships?'

Something else he didn't want to discuss. 'Let's just say I've been a bit burned in the past.'

'And you're still brooding over it enough not to give someone else a chance? She must've hurt you a lot.'

'Yes. She did,' he admitted.

'I'm sorry that you got hurt. But I'm nothing like the usual women you date.'

'Usual?'

She grimaced. 'I haven't been gossiping about you. But the hospital grapevine says you pick women who look like models, women from a much posher background than mine.'

He stared at her. 'You think I'm a snob?'

'No. You treat all our mums the same, whether they're ordinary women or royalty or celebs,' she said. 'I guess what I'm saying is I'm me, so don't go thinking I'll be like her.'

'You're not like her.' He trusted Ella, for a start. Professionally. But letting her into his heart would take a lot longer. Justine had left him with a lot of baggage.

Though he really didn't want to talk to Ella about Justine right now. Especially given their circumstances. How did you tell someone who was expecting your baby that you'd been here before—but the baby hadn't been yours? She'd start reading all kinds of things into that and what he might be thinking now, and he was having a hard time explaining it to himself; he certainly couldn't explain his feelings to her. Wanting to change the subject, he asked, 'What about you?'

Her eyes widened. 'You seriously think I'd date someone else when I'm pregnant with your baby?'

He winced. 'That sounds bad. I mean… You only just found out about the baby. You might've met someone between Hallowe'en and now.'

'No. There isn't anyone.'

'OK.'

And actually the hospital grapevine said she didn't date. Ella was dedicated to her work. Oliver assumed that someone had hurt her badly in the past and she didn't trust love any more, the same way that he didn't trust love. But he could hardly grill her about it. That would be intrusive; besides, right now their relationship was so fragile he didn't want to risk saying the wrong thing and making it worse. 'Have you told your parents?' he asked.

'Not yet. I think I'd prefer to do that face to face—video-calling isn't good enough for news like this,' she said. 'I'm going home for two days at Christmas. I'll tell them then.'

'How do you think they'll take it?'

With sheer disbelief, Ella thought. Her parents knew the situation with her endometriosis and the ruptured cyst. They'd resigned themselves to never having grandchildren, though she'd seen the wistfulness in her mum's eyes every time one of her sisters became a grandmother again. Not that she wanted to discuss any of that with Oliver. Not right now. Because if he knew about her medical issues from the past, he'd try even harder to wrap her in cotton wool and it would drive her crazy.

'They'll be supportive,' she said. She knew that without having to ask. They might be shocked, but they'd definitely be supportive. 'How about yours?'

'It's complicated,' he said.

Another stonewall. Oliver had been hurt by someone in the past and his family situation was complicated. Did that mean maybe his ex had dumped him for his brother, or something? Did he even have a brother or a sister? But, even if she asked him straight out, she knew he'd evade the subject. 'You don't give anything away, do you?'

'I…' He blew out a breath. 'I'm making a mess of this.'

'Yes, you are,' she said. 'It's always better to be honest.' Which was pretty hypocritical of her, considering what she was keeping from him.

He raked a hand through his hair. 'Ella, right now all that matters to me is you and the baby.'

Why couldn't she let herself believe him?

When she didn't say anything, he sighed. 'I'd really like to be there at the scan. But it's your call.'

That was quite a capitulation—and one that clearly hadn't come easily to him. He was used to being in charge at work, so of course he was going to be bossy outside work as well. And maybe she had overreacted a bit. Maybe he really *had* meant to be helpful and trying to look after her, rather than making her feel stupid. But she didn't want to whine about her dyslexia. Plenty of people had more to deal with than she did.

Maybe she should capitulate a bit, too. 'I'll let you know when I've seen my doctor and got a date through,' she said.

'Thank you.' He finished his tea. 'I guess I should let you have the rest of your afternoon in peace. But call me if you need anything, OK? And I'm not trying to be bossy. I'm trying to be supportive.'

'Uh-huh.'

When she'd shown him out, she tidied up and washed up the mugs. She had absolutely no idea how this was going to work out. Oliver was clearly intending to do the right thing and stand by her—but she didn't want him to be with her out of duty. She wanted him there because he *wanted* to be there.

He hadn't said a word about his feelings. He hadn't asked her about hers, either. Which was just as well, because she was all mixed up. The attraction she'd felt towards him hadn't gone away, but she was pretty sure it was one-sided. She didn't want him to pity her for mooning about over him, so she'd been sharper towards him than normal. But then again, if it was that easy to push him away, he clearly didn't want to be with her in the first place.

'It'll work out,' she said quietly, cradling her abdomen protectively with one hand. 'If the worst comes to the worst, I'll go back home to my family in Ireland. But one thing I promise you, baby: even though you weren't planned, you'll always, *always* be loved. And if you're a girl I'm going to call you Joy, because that's what you are to me.'

CHAPTER THREE

ELLA WAS ON a late shift on the Monday morning, and called her GP's surgery as soon as they were open. To her surprise and delight, the GP was able to see her that morning before her shift.

'How are you feeling?' the GP asked when Ella told her she was pregnant.

'Fairly shocked,' Ella admitted. 'I didn't think this would ever happen, after what the doctors told me in London. But, now I've had a couple of days to get used to the idea, I'm thrilled.'

'Good.' The GP smiled. 'Congratulations. Are you having any symptoms?'

'A bit of morning sickness—it's not much fun if one of the dads-to-be on the ward is wearing a ton of aftershave, or if anyone at work's drinking coffee,' Ella admitted.

'I don't need to tell you that you should feel a lot better by the time you're twelve weeks.'

Ella smiled back. 'No. It's weird, because I'm usually the one giving that advice.'

'And you've already done a test?' the GP asked.

'Yes.'

'Then there's not much point in doing a second one,' the GP said. 'Given your medical history, though, I'd like to send you for an early scan. As you work at Teddy's, would you rather go there or would you prefer to book in for your antenatal care somewhere else?'

'Teddy's is fine,' Ella confirmed.

'Good. I'll put a call through to the ultrasound department this morning. Reception will contact you with the date and time.'

'That's great—thank you very much.'

By the time Ella got to Teddy's, the GP's surgery had already sent her a text with the date and time of her scan. Ella wasn't sure whether she was more relieved or shocked to discover that the scan was tomorrow morning, an hour before her shift was due to start.

Someone was bound to see her in the waiting room for the ultrasound, so the whole department would know about the baby very quickly. Which meant that Ella needed to find Annabelle and tell her the news herself. The last thing she wanted was for her best friend to hear about the baby from hospital gossip, especially as she knew what Annabelle had been through over the last few years.

Annabelle was in her office, clearly writing up some reports. Ella knocked on the door, opened it slightly and leaned through the gap. 'I can see you're really busy,' she said, 'but can I have a quick word?'

'Sure,' Annabelle said. 'Is everything all right?'

'Yes—there's just something I wanted to tell you.' Then Ella looked more closely at her friend. 'There's something different about you.'

'How do you mean, different?' Annabelle asked.

'You look happier than I've seen you in a long, long time.'

Annabelle smiled. 'That's because Max and I are back together. For good.'

'Really?' Thrilled for her friend, Ella leaned over the desk and hugged her. 'That's fabulous news.'

'All those years I thought I'd failed him because I couldn't give him children.' Annabelle blew out a breath. 'But he says I'm enough for him, Ella. He doesn't need a family to feel we're complete.'

'I'm so pleased.' Ella paused. 'So this means you're not going to try IVF again?'

'No. We might consider adopting in the future, but we need time to think about it. And time just to enjoy each other,' Annabelle said. 'So what's your news?'

Even though Annabelle seemed to be OK with the idea of not trying for a family, Ella knew that this was still a sensitive subject. 'There isn't an easy way to say this.'

'Oh, no. Please don't tell me you're leaving Teddy's.'

'No.' At least, she hoped she wasn't going to have to leave. 'Annabelle, I wanted you to know before anyone else on the ward does—because everyone's going to know after tomorrow. And I really don't want this to upset you.'

'Now you're really worrying me. Is it another cyst?' Annabelle bit her lip. 'Or—and I *really* hope it isn't— something more sinister?'

Ella took a deep breath. 'No. Nothing like that.'

'Then will you please put me out of my misery?'

'I'm pregnant.'

'Pregnant?' Annabelle's blue eyes widened. 'That's the last thing I expected *you* to tell me. But—how?'

Ella squirmed. 'Basic biology?'

'Apart from the fact that you're not dating anyone—or, if you are, you haven't told me about him—there's your endometriosis and that ruptured cyst and all the damage to your Fallopian tubes,' Annabelle pointed out. 'I thought the doctors in London said there was no chance of you conceiving?'

'They did. But I guess there was a billion to one chance

after all.' A Christmas miracle. One Ella had never dared to dream about.

'I don't know what to say. Are you…well, happy about it?' Annabelle asked cautiously.

Ella nodded. Yet, at the same time, part of her was sad. This wasn't how she'd dreamed of things being when she was a child; she'd imagined having a partner who loved her. That definitely wasn't the situation with Oliver.

'Congratulations. I'm so pleased for you.' Annabelle hugged her. 'How far are you?'

'Seven weeks.'

'Your mum will be over the moon at the idea of being a granny.'

Ella smiled. 'I know. I'm going to tell her at Christmas when I go back to Ireland. Or maybe I'll take a snap of the scan photograph on my phone and send it to her tomorrow.'

'You've got a dating scan tomorrow? That's fantastic. Do you want me to come with you?' Annabelle asked.

'That's lovely of you to offer, but it's fine.'

'Of course. I guess the dad will want to be there.'

Dear Annabelle. She was clearly dying to know who it was, but she wasn't going to push her friend to share all the details until Ella was ready.

'The dad,' Ella said, 'is being just a little bit bossy at the moment and trying to wrap me up in cotton wool.'

Annabelle raised an eyebrow. 'He doesn't know you very well, then?'

'It's complicated.' Ella took a deep breath. 'I'm not actually dating him. And I'm not sure I'm ready for everyone to know who it is.'

'Sienna, mark two?' Annabelle asked wryly. 'Well, that's your right if you want to keep it to yourself. And you know I have your back.'

Ella smiled. 'I know.' Which was precisely why she

was going to tell her best friend the truth. 'Obviously this is totally confidential—it's Oliver.'

'*Oliver?*' Annabelle asked in a scandalised whisper. 'As in our Assistant Head of Obstetrics?'

Ella winced. Was it so unlikely? 'Yes.'

'But… When?'

'The night of the charity ball. We danced together. A lot. He drove me home. And we…' She shrugged. 'Well…'

'I had no idea you even liked him.'

'I've liked him since the moment I met him,' Ella admitted. 'But I never said anything because I always thought he was way out of my league.'

Annabelle scoffed. 'You're lovely, and anyone who says otherwise has me to answer to.'

'But you know what the hospital gossip's like. They say he only dates people a couple of times—and they're usually tall, willowy women who look like models or movie stars. As in the opposite of me.'

'You're beautiful,' Annabelle said loyally.

'Thank you, but we both know I'm not Oliver's type. I'm too short and too round. And he… Well.' Ella had absolutely no idea how Oliver felt about her. He was being overprotective, but was that because of the baby?

'So what are you going to do?' Annabelle asked.

'I'm still working that out,' Ella admitted.

'Is he going to support you?'

'He's pretty much driven me crazy—presenting me with a box of folic acid, telling me to cut back on my shifts…'

'Ah. The protective male instinct coming out. And you sent him away with a flea in his ear?'

Ella nodded. 'You know how hard I worked to get through my exams. I'm not going to give all that up now.'

'So what do you want him to do?'

'Be part of the baby's life,' Ella said promptly. 'And

not boss me about. Except I want him to be there because he wants to be there, not just because he thinks he ought to be there.'

'What does he say?' Annabelle asked.

'It's—' But Ella didn't get the chance to finish the conversation, because one of their colleagues came in, needing Annabelle to come and see a patient.

'We'll talk later,' Annabelle promised, on her way out of the door. Except Ella had a busy shift, starting with a normal delivery and then one that turned complicated, so she didn't have time to catch up with Annabelle.

Everything was fine in her second delivery; there were no signs of complications and no signs of distress as she monitored the baby.

But, as the mum started to push, Ella realised that she was having difficulty delivering the baby's face and head. The classic sign of the baby having a 'turtle neck' told her exactly what the problem was: shoulder dystocia, meaning that the baby's shoulder was stuck behind the mum's pubic bone. And in the meantime it meant that the umbilical cord was squashed, so the baby had less oxygenated blood reaching her.

'Sophie, I need you to stop pushing,' Ella said calmly. She turned to the trainee midwife who was working with her. 'Jennie, please can you go and find Charlie? Tell him we have a baby with shoulder dystocia, then get hold of whichever anaesthetist and neonatal specialist is on call and ask them to come here.'

'What's happening?' Sophie asked, looking anxious.

'Usually, after the baby's head is born, the head and body turns sideways so the baby's shoulders pass comfortably through your pelvis. But sometimes that doesn't happen because the baby's shoulder gets stuck behind your pubic bone,' Ella explained. 'That's what's happened here.

So we need a bit of extra help to get the baby out safely, and that's why I've asked our obstetrician to come in. There will be a few people coming into the room and it'll seem crowded and a bit scary, but please try not to worry. We're just being super-cautious and making sure that someone's there immediately if we need them, though with any luck we won't need any of them.'

'Does this happen very often?' Sophie asked, clearly in distress.

'Maybe one in a hundred and fifty to one in two hundred births,' Ella said. 'Try not to worry, Sophie. I've seen this happen a few times before, and we can still deliver the baby normally—but right now I'm going to have to ask you to stop pushing and change your position a bit so we can get the baby's shoulder unstuck and deliver her safely.'

'Anything you say,' Sophie said. 'I just want my baby here safely.' A tear trickled down her face.

'I know.' Ella squeezed her hand. 'I promise you, it's all going to be fine. Now, I want you to lie on your back, then wriggle down so your bum's right at the very edge of the bed. Can you do that for me?'

'I think so.' Sophie panted a bit, clearly trying to hold back on pushing, and then moved down the bed according to Ella's directions.

Charlie came in with Jennie, followed by the anaesthetist and neonatal specialist. Ella introduced everyone to Sophie. 'Charlie, I want to try the McRoberts manoeuvre first,' she said quietly. It was the most effective method of getting a baby's shoulder unstuck, and would hopefully avoid Sophie having to have an emergency section.

'That's a sound decision,' Charlie said as he quickly assessed the situation. 'I've got another delivery, so if you're confident with this I'll leave you and the team. I'll be in the birthing suite next door—my patient's waters have just broken.

'I'm good, Charlie,' Ella said, then turned her attention back to Sophie as Charlie departed, leaving her to manage the birth.

'Sophie, I'd like you to bend your knees and pull your legs back towards your tummy,' Ella said. 'Jennie's here to help you. What that does is to change the angle of your spine and your pelvis and that gives the baby a little bit more room, and then hopefully we'll be able to get her shoulder out a lot more easily. You'll feel me pushing on your tummy—it shouldn't hurt, just feel like pressure, so tell me straight away if it starts to hurt, OK?'

'All right,' Sophie said.

While Jennie helped move Sophie's legs into position, Ella pressed on Sophie's abdomen just above her pubic bone. It wasn't quite enough to release the baby's stuck shoulder, and she sighed inwardly. 'Sophie, I'm afraid her shoulder's still stuck. I'm going to need to give you an episiotomy to help me get the baby out.'

'I don't care,' Sophie said, 'as long as my baby's all right.'

Which was what Ella was worried about. There was a risk of Sophie tearing and having a postpartum haemorrhage—but more worrying still was that the brachial plexus, a bundle of nerves in the baby's shoulder and arm, could be stretched too much during the birth and be damaged.

'OK. You'll feel a sharp scratch as I give you some local anaesthetic,' Ella said as she worked. 'And you won't feel the episiotomy at all.' Swiftly, she made the incision and then finally managed to deliver the baby's head.

'Here we go—I think someone's all ready to meet her

mum.' She clamped the cord, cut it, and handed the baby to Sophie while mentally assessing the baby's Apgar score.

'Oh, she's so beautiful—my baby,' Sophie said.

The baby yelled, and everyone in the room smiled. 'That's what we like to hear,' Ella said softly. 'Welcome to the world, baby.'

While Ella stitched up the episiotomy, the neonatal specialist checked the baby over. 'I'm pleased to say you have a very healthy little girl,' she said. 'She's absolutely fine.'

Ella helped Sophie get the baby latched on, and the baby took a couple of sucks before falling fast asleep.

'We'll get you settled back on the ward, Sophie,' Ella said. 'But if you're worried about anything at all, at any time, you just call one of us.'

'I will. And thank you,' Sophie said, tears running down her face. 'I'm so glad she's here.'

Oliver called in to one of the side rooms to see Hestia Blythe; he'd delivered her baby the previous evening by Caesarean section, after a long labour that had failed to progress and then the baby had started showing signs of distress.

'How are you both doing?' he asked with a smile.

'Fine, thanks.' Hestia smiled back at him. 'I'm a little bit sore, and I'm afraid I made a bit of a fuss earlier.' She grimaced. 'I feel so stupid, especially because I know how busy the midwives are and I should've just shut up and let them get on with helping people who really need it.'

'You're a new mum who needed a bit of help—you're allowed to make a fuss until you get used to doing things,' Oliver said. 'Nobody minds.'

She gave him a rueful look. 'I needed help to get my knickers on this morning after my shower and it was so, so pathetic. I actually cried my eyes out about it. I mean—how feeble is that?'

'You're not the first and you definitely won't be the last. Remember, you had twenty-four hours of labour and then an emergency section,' Oliver said. 'I'd be very surprised if you didn't need help with things for a day or two. And the tears are perfectly normal with all the hormones rushing round your body.'

'That's what that lovely midwife said—Ella—she was so kind,' Hestia told him. 'She said it was the baby blues kicking in early and everything will seem much better in a couple of days.'

'She's right. When you've had a bit of sleep and a chance to get over the operation, you'll feel a lot more settled,' Oliver agreed. And, yes, Ella was lovely with the patients. He'd noticed that even the most panicky new mums seemed to calm down around her.

'May I have a look at your scar, to see how you're healing?' he asked.

Hestia nodded. 'You kind of lose all your ideas of dignity when you have a baby, don't you?'

He smiled. 'We do try not to make you feel awkward about things, so please tell me if anything I say or do makes you uncomfortable. We want to make your stay here at Teddy's as good as it can be.'

'I didn't mean that,' she said, 'more that you don't feel shy or embarrassed about things any more—you get used to people looking at all the bits of you that aren't normally on view!'

'There is that,' Oliver agreed. He examined her scar. 'I'm pleased to say it looks as if you're healing very nicely. How's the baby?'

'He's feeding really well,' Hestia said. 'I found it a bit tricky to manage at first, but Ella sat down with me and showed me how to get the baby to latch on. She was really patient with me.'

'That's great. May I?' He indicated the crib next to the bed.

'Of course.'

Obviously she saw the goofy smile on his face when he looked at the baby because she said, 'You can pick him up and have a cuddle, if you like.'

'Yes, please.' Oliver grinned. 'This is one of my favourite parts of the job, cuddling a little one I helped to bring into the world. Hello, little man. How are you doing?' He lifted the baby tenderly and stroked the baby's cheek.

The baby yawned and opened his gorgeous dark blue eyes.

It was always a moment Oliver loved, when a newborn returned his gaze. But today it felt particularly special— because in a few months he knew he'd be doing this with his own baby. 'He's gorgeous, Hestia.'

'You're a natural at holding them,' Hestia said. 'Is that from your job, or do you have babies of your own?'

'My job,' he said. Though now he was going to have a baby of his own. And, the more he thought about the idea, the more it brought a smile to his face.

A baby.

His and Ella's.

Right now they weren't quite seeing eye to eye, but he'd make more of an effort. Because this really could work. He liked Ella and he knew she liked him. They were attracted to each other, or Hallowe'en wouldn't have happened. And love…? Oliver had stopped believing in that a long time ago. But he thought they could make a good life together, for the baby's sake.

He just needed to convince Ella.

'I was wondering,' Hestia said. 'My husband and I were

talking, this morning, and you were so good with us last night. If it wasn't for you, we might not have our little boy now. And we'd like to name the baby after you. If that's all right?' she added.

'I'd be honoured,' Oliver said. 'Though I wasn't the only one in Theatre with you, so it'd be a bit greedy of me to take all the glory.'

'You were the one who saved our baby,' Hestia insisted. She peered over at his name tag. 'Oliver. That's such a lovely name.'

Oliver stared down at the baby. If Ella had a boy, would she want to call him Oliver? Or maybe Oliver as a middle name?

The baby started to grizzle and turn his head to the side. 'It looks as if someone's hungry.' He handed little Oliver over to his mum. 'Are you OK latching on now, or would you like me to get one of the midwives?'

'I'll manage—you've all been so great,' Hestia said.

'Good. If you need anything, let us know OK?'

'I will,' she promised. 'But right now all I can think about is my little Oliver here. And how he's the best Christmas present I could've asked for.'

Oliver smiled at her and left the room.

The best Christmas present I could've asked for.

In a way, that was what Ella had given him.

Needing to see her, he went in search of her.

'She's writing up her notes from her last delivery in the office,' Jennie, one of their trainee midwives, told him. 'The baby had shoulder dystocia.'

Which meant extra forms, Oliver knew. 'Did everything go OK?'

'Yes.'

'Good.' He headed for the midwives' office. Ella was sitting at the desk; as usual, she'd dictated something first into her phone, and it looked as if she was listening to her notes and then typing them up a few words at a time. Oliver knew from reading Ella's file that she was dyslexic; he assumed that this was the way she'd learned to manage it, and it was also the reason why she wore coloured glasses when she was reading notes or sitting at a computer.

He rapped on the glass panel of the door to get her attention, then opened it and leaned round it. 'Hi. I hear you just had a baby with shoulder dystocia.'

She nodded. 'There were absolutely no signs of it beforehand. The baby weighed three and a half kilograms and the mum didn't have gestational diabetes.'

'Prediction models aren't much help, as they're based on the baby's actual weight rather than the predicted weight, so don't blame yourself for it. In half of shoulder dystocia cases, we don't have a clue in advance, plus not all of them are big babies or from diabetic mothers,' Oliver said. 'How did it go?'

'Fine. As soon as I realised what was happening, I asked Jennie to get Charlie, the anaesthetist and the neonatal specialist. The McRoberts manoeuvre didn't quite work so I had to give her an episiotomy and guide the baby out, but the baby was fine and there's no sign of a brachial plexus injury. I'm going to keep an eye on Sophie—the mum— for postpartum haemorrhage.'

'Good job.' She looked so tired right now, Oliver thought. Having to concentrate on typing must be hard for her. 'Do you want a hand filling in the shoulder dystocia form?'

She narrowed her eyes at him. 'I'm not that hopeless, Oliver.'

And then the penny dropped. She obviously worried that people thought she was less than capable because of her dyslexia. Maybe in the past people had treated her as if she was stupid; that would explain why she'd overreacted to him buying the folic acid, because it had made her feel that he thought she was stupid.

'You're not hopeless at all, but you look tired,' he said, 'and filling in forms is a hassle even if you don't have to struggle with dyslexia as well.' He remembered what Ella's tutor said in her reference: ignore the exam results because Ella was an excellent midwife and could always tell you every last detail of a case. It just took her a lot longer than most to write it up. The exams must've been a real struggle for her, even if she'd been given extra time or the help of a scribe during the papers. And yet she'd never once given up. 'You could always dictate it to me and I'll type it up for you,' he suggested.

She narrowed her eyes even further. 'Would you make the same offer to anyone else on your team?'

She was worried about him showing favouritism towards her because of the baby? 'Actually, yes, I would,' he said. 'That's the point. We're a team, at Teddy's. And I'm responsible for my team's well-being. Which includes you.' He pulled up a chair next to her, brought the keyboard in front of him and angled the screen so they could both see it. 'Right. Tell me what to type.'

Again she looked wary, and he thought she was going to argue with him; but then she nodded and dictated everything to him. Just as he'd expected, she was meticulous and accurate.

'Thank you,' she said when he'd finished typing.

'Any time. You know your stuff and you pay attention to our mums, so you made that really easy for me.' But she looked so tired, almost forlorn, and it worried him. He wanted to make things better. Now. He gave in to the impulse and rested his palm against her cheek. 'Tell me what you need.'

'Need?'

Her pupils were suddenly huge and his mouth went dry. Was she going to say that she needed him? Because, right now, he needed her, too. Wanted to hold her. Wanted to kiss her.

When she said nothing, he rubbed his thumb lightly against her skin. 'Cup of tea? Sandwich? Because I'm guessing the staff kitchen is a no-go area for you right now.'

'I'd love a cup of tea,' she admitted. 'And a sandwich. Anything really, really bland.'

'Give me five minutes,' he said. 'And, for the record, I'm not trying to be bossy. You've had a busy shift with a tough delivery, and I bet you haven't had the chance of a break today. I want to be there for you and our baby, Ella.'

He'd said the magic word, Ella thought as she watched Oliver leave the office. 'Our', not 'my'. So maybe she wasn't going to have to fight him for her independence.

He came back with the perfect cup of tea, a cheese sandwich and an apple that he'd cored and sliced for her. Ella felt her eyes fill with tears. 'Oh, Oliver.'

'Don't cry.'

But she couldn't stop the tears spilling over. He wrapped his arms round her, holding her close and making her feel cherished and protected, and that only made her want to cry more.

Hormones, that was all it was. And if someone came into the office and saw them, people might start to talk. Although Ella dearly wanted to stay in his arms, she wriggled free. 'Oliver. People are going to start gossiping if they see us like this.'

'No—they'll think you're tired after a long shift, and

I'm doing exactly what I would for any colleague. Being supportive.'

'I guess.' She paused. 'I've got an appointment through for the scan.'

He went very still. 'Are you asking me to come with you?'

'If you want to.'

There was a brief flash of hunger in his eyes. Did that mean he wanted to be there, or did he think it was his duty? She didn't have a clue how he felt about her, and she wasn't ready to ask—just in case the answer was that he saw it as his duty.

'But if anyone asks why, it's because you're supporting your colleague,' she said. 'I'm not ready for the world to know about—well.' She shrugged. There wasn't an 'us'. What should she call it? A fling? A mistake? The most stupid thing she'd ever done in her life?

And yet the end result had been something she'd always thought was beyond her reach. The most precious gift of all. Something that made her heart sing every time she thought about the baby.

'Noted,' he said, his voice expressionless. 'What time?'

'Eleven.'

'I'll be there,' he said. 'Do you want me to meet you in the waiting area outside the ultrasound room, or here?'

'I think the waiting area would be best.' If they went together from here, their colleagues were bound to start speculating, and she really didn't want that. Not until she knew what was really happening between her and Oliver.

'All right.'

'I guess I'd better finish writing up my notes,' she said. 'And then I want to check on Sophie—the mum—to see how she and the baby are doing. And I promised to give a hand with putting up the Christmas decorations in the reception area.'

'I'll let you get on, then.' For a moment, he looked as if he was going to say something else. Then he shook his head as if he'd changed his mind. 'I'll catch you later.'

CHAPTER FOUR

THE NEXT MORNING, Ella woke with butterflies in her stomach. The pregnancy test she'd taken had been positive; but as a midwife she knew that there were all manner of things that could go wrong over the next few weeks. One in four pregnancies ended in a miscarriage. And would the scarring in her Fallopian tubes have caused a problem with the baby?

She managed to force down a slice of toast and was sitting in the waiting room outside the ultrasound suite at five minutes to eleven, having drunk the requested one litre of water. There were Christmas cards pinned on the cork board in the reception area, and some of the tables had been moved to make way for a tree. All the couples sitting in the waiting room now were clearly looking forward to the following Christmas: the first Christmas with their new baby. Right now, Ella didn't know if she and the baby would still be here in Cheltenham with Oliver, or whether they'd be back in Ireland with her family, and it made her feel slightly melancholy.

Would Oliver be on time for the appointment? Or would he need to be in with a patient and have to miss the scan?

She reminded herself that it didn't matter if he couldn't be there; she could manage this perfectly well on her own. She tried to flick through one of the magazines left on the table to distract people who were waiting, but the paper was too shiny for her to be able to read the words easily.

And that was another worry: would her baby inherit her dyslexia? Ella knew that a daughter would have a one in four chance of inheriting the condition, and a son would have a three in four chance. She hated the idea that she could've passed on something that would cause her child difficulties in the future; though at least she was aware of what to look out for, so if necessary she'd be able to get help for her child much earlier than she'd received help, and her child wouldn't go through most of his or her education feeling as clumsy and stupid as Ella had.

She'd just put the magazine back on the table when she heard Oliver say, 'Good morning.'

She looked up and her heart skipped a beat. He really was beautiful: the walking definition of tall, dark and handsome. And she'd never reacted to someone as strongly as she reacted to Oliver.

'Good morning,' she said, trying to sound cool and collected and hoping that he didn't pick up how flustered he made her feel.

'Are you all right? Is there anything I can get you?'

'Thanks, but I'm fine. And, before you ask, yes, I've drunk all the water they asked me to.'

'Let's hope they're running on time so you're not uncomfortable for too long. May I?' He gestured to the chair next to her.

'Of course.' And how ridiculous it was that she longed for him to take her hand, the way that the partners of the other pregnant women in the waiting room seemed to have done. She had to remember that their relationship was limited to an unplanned and inconvenient shared status as a parent: they weren't a proper couple. They probably never would be. The best she could hope for was that Oliver would be there for the baby as he or she grew up. It would be stupid to dream that the man who'd held her yesterday afternoon when she'd cried, the man she was falling for just a little more each day, felt the same way about her. Yesterday he'd been kind, that was all.

A few minutes later, they were called into the ultrasound suite. As they walked into the dimly lit room, the sonographer said, 'Oh, Mr Darrington! I didn't expect to see you.' She looked speculatively at Ella. 'I didn't realise—'

'I'm supporting Ella,' Oliver cut in, 'as I'd support any member of my team whose family lives a long way away.'

'Oh, of course.' The sonographer blushed. 'I'm sorry for—well, making assumptions.'

Ella had wanted to keep everything just between the two of them, but at the same time she felt a prickle of hurt that Oliver hadn't acknowledged the fact that this was his baby, and had fudged it in a way so that he hadn't lied directly but had definitely misdirected the sonographer. She knew it was contrary and ridiculous of her to feel that way, and it was probably due to all the pregnancy hormones rushing round her system. How many times had she had to comfort a pregnant woman in their department who was upset for a totally irrational reason?

Following instructions, she lay on the couch and bared her stomach. The sonographer tucked tissue paper round Ella's clothes to stop them being covered in gel, then put radio-conductive gel on her stomach.

'It's warm,' Ella said in surprise. 'The gel is always cold if we do a scan on the ward.'

The sonographer smiled. 'It always is warm down here because of all the machinery heating up the room. I think it makes things a bit more comfortable for the mums.'

'I agree. We'll have to think of a way of doing that on the ward,' Ella said to Oliver.

The sonographer ran the head of the transceiver over Ella's stomach. 'Good. I can confirm there's just one baby here.'

Ella hadn't even considered that she might be having twins. She had no idea if twins ran in Oliver's family, but she could hardly ask him right then—not without adding to the hospital rumour mill.

'The baby's growing nicely,' the sonographer said, and took some measurements on the screen. 'It's about thirteen millimetres long, so I'd say you're about seven and a half weeks.'

'That ties in with my dates,' Ella said.

'You can see the baby's head and body very clearly.' The sonographer turned the screen round to show them a bean-shaped blob; there was a flicker which Ella knew was the baby's heartbeat. And she was shocked by the rush of sheer emotion that burst through her at the very first sight of her baby.

'The baby's heart rate is one hundred and fifty beats per minute—which you'll know as a midwife is absolutely fine. It's too early to measure the fluid behind the neck for a Nuchal test, as we'd usually do that at about eleven weeks, but we can do a combined screening test for Down's then,' the sonographer said.

Ella only realised then that she'd been holding her breath, waiting to know that everything was all right and her fertility problems hadn't also caused a problem for the baby. 'Thank you. It's really good to know all's well.'

There was a knock on the door and another member of the ultrasound team put her head round the door. 'Sorry to interrupt—can I have a quick word?'

The sonographer went over for a brief discussion. 'I'm so sorry,' she said. 'I just need to pop next door for a moment. I'll be back very soon.'

'Not a problem,' Ella said, feeling a tug of sympathy for whoever was in the other ultrasound room. For the senior sonographer to be called in, it meant the team needed a second opinion on a potential complication.

As the door closed, Oliver took her hand. 'Our baby,' he said in wonder, looking at the screen. 'I've seen so many of these scans since I started working as an ob-gyn, and even performed a few of them myself, but this… This is special.' His voice sounded thick with emotion.

'I know.' It had affected Ella in the same way, and she was amazed by how strongly she felt. She'd only known about this baby for three days and it had turned her world upside down; but at the same time it was the most precious gift anyone could've given her and she was already bonding with the tiny being growing in her womb. She couldn't help tightening her fingers round his.

'Our baby, Ella,' he said again, his voice hoarse, and cupped her face with his free hand.

His touch sent a tingle through her. 'Oliver,' she whispered.

He dipped his head to kiss her; it was soft and sweet and full of longing.

When he broke the kiss, he pulled back just far enough so they could look into each other's eyes. Ella noticed that his pupils were huge. Was it because of the low light in the ultrasound room, or was it because he felt as emotional as she did right at that moment? Did he feel this same pull towards her that she felt towards him? Did they have a chance to make it as a couple—as a family?

'Ella,' he said softly, and kissed her again.

Her heart felt as if it had just done a somersault.

But then they heard the click of the door starting to open, and pulled apart again. Ella felt her cheeks burning, and really hoped that the sonographer hadn't seen anything—or, worse still, that she looked as if she'd just been thoroughly kissed.

Oliver looked both shocked and horrified. Ella could tell instantly that he was regretting the kiss and shrivelled a little inside. How stupid of her to hope that the kiss meant he felt something for her. Clearly he'd just got carried away by the rush of the moment.

'Sorry about that,' the sonographer said brightly. 'I guess as you work in Teddy's, Ella, you already know the answers to the kind of questions my mums normally ask, but is there anything you'd like to ask?'

Ella smiled. 'I'm not going to ask to know whether the baby's a girl or a boy, because apart from the fact I know it's way too early for you to be able to tell, it doesn't matter either way to me.' Though, she wondered, did it make a difference to Oliver? 'But would it be possible to have a photograph, please?'

'Sure. Let's see if we can get you a slightly less blurry picture,' the sonographer said with a smile. Once she'd got a picture she was happy with, she asked, 'How many copies do you need?'

'Two,' Ella said. 'How much are they?'

Before Oliver could embarrass them both by trying to pay, she took out her purse and handed over the money.

The photographs were printed while she wiped her abdomen free of gel and restored order to her clothes.

'Thank you for your support, Oliver,' she said. 'I know you're really busy, so you don't have to hang around and wait for me.'

It was practically a dismissal. So Ella was obviously regretting their kiss, Oliver thought. And she was probably right. They could do with some space. He'd got carried away in the heat of the moment, overwhelmed by seeing the baby on the screen. Right now he needed to take a step back from Ella, metaphorically as well as literally.

'Thanks. I'll see you later on the ward,' he said.

But before he had a chance to leave the sonographer was called next door again.

'Ella,' he said, his voice low and urgent. 'What happened just now—it shouldn't have done. I apologise.'

'Uh-huh.' Her voice was very cool.

And he deserved that coolness. It was all his fault. 'I guess I lost my head a bit. It was the excitement of seeing the baby on the screen and hearing the positive news.'

'We both got carried away,' Ella agreed. 'It won't happen again.' She gestured to the prints. 'I assume you'd like one of these?'

'I would.' It shocked him how very much he wanted the picture. *Their baby.* 'Thank you,' he said when she handed one to him.

'It's the least I could do.'

'I owe you—' he began.

'It's fine. A print of a scan isn't going to bankrupt me.'

That wasn't what he'd meant at all. 'Ella…' He sighed, seeing the determined set of her jaw. 'OK. I'll see you later. And thank you for the photograph.' He wasn't ready to share the news with anyone yet, but having the picture made everything so much more real. He tucked it into his wallet and left the room.

And he'd really have to get his head together.

He'd had no right to kiss her. The reason her fingers had tightened round his was purely because she was emotional about the baby. Seeing the little life they'd created, the strength of the baby's beating heart. That was all.

She wasn't in love with him.

And he wasn't in love with her, he told himself firmly. The attraction he felt towards her was because of the baby, rooted in responsibility rather than passion. He needed to be fair to her and leave her free to find someone else. Someone who hadn't put their heart in permafrost and would be able to give her the love she deserved.

But he'd meet every single one of his responsibilities towards the baby, and he needed to find a good working relationship with Ella, so their child never felt unwanted or a burden. They definitely needed to talk. Later—he really needed to gather his thoughts first.

Annabelle beckoned Ella into her office as she walked past. 'So how did it go?'

Ella beamed and took the scan picture from her purse. 'Look at this! I know, I know, it's too soon to see anything more than a bean-shaped blob.'

'It's gorgeous,' Annabelle said, looking slightly wistful.

Ella bit her lip. 'Oh, Annabelle, I'm sorry. I didn't mean to open up old wounds.' But she'd so wanted to share the picture with someone who'd understand how excited she was.

'You haven't upset me in the slightest.' Annabelle hugged her. 'I'm thrilled for you. Really, truly and honestly.'

'Thank you.' Ella tucked the picture back into her purse.

'So what's the situation between you and Oliver?' Annabelle asked.

'Complicated,' Ella admitted. Even though Annabelle was her best friend, Ella wasn't going to tell her about that kiss today. Oliver had apologised for it and said he'd got carried away in the heat of the moment and it was a mistake, so it'd be pointless for her to wish that it had meant anything more.

'Are you a couple, or not?'

'Not,' Ella said.

'Do you want to be?' Annabelle asked.

That was the crunch question. And the worst part was that Ella couldn't really answer it. 'I don't know. I like him, Annabelle—I like him a lot—but I don't want to lose my independence. I worked so hard to qualify as a midwife, and I hate the way Oliver just expects me to cut back on my shifts and do whatever he says. He obviously hasn't even thought about what it's going to do to my career.'

'I think,' Annabelle said, 'you need to talk to him.'

'You're right. I know,' Ella agreed.

'But, before that,' Annabelle said gently, 'you need to work out what you really want.'

And that was going to be the really hard part. Because right at that moment Ella wanted everything—and she knew that was way too much to ask.

That evening, when she got home, Ella video-called her parents.

'Is everything all right, darling?' Roisin O'Brien asked. 'You always call us on a Thursday, and today's only Tuesday.'

'I know. Mam, I have some news.'

Roisin beamed and asked hopefully, 'You're coming back to Ireland and going to work in the hospital in Limerick?'

Ella smiled. 'Mam, you know I love it here at Teddy's. No, it's not to do with work. Is Da there? Because I need to talk to you both together.'

'Is everything all right?' Roisin asked again.

'Yes.' And no, but she wasn't going to say that.

'Joe! Joe, our Ella's on the computer to talk to us,' Roisin called.

Joe appeared on Ella's screen, next to his wife. 'And how's my beautiful girl, then?'

Ella felt the tears well up. 'Oh, Da.'

Joe looked horrified. 'Ella? Whatever's the matter? I'll hop on the plane and be right over. You just say th—'

'No, Da, it's fine,' she cut in. She swallowed hard. 'Mam, Da—there isn't an easy way to say this, so I'll do what you always say and tell it to you straight. You're going to be grandparents.'

There was a stunned silence for a moment, and then Roisin said, 'But, Ella, the doctors in London said...' Her voice trailed off, and Ella knew what her mother didn't want to voice. The doctors in London had said Ella would never be able to have a child of her own.

'They got it wrong.' Ella picked up the scan photo and held it so her parents could see it. 'I had the scan today—I'm seven and a half weeks. You can't see a lot, just a bean shape, but the sonographer said everything looked fine and the baby's heart was beating just right.'

'We're going to be grandparents.' Joe and Roisin hugged each other.

'You're not angry with me?' Ella asked. 'Because—well, this wasn't supposed to happen?'

'So the baby wasn't planned. It doesn't mean he or she won't be loved to bits,' Roisin said. 'Lots of babies aren't planned. It's grand news, Ella. What about the baby's da? When do we get to meet him?'

Ella hadn't even considered that. 'I'm not sure,' she said carefully. 'It's complicated.'

'Do I need to come and talk to the lad and remind him of his responsibilities?' Joe asked, folding his arms.

'No, Da, and that's not why I called. I just wanted you both to know about the baby. It's early days and a lot of things could still go wrong—but I love you so much and I couldn't keep the news to myself any longer. Please don't say anything to anyone else in the family, not yet—not till I'm twelve weeks, OK?'

'All right. And we love you, too, Ella,' Roisin said. 'If you want us to move over to England to help you with the baby, you just say the word. Or if you want to come home, you've always got a home with us and so has the baby.'

'Oh, Mam.' Ella swallowed back the tears.

'So what does the young man in question have to say for himself?' Joe asked.

'He was at the scan with me today. He's very responsible,' Ella said, guessing what her father was worrying about. She smiled. 'He's trying to wrap me up in cotton wool as much as you do.'

'With about as much success, I'll bet,' Roisin said. 'You get your independent streak from your Granny O'Connor.'

'And your Granny O'Brien,' Joe added, not to be outdone.

Ella laughed. 'Oh, I miss you both so much.'

'You'll be home in a couple of weeks for Christmas,' Roisin said, 'and we can give you a proper hug then. Are you keeping well in yourself?'

'Just a bit of morning sickness.'

'You need crackers by your bedside,' Roisin began, then laughed. 'Hark at me trying to give a midwife advice on pregnancy.'

'You're my Mam,' Ella said. 'Of course you'll tell me, and when I get home you know I want to know *everything* about when you were pregnant with me.'

'She'll talk the hind leg off a donkey,' Joe said.

'As if you won't, too, Joe O'Brien,' Roisin teased back.

'You sort things out with your young man,' Joe said, 'and you bring him home with you for Christmas so we can give him a proper welcome to the family.'

'I'll try,' Ella said. And she knew her parents meant it.

They'd definitely welcome Oliver. Her 'young man'. She couldn't help smiling. If only. 'I love you, Da. And you, Mam.'

'We love you, too,' Roisin said. 'Can we have a copy of that photo—our first picture of our grandbaby?'

'I'll scan it in and send it tonight,' Ella promised. 'As soon as we've finished our video call.'

'Good night, darling,' Roisin said. 'And you call us any time, you hear?'

'I hear. Love you,' Ella said, and ended the call.

It had made her homesick, and she was tearful again by the time she scanned in the photograph and emailed it over to her parents. Part of her wanted to call Oliver and ask him to come with her to Ireland for Christmas; but he probably already had plans. Plans that wouldn't include her. She'd just have to take this whole thing day by day, and hope that things would get easier between them.

Oliver brooded about the situation with Ella and the baby for the rest of Tuesday. It didn't help when he had a text from his mother, asking him if he could please confirm whether he was going to come to the drinks party at Darrington Hall on Thursday night.

He hadn't been to his parents' annual pre-Christmas drinks party for years. But maybe it was time he tried to thaw out his relationship with his family. Particularly as he was about to become a father.

How would his family react to the news? He had no idea. Would they expect him to settle down? Would they try to use the baby as an excuse to make him leave the hospital and spend his time working with his brother, instead of doing the job he'd trained for years and years to do? Would it be the thing that brought them back together again? Or would their awkward relationship be like a marriage under strain and crack even further under the extra pressure of a baby?

It was all such a mess.

It would help if he knew what Ella wanted. Did she regret what had happened between them? Or would she be prepared to try and make a life together?

He didn't have a clue.

And he didn't even know how to begin to ask.

CHAPTER FIVE

By WEDNESDAY MORNING, the frustration was too much for Oliver. Usually he was self-contained, but right now he really needed to talk this over, preferably with someone he could trust to keep this to themselves.

The best person he could think of was Sebastian. Prince Sebastian Falco of Montanari had been one of his best friends since they'd met during Seb's first week at university, when Oliver had been nearing the end of his medical degree; they'd hit it off immediately, despite the four-year difference in their ages. Given his position as the heir to the kingdom of Montanari, Sebastian knew about the importance of privacy. And it didn't matter that Sebastian and Oliver hadn't actually seen each other for a few months; they always picked up their friendship exactly where they'd left off.

Oliver looked at the scan photograph again, then picked up his mobile phone and called Sebastian's private number.

To his relief the prince answered immediately. 'Hello, Olly. How are you?'

All over the place. Not that Oliver was going to admit it. 'Fine, fine,' he fibbed. 'Seb, have I caught you in the middle of something, or do you have a few minutes?'

'I've probably got about ten minutes,' Sebastian said

ruefully, 'and then I really do have to be in a meeting. It's good to hear from you, Olly. How are things?'

'Complicated,' Oliver said wryly.

'Would this be as in female complications?' Sebastian asked. 'Or is it the new job?'

'Both—and thank you for the case of champagne, by the way.'

'It's the least I could do,' Sebastian said. 'So what are these complications? I take it that's why you're ringing me—to get an impartial point of view?'

'And a bit of perspective.' Oliver blew out a breath. He really didn't know where to start. Or maybe he should just do the whole mixed-up lot at once. 'It's crazy at work, what with the winter vomiting virus wiping out half the staff, and Sienna's going on maternity leave any day now. And I'm going to be a father.'

There was silence on the other end of the line.

'Seb? Are you still there?'

Was his friend really that shocked by the news of Oliver's impending fatherhood? Oh, hell. That didn't bode well for his family's reaction. Sebastian was much more laid back than Oliver's parents.

'Sorry, Olly. Someone needed me for a second. You were saying, half of your department's having babies?' Sebastian asked.

'Not half of us—that's the virus wiping everyone out—though it does feel as if everyone's going on leave. Just Sienna. Obviously you know her from when she did the training at the hospital for you.'

'Yes. She did a good job—thank you for recommending her.'

There was something in Sebastian's voice that Oliver couldn't quite work out. Or maybe it wasn't the best line.

He didn't always get great mobile phone reception in his office.

'So Sienna got married when she came back to England?' Sebastian asked.

'No, she's still single. But she knows we're all there for her and she's got a very willing rota of babysitters when the baby arrives. It's due somewhere around the beginning of February.'

'I see.' There was a pause. 'So you're going to be a dad. Should I be offering congratulations or commiserations?'

'Both,' Oliver said wryly. 'Though at least this one's definitely mine.'

'Not a repeat of Justine, then.'

Trust Sebastian to come straight to the point. It was one of the things that Oliver appreciated about his friend: his ability to focus on the important thing and cut through all the irrelevancies. 'No. And Ella's nothing like Justine. She's open and honest. And very independent.'

'So she won't let you boss her about.'

Oliver knew his friend was teasing him—or was he? Was he really as overbearing and bossy as Ella said he was?

'When's the baby due?' Sebastian asked.

'In seven and a half months.'

'It's very early days, then.'

'Yes. Ella only told me a few days ago. She had the dating scan yesterday. Seeing the baby's heart beating on the screen…' It had been a real game-changer. Because now everything was real. *His baby.* And he wanted to be a much better father than his own father had been.

Yet wasn't he making the same mistakes? Insisting that everything should go his way? It was a knee-jerk reaction to the way Justine had behaved—and Ella deserved better.

'So what's the complication with the baby's mum?' Sebastian asked.

Trust the prince to ask the awkward question. 'It's tricky. I'm not her direct boss, but I'm the Assistant Head of the Department.'

'Well, it wouldn't be the first workplace romance in history.'

When Oliver didn't reply, Sebastian continued, 'I assume it *is* a romance?'

'Yes and no.' Oliver sighed. 'I admit, I've been attracted to her since the moment I met her. She's gorgeous—all soft curves and red hair and green eyes.'

'The way you describe her makes her sound like a Picasso painting,' Sebastian commented dryly.

Oliver laughed. 'Hardly. It's not just how she looks— I'm not that shallow. She's *nice*. I can be myself with her. But you know I don't do relationships. So I've kept it platonic.'

'Obviously something changed, or you wouldn't be preparing for fatherhood in seven and a half months' time,' Sebastian pointed out.

'I danced with her at the annual Hallowe'en charity ball. Then I gave her a lift home.' Which sounded pathetic. 'I meant to see her safely indoors and leave, but she invited me in for coffee. And then I just gave in to the urge to kiss her, and…' Oliver sighed. 'I guess one thing led to another.'

'How does she feel about you?'

Good question. One Oliver had been asking himself rather a lot, and he hadn't quite worked out the answer. 'I don't honestly know. Obviously there's something there between us, or we wouldn't be in the position we're in now. But the baby has complicated things a bit. I don't know whether she wants me for *me*,' he said, 'or if she wants me for the baby's sake.'

'Have you tried asking her?'

'No—because, if I'm honest, it's the same for me. I don't know if I want to be with her because I want her, or because I feel responsible for the baby.' Though he wasn't going to tell Sebastian about the kiss during the scan. That complicated things even more. Had they both been caught up in the moment, the excitement of seeing the little life on screen? Or were they both trying to deny the inevitable? Were they meant to be together?

And then there was the issue of why she'd been so sure that he hadn't needed to use contraception. He still hadn't got to the bottom of that. He didn't think Ella was a gold-digger, but there was definitely something she was keeping from him, and he hadn't found the right way to ask her about it without causing a fight. 'Right now, everything's mixed up.'

'I guess only time will tell,' Sebastian said. 'Just make sure you keep the lines of communication open.'

Oliver knew that was sound advice. 'I will.'

'Have you told your family yet?'

'No. It's too early.'

'Fair enough.' Sebastian paused. 'Does Ella know about your family?'

The crunch question. Sebastian knew Oliver kept his background quiet at work, and why. 'No,' Oliver admitted.

'You're going to have to tell her at some point. And them. Especially if she's going to be a part of your future.'

'I know.' He'd been thinking about that. He needed to introduce Ella to his family; and, given that they seemed to be reaching out to him right now, maybe their attitude towards his career might have mellowed and they'd accept him for who he was rather than who they wanted him to be. 'My mother wants me to go to the annual Darrington pre-Christmas cocktail party.'

'Then go,' Sebastian said.

'You know I haven't been for years.' He hated all that meet-and-greet stuff.

'Things are different now. You need to introduce Ella to them. And,' Sebastian counselled, 'a party where there are a lot of people around would be a useful way of doing that.'

'You mean, it's in public so my parents will have to behave impeccably, and there will be enough other people there to dilute them?'

'I didn't say that.' But Oliver could almost hear the smile in his friend's voice, because they both knew what his family was like. Appearances mattered to the Darringtons. Sebastian, being a prince, was perfect friend material in their eyes. Ella came from a very different background, and it probably wouldn't go down well.

Oliver didn't need his parents to approve of Ella. Their relationship—if they could make it a real relationship—was just between the two of them. But he was starting to realise that family was important. Was there a place for his family in his future? Could they learn from the mistakes of the past and build some bridges?

'Olly, I really have to go,' Sebastian said. 'Sorry. I'll call you back when I'm out of my meeting.'

'I'll probably be in a meeting then myself, or in Theatre,' Oliver said. 'But you don't need to call me back, Seb. I think you've already helped me work out the best way forward. Thank you.'

'Any time. Good luck,' Sebastian said. 'And keep me posted on how things go.'

'I will. And thanks again.'

Once he'd put the phone down, Oliver texted his mother.

Confirm will be there on Tomorrow. May I bring a guest? There's someone I'd like you to meet.

The reply came back.

Of course. Look forward to meeting her.

Grilling her, more like, he thought. He definitely wouldn't leave Ella on her own at Darrington Hall. Even if she did protest that he was wrapping her in cotton wool.

'Mummy, look, it's Santa!' The little boy tugged at his mum's hand and pointed to the room on the other side of the floor, and Ella couldn't help smiling at the excitement on his face.

'Santa'—often one of the consultants in a borrowed suit—paid a brief visit to Teddy's every Wednesday afternoon in December, to see the siblings of all the new babies on the ward. The Friends of the Hospital group had raised money for gifts appropriate for different ages—a soft toy, colouring pencils and a pad, or a reading book—and it helped to make the older siblings feel that they were still special despite the new arrival in the family.

So who was it today? Oliver? Max?

Definitely not Oliver, because a couple of minutes later he came striding along the corridor. He paused in the doorway when he saw Ella, and smiled. 'OK?'

Ella nodded, and glanced back at the mum she'd been checking over. She was busy with the baby and talking to her toddler, so Ella stepped out for a second. 'You?'

'Yeah.'

'I wondered if you were, um, helping our friend in the red suit.'

He smiled. 'That would be next week.' For a moment, he took her hand and squeezed it. 'Next year, our baby will see Santa.'

His voice was low enough so that nobody else would've

heard. And that touch, combined with the expression in his eyes and what he'd just said, sent a thrill right through her. Especially when he added, 'And I can't wait. I know five months is still a bit young, but...'

Did that mean he wanted to take the baby to see Santa on his own? Or did he mean the three of them as a family? Not that she could ask. Yesterday, he'd kissed her; but then he'd said it was a mistake. Right now they seemed to be taking one step forward and two steps back.

Or maybe this was her chance to sound him out a little more. 'The year after will be better,' she said. 'Because by then the baby will be talking and know what's going on.'

'We're so getting a train set for the second Christmas,' he said. 'Whether we have a girl or a boy. Wooden trains are the best fun.'

And she could just see him kneeling on the floor with their baby, helping their little one put the train tracks together. Her heart constricted. But would she be there with him?

'You're going to be an amazing mum,' he said. 'Singing nursery rhymes and telling stories with all the voices.'

He'd been thinking about the future, then? Just the baby, or about them too? She let herself get carried away with the fantasy that it was all of them. 'And you're going to be the dad who does all the scary stuff—the highest slide in the park, pushing the swings as fast as they'll go.'

'That sounds good to me,' he said. 'But not that scary. I'll always keep my own safe.'

Right at that second she wasn't sure whether he was talking about the baby or her. And she so wanted it to be both of them.

'Ella—can I borrow you for a second?' Jennie, their trainee midwife, asked.

Oh, help. Ella really hoped that Jennie hadn't overheard any of that conversation.

'Sure,' she said, keeping her fingers crossed that she didn't sound flustered. 'I'll just let my mum know I'll be with you for a little while before I finish writing up her notes. I think they're next for Santa, so they won't miss me. Catch you later, Oliver.'

'Later,' he agreed with a smile.

It was just a work pleasantry, that was all, she reminded herself. She might not even see him again before the end of her shift. But at least they hadn't been fighting. That had to be a start.

Once Ella had helped Jennie and finished writing up her notes, she was called to the birthing suite for another delivery. This was the best job in the world, she thought, watching the little family in front of her: the dad with tears of pride and joy in his eyes, the mum looking tired but radiant, and the baby cuddled up between them. To be able to share these first few precious minutes of a new life was so amazing.

The delivery had been free from complications, the baby had had a perfect Apgar score, and now the three of them were settled back on the ward.

Would Oliver cry when their baby arrived, the way this baby's dad had cried with sheer joy? Or would he be perfectly cool, calm and collected? Given what he'd said to her when Santa came onto the ward, she had a feeling it would be the former. And he had talked about next Christmas, so it sounded as if he wanted to be part of the baby's life.

There was still a lot they weren't saying to each other, but at least they weren't arguing. So maybe they'd manage to work things out between them.

She left the little family to bond and went to write up her notes in the quiet of the office.

She was halfway through when there was a rap on the door. She looked up to see Oliver standing in the doorway.

'Can I have a word?' he asked.

Her heart skipped a beat as she thought about the way he'd kissed her in the ultrasound room yesterday; but then she remembered how quick he'd been to dismiss it as a simple reaction to seeing the baby and hearing the good news. Despite what he'd said to her earlier today about their baby and next Christmas, they hadn't actually resolved their relationship. And she had to be objective about this. Oliver Darrington might be the father of her baby, but he wasn't in love with her. She'd be a fool to dream it would ever happen. She damped down the flare of desire. 'Sure,' she said, as coolly as she could. 'Though I'm in the middle of writing up the birth notes.'

'Did it go well?'

'Very. There were no complications, and I left the new mum and dad bonding with their little girl.' She smiled. 'The dad cried when she was born. It was so lovely to see how happy they were.' And oh, she had to stop talking. The last thing she wanted was for Oliver to guess how she was feeling. 'You wanted something?'

'Yes. What are you doing tomorrow?'

'Cleaning my flat,' she said, 'as it's my day off. And I really ought to do a bit of Christmas shopping. I'm a bit behind, this year.'

'Are you busy in the evening?' he asked.

'Why?'

'Because my parents are having a cocktail party.' He looked awkward. 'I wondered if you'd like to come with me.'

He wanted her to meet his parents?

Ella stared at him in surprise. 'Are you sure? I mean… They didn't invite me.'

'They have now. I asked if I could bring you.'

So he'd already talked to his family about her? Had he told them about the baby, despite the fact he'd suggested she shouldn't tell anyone until she was past the first trimester?

She pushed down the rising panic. Cocktail party, he'd said. She didn't know anyone who actually held cocktail parties. She knew that Oliver had quite a posh accent. But how posh exactly were they? Would she fit in?

As if he'd guessed what she was thinking, he said, 'It's not a big deal. Just a drinks party they hold every year before Christmas.'

It was an annual event? That sounded even scarier. 'It sounds a little bit fancy,' she said.

Oliver's face shuttered. 'All right. So you don't want to meet my family.'

She shook her head. 'No, that's not what I meant, Oliver. I was just thinking that it sounds like quite a big party and your parents will be busy. Wouldn't it be better if I met them at something a bit quieter and more low-key rather than a big event?' And something she could escape from more easily. 'Like, I don't know, meeting at a café in town for a cup of tea?'

'It's probably better,' he said, 'if there are a lot of people there.'

That sounded ominous. Did that mean he thought they were going to hate her, especially when they found out about the baby? Or did they already know about the baby and they weren't pleased?

Clearly her worries showed in her face because he said, 'What I mean is that my family can be a little bit pushy— I guess that's where I get my overbearing streak. I think the first time you meet them will be better if they're a bit diluted. They're the problem, not you.'

That didn't calm Ella's worries in the slightest. Particularly as she knew that her own family would welcome Oliver warmly when she introduced him to them. They'd draw him straight into the middle of things and treat him as if they'd known him for years and years. Her father had already said they wanted to welcome him to the family.

Clearly Oliver's family was very different, and she'd have to tread very carefully.

'Have you told them about the baby?' she asked.

'Not yet.'

'Because they won't approve of me?' The question burst out before she could stop it.

'Because,' he said, 'it's still early days. I'd prefer to wait until you're safely through the first trimester before we tell my family about the baby.'

That was sensible; though it made her feel guilty that everyone in the department already knew. It felt wrong to be sharing this with their colleagues and not Oliver's family, especially as she'd already shared the news with her own family. But how could she explain that? 'OK.' She paused. 'So what do I wear? If it's a big cocktail party...'

'I'll buy you a dress,' Oliver said.

She frowned. 'No—and that's not why I asked. Is the dress I wore to the masked ball suitable?'

'Yes, but I can b—' he began.

'No,' she cut in. 'You really don't need to buy me a dress, Oliver. It's a total waste to buy something you're only ever going to wear to one thing.'

He sighed. 'I'm being bossy again?'

She nodded.

'Got it,' he said. 'Will you allow me to drive you to the party?'

'Yes, but only because you know the way.'

'All right.' His grey eyes were unreadable. 'I'll pick you up tomorrow, then.'

'What time do I need to be ready?'

'The party starts at half-past seven, and it takes about an hour to get there. So I'll pick you up at half-past six.'

'I'll be ready. Should I have dinner first?'

'There will be nibbles there—but yes, I'd say grab a sandwich or something before I pick you up,' Oliver said.

Ella noticed that he didn't suggest eating together first, and pushed down the feeling of hurt. After all, she'd already accused him of being bossy. He'd probably thought she'd bite his head off if he suggested it. 'All right. I'll see you tomorrow then.'

She watched him walk out of the door. Had he just asked her on a date of sorts? Was he thinking about trying to make a go of things between them, and introducing her to his family was the first step? Or was this some kind of test she needed to pass?

'You're overthinking it, you numpty,' she told herself crossly. She knew Oliver didn't play games. He was simply introducing her to his family. Not as the mother of his child, but as... She didn't quite know what as, but it was most likely he'd say she was his colleague or maybe his friend. And then, when he'd worked out how his family reacted to her, he'd find the right way to break the news about the baby. It was nothing to worry about.

'We're going to be just fine,' she said, resting her hand where her bump wasn't even visible yet. 'If they don't like us—well, that's their problem, and we'll deal with it if and when we have to.'

CHAPTER SIX

DESPITE HER BRAVE intentions of the night before, Ella spent Thursday feeling really nervous. What would Oliver's parents be like? Would they accept her? He'd said that his relationship with them was complicated. Would the baby make things worse? Or was he hoping that the baby would be a bonding point?

But then again, how many people thought that having a baby would paper over the cracks in their relationship, only to find instead that the pressure of having a newborn made the cracks burst wide open? And that would be true of any family relationship, not just that of the baby's parents.

She tried not to think about it too much while she cleaned her flat, and it made her feel slightly better when Annabelle sent her a text during her break on the ward.

Good luck for tonight. Am sure O's parents will love you.

Then she went into Cheltenham to do her Christmas shopping, and all her fears came back. Everywhere she looked, she seemed to see new mums proudly pushing a pram with their partners by their side.

Tears pricked her eyelids. She *missed* her parents. And she knew they'd both be doting grandparents, always ready with a cuddle and a story. Would Oliver's parents feel the same way about the baby? Or would it make their strained relationship with Oliver more difficult?

Plus it was still very early days in her pregnancy—especially given the complications of her own medical history, which she hadn't yet felt comfortable enough to share with Oliver. The sonographer hadn't said anything, but what if there was a cyst on her other ovary? What if it grew during the pregnancy and she ended up needing an operation to remove it? She knew that kind of operation wasn't usually done until halfway through the pregnancy, to protect the baby—but what if the cyst ruptured, like the other one had?

'Stop it. You're borrowing trouble, and you know that's stupid,' she told herself crossly.

It had to be hormones making her all tearful and miserable like this, because Ella had never been a whiner. Even on days when the pain of her endometriosis had made it hard for her to crawl out of bed, she'd tried her best to pretend that everything was just fine.

And she needed to be on top form tonight, all smiley and cheerful, so Oliver's family would like her.

Oliver.

Should she get him a Christmas present? They weren't in a relationship exactly, but he was her baby's father. Though Ella didn't have a clue what to buy him. He never shared anything personal at work. Although she knew from the night of the Hallowe'en ball that he liked piano music, she didn't know what he already owned. And she didn't want to buy him something bland and impersonal like a bottle of wine.

She shook herself. She'd worry about that later. For now, she needed to think about meeting his family and hoping she could make them like her.

The shopping and the cleaning took it out of her, and

she ended up falling asleep over her books. She had only just enough time to get ready, grab a sandwich and do her hair and make-up before Oliver arrived at precisely half-past six.

'You look lovely,' he said.

'Thank you.' So did he, in a dinner jacket and bow tie—just as he'd worn to the ball. Evening dress suited him.

And she remembered exactly what it had felt like to slide that shirt off his shoulders and trace his pectoral muscles with her fingertips—and how it had felt when he'd unzipped the dress she was wearing right now...

Oh, help. She really had to keep her imagination and her memory under strict control. Tonight she needed to be on her best behaviour—and that didn't mean doing what she really wanted to do most at that moment and kissing Oliver until they were both dizzy with need and ended up back in her bed. Especially as she wasn't sure at all how he felt about her.

Hormones, she reminded herself. This is all just hormones rushing round and I need to be sensible. 'Um—would you like a drink?' she asked.

'Tea would be good, thanks.' He looked slightly wary. 'I need to talk to you about something.'

This didn't sound good. 'Come in and sit down.' She busied herself making tea; he didn't say anything, which made her feel even more awkward. But she wasn't a coward; she'd face this head on. 'What did you want to talk about?'

'My family,' he said, surprising her. 'I know I don't have to ask you to keep this confidential.'

Because he trusted her? That was a good thing. If he was going to tell her why his relationship with his parents was tricky, it might stop her accidentally making things worse tonight. 'Of course I'll keep whatever you tell me to myself,' she said, wanting to reassure him.

'I don't mention my family at work,' he said, 'because I want people to see me for who I am, not whose son I am.'

She frowned. 'Your dad's famous?'

He coughed. 'My father's the Earl of Darrington.'

It took her a while to process it. 'You mean your family's like a real-life version of the one in *Downton Abbey*?'

'Yes.'

She stared at him, not quite able to believe this. She'd known Oliver was posh, but *this* posh? Oh, help. She didn't quite know how to deal with this.

'So should I have been calling you Lord Darrington all these months?' she asked carefully.

'No. I'm not the oldest son, so I'm just the Hon Oliver Darrington,' he said. 'Addressed as plain Mr Darrington, just as you're addressed as Miss O'Brien.'

'Ms,' she corrected. And as for his 'just the Hon'—she didn't know anyone else who was an Hon. And then a really nasty thought struck her. 'Oliver, you don't think I'm a gold-digger, do you? Because I had absolutely no idea you were—well, from that kind of background.'

Shock spread across his face. 'Of course you're not a gold-digger, Ella. Apart from the fact that nobody at work knows about my background, you're completely open and honest.'

That wasn't quite true. She hadn't been totally honest with him about her past, because she hadn't wanted him to pity her. Guilt trickled through her—but the worry was uppermost. 'So this party tonight's going to be really, really posh?'

He grimaced. 'A bit. And I understand if you'd rather not go. I probably should have told you when I asked you to come with me.'

'I wish you had, because at least then I could've maybe found something more suitable to wear while I was out shopping today.' She gestured to her dress. 'Everyone's going to take one look at me and know this was a sale bargain and probably cost less than their underwear. I'm not going to fit in. And your parents are going to think I'm just after your money. Which,' she added, just in case he was under any kind of misapprehension on that score, 'I'm not.'

Oliver came to stand before her and pulled her to her feet. 'Ella O'Brien, you look beautiful. Nobody whose opinion matters will think anything about what you're wearing other than the fact that you look lovely. You're more than good enough to hold your own at any party, whether it's the pub quiz between Teddy's and the Emergency Department, or the ballroom at Darrington Hall full of…' He spread his hands. 'Well.'

'Lords and ladies?' she asked wryly.

'Not all of them will have a title,' he said. 'But yes. You're more than good enough, Ella.'

There was a slash of colour across his cheeks, telling her that he felt really strongly about this. He really did believe that she could fit in.

And then, the expression in his eyes changed. Turned from fierceness to heat. Achingly slowly, he dipped his head to brush his mouth against hers. There was a sweetness to his kiss, just like when he'd kissed her in the ultrasound room, and Ella found herself melting against him and returning his kiss.

'You're wearing the same dress you wore that night,' Oliver whispered against her mouth. 'That night we made love. The night we made our baby.'

His hand slid down to rest protectively over her abdomen, and Ella's pulse speeded up a notch. On impulse, she rested her hand over his, and he moved slightly so that her fingers were entwined with his, united and protective.

'And you're wearing that suit,' she whispered back. 'I can remember taking your shirt off.'

His eyes darkened. 'Ella. I can't stop thinking about that night. How it felt to be with you.' He stole another kiss. 'The scent of your hair. The feel of your bare skin against mine.' His teeth grazed her earlobe as he whispered, 'I haven't stopped wanting you. And now you're carrying our baby, it makes me want to…'

'Yes.' Oh, yes. She wanted it, too. That shared closeness she'd only ever known with him. Except this time it would be different. Because they'd created a new life, and when he explored her he'd notice the tiny, subtle changes. And she knew he'd tell her about every single one in that amazingly sexy posh voice.

Right now her skin felt too tight. Especially when he kissed her again, pulling her close against him, and her hardened nipples rubbed against him.

'Oliver,' she breathed.

But, when Ella felt Oliver's fingers brush the skin on her back as he began to slide the zip of her dress slowly downward, common sense kicked back in. Yes, she wanted to make love with him. Desperately. But she was supposed to be going to meet his family. She needed to make a good impression. Turning up late, looking as if she'd just had sex, with her mouth all swollen and her hair all mussed— that most definitely wouldn't be the right impression.

'Oliver. We *can't*. We're going to be late.'

He stroked her face. 'Or we can skip the party.'

'But your parents are expecting us. It's rude not to turn up.'

'I know. But I can say I was held up at work.'

'Which isn't true.'

'It's a white lie.'

It sounded as if he didn't want to go to the party, and not just because he wanted to carry her to her bed. She narrowed her eyes at him. 'What else aren't you telling me, Oliver?'

He sighed. 'Nothing, really.'

'You said things were strained between you and your parents. Is not turning up going to make things worse? Or will it be worse when they meet me and realise I'm not from your world?'

He rested his palm against her cheek. 'Trust you to hit the nail on the head. OK. Let's just say that they had other plans for me, so they're not brilliantly happy that I went into medicine.'

She couldn't understand why. 'But you're Assistant Head of Department at a ridiculously young age. Doesn't that tell them how good you are at what you do?'

'I didn't actually tell them about the promotion,' he admitted.

'Why? For pity's sake, Oliver, aren't they massively proud of you? Because they ought to be! You're really good at your job. What you do is *important*.'

Ella was batting Oliver's corner for him, and it made him feel odd. He'd never, ever dated anyone who'd backed him like that before. With Justine, he was always the one doing the protecting; but Ella was different. She was his equal.

Strictly speaking, he and Ella weren't actually dating. But there was more to their relationship than just the shared unexpected parenthood. And the fact that she was backing him like this... Maybe she was the one that he could trust with his heart. The one who'd see him for who he really was. 'You really think that?' he asked.

She put her hands on her hips and rolled her eyes at him.

'Oliver Darrington, you're the one who makes the difference in a tricky birth between someone having a baby, and someone losing their baby. You've saved babies and you've saved their mums, too. And if that's not more important than—than—' She waved a hand in disgust. 'Than having a title, then I don't know what is.'

Even with her lipstick smudged and her hair slightly mussed from their shared kiss, Ella looked magnificent. A pocket Amazonian.

'You,' he said softly, 'are amazing. Never let anyone else ever tell you otherwise.'

'So are you,' Ella said fiercely. 'So we're going to this party, and your family can see that for themselves.'

'Right.' He stole another kiss. 'Though you might want to put some more lipstick on and fiddle with your hair.'

'Give me two minutes,' Ella said.

And she was ready in the time it took him to wash up their undrunk mugs of tea.

Ella didn't manage to get much more out of Oliver about his family on the journey, other than that his older brother Ned was married to Prue and they had three girls. Her bravado dimmed a bit when Oliver explained that Ned was the heir to the earldom and he was the 'spare' until Ned and Prue had a son—particularly when she worked out that if Ned and Prue didn't have a son and something happened to Ned, Oliver would be the future Earl of Darrington; and then if her baby was a boy he would be the heir, which would make her the mother of an earl. Her nerves threatened to outweigh the bravery completely when Oliver drove down the long, narrow driveway lined with trees and she saw just how big Darrington Hall was. Her worries grew as he parked his car among what she recognised as Rolls-Royces and Bentleys. No way could she fit into this kind of world. If his parents didn't approve of his job, they'd approve even less of her.

He helped her from the car, and led her up the steps to the porticoed entrance. They were greeted at the door by a butler wearing white gloves, who took their coats. 'Good to see you again, Master Oliver,' he said, dipping his head in acknowledgement.

'Thank you, Benson,' Oliver said with a smile.

'Everyone's in the ballroom, Master Oliver,' the butler said.

'Thanks, Benson. This way, Ella,' Oliver said.

The reception hall was massive, with a huge sweeping staircase, polished wooden floors, a carpet that looked as if it was an antique worth hundreds of thousands of pounds, and a whole gallery of portraits in heavy gold frames.

'Are they…?' Ella asked, gesturing to them.

'The Earls of Darrington, yes. My father's the one over there.'

The newest portrait. The current Earl had a stern face, Ella thought. And he was wearing very formal dress; she imagined it was what he'd wear in the House of Lords.

He really, really wasn't going to approve of her.

There were serving staff dressed in black and white, carrying silver trays filled with glasses of champagne or exquisite canapés. The trays looked as if they were real silver, Ella thought, rather than the polished chrome used in a restaurant.

She felt even more out of place when they walked into the ballroom itself. Again, the room was massive, with wooden-panelled walls, a huge marble fireplace, more oil paintings in heavy frames and the most enormous crystal chandelier. There was a baby grand piano in the corner of the room, and the man sitting on the piano stool was playing soft jazz, not quite loudly enough to disturb the hum of conversation. And the only time she'd seen a Christmas tree that big was in one of the posh London stores. It looked professionally decorated, too—not like the Christmas trees in her family, strewn with decorations made over the years at school by each child. All the reds and golds of the different decorations matched, and the spacing between baubles was so precise that someone must've used a tape measure.

But then Oliver tucked her hand firmly in the crook of his arm and was walking her over towards a couple at the other side of the room.

'Olls! I thought Mama had been at the sherry when she said you were turning up tonight,' the man said, clapping him on the back.

Even without the words, Ella would've guessed that this was Oliver's brother, because they looked so alike.

'Very funny, Ned. I'd like you to meet Ms Ella O'Brien. Ella, this is my elder brother Ned, and how he managed to persuade lovely Prue here to marry a scoundrel like him is beyond me,' Oliver said, laughing.

'I—um—how do you do, Lord Darrington?' Ella said awkwardly, holding out a hand, really hoping that she'd got the etiquette right. Or should she be curtsying to him? She only just resisted the urge to kick Oliver very hard on the ankle for not giving her anywhere near enough information about how to deal with this.

Viscount Darrington shook her hand. 'Delighted to meet you, Ms O'Brien, or may I call you Ella?'

She could see where Oliver got his charm from, now. 'Ella's fine,' she said, cross with herself for squeaking the words.

'And you must call me Ned,' he said with a warm smile.

'And I'm Prue. We don't stand on ceremony, whatever nonsense Olls might have told you,' Viscountess Darrington said. Then she shook her head in exasperation. 'Did he not even let you get a drink, first? That's terrible. Olls, your manners are shocking. Come with me, Ella— let's leave these heathens to sort themselves out. What would you like? Some champagne?'

'Thank you,' Ella said, 'but I'm on an early shift tomorrow, so I'd rather not be drinking alcohol tonight.'

'Let's sort you out with something soft, then,' Prue said with a smile. 'And I'm sure we have you to thank for Olls actually coming to the party. He normally wriggles out of it.'

'I…um…' Ella didn't know what to say.

'And it's really bad of him to drop you right in the middle of this without any warning,' Prue said. 'This place is a bit overwhelming, the first time you see it—and with all these people about it's even more intimidating.' She shook her head again and tutted. 'I'm so sorry, Ella. If he'd actually told us he was bringing you, I'd have suggested meeting you in Cheltenham for lunch first—somewhere quiet, where we could have had a proper chat and got to know each other a bit before tonight.'

Ella really hadn't expected Oliver's family to be so welcoming, not after he'd said things were strained between them. But Prue Darrington was a real sweetheart, and Ella began to feel just the tiniest bit better about being here.

'I think the invitation was all a bit last-minute,' she said.

Prue rolled her eyes. 'The Darrington men are all the same—they're total rubbish at communicating. But I'm so glad you've come. It's lovely to meet you. And I do like your necklace. It's so pretty.'

Ella wasn't sure whether Prue really meant the compliment or was just being kind, but she was grateful that at least someone here wasn't looking down on her. 'Thank you.'

'I take it you work with Olls?' Prue asked.

Ella nodded. 'I'm a midwife.'

'What a wonderful job to have—to see those first precious moments of life,' Prue said.

'I love it,' Ella confided shyly. 'Oliver says you have three girls?'

'We do. Rose, Poppy and Lily—aged five, three and thirteen months respectively.'

'They're very pretty names,' Ella said.

Prue grinned. 'That's the great thing about having a girl Darrington. You actually get to choose her name yourself.'

Ella blinked. 'You mean, if you'd had a boy, you wouldn't have been able to choose his name, even though you're his mum?'

'The firstborn boy is *always* Edward.' Prue winked. 'Though if we ever have a son, I plan to rebel and always refer to him by his middle name.'

As they walked by a towering floral display, Ella discovered that the heavy perfume of lilies brought on a rush of morning sickness.

'Are you all right?' Prue asked.

'Fine,' Ella fibbed.

'No, you're not. You've gone green. Come on, let's get you a glass of water and somewhere quiet to sit down.'

Prue was as good as her word, and Ella felt better when she'd had a sip of water.

Prue lowered her voice. 'So how far along are you?'

'I don't know what you mean,' Ella said, inwardly horrified that Prue had guessed her secret already.

'Ella, you're a midwife and I have three girls. When someone female goes green at the scent of lilies, either they have hay fever—in which case they'll start sneezing the place down within two seconds—or...' Prue squeezed Ella's hand. 'If it makes you feel any better, I'll tell you a secret. If the party had been last week instead of tonight, I would've turned green as well at the scent of those lilies.'

'You're…?'

Prue nodded, and lifted a finger to her lips. 'Ned and I promised each other not to tell anyone until I'm twelve weeks.'

And that gave Ella the confidence to admit the truth. 'Me, too. Almost eight weeks. But please don't tell anyone,' she said. 'Not even Ned.'

'OK. I promise. But you have to make the same promise,' Prue said. 'You can't even tell Olls for the next three weeks.'

'I promise,' Ella said.

'But this is such fabulous news,' Prue said. 'Our babies will be practically the same age. Which means they'll have a great time romping around this place together.'

'I used to play with my cousins all the time, when I was young,' Ella said. And she loved the idea of her baby having a built-in family like this, just the way that she had.

'My cousins all lived too far away for us to see them that often. And I was the only one, so I was determined to have lots and lots of children,' Prue said. 'Ned's desperate for a boy. Not because of the entailment and all that nonsense about a son and heir, but because he says he's going to need some support when the girls are teens and we all have PMT at the same time and he'll be terrified of us.'

Ella couldn't help laughing. She really, really liked Oliver's sister-in-law, and she had the feeling they were going to become good friends. 'I bet the girls wrap him round their little fingers.'

'They do,' Prue confirmed. 'And you should hear him read them a bedtime story. It's so cute.'

Would Oliver be like that as a father, totally involved with their baby?

Then again, she and Oliver weren't a proper couple—despite the way he'd kissed her tonight.

Ella pushed the thought away as Ned and Oliver came over to join them.

'I wondered where you'd both disappeared to,' Ned said.

'Sorry. I just needed to sit down for a moment,' Ella said. 'It's been a crazy shift at work today. I had a mum with a water birth, and then a scary one where the cord was wrapped round the baby's neck. Luckily there was a happy ending in both cases.' It wasn't strictly true—although that particular shift had happened, it had been a fortnight ago rather than today—but she hoped that the story would keep Ned off the scent.

'We really have to circulate, darling, or Mama will be on the warpath,' Ned said to Prue with a grimace. 'Ella, please excuse us—but do make sure you find us later, because I'd love to get to know you a bit better. And make sure Prue has your mobile number so we can arrange dinner.'

'I will,' Ella promised.

'Are you really all right?' Oliver asked when his brother and sister-in-law had gone.

'Yes.' She gave him a wan smile. 'The lilies got to me.'

'Right.' Understanding filled his gaze.

'Sorry for telling the fib about work.'

'No. I understand. You needed to—otherwise you'd have had to tell them.'

And she'd already told Prue, she thought, feeling guilty. 'I like your brother and sister-in-law,' she said.

'They're good sorts,' Oliver said. He looked her straight in the eye. 'Are you feeling up to meeting my parents?'

Even the idea of it made butterflies stampede through her stomach. It was so important that she got this right and made a good impression, for Oliver's sake. But Prue and Ned had been so nice and welcoming. Surely Oliver's parents would be the same, even if things were strained between them and Oliver? 'Sure,' she said, masking her nerves.

He led her over to the other side of the room. 'Mama, Papa, I'd like to introduce you to Ella O'Brien,' he said.

His voice was much more formal and cool than it had been when he'd introduced her to his brother and sister-in-law, and Ella's heart sank. This didn't bode well.

'Ella, this is my father Edward, the Earl of Darrington, and my mother Catherine, the Countess of Darrington,' Oliver continued.

Instead of greeting her warmly, the way Ned and Prue had, the Earl and Countess of Darrington simply stood there, looking very remote. The Earl nodded at her and the Countess just looked her up and down.

Were they expecting her to curtsey? Did you curtsey to an earl and a countess? Unnerved and flustered, Ella did exactly that. 'Pleased to meet you, Lord and Lady Darrington,' she said awkwardly, hoping she'd got it right.

'Indeed,' the Earl of Darrington said, his voice cool.

Ella noticed that he didn't invite her to use their given names, the way Prue and Ned had done; his approach was much more formal. And she felt as if she'd already made a fool of herself. Perhaps curtseying had been the wrong thing to do.

'So how do you know Oliver?' the Earl asked.

'I'm a midwife. We work together at Teddy's,' she said, acutely aware of the difference between her soft Irish accent and the Earl's cut-glass tones.

'Of course. What do your parents do?' the Countess asked.

'Mama, that's hardly—' Oliver began.

'It's fine,' Ella said. Of course they'd want to know that. 'Mam's a music teacher and Da's a farmer.'

'So you have land in Ireland?' the Countess asked.

'No. Da's a tenant farmer,' Ella said, lifting her chin that little bit higher. She wasn't in the slightest bit ashamed of her background. As far as she was concerned, it didn't matter what your parents did or how much land or money they had—it was who you were as a person and how you treated other people that counted.

And she could understand now why Oliver had a tricky relationship with his parents, and not just because they hadn't wanted him to be a doctor; she knew he thought the same way that she did about people. From his expression, she could tell that he was horrified and angry about the way his parents had reacted to her.

'Ella's a very talented midwife,' Oliver said, his voice very clipped. 'Everyone thinks very highly of her at Teddy's.'

'Indeed,' the Earl drawled. Making it very clear that whatever anyone else thought of her, the Earl and Countess of Darrington didn't think that the daughter of a tenant farmer and a teacher was anywhere near good enough for their son.

'I'm afraid we really ought to mingle. We have rather a lot of guests we haven't welcomed yet,' the Earl said. 'Excuse us, my dear.'

And he and the Countess walked away without even a backward glance.

'I'm so sorry about that,' Oliver said, grimacing.

She swallowed hard. 'It's OK.' Even though it wasn't. Oliver's parents had just snubbed her. Big time. 'I kind of expected it.'

'My parents,' he said, 'aren't the easiest of people. It

really isn't you. That was just plain *rude* of them. Maybe it's because they're stressed about holding a big party.'

Ella didn't think that something as simple as a party would stress the Earl and Countess of Darrington, especially one that had clearly been held every year for a very long time. They would simply snap their fingers and expect things to be done as they ordered. What could there be to worry about? Oliver was just making excuses for them.

Then again, what else could the poor man do?

She was just glad that her own family would be much, much nicer towards Oliver than his parents had been towards her.

Oliver raked a hand through his hair. 'Come on. I'll introduce you to a few others.'

Most of the people at the party seemed to be the movers and shakers of local businesses, plus local landed gentry: the kind of people Ella didn't usually mix with and had nothing in common with. Everyone seemed polite—at least, they weren't as openly hostile towards her as the Earl and Countess had been, but they were still quite reserved with her. It was very obvious that Ella wasn't going to fit into Oliver's world, even though his brother and sister-in-law were nice.

And why did all the men have to wear what smelled like half a bottle of super-strong aftershave? It made her feel queasy again, so she went to splash her face with water.

When she came out of the bathroom, the Countess was waiting outside.

'Feeling a little under the weather?' the Countess enquired, her expression unreadable.

Perhaps Oliver's mother thought she'd been downing too much champagne. Which couldn't have been further from the truth—but the truth was something Ella knew

Oliver didn't want the Countess to know yet. 'It's been a busy day,' Ella prevaricated.

'Perhaps I should offer you some coffee.'

Even the thought of it made Ella gag, and she wasn't quite quick enough to hide the reflex.

'I thought as much,' the Countess said. 'I knew there was a reason why Oliver would want to bring someone, especially as it's been a few years since he's turned up to our pre-Christmas drinks party. How far gone are you?'

Faced with a direct question, Ella couldn't lie. 'It's still early days.'

'Hmm. Obviously Oliver will insist on a paternity test, to make *quite* sure. Both he and Ned have known their fair share of women who, let's say, would like to take advantage of their positions.'

What? Oliver's mother actually thought that Ella was lying about Oliver being the baby's father, and that she was some sort of gold-digger—because her parents were ordinary rather than titled? That was outrageous! But Ella couldn't let rip and give the Countess a piece of her mind. She could hardly make a scene in front of everyone at the party, because it would embarrass Oliver hugely.

So she was just going to have to put up with this. And she really hoped that Oliver would think that she'd been gone a little too long and come in search of her, then rescue her from his mother.

'Of course, if it *is* his,' the Countess continued, 'then as a Darrington the baby will have a position to maintain. If it's a boy, he'll go to the same prep school and public school as Edward and Oliver.'

Over my dead body, Ella thought. No way was she dumping her baby in a boarding school. She wanted her child to go to the local school, where he or she would fit in to a normal world. And her child would most definitely grow up feeling loved and wanted, rather than being palmed off on a nanny.

'And,' the Countess said, 'in that case Oliver will have custody of the child.'

What? The baby was so tiny right now that you couldn't make out more than a bean-shape on an ultrasound scan, and the Countess was already planning to take the baby away from her?

Ella opened her mouth, about to say, 'Absolutely *not*,' when the Countess cut in.

'I'm glad we had this little chat, Miss O'Brien. I think we understand each other now.'

The Countess didn't understand her at all, Ella thought, and clearly didn't want to.

'I'll leave you to think about it,' the Countess finished, and swept off.

That told Ella everything she needed to know.

Even though Prue and Ned had been so nice, there was no way she'd ever fit in here. The last thing she wanted was to deepen the divide between Oliver and his parents. So, even though she was angry on his behalf, she wouldn't tell him what his mother had said and risk things getting even worse. Right now the best thing she could do would be to cool things between them instead of letting herself dream that she and Oliver could possibly have a future. It wasn't going to happen.

But this baby was hers and no way was she going to let Oliver's mother take the baby away from her, whatever the Countess might think. If the Countess tried, then she'd have a real fight on her hands. One which Ella had no intention of losing.

Ella had been gone a little too long for Oliver's liking. Had she got lost in the house? Or had something happened?

Worried, he excused himself from the people he was talking to and went in search of her.

He found her in a corridor on the way back from the bathroom.

'Are you all right?' he asked.

'Fine,' she said.

She didn't look fine to him. She looked upset. 'Has something happened?'

'No—I'm just a bit tired,' she said.

The baby. Of course. He should've realised. And she'd already excused herself a couple of times to splash water on her face. Clearly something was triggering her morning sickness again. The lilies, maybe? She'd mentioned them earlier.

'Do you want to go?' he asked.

'It's fine,' she said. 'I'm happy to wait until you're ready.'

'I'm ready,' he said. Although it had been good to see Ned again, Oliver was seriously upset by the way his parents had been so cool to Ella, dismissing her. Maybe they were worried he was going to get hurt again, the way he had with Justine—but, as they'd been the ones to introduce him to Justine in the first place and had put so much pressure on them to get together, they were hardly in a position to judge Ella. And he was still furious about the way his mother had grilled Ella about her background. As if it mattered in the slightest what her parents did.

'I really ought to find your parents and thank them for inviting me,' she said.

Oliver would rather leave right now, but he knew Ella was right. Manners were important. It was a pity that his parents seemed to have forgotten that tonight. Though he'd make that point to them later, when Ella wasn't around to be embarrassed by his bluntness.

Thankfully they managed to keep their leave-taking really brief. But Ella was quiet all the way back to Cheltenham. And, when he parked outside her flat, she didn't invite him in for coffee.

Maybe she was tired. It was common for women to be really, really tired in early pregnancy, he reminded himself.

Yet he couldn't shake the feeling that something was wrong. Before the party, he'd kissed her—and she'd definitely responded. Kissed him back. They'd been very close to him picking her up and carrying her to her bed. And the way she'd been so firmly on his side about his career, making him feel that they were in an equal partnership and she'd fight his corner just as hard as he'd fight hers... He'd felt that they'd moved closer, were nearer to understanding each other better and getting to the point where they could agree to make a go of things. And now he realised he knew what he wanted: to be part of her life as well as the baby's. To make a proper family with her.

Right now she'd become remote again. This felt like one step forward and two steps back. Was it because his parents had been so awful? Did she really hate the world he came from? He knew if he asked her what was wrong, she'd say everything was fine. If he tried to kiss her, he had a feeling that this time she wouldn't respond—that he'd be deepening the chasm between them.

How could he get her to talk to him without making things worse?

'Thank you for this evening,' she said politely. 'I'll see you on the ward.'

Maybe the best thing to do now would be to give her some space. 'Sure,' he said, and waited until she was safely indoors before he drove back to his own place.

Was he overreacting, or was Ella going cool on him?

No. He was being ridiculous and paranoid. She'd told

him she was tired. And Ella was straightforward. He was just seeing things completely out of context, because seeing his parents always rubbed him up the wrong way. He'd hoped that tonight he could re-establish a better relationship with his parents, or at least the beginnings of one. But they hadn't changed. Right now, he was just out of sorts and seeing shadows where there weren't any. Tomorrow, he'd see Ella on the ward and she'd be her usual sunny self, and everything would be just fine.

It *would*.

CHAPTER SEVEN

ELLA SLEPT BADLY that night. She kept waking up, shivering, after horrible dreams of Oliver delivering the baby and then his mother snatching the child before he could give it to Ella and slamming the door behind her.

When her alarm clanged, Ella was feeling out of sorts and upset. A shower and washing her hair didn't make her feel much better, and she could barely face a single slice of dry toast for breakfast.

She drove in to work and was relieved to discover that Oliver was in a meeting, so she wouldn't have to face him. Even though part of her wanted to tell him about what his mother had said—and to get a bit of reassurance about her nightmare—she knew that wouldn't be fair to him. It'd be like asking him to choose between her and his family. Annabelle was off duty, so Ella couldn't discuss it with her, either. Annabelle had texted her that morning.

How did it go?

Ella had texted back with a total fib, saying it was all fine. She didn't want to burden her best friend, especially as she knew how hard things had been for Annabelle and Max. She was glad it had worked out for them, but at the same time she felt slightly wistful, as she couldn't see how things could ever work out between herself and Oliver. Prue and Ned had been kind, but his parents would never accept her, and Ella didn't want to be responsible for the final rift between Oliver and his parents.

'Hey, sweetie. Are you doing OK?'

Ella looked up to see their heavily pregnant neonatal cardiothoracic surgeon, standing before her. 'Morning, Sienna. Of course I'm OK. Why wouldn't I…?' Her voice tailed off as she realised what Sienna meant. 'Oh. You know.'

''Fraid so.' Sienna patted her arm. 'You've replaced me as the hottest topic of gossip at the Royal Cheltenham, right now.'

Ella bit her lip. 'Hopefully everyone will find something else to think about soon.'

'Of course they will. How did the scan go?'

'Good, thanks. Everything's positive.'

'That's great.' Sienna smiled at her. 'I'm glad that Oliver supported you, too.'

Oh, help. They'd used the cover story that her family was far away so Oliver was supporting her, but had everyone guessed the truth—that Oliver had been there as the baby's father? 'He's the Assistant Head of Obstetrics, so I guess he feels responsible for his staff,' Ella said hesitantly.

'He's a good man. He offered to go with me for my scans, too.'

So Sienna *didn't* know that Oliver was the father of Ella's baby. Which meant that nobody else did either—because Ella knew that Annabelle would've kept her confidence. 'Thanks for not asking.'

'About who the dad is?' Sienna laughed. 'Given my situation, I could hardly be that hypocritical. Sometimes this is just how things happen—and it's much better for a baby to have one parent who really loves them, than two who fight all the time.'

That sounded personal, but Ella wasn't going to intrude by asking. 'Yes, you're right.'

'I just wanted to say, if you need a confidential ear at any time, you know where I am—I know I'm going on leave soon, but I'll still be around.'

'Thanks, Sienna.' It was kind of her to offer, even though Ella thought that the doctor was going to be way too busy with her newborn baby. 'And I'm still on your babysitter list—the bump won't change that.'

'Glad to hear it.' Sienna patted her arm again. 'It'll be good practice for you. We're both used to newborns, but we're also used to handing the babies over and I think it's going to be a bit of a shock to our systems.'

'Ah, but I get to teach new mums how to change nappies and put on a sleep suit,' Ella pointed out.

'Then you have the advantage over me. I know who to call when I get stuck, then.' Sienna smiled. 'Right, I'm due in Theatre. I just wanted to catch you first and see how you were getting on.'

Tears pricked Ella's eyelids. 'That's so kind.'

'And invest in tissues,' Sienna advised. 'You wouldn't believe the stupid things that are going to make you cry. Or how often.'

'I believe you—especially now, because you were right about tins smelling, too,' Ella admitted wryly.

'It'll be fine,' Sienna reassured her. 'See you later.'

'Ella, could we have a wo—?' Oliver began.

She lifted her hands as if shoving him away. 'Sorry— I've been called down to Ultrasound.'

He couldn't argue with that.

But the next time he saw her in a corridor, Ella couldn't

stop to have a quick word because she was in a rush on the way to help Jennie, their trainee midwife.

Was he being paranoid, or was she avoiding him?

And she'd been so quiet on the way back to Cheltenham last night.

He'd shared a part of his life with her that he'd always kept private; but, instead of bringing her closer to him, it seemed to have driven her further away.

The third time Oliver tried to talk to Ella, she was backing away as soon as he started speaking. 'Sorry, Oliver. I can't talk right now. I've been called to the Emergency Department.'

'If that was to see the mum with the suspected placental abruption,' he said grimly, 'then you're working with me.'

She bit her lip. 'Oh. I thought I'd be working with Charlie.'

So yet again she'd been hoping to avoid him. 'No. He's in the middle of a complicated delivery.' Hurt made him snap at her. 'So you'll just have to put up with it being me, won't you?'

She gave him a speaking look, but said nothing.

Oliver sighed inwardly. He hated to think that their working relationship was as bad as their personal relationship right now. He knew he should apologise for being abrupt with her, but her coolness had really got to him.

'Ella,' he said when they got into the lift. 'Are you going to be OK with this?'

'An abruption? I've come across them before,' she said coolly.

Oh, great. She'd misunderstood and was about to go prickly on him. 'I don't mean clinically. I know you know your stuff,' he said. 'I meant emotionally. You're pregnant and this might not have a good outcome. If you'd rather someone else took this case, I'll organise that for you.'

'No, it's fine.' She took his hand and squeezed it briefly. 'But thank you for thinking about that.'

Her touch flustered him so much that he didn't say a word until they were in the Emergency Department with Mike Wetherby.

'Courtney Saunders, age thirty-six, and she's currently thirty-four weeks,' Mike explained. 'This is her second baby; her last pregnancy and birth were straightforward, and this pregnancy's been straightforward so far but today she slipped on the ice while she was getting off the bus and had quite a bad fall. She tried to protect the baby by throwing herself sideways; she banged her hip and her head. I've sorted that side of it out for her, and obviously there's still a bit of tachycardia but I think that's probably stress.'

Though it could also be a precursor to other complications, Oliver knew. 'How's the baby doing?'

'That's why I called you,' Mike said. 'She says she hasn't felt the baby move much since the fall, her back hurts, and she thinks she's having Braxton Hicks.'

'But you don't think it's Braxton Hicks?' Oliver asked.

'I have a bad feeling about this,' Mike said. 'She doesn't have any signs of bleeding but, given the fall and the length of her pregnancy, I think it might be a concealed abruption. That's why I called you guys rather than doing a manual exam myself.'

'Good call,' Oliver said. If it was an abruption, a manual exam would make things much worse. 'Have you managed to contact her partner or a friend to be with her?'

'We tried her partner, but he's in a meeting, so we've left a message for him either to call us or to come straight in,' Mike said. 'I'll introduce you to Courtney.'

Once Mike had introduced Oliver and Ella and headed off to treat his next patient, Oliver said, 'Mrs Saunders—

may I call you Courtney?' At her nod, he continued, 'I'd like to examine you, if I may.'

Courtney gave her consent, and Oliver examined her gently. 'Tell me if there's any pain or tenderness,' he said.

'I'm fine. I can put up with being a bit sore and the Braxton Hicks. But I'm scared about the baby,' she said.

Ella took her hand to reassure her. 'That's why we're here. Oliver's the Assistant Head of Obstetrics, so he's really good at his job.'

'Assistant Head of Obstetrics?' Courtney looked panicky. 'Does that mean it's really serious?'

'It simply means,' Oliver said gently, 'that all my other obstetricians are in Theatre or in clinics right now and I happened to be the doctor who was free. It's nothing sinister, I promise. But what I'm going to do first is reassure you by checking the baby, OK? Once I've listened to the heartbeat, Ella's going to put some wires on you so we can monitor how the baby's doing and keep an eye on—do you know if it's a boy or a girl?'

Courtney shook her head. 'We didn't want to know. But Alex—he's my oldest—he tells everyone he's going to have a little sister.'

'Baby Saunders, then,' Oliver said with a smile. 'And we'll also measure how your contractions are doing.' He took the Pinard stethoscope and listened to the baby's heartbeat, then smiled at Courtney. 'That's a nice strong heartbeat, so that's good news.' It was a little slow for his liking, but he wasn't going to worry Courtney about that just now. Not until he'd checked the ultrasound. 'Before Ella puts the wires on, I'd also like to give you an ultrasound scan—it's just like the ones you've had before, when you came in at twenty weeks.'

And the scan showed him the one thing he'd hoped it wouldn't. He glanced across at Ella who mouthed, 'Abruption?' At his tiny nod, she mouthed, 'Line in and cross-match?'

He was glad she was so quick to pick things up—and he was even more glad that she was professional enough not to let the difficulties between them affect their patient.

He turned the screen so that Courtney could see it. 'When you fell, Courtney, it caused part of the placenta to start to come away from the wall of your womb—this dark area here shows bleeding behind the womb, which is why you're not seeing any spotting,' he said. 'It's what we call a placental abruption.'

Courtney turned pale. 'Can you stitch it back or something?'

'Unfortunately we can't reattach the placenta,' he said. 'If a mum has a small tear in the placenta and the baby's doing OK, we can send her home to wait it out, or we can admit her to Teddy's and see how things go—but this is quite a big tear. It means that right now your baby isn't getting enough oxygen and nutrients from the placenta, and the baby's heartbeat is getting slower.'

'Is my baby going to die?' Courtney asked, her eyes wide with panic.

'We're going to do our best to keep your baby safe,' Ella said.

'And the safest thing for me to do is to deliver the baby now through an emergency Caesarean section,' Oliver finished.

'But it's too early for me to have the baby!' Courtney said. 'I'm only thirty-four weeks—there's another six weeks to go yet.'

'The baby's going to be small,' Oliver said, 'but I promise you at thirty-four weeks Baby Saunders will manage just fine. I'm going to give you steroids to help mature the baby's lungs.'

'Like bodybuilders use?' Courtney asked.

'No, they're corticosteroids, like the ones the body produces naturally or people with asthma take to help with their airways,' Ella explained. 'Babies born before thirty-seven weeks sometimes have trouble breathing because their lungs aren't developed fully. The steroids help the lungs develop so the baby doesn't have breathing problems.'

Oliver didn't chip in; he was enjoying watching Ella in action. She was so good with patients, explaining things simply in terms they could understand.

She'd be a good mum, too, he thought wistfully. But would she give him the chance to be a good dad?

He shook himself. Now wasn't the time. Their patient had to come first. But he'd try to find a good time for him and Ella to talk. They really, really needed to talk about the baby—and about them.

'What happens is we give you an injection,' Ella continued, 'and the steroids go through your bloodstream and through the placenta into the baby's body and lungs. And as well as being able to breathe better, the baby can suck better and take in more milk.'

'So the baby won't have side-effects?' Courtney asked.

'No, and neither will you,' Ella reassured her.

'But Ryan isn't here yet. He can't miss our baby being born,' Courtney said, a tear running down her cheek.

'I'll try him again,' Ella said, and squeezed her hand. 'I'm just going to put a butterfly in the back of your hand so we can give you any drugs we need, and then I'll call him myself—Mike said he was in a meeting so they left a message, but I'll make sure I actually speak to him.' She smiled at Courtney. 'I know this is really scary, but you're in the best place.'

Once Ella had put the line in, cross-matched Courtney's blood and set up continuous foetal monitoring for the baby's heartbeat and Courtney's contractions, she went off to call Courtney's partner.

'I can't believe this is happening. I wish I'd stopped work last week instead of trying to keep going a bit longer,' Courtney said.

'Hey, it could've happened anyway,' Oliver said. 'You might have slipped on your front doorstep, or when you were taking Alex out to the park.' He sat next to her and held her hand. 'There is something else I need to talk to you about, Courtney. With an abruption like this, it's possible that you might lose a lot of blood—we can't tell from the scan how much blood you've already lost. That's why Ella cross-matched you, so we can make sure we can sort that out and give you more blood if you need it. But if I can't stop the bleeding once I've delivered the baby, I might have to give you a hysterectomy.'

Courtney looked dismayed. 'You mean—like someone who's near the menopause?'

'Sort of,' Oliver said. 'I know you're very young and you might want to have more children, so I'm hoping it'll all be straightforward. But I do need to prepare you for the worst-case scenario too—because if that happens then a hysterectomy might be the only way I can save your life.'

'So this abruption thing could kill me as well as the baby?'

'That's the very worst-case scenario,' Oliver stressed. 'In most cases it's fine. But I do need you to sign a consent form just in case the very worst happens.'

'I…' Courtney shook her head, looking dazed. 'It's a lot to take in. This morning I was planning to work for another month, and now I've fallen when I got off the bus I might die and so might the baby.'

'Very, very worst-case,' Oliver said. 'But that's why I

want to deliver the baby now, to give him or her the best possible chance.'

'There isn't really a choice, is there?' she asked miserably. 'All right. I'll sign your form.'

By the time she'd signed the form and Oliver had administered the steroids, Ella came back into the room, smiling. 'I've spoken to Ryan. He's on his way now and he says to tell you he loves you and everything's going to be all right.'

A tear trickled down Courtney's face. 'Even though I nearly killed our baby?'

'You did nothing of the sort. It was an accident,' Ella reassured her. 'And your man will be here really soon. He says to tell you he's going to make the world speed record for getting across town.'

Courtney's lower lip wobbled, but she tried her best to smile.

'So what happens now is the anaesthetist is on her way. She's going to give you an anaesthetic, and then Oliver will make an incision here—' she sketched the shape on Courtney's tummy '—so he can deliver the baby.'

'Can Ryan be there?' Courtney asked.

'If he does that world speed record,' Ella said with a smile, 'then he can be there and he can cut the cord. I'll be there, too, to look after Baby Saunders. Once I've checked the baby over, you can both get to see him or her and have a cuddle.'

'What if—if it's the worst-case scenario?' Courtney asked, a catch in her voice.

'Then I'll take Ryan off to one side with the baby so Oliver can sort everything out. But he's the best surgeon I know. You're in good hands.'

If only she had as much confidence in him personally as she had in him professionally, Oliver thought. Though part of it was his own fault. He'd held back from her. If he told her about Justine, then maybe she'd understand why he was having a hard time getting his head round the fact that he was going to be a dad—and why he needed to feel that he was in control of everything. But then again, letting her close enough to meet his family had backfired.

This whole thing was a mess.

But doing the job he did, seeing how important family was to the women he helped to give birth and their partners… It was beginning to make him realise that he wanted this, too. He didn't want to be just a dad. He wanted to be a partner, too. He wanted to be loved for who he was.

But what did Ella want? Could they make a go of things together? Could they become a family, the kind of family that he hadn't grown up in but suspected that she had?

By the time the anaesthetist had administered the spinal block, Ryan had arrived for a tearful reunion with his wife. Oliver glanced at Ella and saw the wistfulness on her face. So was this affecting her, too?

Their talk would have to wait until after this operation. But Oliver was determined to sit down and talk to Ella properly and find out what she wanted—and, with any luck, it would be the same thing that he wanted. And then they could move forward properly. Together.

Thankfully, delivering the baby and the placenta stopped the bleeding, so he didn't have to give Courtney a hysterectomy. And their little girl, although tiny and in need of a day or two in the neonatal unit, looked as if she was going to do very well indeed.

Once he'd finished the operation and Courtney had gone through to the recovery room, he was on his own with Ella.

'Can we take ten minutes?' he asked. 'I'll buy you a cup of tea, if you like.'

'Thanks, but I need to be elsewhere,' she said. 'I promised to help Jennie with her studies.'

Again? His heart sank. This sounded like another evasion tactic. Maybe he was wrong about this after all, and she didn't want the same thing that he did. 'Ella, I think we need to talk.'

'No need,' she said with a brisk smile. 'Everything's fine.'

He didn't think so; and, from the expression in her eyes, neither did she.

'How about dinner tonight?'

'Sorry,' she said. 'I really do have to go.'

Which left Oliver to walk back to his office alone.

He sat at his desk, trying to concentrate on his pile of admin, and wondering how everything between him and Ella had gone so wrong. Was it his imagination, or was she finding excuses to be anywhere but near him?

And how was he ever going to persuade her to give him a chance?

He was beginning to think that he needed a Christmas miracle. Except they were in very short supply, and in any case he ought to be able to sort this out on his own.

CHAPTER EIGHT

'YOU LOOK TERRIBLE, ELLA,' Annabelle informed her best friend. 'Rough night?'

'I'm fine,' Ella fibbed.

'I've known you for a lot of years now,' Annabelle said softly, 'and you're not fine. What's wrong?'

Ella grimaced. It was all so complicated. Where did she even start?

'That was a pretty stupid question,' Annabelle said. 'Obviously it's Oliver.'

'Not so much Oliver as his family,' Ella admitted.

Annabelle winced. 'I thought you said Thursday night went OK?'

'Bits of it did,' Ella said. 'His brother's nice, and so is his sister-in-law.'

'So the problem's his parents?'

Ella nodded miserably. But she couldn't tell Annabelle the whole story. It wasn't hers to tell, and it wouldn't be fair to break Oliver's confidence; Ella was the only person in the department who knew about his background. But she could tell Annabelle some of it, and maybe Annabelle would have some ideas about how to deal with it. 'His mum wants me to have a paternity test.'

'What?' Annabelle looked shocked. 'That's ridiculous.'

But it didn't bother Ella anywhere near as much as the

other thing that the Countess had suggested. 'And she wants Oliver to have custody of the baby.'

Annabelle frowned. 'What does Oliver say about it?'

'He doesn't know,' Ella admitted. 'He wasn't there when she said it.'

'Then talk to him about it. Tell him what she said.'

'That's the problem. I can't,' Ella said. 'He doesn't get on that well with his parents.'

'Then obviously he'll take your side. And no way is he going to take the baby from you.'

Oh, but he could. Especially if she had a boy and Prue had a girl—because then Ella's baby could be the future Earl of Darrington. But explaining that wouldn't be fair to Oliver. 'It's complicated,' Ella hedged. 'And I don't want to make things worse between Oliver and his parents. It wouldn't be fair to make him choose sides.'

'Talk to him,' Annabelle advised. 'And if Oliver Darrington's even half the man I think he is, he'll tell his mother to back off and to start treating you with a bit of courtesy.'

'I'm not even officially his girlfriend,' Ella pointed out.

'He took you to meet his family. Which he wouldn't have done if he wasn't serious about trying to make a go of things with you,' Annabelle countered.

But Oliver hadn't said anything about his feelings. And Ella didn't want to try to make a go of it just for the sake of the baby. Sienna's words rang all too true: *It's much better for a baby to have one parent who really loves them, than two who fight all the time.*

But, before she and Annabelle could discuss it any more, Jennie rushed over to them. 'Ella, you're needed in Room One,' she said. 'It's Georgina.'

'Georgina? As in Georgie, our mum-to-be with quads?' Ella asked. Georgina was one of Ella's special patients;

after IVF treatment, the two embryos implanted had each split into identical twins, so Georgina was expecting quadruplets. 'But she's not due in for another appointment until next week.'

'She thinks she's in labour,' Jennie said.

It was way too early for Georgina to be in labour. 'I'm coming now,' Ella said. She squeezed Annabelle's hand. 'Thanks for letting me talk. I'll catch up with you later.'

'Sure. Call me if you need anything.'

'I will,' Ella promised.

She went into Room One, where Georgina was sitting on the bed, looking worried. The younger woman's face brightened when she saw Ella.

'How are you doing, Georgie?' Ella asked.

'A bit scared. I think I'm in labour,' Georgina said.

'Is Leo not with you?' Georgina's partner had been to every single appointment with her.

'He's in New York. I called him and he's getting the first plane back.' Georgina bit her lip. 'Mum's got the vomiting bug that's going round, and she doesn't want to give it to me, or she'd be here to hold my hand—but she's texted me a dozen times since I told her I was coming in.'

But texting wasn't the same as having someone with you, especially if you were scared, Ella knew. 'OK. Let's have a look at what your lovely babies are up to,' Ella said with a smile. 'Jennie, can you see if Charlie's around, please? He'll want to see his patient immediately. And can you get the portable scanner, please?'

'Sure,' the trainee midwife said.

'So are you having contractions, Georgie?' Ella asked. 'And have you timed them?'

'I'm not sure—I think I'm getting twinges or something, but it doesn't hurt as much as I expected and they're all over the place. But, Ella, my tummy feels *weird*,' Georgina said. 'It's all tight and shiny. My back aches. And I feel as if I've put on half a stone overnight.'

Alarm bells rang in the back of Ella's head. She didn't want to worry Georgina, but this didn't sound like the beginnings of labour. It sounded like a complication—and, given that Georgina was carrying four babies, this could be a very tricky complication. 'Would you mind baring your tummy for me so I can have a look?' she asked, keeping her voice light and cheery.

'Of course,' Georgina said, and pulled up her top while she leaned back against the pillows.

Georgina's abdomen definitely looked tight and shiny, as she'd said. But Ella wasn't sure this was labour. She had a nasty feeling that one of the quads might be in trouble.

'As soon as Charlie gets here,' Ella said, 'we'll have a look on the ultrasound and see if they're all waving at you this time.'

Georgina smiled, but Ella could tell that the young mum-to-be was panicking.

'I'll take your blood pressure while we're waiting for Charlie,' she said.

At least Georgina's blood pressure was normal, but Ella would be a lot happier once she'd monitored all the babies.

Just then, Oliver walked in with Jennie, pushing the portable scanner. Ella's heart skipped a beat when she saw him.

'Sorry, Charlie's in Theatre. Will I do?' he asked.

Provided they could keep their private life out of it, yes. 'Georgie, this is Oliver Darrington, our Assistant Head of Obstetrics,' Ella said. 'Oliver, this is Georgie. She's twenty-eight weeks and she's expecting quads.'

'Congratulations,' Oliver said, smiling at her.

'Thank you,' Georgina said.

'Georgie thinks she might be in labour,' Ella said. 'Her

blood pressure's fine, but we need to do a scan to see what the babies are up to.'

'OK. I'm sorry, Georgie, our gel's a bit cold,' Oliver apologised. 'May I?'

'Sure.'

Once the scan of the babies was on the screen, Ella spotted the problem immediately. The two girl quads were fine, but the two boys were definitely struggling; one of them had a lot of amniotic fluid in the sac, while the other had very little and was practically stuck against the wall of Georgie's womb. The bigger boy twin had a full bladder; Ella couldn't see the smaller twin's bladder, but if her suspicions were right it wasn't full.

'Oliver, can we have a quick word?' she asked, not wanting to worry Georgina by discussing her fears in front of her.

'Sure. Would you excuse us a moment, Georgie?' Oliver asked with a smile.

Georgie nodded.

'Jennie, perhaps you can get Georgie a drink and make her comfortable for the next couple of minutes?' Ella asked.

'Thanks,' Georgina said. 'I have been feeling a bit thirsty, the last day or two.'

It was another maternal sign for twin-to-twin transfusion, Ella knew, and her misgivings increased. She waited until they were outside the room and the door was closed before she turned to Oliver. 'I've been Georgie's named midwife since day one and Charlie's her named doctor—the quads have all been doing just fine, and Georgie was only in for a scan last week,' Ella said. 'When she told me her symptoms this morning and I examined her, I wondered if it might be twin-to-twin transfusion.'

'Good call. The scan pretty much proved that,' Oliver said.

'But how could it happen so fast? Everything was fine last week. I've kept a really close eye on her because obviously with carrying quads she's a high-risk mum.'

'She's in her last trimester,' Oliver said, 'so it's an acute form of the condition rather than a chronic one—and acute TTT can happen practically overnight.'

'So what are the options?' Ella asked. 'I've seen less than half a dozen cases of TTT in my career. Do we deliver the babies early, or do you put a hole in the membrane between the twins, or could you do laser surgery on the placenta to separate their bloodstreams?'

'It's a difficult call,' Oliver said. 'If you put a hole in the membrane so the twins share one sac, there's a risk of entangling the umbilical cords, and that's something I'd rather do at an earlier stage than Georgina's at. This has all happened really quickly, so there's a possibility that the recipient quad has a heart problem, because the excess blood and fluid will have put strain on his heart.' He frowned. 'I'd like to call Juliet Turner in.'

'Juliet Turner?' Ella asked.

'She's a neonatal specialist surgeon and she's got a fabulous reputation for her work in utero. She might be able to operate on the quads if need be.'

'What aren't you telling me?'

'She's in Australia,' Oliver admitted.

'So it'll be at least a day before she can get here—*if* she agrees to come,' Ella pointed out. 'And you're just expecting the poor woman to drop everything and travel halfway round the world to come and treat Georgie's babies?'

'Juliet's a professional.'

'Surely there's someone closer than Australia?' Ella asked.

'Juliet's the best,' Oliver said simply, 'which is the whole point of Teddy's. We can keep Georgina and the babies comfortable until she gets here.'

Ella was about to say that Juliet Turner might already have commitments which prevented her from rushing all the way from Australia to Cheltenham, but Oliver had the kind of stubborn expression that told her he'd talk the surgeon into changing any commitments for the sake of Georgina and the quads.

'OK,' she said. 'And I guess that gives Leo—the quads' dad—a chance to get here from New York. Let's tell her together.'

She went back in with Oliver and sat on the bed, taking Georgina's hand.

'Everything's not all right, is it?' Georgina asked. 'What's happening to my babies?'

'It's something called twin-to-twin transfusion,' Ella explained. 'You know you've got two sets of identical twins.'

'Two boys and two girls—Graham, Rupert, Lily and Rose,' Georgina said.

'Lovely names,' Oliver said. 'Two of my nieces are called Lily and Rose.'

'What's wrong with them?' Georgina asked.

'Lily and Rose are both fine,' Ella reassured her. 'But Graham and Rupert have a problem.

Normally identical twins share a placenta, and the blood flows evenly between the babies, so they both get the same amount of blood flow and nutrition. But sometimes there's a problem with the blood vessels so one twin gets too much and one doesn't get enough. The twin that gets too much blood wees more, and that produces more amniotic fluid round him, and the twin that doesn't get enough wees less and has less amniotic fluid. That's why it's called twin-to-twin transfusion.'

'Are they—will they be all right?' Georgina asked. 'And was it something I did?'

'It's definitely not anything you did,' Oliver said. 'It just happens, sometimes.'

'You did the best thing by coming straight in to us when you weren't feeling right,' Ella added.

'And we'll do our very best to keep them healthy,' Oliver said. 'There are several things we can do, but I'd like to bring in a specialist who's very, very experienced at doing surgery in the womb.'

'You're going to operate on one of the boys while they're still inside me?' Georgina asked, looking shocked.

'That depends on what Juliet thinks is the best thing to do,' Oliver said, 'but it's a possibility. You can discuss your options with Dr Warren, too. I know he's been your named doctor since day one, so it's important that you talk to him.'

'So when's this going to happen?' Georgina asked. 'Today? Because I want Leo here.'

'Ella told me he's coming from New York. Don't worry, it won't be today,' Oliver said, 'so there's plenty of time for him to get here.'

'We're going to keep you in for a few days,' Ella said. 'I want to monitor the babies, so we'll be hooking you up with some wires, and we'll keep you comfortable until Juliet gets here.'

'Can't Charlie do the operation?' Georgina asked.

'Juliet has much more experience,' Oliver said. 'And I'm sure Charlie will be in to see you as soon as he's out of Theatre and he will explain everything. I'm due in clinic, but if you need me then Ella will give me a call.'

'Thank you,' Georgina said.

Charlie came in as soon as he was out of Theatre. 'I'm so sorry I wasn't here, Georgie.' Standing by the bed, he quickly read her case notes. He had been informed there was a situation on the way from Theatre. 'Ella, who diagnosed the TTT?'

Ella filled him in on everything except Juliet's potential involvement; it wasn't her place to tell Charlie.

'I understand it's a little overwhelming, Georgie,' Charlie said. 'But there are treatment options. Don't think the worst. We might not have to deliver the babies early.'

'Oliver said the babies might have an operation in my womb,' Georgina said.

'It's a possibility, but we'll discuss every option with you and Leo and we'll go ahead the way you want us to go,' Charlie reassured her.

Ella stayed with Georgina until the end of her shift; but then she discovered that Lexie, the midwife who was meant to take over from her for the night shift, had gone down with the vomiting bug.

'Don't worry. I'll stay with you, Georgie,' Ella promised.

'But—you've been working all day.'

'That's fine,' Ella said with a smile. 'You're one of my mums, and I'm not leaving you while you're worried.'

Clearly Oliver wasn't happy about the situation when he heard about it, because he came to the door of Georgina's room. 'A word, Ella?'

'How did you get on with Juliet?' she asked, hoping to head him off.

'She'll be here on Monday. But that wasn't what I wanted to talk to you about.' He sighed. 'Ella, you can't work a double shift.'

Ordering her about *again*. 'Watch me,' Ella said grimly. 'You know the situation. Lexie's gone down with the virus.'

'Health and Safety would have the biggest hissy fit in the world.'

Ella shrugged. 'Their problem. I'm not leaving Georgie.'

'I can get an agency nurse in to cover Lexie's shift. Ella, you need to look after yourself.' His face tightened. 'And our baby.'

'Georgie's worried as it is,' Ella pointed out. 'I'm not leaving her to be looked after by someone she's never met before. She knows me and she's comfortable with me.'

'And you're putting your health at risk.'

'OK, then. I'm off duty—and I'm visiting someone in Teddy's.'

'Now you're being ridiculous.' Oliver scowled at her.

'I'm not. I care about my mums, and I'm not deserting someone who right now is on her own and worried sick about her babies. Georgie's mum has the vomiting bug, so she can't come in, and her husband's on a plane back from New York. That means that Georgie's on her own, knowing there's something wrong with one of her babies and worrying that the worst is going to happen. I'm not just walking out of that door and leaving her to it.'

Oliver sighed. Why did Ella feel that she had to prove herself over and over again? 'You're a good midwife, Ella. Everyone in Teddy's knows that.'

She lifted her chin. 'Thank you.'

'But you also have to remember that you're pregnant. You can't work a twenty-four-hour shift. I wouldn't let a non-pregnant member of staff do that, let alone one who's pregnant.'

Ella shrugged. 'Then I'm a visitor who's staying.'

A stubborn visitor. 'Just promise me you'll put your feet up, you won't rush around, and you'll eat properly.'

'I'm not stupid, Oliver.'

'I know that.'

'I'm not going to do anything reckless or anything that

could hurt the baby. But I can't just walk away and leave Georgie worrying. Can't you see that?'

Yes, he could. Because Ella was sweet and kind and was always the first to offer help. 'All right,' he said. 'You can stay with her as a visitor, provided you put your feet up and rest properly. But you are absolutely *not* working. I'll get agency cover.'

'As long as the agency midwife knows that I'm Georgie's named midwife and to run everything past me,' Ella insisted.

If he didn't agree, he knew Ella would find a way of breaking the rules and work a double shift. 'All right,' he said.

But two could play that game. And he made quite sure that Ella had a proper evening meal, because he brought it in to her himself on a tray. 'No arguments,' he said.

And he could see in her expression that she knew he'd call her on the situation in front of Georgie if she refused the meal—and he'd stay until she'd eaten it, if he had to. 'Thank you,' she said. 'That's really kind of you and it looks scrumptious.'

When Oliver had left the room and closed the door behind him, Georgie asked, 'What's with the special treatment? Are you two an item?'

Not really, Ella thought. She wished they were, but it wasn't going to happen because his parents would never accept her. So she couldn't answer Georgie's question honestly. 'Oliver looks after all his team,' she said. Which was true: sometimes she wondered what drove him to be so protective. 'And I'm pregnant.'

'Congratulations,' Georgie asked. 'When's it due? That is, I take it you're having just one and not quads?'

Ella smiled. 'No, just the one baby. It's early days. The

baby's so tiny at the moment it looks like a little bean on the scan.' She took her phone from her pocket and flicked through to the photograph she'd taken of the scan picture. 'Look, that's my little one.'

'Your first?'

Ella nodded. 'And that's scary enough. I can't imagine what it's like to be expecting quads.'

'Really scary,' Georgie said. 'I never thought we'd be able to have children at all. It was a miracle that two embryos took—and even more of a miracle that both of them then became twins.'

Her baby was a miracle, too, Ella thought. Not that she wanted to discuss that. 'Two girls and two boys—and they'll all grow up close. That's nice.'

'All the way through, I've been so scared that we'd lose one of them,' Georgie said. 'All the stories you see on the Internet.'

'Which do nothing but make new mums worry,' Ella said. 'Ignore them.'

'I had—but now with this twin-to-twin thing…'

Ella took her hand. 'Try not to worry. Oliver says Juliet's the best and she'll be able to keep your boys safe.'

'I hope so,' Georgie said.

Oliver came in twice more that evening—the first to check that everything was fine, and the second to bring both Georgie and Ella a mug of hot chocolate.

And then the penny dropped for Ella.

Oliver was officially off duty right now and had been for a while, but he was still here at the hospital. Was he checking up on her? She pushed the thought away. Of course it wasn't that he didn't trust her. She'd made him aware of his bossy tendencies, so it was more likely that he was worried about her but he was trying not to make the sort of fuss that would annoy her.

'Shouldn't you be at home by now?' she asked. She saw the flash of guilt in his eyes, and knew that her guess had been right.

'I'm catching up on some paperwork, so I thought I'd take a break and keep you both company for a bit.'

'Oliver, it's ten o'clock and you're on an early shift tomorrow.'

His expression said very clearly, *Yes, and you've been in all day.*

'Go home,' she said gently, 'and get some sleep.'

'Are you sure you're going to be all right here?'

'I'm sure. And I'm on a late tomorrow, so I'm going to laze around all morning.' She knew he'd pick up what she wasn't saying in front of Georgie: *don't fuss.* Though, at the same time, it warmed her that he was concerned and trying not to be overbearing about it.

If only his family was different...

But that wasn't fair. It wasn't his fault.

'I'll see you later, then,' he said. 'Call me if you need anything.'

'I will,' she promised.

But he came in again on his way out of the department, this time carrying a blanket, which he proceeded to tuck round her. Georgie had fallen asleep, so he simply mouthed, 'Call me,' rested the backs of his fingers briefly against her cheek, and left the room as quietly as he could.

Ella had to blink back the tears. This was the man she'd fallen for—kind, considerate and caring. But his parents would never accept her in his life. She couldn't ask him to choose between them. Somehow, she'd have to find a way of backing off without either of them getting hurt.

Except she had a nasty feeling it was already too late for that.

She dozed in the chair next to Georgie's bed, waking

only when the agency midwife came in to check on them, until Leo arrived at the crack of dawn the next morning. Ella talked him through what was happening with the babies, drawing diagrams and labelling them to help him understand.

'Sorry, my writing's terrible,' she said, wincing. At times like this, she really resented her dyslexia.

'It's because you're a medic,' Leo said with a smile. 'All medics have terrible handwriting.'

'I guess,' she said.

She stayed with Georgie and Leo until the midwife from the early shift took over.

'Thank you for staying with me,' Georgie said. 'That was above and beyond the call of duty.'

'Any time,' Ella said, meaning it. 'I'm going home for a nap now, but if you need me just ask one of the midwives to call me, OK?'

'You're the best, Ella,' Leo said, giving her a hug. 'Thank you.'

'No problem. Sit and cuddle your wife,' she said with a smile.

CHAPTER NINE

ELLA'S CAR HAD frozen over during the night. With a sigh, she scraped the ice off the windscreen and climbed into the car. Fortunately she was on a late today so she could go home, have a cup of tea and a bath, then set her alarm and have a sleep before her shift.

As she drove back towards her flat, she noticed a car coming up to the junction of a side road on her left. To her shock, it didn't manage to stop at the junction but slid on the ice and crashed straight into her. The impact pushed her right across the road into a line of parked cars.

She checked to see it was safe to get out of the car, then did so. She could see straight away that her car was undriveable and she'd need to call the insurance company to tow her car away.

The other driver came over to her. 'I'm so sorry, love. The road wasn't gritted and I just couldn't stop,' he said.

'The roads are pretty bad. I guess we'd better swap insurance details,' she said tiredly and reached into the car for her handbag. She took out a pen and notebook, but when she took out her reading glasses she saw that the coloured lenses had cracked during the impact. She didn't have a spare pair with her, so now she was going to make a mess of this and probably get half the numbers in the wrong place.

'Are you all right, love?' the other driver asked, clearly seeing that she was close to tears.

'I'm dyslexic,' she said, gesturing to her ruined glasses, 'and without these I'm going to get everything wrong.'

'Let me do it,' he said. 'It's the least I can do, seeing as it was my fault. You sit down in the warm, love, and I'll sort it out.'

He wrote down all the information for her, called the police to inform them about the accident and her insurance company so they could arrange to pick up her car, and waited with her until the tow truck arrived. Thankfully it turned up only half an hour later, but by then Ella was shivering and desperately tired.

'Are you sure you're all right? You've not banged your head or anything?' the tow truck driver asked.

'No, just my reading glasses are wrecked,' she said wearily. 'I was lucky. It could've been an awful lot worse.'

'We've had so many cars sliding off the road this morning—the gritters clearly didn't think it was going to freeze this badly last night,' the tow truck driver said. He took her car to the repair garage and then drove her back to her flat. 'I'm only supposed to take you to one or the other,' he said, 'but I remember you. You delivered my youngest last year. My wife had a rough time and you were brilliant with her.'

Ella was really grateful. 'Thank you so much. Do you want a cup of tea or something?'

'That's kind of you, but I'd better not. I've got half a dozen other crashes to go to,' he said wryly. 'Take care.'

Ella let herself into her flat, started running a bath and put the kettle on. Then, when she undressed, she realised there was blood in her knickers.

She was spotting.

Ice slid down her spine. She'd felt a sharp jerk across her

shoulder and abdomen from the seatbelt when the other car had crashed into her, but her car's airbag hadn't gone off and she hadn't banged herself against the steering wheel. She hadn't thought the crash was bad enough to warrant going to hospital; she'd felt OK at the time, there had probably been dozens of other accidents on the icy roads and there were drivers more in need of urgent medical attention than her.

But now she was spotting, at eight weeks of pregnancy, and that wasn't a good thing.

Oh, God. Please don't let her lose the baby. It hadn't been planned, but it was oh, so wanted.

'Hang on in there, little one,' she whispered, with one hand wrapped protectively round her bump.

With shaking hands, she rang Annabelle, but her best friend wasn't answering her home phone or her mobile. Ella was sure that Annabelle was off duty today; but maybe she was out with Max somewhere and her phone was accidentally in silent mode.

Ella didn't want to ring an ambulance, because she knew how busy the hospital was right now, and someone else could need to go to the emergency department more urgently. Maybe she should get a taxi in to the Royal Cheltenham?

But right now she was so scared. She really didn't want to do this on her own.

Oliver.

Given how things were between them and that he'd been so fed up that she'd stayed with Georgina all night after her shift, worrying that she was overdoing things and putting the baby at risk, Oliver was the last person she wanted to call. But her brain was on a go-slow and she couldn't think of anyone else. Plus he was the baby's father—he had the right to know that there was a problem.

It took her three attempts before she managed to call his mobile.

'Darrington,' Oliver said absently, as if he hadn't even looked at the screen.

'It's Ella,' she said.

'Ella? Is everything all right?'

Her teeth had started to chatter and she could hardly get the words out.

'Ella, what's happened?' he asked urgently.

'A c-car crashed into me on the way h-home, and now I'm s-spotting.'

'Are you at home?'

'Y-yes.'

'I'm on my way to you right now,' he said. 'Try not to worry. I'll call you when I'm in the car so you're not going to be on your own while you're waiting, and I'll be with you very, very soon, OK?'

Ella had had a car accident and she was spotting. That wasn't good.

Please, please don't let her lose the baby, Oliver begged inwardly.

The shock of her news had made him realise just how much he wanted the baby.

He headed out to Reception and was really grateful that Annabelle was there; she'd changed duty at the last minute to help cover sick leave.

'Is everything all right?' she asked.

'No. Ella's been in an accident. She just called me and said she's spotting. I'm going to get her now, so please can you make sure the portable scanner's in one of the rooms and keep it free? I'm bringing her straight in to Teddy's.'

'Got you. Give her my love and tell her not to worry,' Annabelle said. 'Drive safely.'

'I will.'

As soon as he was in the car, Oliver switched his phone over to the hands-free system and called Ella as he drove to her flat. He could hear the tears in her voice when she answered; it ripped him apart that she was crying and right now he couldn't comfort her properly or do anything to fix this. But until he'd done the scan and knew what was going on, he couldn't give her the reassurance he really wanted to give her.

'Ella, I'm on my way now,' he said. 'Teddy's is on standby and Annabelle's there—she sends her love.'

'But Annabelle's off duty.'

'No, she swapped duty yesterday to help me out with sick leave cover,' he said.

He heard a sob. 'I'm meant to be on a late today.'

'Don't worry about that right now,' he soothed. 'We can sort it out later.'

'I never meant for this to happen when I stayed with Georgie,' she said. 'I would never, ever put the baby at risk.'

'I know and you did the right thing—the kind thing,' he said. 'You'd have been worrying yourself silly about Georgie and the quads if you'd just gone home.' Because that was who Ella was: dedicated to her job.

'The crash wasn't my fault, Oliver. It really wasn't. The other driver just couldn't stop at the junction and ploughed into me.'

Why did she seem to think he was angry with her? 'Ella, I'm not going to shout at you.'

'You were near shouting at me yesterday.'

She had a point. He'd gone into overprotective mode when she'd suggested working a double shift. 'I'm sorry. I'm a grumpy sod and you have the right to tell me to shut up when I start ranting,' he said.

To his relief, he heard what sounded almost like a wry chuckle. But then there was another muffled sob. 'Hold on, honey. I'm going to be there very soon,' he said. 'And, Ella, I'm glad you called me.'

'Really?' She didn't sound as if she believed him.

'Really,' he said firmly.

He kept her talking all the way from his house to her flat. When he got there, he didn't bother about a parking permit—he'd willingly pay a dozen parking fines if he had to—but just ran over to her door and rang the bell. When she opened her door, he pulled her straight into his arms and held her close. 'Everything's going to be all right, I promise.'

'I don't want to lose the baby.' Her shoulders heaved.

'You're not going to lose the baby, not if I have anything to do with it,' he said. 'Let's go.' He locked the front door behind her, held her close all the way to his car, helped her in and then drove to the Royal Cheltenham, holding her hand between gear changes. She was trembling and he desperately wanted to hold her; but he knew that if he stopped to comfort her it would be that much longer before he could give her a scan and see what was going on. 'We're not going to the Emergency Department. I'll do the scan myself at Teddy's so you don't have to wait.'

'I'm so scared, Oliver. I want this baby so much.'

'Me, too,' he said. More than that, he wanted Ella as well. Whatever had caused her to back off from him since the party, they could fix it—because she was more important to him than anything or anyone else. 'It's going to be OK, Ella. I promise you.'

She was crying silently, and he hated the fact that he couldn't do anything more to help; but, at the same time, he needed to get her to hospital safely.

It seemed to take for ever to get to Teddy's, even though

he knew it couldn't have been more than twenty minutes. But at last they were there and he parked as close to the entrance as possible, then grabbed a wheelchair from the entrance.

'I can walk,' Ella protested.

'I know, but this is faster. Let me do this, Ella. Please. I won't smother you in cotton wool, but I want to get you in there for that scan.' His voice cracked and he wondered if she'd heard it and realised that he was as emotional about the situation as she was. And, actually, maybe she needed to know it. 'Not just for you. For me. I need to be sure you're both all right.'

He was almost breaking into a run by the time they got to Teddy's.

'Later,' he said to the nurse on the reception desk, who looked at Ella in shock as he wheeled her through. 'I'll explain later.'

Annabelle had texted him to say that Room Three was reserved for him, if she wasn't there when he brought Ella in. Oliver wheeled Ella into the room, scooped her out of the wheelchair and laid her on the bed. The fact that she made no protest this time really scared him.

'Can you bare your tummy—?' he began, but she was already doing it.

Please, please, let the baby be all right, he begged inwardly, and smeared the gel over her stomach.

His hands were actually shaking as he stroked the head of the transceiver across her abdomen.

But then he could see the little bean shape, and the heart was beating strongly.

Thank you, he said silently, and moved the screen so Ella could see it, too. 'Look,' he said. 'It's going to be OK. There's a really strong heartbeat, not too fast and not too slow. Everything's going to be fine, Ella.'

Her shoulders heaved, and then she was crying in earnest. He held her close, stroking her hair, and realised that tears were running down his cheeks, too.

He wanted this baby. So did she, desperately. Surely there was a good chance that they could make a decent life together—the three of them, because now he realised how much he wanted that, too.

Finally Ella was all cried out—and then she realised that Oliver was still holding her. And she'd soaked his shirt. And was it her imagination, or were his eyes wet, too? She'd been so frightened that she hadn't been able to focus much on what he'd said to her, but had he said that he was scared, too?

She wasn't sure, and her first instinct was to back away in case she was making a fool of herself again. 'We ought to—well, someone else might need this room.'

'I want to admit you now and keep you in overnight,' he said, 'for observation.'

She shook her head. 'I'll be fine.'

'You're on bed-rest. Don't argue,' he said, 'and there's no way in hell you're working your shift today, so don't even suggest it.'

'But someone else might need the bed on the ward more than I do.'

'Ella, you're pregnant and you were in a car crash.'

'A minor crash. At low speed.'

'Bad enough that they had to get a tow-truck for your car,' he said. 'And you were spotting. If any of your mums came in presenting like that, what would you say?'

'Go home and rest,' she said, 'and come back if you're worried.'

'And if it was a mum you knew damn well didn't know the meaning of the word rest?'

'Then I'd suggest staying in,' she admitted.

'I know you think I'm wrapping you up in cotton wool,' he said, 'and I know that drives you mad—but what I don't get is why you won't let anyone look after you.'

'It's a long story,' she said.

He shrugged. 'I've got all the time in the world.'

He really expected her to tell him? Panic flooded through her. 'I don't know where to start.'

'Try the beginning,' he said. 'Or the middle—or anywhere that feels comfortable—and you can take it from there.'

She knew where to start, then. 'The baby. I didn't try to trap you.'

'I know. You're not Justine.'

She frowned. 'Justine?'

'It's a long story.'

What was sauce for the goose… 'I've got time,' she said. 'And maybe if you tell me, it'll give me the courage to tell you.'

He looked at her for a long moment, then finally nodded. 'OK. I'll go first. Justine was the daughter of my parents' friends. They'd kind of earmarked her for me as a suitable future wife, even though I wasn't ready to settle down and I wanted to get all my training out of the way first so I could qualify as an obstetrician. They fast-tracked me and I was just about to take my last exams when Justine told me she was pregnant.'

Ella went cold. So this wasn't the first time Oliver had been faced with an unexpected baby; it also went some way to explaining why Oliver's mother had been so disapproving about the baby, if the Countess had been in that position before. But as far as Ella knew Oliver didn't have a child. What had happened?

'I really wasn't ready to be a dad,' Oliver said. 'I'd

been so focused on my studies. But I did the right thing and stood by her.'

'Like you're standing by me?' she couldn't help asking.

He didn't answer that, and she went colder still.

'So we found a nice flat, moved in together, and sorted out a room for the baby.'

Oliver definitely wouldn't have abandoned the baby. This must have ended in tragedy—or maybe Justine had refused him access to the baby and that was why the Countess had been adamant that Oliver should have custody.

His grey eyes were filled with pain and she squeezed his hand. Clearly the memories hurt him, and she didn't want that. 'You don't have to tell me anything more.'

'Yes, I do,' he said. 'I don't want there to be any more secrets between us. I should've told you about this a long time ago.' He dragged in a breath. 'We'd planned to get married after the baby was born. But then one day she accidentally picked up my phone instead of hers and went out. I assumed that the phone on the table was mine and was about to put it in my pocket when a text came through.' He grimaced. 'Obviously I didn't set out to spy on her and read her texts, because I trusted her, but the message came up on her lock screen and I read it before I realised it was a private message for her.' He looked away. 'It was from another man, and the wording made it clear they were having an affair. I tackled her about it when she got home and she admitted the baby was his, not mine.'

'So that's why—' She stopped abruptly. Now wasn't the time to tell him that his mother wanted her to have a paternity test.

'Why what?'

'Nothing. I'm so sorry, Oliver. That was a vile thing to do to you. But why would she lie to you like that?'

He shrugged. 'You've been to Darrington Hall and met my family. I guess it was the kind of lifestyle she wanted and the other guy couldn't give her that.'

Now Ella could understand his mother's comments about gold-diggers. But did Oliver think she was a gold-digger too—despite the fact that she'd told him she wasn't? He'd been in that situation before. And now she realised why he'd been so controlling with her when she'd told him about the baby, because Justine had taken all his choices away. Ella had reacted by being stubbornly independent, and they'd been at cross purposes when it needn't have been like that at all.

'It's still horrible for you. And not all women think like that, you know.'

'I know.' His fingers tightened round hers. 'You don't.'

She was relieved that he realised that. 'Was the—was the baby all right?'

'Yes. I moved out and the other guy moved in—but from what I hear it didn't last.'

And then a really horrible thought hit her. Was Oliver still in love with Justine? Was that why he couldn't move on? She didn't want to ask him, because she was too scared that the answer might be 'yes'.

As if he'd guessed at her thoughts, he said, 'You're not Justine, and I don't have a shred of doubt that this baby's mine. I'm just sorry I haven't been able to get my head round things properly and support you the way I should've done.'

Relief made her sag back against the bed. 'Now you've told me what happened to you before, I can understand why you reacted the way you did.'

'Though I did wonder if you were lying to me,' he said, 'when you said it was safe and I assumed you were on the Pill.'

'I thought it *was* safe,' Ella said. 'I honestly never thought I'd ever get pregnant.'

'That's what I don't understand. I haven't found the right way to ask you because…' He grimaced. 'Ella, I didn't want to fight with you over it. But, once you'd told me you were pregnant, I couldn't work out why you were so sure that I didn't need contraception and yet you weren't on the Pill. I knew there was something, but asking you straight out felt intrusive and as if I was accusing you of something, and I didn't want that.'

He'd been honest with her, so now she needed to be honest with him. At least she wouldn't have to explain the medical side too much because it was Oliver's speciality and he understood it. 'I have endometriosis. It caused a lot of scarring on my Fallopian tubes over the years, and then I had an ovarian cyst that ruptured during my training. The doctors in London told me that I was infertile.'

'So that's why you said I didn't…'

'…need a condom,' she finished. 'Yes.'

'I'm sorry. Endometriosis is pretty debilitating, and to get news like that when you're so young…'

'Yes.' She'd cried herself to sleep for weeks afterwards. 'Worse was that it disrupted my studies.'

'Didn't you tell your tutors? They would've understood.'

She grimaced. 'You've read my file, so you know I'm dyslexic.'

He nodded.

'I wasn't diagnosed with dyslexia until I was fifteen. Everyone just thought I was a bit slow because I had trouble reading and I'm clumsy. I was always the last to be picked for the netball team in PE lessons, because I could never catch a ball, and you really don't want to see me trying to throw one.' She shrugged. 'Anyway, the September I turned fifteen we all knew I wasn't going to do well over the next two years, so I wasn't going to get good grades in my exams. But I was good with people and had the gift of the gab, so everyone thought I ought to go and work in the local pub, at first in the kitchen and then in the bar when I was old enough.'

'Right.'

'Except I had a new science teacher that year, and she took me to one side after the first week and asked me all kinds of questions. She was the first teacher ever at school who seemed to think I wasn't slow.' And it had been so liberating. Suddenly it had been possible to dream. 'She said she thought I had dyslexia, because I was fine at answering questions on stuff we'd talked about in class but when she looked at my written work it wasn't anywhere near the same standard, and my writing was terrible. Nobody had ever tested me for dyslexia—they'd never even considered it. So my teacher talked to my parents and the Special Needs department at school and they got me tested.'

'And it turned out she was right?'

She nodded. 'They gave me coloured glasses and got my test papers printed on pastel colours instead of bright white, and suddenly bookwork wasn't quite so much of a struggle any more.' She smiled. 'I'd always wanted to be a midwife like my Aunty Bridget, but nobody ever thought I was clever enough to do it. But I got through my exams, I stayed on at sixth form and I actually got accepted at uni. I was already getting help for my dyslexia, because they let me record all my lectures to help me revise, so I didn't feel I could go to my tutors and say there was another problem as well. It felt like one excuse too many.'

Now Oliver began to understand why Ella was so independent. She'd had to fight hard to get where she was, and she'd no doubt been wrapped in cotton wool as the child who always underachieved—as well as being told that she was stupid by people who should never have judged her in the first place.

'And I guess,' she said, 'there was a part of me that didn't want to admit it because then I'd have to admit I wasn't a real woman—that I'd never be able to give my partner a child of his own.'

'Ella, being infertile doesn't make you any less of a woman,' Oliver said.

'That's easy for you to say, being a man,' she said softly. 'I knew my parents were desperate for grandchildren and I'd let them down, too.'

'That's seriously what they believe?'

'No, of course not! They said it didn't matter if I didn't have children,' Ella said, 'but I've seen my mum's face whenever she talks about her great-nieces and great-nephews. Just for a second there's this wistfulness. She couldn't have any more children after me, so me not being able to have children meant that she'd never have grandchildren. So she and Da were thrilled to bits when I told them about the baby.'

Oliver was shocked. Hadn't they agreed to wait to tell their family until she'd got through the first trimester? 'You've told them already?'

'I'm sorry. I just couldn't wait,' she said simply. 'I know things are tricky for you with your parents, but mine aren't like that—they're so pleased.'

She'd thought she was infertile but, because of him, she was having a baby. It was almost like the Justine situation again except there wasn't any cheating, this time. Justine had wanted the lifestyle and not him. Did Ella want the baby and not him?

He shook himself. But he wanted this baby, too. And, before the Hallowe'en Masquerade Ball, he and Ella had been friends. So maybe they could make this work, the way it hadn't with Justine.

'My parents are dying to meet you,' Ella said.

'So do I need to ask your father officially for your hand in marriage?' Oliver asked.

She blinked at him. 'What?'

'It's the practical solution,' Oliver said. 'We both want this baby. We get along well, for the most part. So we'll get married and give the baby a stable home.'

We both want this baby... Get married... A stable home.

But Oliver hadn't said a word about love. Or actually *asked* her to marry him.

And all Ella could think of was what Sienna had said about it being better for a baby to have one parent who loved it to bits than two parents who fought all the time. Given the situation with Oliver's parents, there was a good chance that she and Oliver would fight. A lot.

Marrying her meant he'd get custody of the baby: exactly what his mother wanted.

Even though Ella understood now what might have driven the Countess to take that view, she also didn't want her life taken over by the Darringtons—to have to give her baby the name they chose, send the baby to the school they chose, and give up her job to take on the role they chose.

If Oliver had said one word to her about love, it would've been different.

But he hadn't. And she couldn't marry someone who didn't love her. It wouldn't be a real relationship. That wasn't what she wanted.

'No,' she said.

CHAPTER TEN

OLIVER STARED AT ELLA, not quite believing what he was hearing.

He'd proposed to her—and she'd refused.

'Why?' he asked.

'I'm not marrying you just for the baby's sake. And I'm perfectly happy for my baby to be an O'Brien.' Her expression was closed.

'But—this is my baby, too.' He looked at her, shocked. 'Or are you telling me…?'

She blew out a breath. 'Now I know what your ex did, I can understand why you're worrying that it's history repeating itself, but don't you know me better than that?'

He'd thought he knew her. But maybe he didn't. And maybe she did have one thing in common with Justine, then: her feelings for him weren't the same as his for her. 'I asked you to marry me.'

'For the baby's sake.' She swallowed hard. 'Like your mother—' She stopped abruptly.

'What about my mother?'

'Nothing.'

'It doesn't sound like nothing to me.'

'All right—if you must know,' Ella said, 'she wants the baby.'

'What?' He'd never heard anything more ridiculous in his life. His mother didn't even *know* about the baby.

'Provided you have a paternity test first to make quite sure it's yours,' Ella continued. 'And then you'll sue me for custody.'

This was getting more and more surreal. 'What? Why?'

'Because Darrington babies have a position to maintain.'

'That's ridiculous. Of course my mother wouldn't say anything like that,' Oliver said. 'And when did she say anything to you? I was with you nearly all the time at Darrington.'

'Not all the time. Not when I'd gone to splash my face with water.'

'You're saying my mother accosted you in the bathroom?' That definitely wasn't his mother's style.

'She'd been watching me and she'd worked out that I was going green around the lilies. And I was the first person you'd brought there in years, so there was obviously a reason why you wanted them to meet me.'

Oliver shook his head, unable to take this in.

'Believe what you like,' she said. 'But I'm not marrying you.' She turned away.

Oliver raked a hand through his hair. What the hell was going on? 'Ella—'

'I could do with some rest,' she said.

Because she'd just had a car crash and a nasty scare about the baby. And she'd been here at the hospital all night, keeping Georgie company until Leo arrived from New York.

Of course she could do with some rest. She must be exhausted, physically and mentally and emotionally.

Maybe that was why she was flinging around these wild accusations—she was sleep-deprived and still worried sick about the baby, and saying the first thing that came into her head instead of thinking about it. Maybe if he gave her some space and some time to sleep, she'd get her head round things and talk this over sensibly with him.

'I'll arrange for you to be moved to a side room,' he said stiffly, and left the treatment room.

'Is everything OK?' Annabelle asked, coming over to him as he strode through the department.

'With the baby? Yes.'

She frowned. 'Is Ella all right?'

'She needs to be moved to a side room and kept in overnight for observation,' Oliver said. 'Excuse me.'

'Oliver—'

'Not now,' he said, and headed for his office. And for once he actually closed his door. Usually he was happy to be interrupted by any member of staff who needed him, but right now he needed to lose himself in paperwork and not have to deal with another human being.

He was halfway through a pile of admin when his phone buzzed; he glanced at the screen.

Darrington Hall.

Why were his parents calling him?

For a moment, he thought about just ignoring the call. But then again it might be important. With a sigh, he answered.

'Oliver. I was just checking if you were coming home for Christmas,' his mother said.

He nearly laughed. Darrington Hall hadn't been 'home' for a long, long time. 'I'm afraid not,' he said. 'I'm on duty.'

'Can't you change it?'

'No,' he said. But something was eating at him. Had his mother really had a fight with Ella outside the bathroom? He'd thought at the time that Ella had been gone a long while. And she'd been very cool with him after that.

If his mother had just warned her off him, that would explain why she'd gone cold on him. 'Mama—did you tell Ella you wanted her to have a paternity test?'

'I… Why would I do that?'

He noticed that his mother hadn't denied all knowledge of Ella being pregnant. He was pretty sure that Ella wouldn't have volunteered the information willingly, the way she had with her own family. And he knew exactly what would've driven his mother to talk about a paternity test. 'Justine,' he said succinctly.

'Well, I don't want to see you trapped again.'

It was the nearest his mother would get to admitting what she'd said. 'Ella isn't trying to trap me,' Oliver said. She'd just refused to marry him. He paused. Now he thought about it, that stuff about Darrington babies having a position to maintain sounded just like the sort of thing his mother would say. 'What position does a Darrington baby have to maintain?'

'I don't know what you mean.'

That definitely sounded like bluster. 'Mother, I'm not the heir to Darrington.'

'You will be if Edward and Prudence don't get their skates on and produce a boy.'

He let that pass. 'And, for the record, I have no intention of suing Ella for custody.'

'Custody?'

'Yes. Did you tell her we wanted custody? Because Darrington babies have a position to maintain?' he repeated.

'I—Oliver, you know it would be for the best. We could hire a nanny. There's plenty of space here—'

'No,' he cut in. 'Ella is the mother of my child, and the baby stays with her.'

'I see.' His mother's tone became frosty.

He sighed. 'Mama, I know we don't see eye-to-eye

about my job. But I've been either a medical student or a qualified doctor for seventeen years now. Half a lifetime, almost. I'm not going to change my mind about what I do. And you need to start trusting me, because I'm doing what's right for me.'

'But, Oliver, Ella's—'

'Ella's lovely,' he said, 'as you'd know if you actually gave her a chance, the way Ned and Prue did. Think about it. Yes, things went wrong with Justine. On paper she was the perfect match, and you pushed us together—and it went wrong. This time, I'm making my own choice. I don't care if Ella's parents don't have the same pedigree that you do. It doesn't matter where you come from, Mama—what matters is who you are and how you treat other people.'

And he hadn't treated Ella very kindly just now.

'I'm going to be a father,' he said quietly. 'And I'd like my baby to know both sets of grandparents. Properly. I'd like to build some bridges with you and Papa. But in turn you need to respect that I'm old enough and wise enough to make my own decisions.'

'And your own mistakes?' the Countess asked coldly.

'Ella isn't a mistake,' he said. 'And neither is my career.'

'So you're giving me an ultimatum?'

'No. I'm giving you a chance to get to know the woman I love, and our baby,' he said. 'It's not going to happen overnight and we're all going to have to learn to compromise a bit, but I guess that's part of what being a real family means.'

'Oliver…'

'I'm on leave at New Year,' he said. 'Maybe we could start with lunch. Something small, informal and friendly. Just you, Papa, Ned and Prue and the girls, and us. Nobody else. Just family. You can get to know Ella a bit better—and we'll take it from there.'

'Just family, New Year,' the Countess echoed.

'A new year and a new beginning,' he said softly.

For a long time, she said nothing, and he thought she was going to throw it all back in his face.

But then she sighed. 'All right.'

'Good. I'll speak to you soon,' he said.

But, more importantly, he needed to talk to Ella. To apologise for ever having doubted her. He wasn't going to take her an armful of flowers—apart from the fact that there was a ban on flowers while the vomiting bug was still around, flowers weren't going to fix things. The only way to fix things was by total honesty.

He just hoped that she'd hear him out.

When he went back onto the ward, Annabelle was there. 'Which room is Ella in?' he asked.

'I'm not entirely sure I should tell you,' she said, narrowing her eyes at him. 'At the moment, Oliver Darrington, I'd quite like to shake you until your teeth rattle.'

He blinked, not used to his head nurse being so fierce. 'What have I done?'

She scoffed. 'Are you really that dense? You made Ella cry.'

He winced. 'I need to talk to her.'

'You need,' Annabelle said crisply, 'to grovel.'

'That, too,' he said.

'She's in here.' Annabelle indicated the side room. 'But if you make her cry any more, I'll throw you out personally, and I don't care if you're the Assistant Head of Obstetrics.'

'You won't have to do that,' Oliver said.

'Hmm,' Annabelle said, and watched him as he walked into the room.

He closed the door behind him, noting that Ella was in tears.

'Hey,' he said softly.

She looked at him and scrubbed at her eyes with the back of one hand. 'What do you want?'

'To talk. To apologise.' He paused. 'Annabelle says I need to grovel.'

Ella's face was tight. 'It doesn't matter.'

'Why are you crying?'

'It doesn't matter,' she repeated.

'Yes, it does,' he said. 'Are you crying because I walked out?'

She didn't answer.

'Because, earlier,' he said, 'you seemed to think that me walking out on you would make you happy. What do you want, Ella?'

'Something you can't give me,' she said. 'You don't do relationships. I was stupid to think that maybe I could change your mind on that score, especially now I know why you don't date anyone more than twice.'

'But that's what I want, too,' he said, coming to sit beside her. 'I want a proper relationship. I want to be a proper family. With you.'

'Your family will never accept me,' she said. 'Your brother and Prue are nice, but your mum hates me and your dad despises me, so it's never going to work. It's just going to cause endless rows between you and them, and that's going to make things difficult between you and me.'

'My parents,' he said, 'are difficult, but they're going to learn to change. And I'm sorry that my mother harangued you outside the bathroom and said I'd insist on custody after a paternity test.'

She frowned. 'But you said she wouldn't say things like that.'

'I didn't want to think she'd say it,' he said, 'but what you said rang pretty true. Oh, and she's sorry, by the way.'

Ella stared at him, looking surprised. 'You've spoken to your mother?'

'Technically, she rang me,' he said. 'So I asked her about what she'd said to you. And I told her very bluntly that you're the mother of my child and the baby stays with you.'

'So you're not going to sue me for custody?'

'I was rather hoping,' he said, 'that we could do better than that. That we could be a family.'

She shook her head. 'I'm not marrying you for the baby's sake, Oliver. That won't work, either. We'll end up resenting each other and it won't be good for the baby.'

'That isn't why I asked you, actually,' he said. 'I asked you because I want to marry you for you. Because I love you.'

She scoffed. 'We had a one-night stand with consequences neither of us was expecting. That's not love, Oliver.'

'Agreed, but that's got nothing to do with it. I've known you for eighteen months,' he said. 'The first moment I saw you, I noticed you. That glorious hair, those beautiful eyes, and a mouth that made my knees weak.'

She looked stunned.

'And then I got to know this bright, warm midwife who's a joy to work with,' Oliver continued. 'She's great with the mums and makes them all feel a million times better when they're panicking, she's great at explaining things to our trainees and gives them confidence when they don't think they can do things, and she thinks on her feet so she can second-guess what senior staff need, too—and I admit, that's why I didn't ask you out months ago, because I know I'm rubbish at relationships and I didn't want to mess up things at work. But then it was the night of the ball—and yes, I'm shallow, because it's the first time I saw you all dressed up and I couldn't think straight. Especially when

I danced with you. I wanted to go and reclaim you from every other guy you danced with,' he told her.

'Really?'

'Really,' he confirmed. 'I couldn't resist you. And then it got complicated, because I realised what I'd done, and I'd messed everything up, and I didn't know how to make things right between us again.'

'And then I told you about the baby—and that must've brought back memories of Justine,' she said quietly.

'It did, though I never doubted you for a second and I don't want to do a paternity test. The night of the party, when you made me feel you really believed in me and supported me—I've never had that from anyone before. It threw me. And it made me realise that maybe you were the one I could trust with my heart. Except then you started avoiding me, and when I asked you to marry me you said no.'

'Because you never said a word about your feelings,' she said. 'I thought you were asking me to marry you out of duty, just because you thought it was the right thing to do. You said we got on well and we could give the baby a stable home—but that's not enough, Oliver. You need love as well, to make a family.'

'I'm not very good at talking about my feelings,' he said. 'But I do love you, Ella. And I do want to be a family with you and the baby. Not like the way I grew up, with my parents very distant and leaving most of the care to hired staff. I want to take the baby to the park with you, and feed the ducks together, and read bedtime stories, and be there in the playground on the first day our little one starts school.'

'The local school?' she checked.

'Definitely the local school,' he said. 'I want to be a family with you and our baby.'

* * *

He meant it, Ella realised.

Oliver really did love her. He wanted to make a life with her and the baby—not because he thought it was the right thing to do, but because he *wanted* to be with them. That day on the ward when he'd talked about taking their baby to see Santa: that had been the real Oliver. The hidden Oliver.

Ella felt her heart contract sharply. 'I love you, too, Oliver,' she said. 'I fell for you months ago.'

'But you never said anything.'

'I thought I was out of your league,' she said. 'The hospital rumour mill said you only ever dated supermodels.'

He laughed. 'Hardly. Anyway, you could hold your own against any supermodel.'

'I'm too short and too curvy,' she said.

'No way. You're beautiful,' he said. 'And I don't want a supermodel. I want you. I love you.'

She stroked his face. 'I love you, too.'

'Even though I'm a grumpy control freak?'

'Even though you're a grumpy control freak,' she said. 'And I guess that's why I called you today when I started bleeding, because I trust you and I knew you'd be there for me. Just as I hope you know I'll always be there for you.'

'Then I'll ask you the same question I asked earlier, except this time I'll do it properly.' He knelt down on one knee. 'Ella O'Brien, you're the love of my life and I want to make a family with you—will you marry me?'

And this time she knew he meant it. That this was going to be a real marriage, not papering over the cracks. 'Yes.'

There was a rap on the door and Annabelle came in. She frowned as she took in the tears on Ella's face. 'Oliver Darrington, I warned you not to make Ella cry,' she said, putting her hands on her hips. 'And you didn't listen. So that's it. *Out.*'

'Annabelle, I'm not crying because I'm miserable,' Ella said, hastily. 'I'm crying because I'm happy.'

Annabelle looked confused. 'So he grovelled?'

'I probably still need to do a bit more grovelling,' Oliver admitted, 'but we're getting there—and we're looking for a matron of honour. I don't suppose you know anyone who might be up for the job? Someone, say, in this room?'

Annabelle's jaw dropped and she stared at each of them in turn. 'You're getting married?'

'You're the first to know,' Ella said. 'Would you be our matron of honour?'

'And godmother to Baby Darrington?' Oliver added.

Annabelle smiled. 'Absolutely yes. To both.'

EPILOGUE

A year later

'BA-BA! DA-DA!' five-month-old Harry crowed, waving his chubby little hands as his father walked into the living room.

'Hello, Harrykins.' Oliver swept his son up into his arms and gave him a resounding kiss. 'Have you been good for Mummy today?'

'Ba-ba,' Harry said solemnly.

'I'm glad to hear it.' Oliver blew a raspberry on the baby's cheek, making him giggle, and put him back in his bouncy chair.

'And good afternoon to you, Mrs Darrington,' he said, taking Ella into his arms and kissing her. 'Guess what I managed to borrow today?'

'Reindeer? Sleigh? A snow machine?'

'Not far off,' he said. 'Wait. Close your eyes. And no peeking.'

Ella smiled and followed his directions.

'OK. You can look now,' he said. 'Ho-ho-ho.'

She burst out laughing, seeing him wearing the Santa outfit from the ward.

Harry, on the other hand, took one look at the strange

man in the red hooded suit and white beard, and burst into tears.

Swiftly, Oliver pulled the hood back and removed the beard. 'Harrykins, it's all right. It's Daddy.' He looked at Ella. 'Sorry. I had no idea it'd scare him like this.'

'He's still only five months old and he doesn't really know what's going on. Next Christmas,' she said, 'he'll be old enough to appreciate it and you'll get the reaction you were expecting today.' She scooped the baby into her arms and rocked him gently. 'Harry, it's OK. It really *is* Daddy.'

Harry simply screamed.

Thirty seconds later, the doorbell went.

'I'll go,' Oliver said.

'Oliver Darrington, why are you half dressed as Father Christmas?' the Countess of Darrington asked in crisp tones on the doorstep. 'And why is my grandson wailing like that?'

'Those two things are connected, and I'm an idiot,' Oliver said. 'Hello, Mama. I didn't realise you were coming over tonight.'

'Your father and I just collected Joe and Roisin from the airport,' Catherine said. 'Or had you forgotten they were coming?'

'He was too excited about being Harry's very first Father Christmas to remember that you're all going to be here for dinner tonight,' Ella said with a grin, walking into the doorway with a still-sobbing Harry. 'And you need to take that suit off, Oliver, and hide it before Prue, Ned and the children get here, because the girls are still young enough to believe in Santa and I don't want to spoil it for them.'

'Tsk. Go and sort yourself out, Oliver. Give the boy to me,' Catherine said, holding out her arms, and Ella duly handed over the baby. 'There, there, Harry. Nobody's going to scare you when Granny Darrington's around.'

Probably, Oliver thought, because his mother was the scariest thing around.

Two seconds later, Harry stopped crying and started gurgling at his grandmother.

And Oliver couldn't quite be annoyed that his mother seemed to have a knack for soothing the baby, because it was so nice to see his family all on such good terms.

'I'll put the kettle on,' Ella said. 'Catherine, I bought some of that horrible lapsang souchong you like, this morning.'

'Thank you, my dear,' Catherine said.

'And there's some good proper tea for me, I hope,' Roisin chipped in, walking into the hallway and overhearing the conversation.

'Of course, Mum.' Ella kissed her mother warmly.

'Your turn for a cuddle, Roisin,' Catherine said, handing over the baby. 'And I'll make the tea, Ella. That baby's had you running round all day and you ought to put your feet up.'

Oliver hid a smile. If anyone had told him a year ago that the two most important women in his life would become fast friends, he would never have believed it. But he'd gradually rebuilt his relationship with his parents, starting with the quiet family lunch he'd suggested at New Year. Things had still been a little strained between them until one day when the baby had started kicking, and Ella had gone over to Catherine, taken her hand and placed it on the bump, saying, 'Baby Darrington, say hello to Granny Darrington.' Catherine had been rewarded by some very firm kicks, and from that point on she'd warmed to Ella.

The O'Briens had instantly adopted Oliver as one of their own and, although Oliver had been wary about the first meeting between Roisin and Catherine, to his surprise they'd got on really well. Roisin was too straightforward for there to be any misunderstandings; and, once Catherine had discovered just how well Roisin played the piano, they'd bonded over a shared love of music and their future grandbaby.

Prue and Ned had also had a son, a couple of weeks before Ella had Harry, so Oliver was no longer the 'spare'. To his delight, having that pressure taken off meant that his parents had finally accepted what he did for a living. Catherine had even suggested that the next Darrington Christmas cocktail party should be a fundraiser for Teddy's. She'd been backed by Ella, Prue and Roisin; and the O'Briens had come over from Ireland this week to help with the last-minute arrangements for the party.

Life, Oliver thought, didn't get any better than this.

Knowing that his father and Joe were bringing in the luggage, and Catherine and Roisin were in the kitchen with the baby, he scooped Ella into his arms and swung her round before kissing her. 'Hey. Happy Christmas. I love you.'

She kissed him back. 'Happy Christmas, Oliver. I love you, too.' She smiled. 'I thought last year I had the best present ever, when I found out that I was expecting our Harry, but I was wrong. Because this is the best present ever—our family, all together.'

'Our family, all together,' he agreed, and kissed her again.

* * * * *

MIDWIFE'S
MISTLETOE BABY

FIONA McARTHUR

Dedicated to my darling husband, Ian.
Because I love you xx Fiona

PROLOGUE

March

RAYNE WALTERS BREATHED a sigh of relief as he passed through immigration and then customs at Sydney airport, deftly texted—I'm through—and walked swiftly towards the exit. Simon would be quick to pick him up. Very efficient was Simon.

He'd had that feeling of disaster closing in since the hiccough at LA when he'd thought he'd left it too late. But the customs officers had just hesitated and then frowned at him and waved him through.

He needed to get to Simon, the one person he wanted to know the truth, before it all exploded in his face. Hopefully not until he made it back to the States. Though they were the same age, and the same height, Simon was like a brother and mentor when he'd needed to make life choices for good rather than fast decisions.

But this choice was already made. He just wanted it not to come as a shock to the one other person whose good opinion mattered. He wasn't looking forward to

Simon's reaction, and there would be anger, but the steps were already in motion.

A silver car swung towards him. There he was. He lifted his hand and he could see Simon's smile as he pulled over.

'Good to see you, mate.'

'You too.' They'd never been demonstrative, Rayne had found it too hard——but their friendship in Simon's formative years had been such a light in his grey days, and a few hilarious hell-bent nights, so that just seeing Simon made him feel better.

They pulled out into the traffic and his friend spoke without looking at him. 'So what's so urgent you need to fly halfway around the world you couldn't tell me on the phone? I can't believe you're going back tomorrow morning.'

Rayne glanced at the heavy traffic and decided this mightn't be a good time to distract Simon with his own impending disaster. Or was that just an excuse to put off the moment? 'Can we wait till we get to your place?'

He watched Simon frown and then nod. 'Sure. Though Maeve's there. She's just had a break-up so I hope a sister in my house won't cramp your style.'

Maeve. Little Maeve, Geez. It was good to think of someone other than himself for a minute. She'd been hot as a teenager and he could imagine she'd be drop-dead gorgeous by now. All of Simon's sisters were but he'd always had a soft spot for Maeve, the youngest. He'd bet, didn't know why, that Maeve had a big front of confidence when, in fact, he'd suspected she was a lot softer than the rest of the strong females in the house.

Though there'd been a few tricky moments when she'd made sure he knew she fancied him—not politic when you were years older than her. He'd got pretty good at not leaving Simon's side while Maeve had been around. 'I haven't seen Maeve for maybe ten years. She was probably about fifteen and a self-assured little miss then.'

'Most of the time she is. Still a marshmallow underneath, though. But she makes me laugh.'

She'd made Rayne laugh too, but he'd never mentioned his avoidance techniques to Simon. He doubted Simon would have laughed at that. Rayne knew Simon thrived on protecting his sisters. It had never been said but the *Keep away from my sisters* sign was clearly planted between them. And Rayne respected that.

'How are your parents?' It was always odd, asking, because he'd only had his mum, and Simon had two sets of parents. Simon's father, who Rayne had known as a kid, had turned out to be Simon's stepdad and he remembered very well how bitter Simon had been about all the lies. Bitter enough to change his last name.

But Simon's mum had chosen to go with someone she'd thought could give her accidental child the life she wanted him to have, and had been very happy with Simon's wealthy stepdad. Simon's birth father hadn't known of his son's existence until Simon had accidentally found out and gone looking for him.

No such fairy-tale for himself. 'Your father is dead and not worth crying over,' was all his mother had ever said.

'You know Dad and Mum moved to Boston?' Simon's voice broke into his thoughts. 'Dad's bypass went well and Mum's keeping us posted.'

'Good stuff.' Rayne glanced at his friend and enjoyed the smile that lit Simon's face. Funnily, he'd never been jealous of Simon's solid family background. Just glad that he could count this man as his friend and know he wouldn't be judged. Except maybe in the next half-hour when he broke the news.

Simon went on. 'And Angus and the Lyrebird Lake contingent are great. I saw them all at Christmas.' More smiles. He was glad it had all worked out for Simon.

Then the question Rayne didn't want. 'And your mum? She been better since you moved her out to live with you?' Another glance his way and he felt his face freeze as Simon looked at him.

'Fine.' If he started there then the whole thing would come out in the car and he just needed a few more minutes of soaking up the good vibes.

Instead, they talked about work.

About Simon's antenatal breech clinic he was running at Sydney Central. He'd uncovered a passion for helping women avoid unnecessary Caesareans for breech babies when possible and was becoming one of the leaders in re-establishing the practice of experienced care for normal breech births.

'So how's your job going?' Simon looked across. 'Still the dream job, making fistloads of money doing what you love?'

'Santa Monica's great. The house is finished and looking great.' Funny how unimportant that was in the big picture. 'My boss wants me to think about becoming one of the directors on the board.' That wouldn't happen now. He shook that thought off for later.

'The operating rooms there are state-of-the-art and we're developing a new procedure for cleft pallet repair that's healing twice as fast.'

'You still doing the community work on Friday down at South Central?'

'Yep. The kids are great, and we're slipping in one case a week as a teaching case into the OR in Santa Monica.' He didn't even want to think about letting the kids down there but he did have a very promising registrar he was hoping he could talk to, and who could possibly take over, before it all went down.

They turned off the airport link road and in less than five minutes were driving into Simon's garage. Simon lived across the road from the huge expanse of Botany Bay Rayne had just flown in over. He felt his gut kick with impending doom. Another huge jet flew overhead as the automatic garage door descended and that wasn't all that was about to go down.

He'd be on one of those jets heading back to America tomorrow morning. Nearly thirty hours' flying for one conversation. But, then, he'd have plenty of time to sit around when he got back.

Simon ushered him into the house and through into the den as he called out to his sister. 'We're back.'

Her voice floated down the stairs. 'Getting dressed.' Traces of the voice he remembered with a definite womanly depth to it and the melody of it made him smile.

'Drink?' Simon pointed to the tray with whisky glass and decanter and Rayne nodded. He'd had two on the plane. Mostly he'd avoided alcohol since med school but he felt the need for a shot to stiffen his spine for the conversation ahead.

'Thanks.' He crossed the room and poured a finger depth. Waved the bottle in Simon's direction. 'You?'

'Nope. I'm not technically on call but my next breech mum is due any day now. I'll have the soda water to keep you company.' Rayne poured him a glass of the sparkling water from the bar fridge.

They sat down. Rayne lifted his glass. 'Good seeing you.' And it was all about to change.

'You too. Now, what's this about?'

Rayne opened his mouth just as Simon's mobile phone vibrated with an incoming call. Damn. Instead, he took a big swallow of his drink.

Simon frowned at him. Looked at the caller, shrugged his inability to ignore it, and stood up to take the call.

Rayne knew if it hadn't been important he wouldn't have answered. Stared down into the dregs of the amber fluid in his glass. Things happened. Shame it had to happen now. That was his life.

'Sorry, Rayne. I have to go. That's my patient with the breech baby. I said I'd be there. Back as soon as I can.' He glanced at the glass. 'Go easy. I'll still be your mate, no matter what it is.'

Rayne put the glass down. 'Good luck.' With that! He had no doubt about Simon's professional skill. But he doubted he'd be happy with his friend when he knew.

Rayne watched Simon walk from the room and he was still staring pensively at the door two minutes later when the woman of his dreams sashayed in and the world changed for ever.

One moment. That was all it took. Nothing could have warned him what was about to happen or have prevented him, after one shell-shocked moment, standing up. Not all the disasters in the universe mattered as he walked towards the vision little Maeve had become.

A siren. Calling him without the need for actual words. Her hair loose, thick black waves dancing on her shoulders, and she wore some floating, shimmering, soft shift of apricot that allowed a tantalising glimpse of amazing porcelain cleavage—and no bra, he was pretty sure. A flash of delicious thigh, and then covered again in deceptive modesty. He could feel his heart pound in his throat. Tried to bring it all back to normality but he couldn't. Poleaxed by not-so-little Maeve.

Maeve paused before entering the room. Drew a breath. She'd spent the day getting ready for this moment. Hair. Nails. Last-minute beauty appointments that had filled the day nicely. When Simon had told her yesterday that Rayne was coming she'd felt her spirits lift miraculously. Gone was the lethargy of self-recriminations

from the last month. She really needed to get over that
ridiculous inferiority complex she couldn't seem to
shake as the youngest of four high achieving girls.

Here was one man who had never disappointed her.
Even though she'd been embarrassingly eager to pes-
ter him as a gawky teenager, he'd always made her feel
like a princess, and she wanted to look her best. Feel
good about herself. Get on with her life after the last
fiasco and drop all those stupid regrets that were doing
her head in.

She hoped he hadn't changed. She'd hero-worshiped
the guy since the day he'd picked up the lunch box she'd
dropped the first time she'd seen him. Her parents' reservations about Rayne's background and bad-boy status
had only made him more irresistible. At fifteen, twenty
had been way out of her reach in age.

Well, things should be different this time and she
was going to make sure they were at least on an even
footing!

Maybe that's where the trill of excitement was coming from and she could feel the smile on her face from
anticipation as she stepped into view.

That was the last sane thought. A glance across a
room, a searing moment of connection that had her
pinned in the doorway so that she stopped and leant
against the architrave, suddenly in need of support—a
premonition that maybe she'd be biting off more than
she could chew even flirting with Rayne. This black-

shirted, open-collared hunk was no pretty boy she could order around. And yet it was still Rayne.

He rose and stepped towards her, a head taller than her, shoulders like a front-row forward, and those eyes. Black pools of definite appreciation as he crossed the room in that distinctive prowl of a walk he'd always had until he stood beside her.

A long slow smile. 'Are you here to ruin my life even more?'

God. That voice. Her skin prickled. Could feel her eyebrows lift. Taking in the glory of him. 'Maybe. Maybe I'm the kind of ruin you've been searching for?'

Goodness knew where those words had come from but they slid from her mouth the way her lunch box had dropped from her fingers around ten years ago. The guy was jaw-droppingly gorgeous. And sexy as all get-out!

'My, my. Look at little Maeve.'

And look at big Rayne. Her girl parts quivered.

'Wow!' His voice was low, amused and definitely admiring—and who didn't like someone admiring?— and the pleasure in the word tickled her skin like he'd brushed her all over. Felt impending kismet again. Felt his eyes glide, not missing a thing.

She looked up. Mesmerised. Skidded away from the eyes—too amazing, instead appreciated the black-as-night hair, that strong nose and determined jaw, and those shoulders that blocked her vision of the world. A shiver ran through her. She was like a lamb beckoning to the wolf.

Another long slow smile that could have melted her bra straps if she'd had one on, then he grew sexy-serious. 'Haven't you grown into a beautiful woman? I think we should meet all over again.' A tilt of those sculpted lips and he held out his hand. 'I'm Rayne. And you are?'

Moistened her lips. 'Maeve.' Pretended her throat wasn't as dry as a desert. Held out her own hand and he took her fingers and kissed above her knuckles smoothly so that she sucked her breath in.

Then he allowed her hand to fall. 'Maeve.' The way he said it raised the hair on her arms again. Like ballet dancers *en pointe*. 'Did you know your name means *she who intoxicates*? I read that somewhere, but not until this moment did I believe it.'

She should have laughed and told him he was corny but she was still shaking like a starstruck mute. Finally she retaliated. 'Rain. As in wet?'

He laughed. 'Rayne as in R.A.Y.N.E. My mother hated me.'

'How is your mother?'

His eyes flickered. 'Fine.' Then he seemed to shake off whatever had distracted him and his smile was slow and lethal. 'Would you like to have a drink with me?'

And of course she said, 'Yes!'

She watched him cross the room to Simon's bar and that made her think, only for a millisecond, about her brother. 'Where's Simon?' Thank goodness her brother hadn't seen that explosion of instant lust between them or he'd be playing bomb demolition expert as soon as he cottoned on.

'His breech lady has gone into labour and he's meeting her at the hospital.'

Maeve ticked that obstacle out of the way. A good hour at least but most probably four. She was still languid with residual oxytocin from the Rayne storm as she sank onto the lounge. Then realised she probably should have sat in Simon's favourite chair, opposite, because if Rayne sat next to her here she doubted she'd be able to keep her hands off him.

He sat down next to her and the force field between them glowed like the lights on the runway across the bay. He handed her a quarter-glass of whisky and toasted her with his own. Their fingers touched and sizzled and their eyes clashed as they sipped.

'Curiouser and curiouser,' he drawled, and smiled full into her face.

OMG. She licked her lips again and he leaned and took her glass from her hand again and put it down on the coffee table. 'You really shouldn't do that.' Then lifted his finger and gently brushed her bottom lip with aching slowness as he murmured, 'I've been remiss.'

He was coming closer. 'In what way?' *Who owned that breathy whisper?*

'I didn't kiss my old friend hello.' And his face filled her vision and she didn't make any protest before his lips touched, returned and then scorched hers.

In those first few seconds of connection she could feel a leashed desperation about him that she didn't understand, because they had plenty of time, an hour at least, but then all thoughts fled as sensation swamped her.

Rayne's mouth was like no other mouth she'd ever known. Hadn't even dreamt about. Like velvet steel, smoothly tempered with a suede finish, and the crescendo was deceptively gradual as it steered them both in a sensual duel of lips and tongue and inhalation of whisky breath into a world that beckoned like a light at the end of the tunnel. She hadn't even known there was a tunnel!

Everything she'd imagined could be out there beckoned and promised so much more. She wanted more, desperately needed more, and lifted her hands to clasp the back of his head, revel in his thick wavy hair sliding through her fingers as she pulled him even closer.

His hands slid down her ribs, across her belly and up under and then circling her breasts through the thin fabric of her silk overshirt. His fingers tightened in deliciously powerful appreciation then he pulled away reluctantly.

'Silk? I'd hate to spoil this so I'd better stop.'

'I'll buy another one,' she murmured against his lips.

Rayne forced his hands to draw back. It was supposed to be a hello kiss. Holy hell, what was he doing? He'd barely spoken to the woman in ten years and his next stop was definitely lower down. They'd be naked on the floor before he realised it if he didn't watch out. 'Maybe we should draw a breath?'

She sat back with a little moue of disappointment, followed by one of those delicious tip-of-the-tongue lip-checks that drove him wild. He was very tempted to throw caution to the winds, and her to the floor, and have his wicked way with the siren. Then he saw Simon's glass of sparkling water sitting forlornly on the table and remembered his unspoken promise. Forced himself to sit back. He'd be better having a cold glass of water himself.

'I'm starving!' He wasn't, but appealing to a woman's need to feed a man was always a good ploy to slow the world down.

She shrugged and he wanted to laugh out loud. Still a princess. Gloriously a princess. 'Kitchen's through there.' A languid hand in vague direction. 'I'm not much of a cook but you could make yourself something.'

Observed her eyes skid away from his. Decided she was lying. 'Don't you know the way to a man's heart is through his stomach?'

'And the way to a woman's heart is more of that hello kissing.' She sighed and stood up. 'But come on, I'll feed you. And then I'm going to kiss you again before my brother comes home. You'll owe me.'

He did laugh at that. 'I'll pay what I have to pay.' And he thought, I am not sleeping with this woman but thank God I brought condoms.

* * *

Maeve had lied about not being able to cook. She'd done French, Italian and Spanish culinary courses, could make anything out of nothing, and Simon's fridge was definitely not made up of nothing. 'Spanish omelette, French salad and garlic pizza bread?'

'Hold the garlic pizza bread.'

She grinned at him, starting to come down from the deluge of sensations that had saturated her brain. She'd planned on being admired, building her self-esteem with a safe yet sexy target, not ending up in bed with the guy. 'Good choice.' Heard the words and decided they applied to herself as well. It would be a good choice not to end up in bed either.

Then set about achieving a beautifully presented light meal perfect for a world traveller just off a plane.

'Oh, my.' He glanced down at his plate in awe. 'She cooks well.'

'Only when I feel like it.' And spun away, but he caught her wrist. Lifted it to his mouth and kissed the delicate inside skin once, twice, three times, and Maeve thought she was going to swoon. She tugged her hand free because she needed to think and she hadn't stopped *feeling* since she'd seen this man. She mimicked him. 'He kisses well.'

He winked at her. 'Only when he feels like it.'

She leaned into him. 'We'll work on that. Eat your dinner like a good boy.' *While I get some distance, fan my face and figure out why I'm acting like he's my chance at salvation. Or is that damnation?*

Five minutes later Rayne sat back from his empty plate. He had been hungry. Or the food was too good to possibly leave. 'Thank you.'

He needed a strategy of space between him and this woman. What the heck was going on to cause this onslaught of attraction between them? His own dire circumstances? The thought that she might be the last beautiful thing he would see or touch for a long time?

And her? Well, she was vulnerable. Simon had suggested that. But vulnerable wasn't the word he would have used. Stunning, intoxicating, black-widow dangerous?

He stood up and put his plate in the sink. Rinsed it, like he always did because he'd been responsible for any cleaning he'd wanted done for a long time, and internally he smiled because she didn't say, *Leave that, I'll do it,* like most women would have. She leant on the doorframe and watched him do it.

'Simon said you've just finished a relationship?' Seemed like his subconscious wanted to get to the bottom of it because his conscious mind hadn't been going to ask that question.

'Hmm. It didn't end well, and I've been a dishrag poor Simon had to put up with for the last month. You've no idea the lift I got when Simon said you were coming.'

No subterfuge there. He had the feeling she didn't

know the meaning of the word. 'Thank you. But you know I'm here only for one night. I fly back tomorrow.'

She turned her head to look at him. 'Do you have to?'

That was ironic. 'No choice.' Literally. 'And I won't be back for a long time.' A very long time maybe.

She nodded. 'Then we'd best make the most of tonight.'

He choked back a laugh. 'What on earth can you mean?'

'Catch up on what we've both been doing, of course. Before Simon monopolises you.' She was saying one thing but her body was saying something else as she sashayed into the lounge again, and he may as well have had a leash around his neck because he followed her with indecent haste and growing fatalism.

'Simon will be back soon.' A brief attempt to return to reality but she was standing in the centre of the room looking suddenly unsure, and that brief fragility pierced him like no other reaction could have. Before he knew it he had his arms around her, cradling her against his chest, soothing the black hair away from her face. Silk skin, glorious cheekbones, a determined little chin. And she felt so damn perfect in his arms as she snuggled into him.

'Take me to bed, Rayne. Make me feel like a woman again.'

'That would be too easy.' He kissed her forehead. 'I don't think that's a good idea, sweetheart.'

'I'm a big girl, Rayne. Covered for contraception. Unattached and in sound mind. Do I have to beg?'

He looked at her, squeezed her to him. Thought about the near future and how he would never get this chance again because things would never be the same. He would never be the same. Searched her face for any change of mind. No. Bloody hell. She didn't have to beg.

So he picked her up in his arms, and she lifted her hands to clasp him around his neck, and he kissed her gorgeous mouth and they lost a few more minutes in a hazy dream of connection. Finally he got the words out. 'So which bedroom is yours?'

She laughed. 'Up two flights of stairs. Want me to walk?'

'Much as I have enjoyed watching you walk, I'd prefer to carry you.'

And with impressive ease he did. Maeve rested her head back on that solid shoulder and gazed up at the chiselled features and strong nose. And those sinful lips. OMG, did she know what she was doing? Well, there was no way she wanted this to stop. This chemistry had been building since that first searing glance that had jerked and stunned them both like two people on the same elastic. She tightened her hands around his neck.

He felt so powerful—not pretty and perfect like Sean had been—but she didn't want to think about Sean. About the pale comparison of a man she'd wasted her heart on when she should have always known Rayne would stand head and shoulders above any other man.

Speaking of shoulders, he used one to push open the door she indicated, knocked it shut with his foot, and strode across the room to the big double bed she thought he would toss her onto, but he smiled, glanced around the room and lowered her gently until her feet were on the floor.

His breathing hadn't changed and he looked as if he could have done it all again without working a sweat.

Ooh la la. 'I'm impressed.'

He raised his brows quizzically and freed the French drapes until they floated down to cover the double window in a flounced bat of their lacy eyelids and the room dimmed to a rosy glow from the streetlights outside. Slid his wallet out of his pocket and put it on the windowsill after retrieving a small foil packet.

Then he pulled her towards him and spun her until her spine was against the wall and her breasts were pressed into his hardness. Shook his head and smiled full into her eyes. Felt her knees knock as he said, 'You are the sexiest woman I have ever seen.'

She thought, *And you are the sexiest man*, as she lifted her lips to his, and thank goodness he didn't wait to be asked twice. Like falling into a swirling maelstrom of luscious sensation, Maeve felt reality disappear like a leaf sucked into a drainpipe then she heard him say something. Realised he'd created physical distance between them. Her mind struggled to process sound to speech.

'Miss Maeve, are you sure you want to proceed?'

It was a jolting and slightly disappointing thing to say

in the bubble of sensuality he'd created and she looked up at him. Surprised a look of anguish she hadn't expected. 'Are you trying to spoil this for a particular reason?'

A distance she didn't like flashed in his eyes. 'Maybe.'

She pulled his head forward with her hands in his hair. 'Well, don't!'

Rayne shrugged, smiled that lethal smile of his, and instead he lifted her silk shift over her head in a slow sexy exposure, leaving the covering camisole and the dark shadow of her breasts plainly visible through it.

He trailed the backs of his fingers up the sides of her chest and she shivered, wanted him to rip it off so she could feel his hands on her skin. And he knew it.

This time the backs of his fingers trailed down and caught the hem of the camisole, catching the final layer, leaving her top half naked to the air on her sensitised skin.

She heard him suck in his breath, heard it catch in his throat as he glimpsed her body for the first time— and the tiny peach G-string that was all that was left.

Her turn. He had way too many clothes on and she needed to look and feel his skin with a sudden hunger she had no control over.

She reached up and danced her fingers swiftly down the fastening of his black shirt, as if unbuttoning for the Olympics way ahead of any other competitor, because she'd never felt such urgency to slip her hands inside a man's shirt. Never wanted to connect as badly as now with the taut skin-covered muscle and bone of a man. The man.

This was Rayne. The Rayne. And he felt as fabulous as she'd known he would and the faster she did this the faster he would kiss her again. Her fingers seemed to glow wherever she touched and she loved the heat between them like a shivering woman loved a fire.

While her fingers were gliding with relish he'd unzipped and was kicking away his trousers. They stood there, glued together, two layers of mist-like fabric between their groins, two flimsy, ineffectual barriers that only inflamed them more, and his mouth recommenced its onslaught and she was lost.

Until he shifted. Moved that wicked mouth and tongue lower, a salutation of her chin, her neck, her collarbone, a slow, languorous, teasing circle around her breast and exquisite tantalising pleasure she'd never imagined engulfed her as he took the rosy peak and flicked it with delicate precision.

She gasped.

His hands encircled her ribs, the strong thumbs pushing her breasts into perky attention for his favours. Peaks of sensitive supplication and he took advantage until she was writhing, aching for him, helpless against the wall at her back, unable to be silent.

She. Could. Not. Get. Enough.

Rayne lifted his head, heard the moan of a woman enthralled, saw the wildness in her eyes, felt his own need soar to meet hers, dropped his hands to the lace around her hips and slid those wicked panties slowly down her legs, savoured the silk of her skin, the tautness of her thighs under his fingers, and then the scrap of material fell in a ridiculously tiny heap at her feet. There was something so incredibly sinful about that fluttering puddle of fabric, and he'd bet he'd think about it later, many times, as he reached for the condom and dropped his own briefs swiftly.

Then his hands slid back to her buttocks. Those round globes of perfection that fitted his hands perfectly. Felt the weight of her, lifted, supported her body in his hands, and the power of that feeling expanded with the strain in his arms and exultantly, slowly, her back slid up the wall and she rose to meet him.

Rayne slowly and relentlessly pinned her with his body and she wrapped her legs around him the way he had known, instinctively, she would, and it felt as incredible as he'd also known it could be, except it was more. So much more. And they began to dance the ancient dance of well-matched mates.

The rising sun striped the curtains with a golden beam of new light and Maeve awoke in love. Some time in the night it had come to her and it was as indestructible as a glittering diamond in her chest. How had that happened?

Obviously she'd always loved him.

And it was nothing like the feelings she'd had for

other men. This was one hundred per cent 'you light my fire, I know you would cherish me if you loved me back, I want to have babies with you' love. So it looked like she'd have to pack her bags and follow the man to the States.

At least her mother lived there.

But Rayne was gone from their tumbled bed and someone was talking loudly downstairs.

Maeve sat up amidst the pillows he'd packed around her, realised she was naked and slightly stiff, began to smile and then realised the loud voice downstairs was Simon's.

A minute later she'd thrown a robe over her nakedness and hurried into Simon's study, where two burly federal policemen had Rayne in… handcuffs?

The breath jammed in her throat and she leant against the doorframe that had supported her last night. Needed it even more now.

Simon was saying, 'What the hell? Rayne? This has to be a mistake.'

'No mistake. Just didn't get time to explain.' Rayne glanced across as Maeve entered and shut his eyes for a moment as if seeing her just made everything worse. Not how she wanted to be remembered by him.

Then his thick lashes lifted as he stared. 'Bye, Maeve,' looked right through her and then away.

Simon glanced between the two, dawning suspicion followed swiftly by disbelief and then anger. 'So you knew they'd come and you…' He couldn't finish the sentence. Sent Maeve an, 'I'll talk to you later' look, but the federal policemen were already nudging Rayne towards the door.

Simon was still in the clothes he'd left in last night so he hadn't been home long. Rayne was fully dressed, again in sexy black, and shaved, had his small cabin bag, so it looked like he'd been downstairs, waiting. She would never know if it was for Simon or the police.

She wondered whether the police hadn't come he would have woken her to say goodbye. The obvious negative left her feeling incredibly cold in the belly after the conflagration they'd shared last night and her epiphany this morning.

He'd said he was going and wouldn't be back for a while but she'd never imagined this scenario.

Then he really was gone and Simon was shaking his head.

CHAPTER ONE

Nine months later.
Looking for Maeve.

RAYNE'S MOTHER DIED of a heroin overdose on the fifteenth of December. He was released from prison the day after, when the posted envelope of papers arrived at the Santa Monica police station, and he put his head in his hands at his inability to save her. The authorities hadn't been apologetic—he should have proclaimed his innocence, but he'd just refused to speak.

Her last written words to him…

My Rayne
I love you. You are my shining star. I would never have survived in prison but it seems I can't survive on the outside either with you in there. I'm so sorry it took me so long to fix it.

With the other letter and proof of her guilt she'd kept, the charges on Rayne were dropped and he buried her a week later in Santa Monica. It had been the only place she'd known some happiness, and it was fine to leave her there in peace.

He had detoured to see his old boss, who had been devastated by the charges against him, explained briefly that he'd known she wouldn't survive in jail, and the man promised to start proceedings for the restoration of his licence to practise. Undo what damage he could, and as he'd been able to keep most of the sensation out of the papers, that was no mean offer.

Then Rayne gave all his mother's clothes and belongings to the Goodwill Society and ordered her the biggest monumental angel he could for the top of her grave. It would have made her smile.

Then he put the house up for sale and bought a ticket for Australia and Maeve. The woman he couldn't forget after just one night. Not because he was looking for happily ever after but because he owed it to her and Simon to explain. And if he was going to start a new life he had to know what was left of his old one. If anything.

All he knew was the man he was now was no fit partner for Maeve and he had no doubt Simon would say the same.

On arrival it had taken him two days of dogged investigation before he'd traced Maeve to Lyrebird Lake and he would have thought of it earlier if he'd allowed himself to think of Simon first.

Simon's birth father lived there and Simon often

spent Christmas with them—he should have remembered that. With Maeve's mother in the US it made sense she was with her brother.

Who knew if she'd say yes to seeing him after the way he'd left, if either of them would? He guessed he couldn't blame them when they didn't know the facts, but he had to know they were both all right. Maybe he should have opened the letters Maeve had sent and not refused the phone calls Simon had tried, but staying isolated from others and keeping the outside world out of his head had been the only way he'd got through it.

Looked down at the wad of letters in his hand and decided against opening the letters now in case she refused to see him in writing.

Two hundred miles away from Lyrebird Lake, and driving just over the legal speed limit, Rayne pressed a little harder on the accelerator pedal. The black Chev, a souped-up version of his first car from years ago, throttled back with a throaty grumble.

He didn't even know if Maeve had a partner, had maybe even married, but he had to find out. She would refuse to see him. It was ridiculous to be propelled on with great urgency when it had been so long, but he was. He should wait until after the holiday season but he couldn't.

The picture in his head of her leaning against the doorframe as he'd been led away had tortured him since that night. The fact that he'd finally discovered the woman he needed to make him whole had been there all the time in his past, and he'd let her down in the most cowardly way by not telling her what would happen.

He couldn't forgive himself so how did he think that Maeve and her brother would forgive him? All he just knew was he had to find her and explain. Try to explain.

So clearly he remembered her vulnerability before he'd carried her up those stairs. Blindingly he saw her need to see herself the way he saw her. Perhaps it was too late.

If she had moved on, then he would have to go, but he needed her to know the fault was all his before they said a final goodbye. It wasn't too late to at least tell her she couldn't have been more perfect on that night all those months ago.

A police highway patrol car passed in the opposite direction. The officer glanced across at him and Rayne slowed. Stupid. To arrive minutes later after nine months wouldn't make the difference but if he was pulled over for speeding then the whole catastrophe could start again. International drivers licence. Passports. He didn't want the hassle.

It was lucky the salesman had filled the fuel tank last night because he'd only just realised it was early Christmas morning. Every fuel stop was shut. He had no food or drinks except the water he'd brought with him. Big deal except he was gatecrashing Simon's family at a time visitors didn't usually drop in. Hopefully the rest of the family weren't assembled when he arrived.

It wasn't the first time he'd done this. He remembered Simon taking him home to his other parents' one year while they'd been in high school. Rayne's mother had ended up in rehab over the holiday break, it had always been the hardest time of the year for her to stay straight, and his friend, Simon, had come to check on him.

He'd been sixteen and sitting quietly watching television when Simon had knocked at the door, scolded him for not letting him know, and dragged him reluctantly back to his house for the best Christmas he'd ever had.

Simon's parents had ensured he'd had a small Christmas sack at the end of his bed on Christmas morning and Maeve had made him a card and given him a Cellophane bag of coconut ice she'd made for everyone that year. He'd loved the confectionary ever since.

Well, here he was again, gatecrashing. Unwanted.

It was anything but funny. The truly ridiculous part was that in his head he'd had an unwilling relationship with Maeve for the last nine months. She'd made an irreversible imprint on him in those hours he'd held her in his arms. Blown him away, and he was still in pieces from it. He'd kept telling himself they'd only connected in his last desperate attempt to hold onto someone good before the bad came but he had no doubt she would always hold a sacred piece of his heart.

In prison he'd separated his old life out of his head. Had kept it from being contaminated by his present. Refused any visitors and stored the mail. But when his defences had been down, when he'd drifted off to sleep, Maeve had slid in beside him, been with him in the morning when he'd woken up, and at night when he'd dreamt. He'd had no control over that.

But he'd changed. Hardened. Couldn't help being affected by the experience, and she didn't need a man like he'd become—so he doubted he'd stay. Just explain and then head back to Sydney to sort out his life. Start fresh when he could find some momentum for beginning. Wasn't even sure he would return to paediatrics. Felt the need for something physical. Something to use up the coil of explosive energy he'd been accumulating over the last nine months.

So maybe he'd go somewhere in between for a while where he could just soak up nature and the great outdoors now that he had the freedom to enjoy it.

Funny how things were never as important until you couldn't have them. He'd lusted after a timeless rainforest, or a deserted mountain stream, or a lighthouse with endless ocean to soothe his soul.

Or Maeve, a voice whispered. No.

CHAPTER TWO

Maeve

MAEVE PATTED HER round and rolling belly to soothe the child within. Christmas in Lyrebird Lake. She should have been ecstatic and excited about the imminent birth of her baby.

Ecstatic about the fact that only yesterday Simon had declared his love to Tara and was engaged to a woman she couldn't wait to call her sister. She put her fingers over the small muscle at the corner of her eye, which was twitching. But instead she was a mess.

Her only brother, or half-brother, she supposed she should acknowledge that, seeing she was living in Lyrebird Lake where his birth father lived, was engaged to be married. That was very exciting news.

And it wasn't like Simon's family hadn't made her welcome. But it wasn't normal to land on people who didn't know you for one of the biggest moments of your life even if Simon had always raved about Lyrebird Lake.

The place was worth raving about. She'd never been so instantly received for who she was, even in her own family, she thought with a tinge of uneasy disloyalty, but that explained why Simon had always been the least judgemental of all her siblings.

Until she'd slept with Rayne, that was.

Simon's other family didn't know the meaning of the word judgmental. Certainly less than her mother, but that was the way mum was, and she accepted that.

And she and Simon had re-established some of their previous closeness, mostly thanks to Tara.

The fabulous Tara. Her new friend and personal midwife was a doll and she couldn't imagine anyone she would rather have in the family.

She, Maeve, was an absolute bitch to be depressed by the news but it was so hard to see them so happy when she was so miserable.

She gave herself a little mental shake. Stop it.

Glanced out the window to the manger on the lawn. It was Christmas morning, and after nearly four weeks of settling in there was no place more welcoming or peaceful to have her baby.

So what was wrong with her?

It was all very well being a midwife, knowing what was coming, but she had this mental vision of her hand being held and it wasn't going to be Simon's. Have her brother, in the room while she laboured? Not happening, even if he was an obstetrician.

No. It would be Tara's hand that steadied her, which

was good but not what she'd secretly and hopelessly dreamt of.

That scene she'd replayed over in her head a thousand times, him crossing the floor to her after that first glance, and later the feel of his arms around her as he'd carried her so easily up the stairs, the absolutely incredible dominance yet tenderness of his lovemaking. Gooseflesh shimmered on her arms.

She shook her head. The birth would be fine. It was okay.

She tried to shake the thought of needing Rayne to get through labour from her mind but it clung like a burr and refused to budge as if caught in the whorls of her cerebral convolutions.

Which was ridiculous because the fact was Rayne didn't want her.

He'd refused to answer her letters or take the call the one time she'd tried to call the prison, had had to go through the horror of finding out his prison number, been transferred to another section, the interminable wait and then the coldness of his refusal to speak to her.

Obviously he didn't want her!

Simon had told her he'd found out he would be in prison for at least two years, maybe even five, and that the charges had been drug related. She, for one, still didn't believe it.

But she hated the fact Rayne didn't want to see her.

Her belly tightened mildly in sympathy, like it had been tightening for the last couple of weeks every now and then, and she patted the taut, round bulge. *It's okay, baby. Mummy will be sensible. She'll get over your father one day.* But that wasn't going to happen if she stayed here mooning.

Maeve sat up and eased her legs out of the bed until her feet were on the floor. Grunted quietly with the effort and then smiled ruefully at herself for the noisy exertion of late pregnancy.

She needed to go for a walk. Free her mind outside the room. Stay fit for the most strenuous exertion of her life.

It was time to greet Christmas morning with a smile and a gentle, ambling welcome in the morning air before the Queensland heat glued her to the cool chair under the tree in the back yard. The tables were ready to be set for breakfast and later lunch with Simon's family and she would put on a smiling face.

She wondered if Tara was up yet. Her friend had come in late last night with Simon, she'd heard them laughing quietly and the thought made her smile. Two gorgeous people in love. The smile slipped from her face and she dressed as fast as she could in her unbalanced awkwardness and for once didn't worry about make-up.

Self-pity was weak and she needed to get over herself. She was the lucky one, having a baby when lots of women ached for the chance, and she couldn't wait.

It wasn't as if she didn't have a family who loved her, even if her mum was in the States.

But she had dear Louisa, Simon's tiny but sprightly grandmother, spoiling them all with her old-fashioned country hospitality and simple joy in kinfolk. She, Maeve, was twenty-five and needed to grow up and enjoy simple pleasures like Louisa did.

Once outside, she set off towards the town and the air was still refreshingly cool. Normally she would have walked around the lake but it was Sunday, and Simon liked the Sunday papers. Did they print newspapers on Christmas Day? Would the shop even be open? She hadn't thought of that before she'd left but if it didn't then that was okay.

It was easier not to think in the fresh air and distractions of walking with a watermelon-sized belly out front cleared the self-absorbtion.

Maeve saw the black, low-to-the-ground, old-fashioned utility as it turned into the main street and smiled. A hot rod like you saw at car shows with wide silver wheels and those long red bench seats in the front designed for drive-in movies. It growled down the road like something out of *Happy Days*, she thought to herself. The square lines and rumbling motor made it stand out from the more family-orientated vehicles she usually saw. Something about it piqued her curiosity.

She stared at the profile of the man driving and then her whole world tilted. Shock had her clutching her throat with her fingers and then their eyes met. Her heart suddenly thumped like the engine of the black beast and the utility swerved to the edge of the road and pulled up. The engine stopped and so did her breath—then her chest bumped and she swayed with the shock.

It was Maeve! The connection was instantaneous. Like the first time. But she was different. He blinked. Pregnant! Very pregnant!

Rayne was out of the car and beside her in seconds, saw the colour drain from her face, saw her eyes roll back. He reached her just as she began to crumple. Thank God. She slumped into his arms and he caught her urgently and lifted her back against his chest, felt and smelt the pure sweetness of her hair against his face as he turned, noticed the extra weight of her belly with a grimace as he struggled with the door catch without dropping her. Finally he eased her backwards onto the passenger seat and laid her head gently back along the seat.

He stared at the porcelain beauty of the woman he'd dreamed about throughout that long horrible time of incarceration.

Maeve.

Pregnant by someone else. The hollow bitterness of envy. The swell of fierce emotion and the wish it had been him. He patted her hands, patted her cheek, and slowly she stirred.

Unable to help the impossible dream, he began to count dates in his head. He frowned. Pushed away a sudden, piercing joy, worked out the dates again. But they'd both used contraception. It couldn't be…

She groaned. Stirred more vigorously. Her glorious long eyelashes fluttered and she opened her eyes. They widened with recognition.

Then she gagged and he reached in and lifted her shoulders so she was sitting on the seat and could gag out the door. She didn't look at him again. Just sat with her shoulders bowed and her head in her hands.

He reached past her to the glove box and removed a small packet of tissues. Nudged her fingers and put them into her hand. She took them, but even after she'd finished wiping her mouth she still didn't look at him and he glanced around the street to see if anyone had noticed. Thank God for quiet Sunday mornings. Quiet Christmas morning, actually.

Well, that was unexpected. Something going right!

Seeing Maeve outside and alone. So unplanned. Looking down at her, he couldn't believe she was here in front of him. His eyes were drawn to the fragile V of the nape of her neck, the black hair falling forward away from the smoothness of her ivory skin, and he realised his heart was thumping like a piston in his chest. Like he'd run a marathon. Like he'd seen a vision of the future that was so bright he was blinded. Fool.

It felt like a dream. A stupid, infantile, Christmas fantasy... In reality, though, the woman of his dreams had, in fact, fainted and then thrown up at the very sight of him! He needed to get a grip.

CHAPTER THREE

After faint...

'WHERE DID YOU come from?' Maeve opened her eyes. Barely raised her voice because her throat was closed with sudden tears. She kept her head down. Couldn't believe she'd fainted and thrown up as a first impression. Well, he shouldn't have appeared out of nowhere.

'America. Earlier this week. You're pregnant!'

Der. 'Does Simon know?'

'That you're pregnant?'

She sighed. Her head felt it was going to explode. Not so much with the headache that shimmered behind her eyes but with the thoughts that were ricocheting around like marbles in her head. Just what she needed. A smart-alec answer when she had a million questions.

Awkwardly she sat straighter and shifted her bottom on the seat in an attempt to stand. Frustratingly she couldn't get enough purchase until he put his hand down and took hers.

She looked at his brown, manly fingers so much

larger than the thin white ones they enclosed. Rayne was here. She could feel the warmth from his skin on hers. Really here.

He squeezed her fingers and then pulled steadily so she floated from the car like a feather from a bottle. She'd forgotten how strong he was. How easily he could move her body around. 'I assume you caught me when everything went black?'

'Thank goodness.' She looked up at the shudder in his voice. 'Imagine if I hadn't.'

She instantly dropped her other hand to her stomach and the baby moved as if to reassure her. Her shoulders drooped again with relief.

'You're pregnant,' he said again.

Now she looked at him. Saw the rampant confusion in a face she'd never seen confusion in before. 'I told you that. In the letters.'

His face shuttered. A long pause. 'I didn't open your letters.'

Maeve was dumbstruck, temporarily unable to speak. He hadn't opened her letters? The hours she'd spent composing and crunching and rewriting and weeping over them before she'd posted them. Wow!

That explained the lack of reply, she thought with a spurt of temper, but it also created huge questions as to just how important she'd been to him. Obviously not very. Not even being locked away in prison had been enough to tempt him to open her letters. She felt the nausea rise again.

He'd refused to talk to Simon too and she knew her brother had been hurt about that. He had hoped for some reassurance from Rayne that somewhere there was an explanation.

The guy was lower than she thought. She needed to protect Simon from being upset a day after his happiest day. That was a real worry. Or a diversion for her mind.

She tried to compose herself, get her thoughts together...

'I don't think you should see Simon until I can warn him you're back.'

Rayne straightened. Lifted his chin. 'I'm not going to hide.'

'It's not about you.' She could feel the unfairness expand in her. This was not how she dreamed their first meeting would be. Why couldn't he have warned her he was coming? Given her a chance to have her defences sorted? Dressed nicely? Put her make-up on, for goodness' sake? She'd just walked out of the house in her expander jeans and a swing top. And trainers. She groaned.

'Are you okay?'

She looked up. Saw the broad shoulders, bulging muscles in his arms, that chest she'd dreamt of for three quarters of a year. He was here and she wanted to be scooped up and cradled against that chest but he wasn't saying the right things. 'You can't see Simon yet. He's just got engaged. He's happy. I won't let you do that. You've upset him enough.'

He'd upset her too, though upset was an understatement. Hurt badly. Devastated. But then you reappeared at the right moment, a tiny voice whispered. The exact right moment. Just in time.

She saw a flicker of pain cross his face and she closed her eyes. What was she doing? Why was she being like this? Was she trying to drive him away?

She needed to think. It overwhelmed her that Rayne was here. As if she'd conjured up him by her need this morning and now she didn't know what she should think. And he hadn't known she was pregnant!

Rayne was having all sorts of problems keeping his thoughts straight. He could see she was at a loss too. 'Maeve!'

'What?'

He needed to know. Couldn't believe it but didn't want to believe it was someone else. 'Are you pregnant with my baby?'

She hunched her shoulders as if to keep him out. 'It's my baby. You didn't want to know about it.'

He pulled her in close to him and put both arms around her. Lifted her chin to look at him. 'For God's sake, woman.' Resisted the urge to shake her. 'Are you pregnant with my baby?'

'Yes. Now let go of me, Rayne.' His loosened his fingers. Felt her pull away coolly. Create distance between them like a crack from a beautiful glacier breaking away from its mountain, and his heart, a heart that had been a solid rock inside him, cracked too.

Maeve turned her back on him and climbed awkwardly into his car. The realisation that she couldn't protect Simon from this shock forever hit her.

'Come on. Let's get it over with. You need to see Simon and then we need to talk.'

Simon came out of the house when the car pulled up and a petite blonde woman followed him. Rayne remembered now that Maeve had said Simon was engaged. This would be some first introduction.

Rayne climbed out and walked around to open the passenger door; he glanced at his old friend, who looked less than pleased, and then back at the woman's hand he wanted to hold more than anything else in the world.

For an icy moment there he thought she wasn't going to allow him that privilege—right when he needed her most—but then she uncurled her closed fist and allowed her fingers to slide in beside his. By the time Simon had arrived she was standing beside him. Solidarity he hadn't expected.

'They let you out?' There was no Christmas spirit in that statement, Rayne thought sardonically to himself, though couldn't say he could blame him, considering Maeve's condition.

He stared into Simon's face. Felt the coolness between them like an open wound. 'I wanted to explain.' He shrugged. 'It just didn't happen.'

'Instead, you slept with my sister.'

'There's that.' To hell with this.

He just wanted it over. Tell Simon the truth. Let Maeve know at least the father of her baby wasn't a criminal. At the very least. Then get the hell away from here because these people didn't deserve him to infect their live with the disaster that seemed to follow him around.

'When my mother died there wasn't a reason for me to be in there any more. She told them the truth before she overdosed and they dropped the charges.'

Maeve's breath drew in beside him. 'Your mother died?' Felt her hand, a precious hand he'd forgotten he still held, tighten in his. She squeezed his fingers and he looked down at her. Saw the genuine sympathy and felt more upset than he had for the last horrific year. How could she be so quick to feel sorry for him when he'd ruined her life with his own selfishness? That thought hurt even more.

'You took the rap for your mother!' Simon's curt statement wasn't a question. 'Of course you did.' He slapped himself on the forehead. Repeated, 'Of course you did.'

He didn't want to talk about his mother. Didn't want sympathy. He spoke to Simon. 'I understand you not wanting me here.'

He forced himself to let go of Maeve's hand. 'Take Maeve inside. She fainted earlier, though she didn't fall.' He heard Simon's swift intake of breath and saw the blonde woman, from hanging back, shift into gear to swift concern.

He felt Maeve's glance. Her hand brushed the woman's gesture away. 'No. We need to talk.'

'I'll come back later when you've had a chance to rest. I'll find somewhere to stay for tonight.'

And give myself a chance to think, at least, he thought. He reached into his wallet and pulled out a piece of paper on which he'd written his number. 'This is my mobile number. Phone me when you've rested.' And then he spun on his heel and walked away from the lot of them, wishing he had warned them he was coming, though he wasn't sure it would have gone over any better if he had.

Well, they knew the truth now. He'd done what he'd come to do. Learnt something he'd never envisaged and was still grappling with that momentous news. He allowed himself one long sweeping glance over the woman he had dreamed about every night, soaking in the splendour that was Maeve. Her breasts full and ripe for his child, her belly swollen and taut, and her face pale with the distress he'd caused her.

Maeve allowed Tara to steer her back inside, up the hallway to her bedroom, because suddenly she felt as weak as a kitten. Simon was still standing on the street, watching the black utility disappear down the road with a frown on his face, but she'd worry about Simon later.

An almost silent whistle from Tara beside her drew

her attention as she sat down on her bed. 'So that's Rayne. Not quite what I imagined. A tad larger than life.' Tara squeezed her arm in sympathy. 'You look pale from shock.'

Maeve grimaced in agreement. Glanced at Tara, calm and methodical as usual as she helped her take off her shoes. 'It was a shock. And highly embarrassing. Not only did I faint but then proceeded to throw up in front of him.'

She felt the assessing glance Tara cast over her. 'For a very pregnant lady you've had a busy morning and it hasn't really started yet.'

It was barely seven o'clock. 'Lucky I got up early. It was supposed to be a gentle Christmas morning walk for Simon's newspaper.'

'The shop won't be open. But your Rayne is a Christmas present with a difference.' Tara laughed. 'What was it you said when you described him to me? A head taller and shoulders like a front-row forward and those dark eyes. No wonder you fell for him, boots and all.'

A fallen woman. And still in love with him, boots and all. 'Is it mad that even after ten minutes with him after all this time, I wanted to go with him? That I feel like we've been together for so much more than one night? That I can even feel that when he's just been away? When even I know that's too simplistic and whitewashed.'

She saw Tara look towards the bedside table, cross to her glass of water and bring it back for her. 'Even from where I was standing, I could feel the energy between you two. I wouldn't be surprised if Simon felt it too.'

'Thanks for that, at least.' She took a sip of water and it did make her feel a little clearer. 'Problem is, I was okay to sleep with but not okay to tell that he was going to prison.'

'Well.' Tara looked thoughtful. 'It seems he has got an explanation if he took the blame for his mother. And things are different now. He can't just walk away and think you'll be better off without him without even discussing it.'

She touched Maeve's shoulder in sympathy. 'And you have been carrying his child. So I guess at least a part of him has been with you since then.' Tara gave her a quick hug. 'He looks tough and self-sufficient but doesn't look a bad man.'

She knew he wasn't. From the bottom of her heart. 'He's not. I believe he's a good man.' She stroked her belly gently. 'I have to believe that if he's going to be part of our lives. And until this…' she patted her belly again '…Simon wouldn't hear a wrong word said about him.' She glanced at Tara and smiled to lighten the dramatic morning. 'And we both know Simon has good taste.'

Tara blushed but brushed that aside. 'Did he say he wants to be a part of your lives?'

In what brief window of opportunity? 'We didn't get that far. What with me fainting like a goose at the sight of him.' Maeve shook her head. Thought about it. 'He said he hadn't opened my mail. That he didn't know I was pregnant.' She thought some more. 'But he didn't look horrified when I told him.'

'Helpful. Though why he wouldn't open your mail has me puzzled.'

Me, too. 'I'll be asking that when he comes back. And it's Christmas morning.' She suddenly thought of the impact of her commotion on everyone else's day. That's what Lyrebird Lake did to you. Made you begin to think more of other people. 'I hope it doesn't spoil your first Christmas with Simon. I feel like I'm gatecrashing your engagement celebrations with my dramas.'

'Nothing can spoil that.' A lovely smile from Tara. 'I'm just glad we're here for you. No better time for family. And Simon will be fine.'

Tara had said family. The idea shone like a star in a dark night sky. It was a good time for family. Tara had probably meant Simon's family but Maeve was thinking of her own. Rayne and her and their baby as a family.

To Maeve it had felt like she'd been marking time for Rayne to arrive and now he was here he was her family. As long as he could handle that idea. Well, he'd just have to get used to it.

She heard Simon's footsteps approaching and as he paused at her bedroom door Maeve felt his assessing glance.

She looked at him. 'Rayne went to gaol for his mother! That's what he'd come to tell you that night.'

Simon nodded. 'So it seems. Fool. He didn't get around to it and if he had I would have tried to talk him out of it. I'm not surprised he didn't rush into an explanation. He knew I would have told him that taking the blame for his mother wouldn't help her at all.'

What kind of man made that sort of sacrifice without flinching? Actually, her man. 'He went to prison for her. Lost his job and his reputation.' And me, she thought, but didn't say it. Well, he hadn't lost her yet.

Simon rubbed the back of his head. 'That news just makes me more angry with him. But I'll get over it.' He rubbed again. 'Obviously I'm still battling with the idea I didn't suspect Rayne would do that. Now it's glaringly obvious. So I let him down too.'

He put his finger up and pointed at her. 'Maybe you should do what he suggested. Lie down. You're as pale as a ghost and the family won't be here for another two hours for breakfast.'

Maybe she would. Because she had plans for tonight. 'I want Rayne to spend Christmas with us.'

Simon didn't look as surprised as she'd thought he would. He glanced at Tara and Maeve caught the almost imperceptible nod between them. 'Thought you might—just don't rush into anything,' was all he said.

Rayne threw his duffle bag on the floor of the sparse hotel room and himself onto the single bed on his back. He'd had to knock on the residence door to ask if they were opening today. The guy had said not officially and let him in. Given him a room and said he'd fix him up tomorrow.

Rayne pulled the packet of letters from his pocket and eased open the first one. Started to read about Maeve's pregnancy. After ten minutes, and an aching, burning feeling in his gut, he loosened his belt and lay down on the bed. His mind expanded with images, good and bad, of his time with Maeve and what she'd gone through because he hadn't been there for her. He couldn't stomach it. He searched for something else to think about until he got over the pain.

He reached his hands arms up behind his head and sighed. One thing about prison, you lost your finicky ways about where you could sleep.

It was a typical country pub. With typical country hospitality, seeing he could be sleeping on a park bench if they hadn't let him in.

Squeaky cast-iron bedframe with yellowed porcelain decoration in the middle, thin, lumpy mattress, used-to-be white sheets and a wrinkled bedspread. A hook for clothes and a bathroom down the hall to share, except that no one else was such a loser they were in there for Christmas.

He wouldn't be here long. Wasn't sure he should be in Lyrebird Lake at all. But thank God he'd come.

Maeve was having his baby. Maeve, who was anything but 'little Princess Maeve'. How the hell had that happened when they'd been so careful?

Funnily, he didn't even consider it could be anyone

else's because the dates matched and after what they had shared—Lord, what they had shared in one incredible night—if a persistent sperm was going to get through any night that would be the one. He half laughed out loud—a strangled, confused noise—thankful that nobody else would hear or care about it.

A ridiculous mix of horror that a child had been dumped with him for a parent, regret at how distressed Simon must have been at his supposed friend's perfidy, ghastly regret that Maeve had had to face Simon without him and spend a pregnancy without his support.

But on top, like a life-raft shining light in the dark ocean, was an insidious, floating joy that glorious Maeve had kept his child and he was going to be a father. And she'd held his hand in front of Simon.

Though the next steps held a whole bag of dilemmas. What was he going to do about it? What could he do about it? Of course he would support them, money wasn't a problem. Hell, he'd buy her a house and put it in her name, or the baby's name, whatever she wanted. But what else?

Suddenly his whole world had changed, from that of a lost soul who hadn't been able to help his own mother—the one person he'd tried so hard to save—to a social pariah without any commitments and little motivation to slip back into his previous life, and now to a man with the greatest responsibility of all. Protecting another woman, keeping in mind he hadn't been able to save the last one, and this time his child as well, was something which scared him to the core.

Of course, that was if they could possibly work something out, and if she'd let him, but at least she wanted to talk. He wasn't so sure Simon wanted to and he really couldn't blame him.

It was a lot to take in. And a lot to lose when you thought you'd already lost it all.

Maeve saw Rayne arrive because she was standing at the window of her bedroom, waiting. It was nine-thirty and everyone had arrived for breakfast and the huge pile of family presents were to be opened after that.

She shook her head as the black car stopped, so antique it was trendy again, big and bulky and mean looking, very *James Dean, I'm a bad boy*, Rayne really needed to get over that image. Especially now he was going to be a father. She smiled ironically through the window. Though if Rayne had a son her child would probably love that car as he grew up.

She turned away from the window and glanced at the mirror across the room. So it seemed after only one sight of Rayne she was thinking of her child growing up with him.

She saw her reflection wincing back at her. The worried frown on her brow. Saw the shine reflected on her face and she crossed the room to re-powder her nose.

Was she doing the right thing, going with her feelings? she thought as she dabbed. Should she believe so gullibly that there might be a future with Rayne? Take it slowly, her brother had said. Maybe Simon was right.

She reapplied her lip gloss. At least she'd been the first point of call as soon as he was free, and that had been before he'd known she was having his baby.

Or was she having herself on. Maybe it was Simon, his best friend from his childhood, not her he'd really come to see. He had travelled across the world last time for a conversation with Simon that hadn't happened. This morning he'd just seen her on the side of the road first.

When it all boiled down to it. how much did Rayne know about her or could care after just one night? One long night when they hadn't done much talking at all.

Nope. She wasn't a stand-out-in-the-crowd success story.

With a mother who expected perfection and three older, very confident sisters, she'd always wanted to shine in the crowd. Had hidden her shyness under a polished and bolshie exterior that had said, *Look at me*, had forced herself to be outgoing. Maybe that was why her relationships with men had seemed to end up in disaster.

Once they'd got to know her and realised she wasn't who they'd thought she was.

That was her problem. Being the youngest of five very successful siblings, she'd always seen herself falling a little short. But finally, when she'd settled on midwifery, incredibly she'd loved it. But her job had gone down the tube with this baby for a while yet—so she'd blown that too.

The hardest thing about Rayne walking away without a backward glance had been those voices in her head saying it had been easy for him to do that. Too easy.

She turned away from the mirror with a sigh. And then there was Rayne's consummate ease in keeping the whole impending disaster of his court appearance and sentencing from her.

But what if she had the chance to show him the real woman underneath? Maybe he'd show her the real man? Maybe it could work because there was no doubting physical chemistry was there in spades between them. Or had been before she'd turned into a balloon. They'd just have to see if that was enough to build on with their child.

She slid her hand gently over the mound of her stomach and held the weight briefly in her palm.

You are the most important person, baby, but maybe your daddy just needs to have someone with faith in him to be the perfect father. And I do have that faith and he'll have to prove otherwise before we are going to be walked away from again.

CHAPTER FOUR

Christmas Day

RAYNE PULLED UP outside the place Maeve had called the manse. The phone call had come sooner than he'd expected. Apparently he was down for family breakfast *and* lunch. He wasn't sure if could mentally do that but he'd see how it turned out.

As he gently closed the door of the car he glanced at motorised nodding animals in the Christmas manger on the lawn and shook his head. There was a little straw-filled crib with a tiny swaddled baby in it, and for a minute he thought it was a real baby; rubbed his eyes and, of course, it was a doll. He was seeing babies everywhere. Not surprising really.

But there were definite adoring looks and nods from the mechanical Mary and Joseph, and the three wise men and those crazy manger animals nodded along.

He could imagine during the weeks leading up to Christmas it wouldn't be unusual for children to drop by on the way home from school to check out the display.

He'd sort of noticed the display but not really when he'd been here earlier. He stopped for a moment and took in the full glory of the scene. Geez. Now, that was schmaltz with a capital S.

It was so over the top, with the solar mini-train circling the yard carrying fake presents, the fairy-lights all over the house and around the manger, and the giant blue star on the main building roof, totally the opposite of Maeve and Simon's mother's idea of colour-coordinated, understated elegance. Or his own poor mother's belief it was all a waste of time.

Imagine a family who was willing to put that much effort into decorations that only hung around for a month and then had to be packed away again. He couldn't help but speculate how much they'd be willing to put into things that were really important.

It was so hard to imagine that sort of close-knit caring. The kind he'd seen between Maeve and Simon's family every time he'd visited their house.

He'd always told Simon he was lucky, having two families and six sisters, and Simon had said he could share them as long as he didn't chat them up.

Well, that one had been blown out of the water with Maeve, he thought with a grimace, though he and Maeve hadn't done much chatting.

He sighed. Pulled back his shoulders and lifted his chin. Started to walk again. Not something to be proud of. Well, that's what he was here for. To make right what he could. Maeve had said they needed to talk but he wasn't so sure Simon was going to come to the party.

The front screen door opened and Simon met him as he came up the steps. And held out his hand. There was a definite welcome there he hadn't expected. Holy hell. Rayne's throat burned and he swallowed.

Simon shrugged and smiled. 'Can't say I've been happy but it is good to see you.' Then he stepped in and hugged him.

Rayne's choked throat felt like someone had shoved a carpenter's wood rasp down his neck, not that he'd ever cried, even when he'd buried his mother, so it was an unfamiliar and uncomfortable feeling, but he hadn't expected this. He gripped Simon's hand so hard his friend winced and he loosened his fingers. Dropped the handshake.

'Um. Thanks. That was unexpected.'

'I've had time to cool down. And I'm sorry about your mother.' A hard stare. 'You taking the blame for her is something we'll talk about another time.'

His throat still felt tight. He so hadn't expected this. 'Maeve is incredible.'

Simon snorted. 'Or incredibly stupid. We'll see which one.' He shrugged, definitely warmer than earlier that morning, and gestured to the door. 'Now come in. It's Christmas and you're about to meet the rest of the family. By the way, my dad knows all about you.' Simon raised his brows.

Raised his own back. 'Nice.' Not. Rayne glanced

over his shoulder at the road but there was only his car on the street. He'd hoped as there were no other cars he could come and go before the family arrived.

Simon must have seen his look because he said, 'Everyone walks most places around here. They're all out the back.'

They walked through the house down a central hallway, past some mistletoe he needed to avoid unless Maeve was there, with at least three rooms each side, and into a large kitchen, heavily decorated for Christmas, complete with multi-coloured gifts under the tree. At the kitchen bench a tiny, round, older lady with a Santa hat on her white hair was carving ham slices onto a plate. The young blonde woman he'd seen earlier that morning was piling fried eggs onto another carving plate.

'This is Rayne, Louisa. My grandmother, Rayne.'

The older lady looked up and glowed at Simon and then with twinkling eyes skimmed Rayne from head to toe with apparent delight. 'Maeve's mystery man. You are very welcome, my dear. And just in time for breakfast. Merry Christmas.'

Just in time for breakfast? His stomach rumbled. He hadn't even thought about food. She was a jolly little thing and jolliness had been hard to come by lately. He couldn't help a small smile. 'Merry Christmas to you.'

Simon's voice warmed even more. 'And this divine being is my fiancée, Tara. Tara's a midwife at the birth centre and has been looking after Maeve's pregnancy since she arrived. If you're good, we might even invite you to our wedding.'

'Hello, Rayne. Welcome. Merry Christmas.' And Tara, a much younger small blonde woman with wise eyes, smiled a smile that said, *I know how hard it is for you at this moment*. And, incredibly, he actually believed her. Now, that was strange.

Tara handed him the heaped plate. 'Take this out with you when you go, could you, please, and try to find a spot on the table for it.'

He took the plate and she gestured Simon to a basket of rolls, which he obligingly picked up right after he'd kissed her swiftly on her mouth. She laughed and shooed him off and Rayne looked away. He couldn't ever imagine being so easy with Maeve.

There was a brief lull in the conversation when they opened the screen door out into the back yard, but Rayne had spotted Maeve and the voices were fading anyway as his eyes drank in the sight of her.

Damn, she looked amazing in a red summer dress, like a ripe plum, the material ballooned over her magnificent belly and shimmered when she shifted. A green Christmas scarf draped her gorgeous shoulders. She looked like his fantasy Mrs Santa Claus and he had to hold himself back as Simon introduced him to his other family.

A tall, powerfully built man crossed to them. He put his hand out to Rayne and he took it. Shook firmly and stepped back. Yep. That had to be Simon's natural father. Same mouth and nose. A chip off the old block, and he reminded him of an army major he'd know once. 'Pleased to meet you, sir.'

'Angus, not sir. And I understand you're a paediatrician?'

'Not for nearly a year.'

'Maybe we'll get a chance to talk about that while you're here. You could think of having a breather here while you settle back into some kind of routine.'

Not likely. He already wanted to run. 'Perhaps.'

A vivacious redhead swooped in and gave him a hug. He tried awkwardly to return it but he'd never been a hugger. Her head only came up to his chin. 'Merry Christmas, Rayne. I'm Simon's stepmother, Mia.'

She stepped back and waved to two young miniatures of herself at the table. 'And our daughters Amber and Layla. So there will be nine of us for breakfast.'

It felt like a lot more but, really, the only person he wanted to talk to there was Maeve, who was watching him with an enigmatic expression, and it looked like they'd have to eat before he'd get any chance of that.

Tara and Louisa brought the last two plates and they all began to sit at the long table under the tree, but as he crossed to Maeve she moved towards the table as if she felt more confident there. With definite intent he held her chair and then settled himself beside her.

He glanced around and hoped nobody could see he really didn't want to be here, then he pulled himself up. It was Christmas.

One of the little girls said grace, and he acknowledged the nice touch, especially as he would have been stumped if someone had asked him, and the table groaned with food. He hadn't seen this much food since that Christmas at Simon's all those years ago.

When grace was over he turned to Maeve. She was why he was here. Funny how Simon had slipped back into second place, though it was good to see him too. His only friend in the world, and he'd thought he'd lost him.

But Maeve. She looked even better up close. Much more colour in her cheeks than earlier. He lowered his voice because he imagined she wouldn't want to draw attention to the fact she'd fainted that morning. 'Are you okay?'

A brief glimpse of her confusion as she looked at him. 'I'm fine.'

'Fine as in Freaked Out, Insecure, Neurotic and Emotional?' He tried a poor attempt at a joke.

A longer look. 'They been showing you movies in there?'

He felt his face freeze. His body go cold with the memories. 'No.'

Then he saw the distress that filled her eyes and her hand came across and touched his. Stayed for a second, warmed him like an injection of heat up his arm, and then shifted back to her lap. 'I'm sorry. It was a stupid joke.'

'Ditto. From another movie.' He forced a smile. 'It's fine.'

Her face softened. 'You sure? You know what "fine" means?'

He so didn't want to play, even though he'd started it. 'How long do we have to stay? I need to talk to you.'

She glanced around to make sure nobody had heard. It wasn't a problem because everyone was talking and laughing full steam ahead and the little girls were bouncing in their seats. Maeve's eyes softened when she looked at them. 'Until after the presents, and then I don't have to be back here until this afternoon.'

'So you'll come with me for a couple of hours. Talk in private? Sort what we can?'

He felt her assessing look. 'We can do that. Not sure how much we can sort in a couple of hours. As long as you get me back here before Christmas lunch at three o'clock. I promised to make the brandy sauce.' She glanced under her brows at him. 'I can cook when I feel like it, you know.'

'Oh. I know.'

It was all still there. Maeve could feel the vibration of chemistry between them. Just an inch or two between her skin touching his skin and even then his heat was radiating into her shoulder in waves without the contact. And all this at the Christmas breakfast table in front of Simon's family.

How could this man make her so aware of every part

of her body, and why him? He curled her toes, made her nipples peak, her belly twist and jump, and that was without the baby doing its own gyrations in there. It was darned awkward and the only consolation was he didn't look any more comfortable than she was.

But this was way more important than incredible sex. This was about the future, and even she had to admit she hadn't given the future a thought last time they'd been together. He'd been pretty adamant there hadn't been a future if she remembered rightly, though she had expected a little more pillow talk the next day rather than him being marched away by federal police.

She caught Tara's concerned eyes on her and shrugged. She'd be okay. Early days yet. But to think that this morning she'd been crying into her pillow, wanting him to be here for the birth, and here he was within an inch of her. It was a lot to take in. And she couldn't help the tiny beam of light that suggested she'd been given a blessing to be thankful for.

Someone asked her to pass a plate of tomatoes. There was a lot of eating going on all around them and she and Rayne hadn't started yet. Maybe they'd better.

Rayne must have thought the same because he passed her the ham and she took a small piece, glanced at his plate, and saw at least he was preparing to be fed. Then he passed her the eggs and she took one of those as well. Though she didn't feel like putting anything into her mouth. Her belly was squirming too much.

People were putting their knives and forks together

and sitting back. Leaning forward again and pouring coffee and juice. Maeve reached over and brought the rolls over in front of her, gave one to Rayne and one to herself without thinking and then realised she was acting like an old housewife looking after her husband.

He lifted his brows and smiled sardonically at her and she shrugged. 'Enjoy.' Reminded herself that she'd been a confident woman the last time he'd seen her and she needed to keep that persona even more now she was fighting for her baby's future. But what if she wasn't enough? What if he still left after their talk today? Surely he wouldn't leave this afternoon after just getting here.

'How long can you stay around here?'

He paused with his fork halfway to his mouth. Good timing at least. 'When is the baby due?'

'Tomorrow.'

His face paled and she thought, *Tell me about it, buster, I'm the one who has to do it.* 'But I expect I'll go overdue. Does it matter what date?'

He shook his head, clearly rattled by the impending birth. Put his fork down. Couldn't he see her belly looked like it was about to explode?

Then he said quietly, aware that a few ears were straining their way, 'I have no commitments, if that's what you mean.'

She sniffed at that. 'You do now.'

He glanced around the table. Saw Simon and his

father watching them. 'I'll be here for as long as you want me to be here. It's the least I can do.'

If only he hadn't added that last sentence. The relief she'd felt hearing him say he'd stay as long as she needed him was lost with the tone of sacrifice. Before she could comment, and it would have been unwise whatever she'd been going to say, at the very least, he touched her hand.

'Sorry. That came out wrong. It's just that I'm still getting used to you expecting a baby. And this table is killing me.'

Just then Mia stood up. 'The girls want to know how long before everyone is finished.'

Maeve pushed her plate away thankfully. 'I'm done.'

Rayne stood up. 'Let me help clear.' And he began very efficiently scraping and collecting plates, and she remembered him rinsing his plate at Simon's house.

At least he was house-trained, she thought with an internal smile as she began to gather up side plates, probably a lot more than she was. It was a warming thought that maybe there was stuff that they could do for each other, maybe there were things they could share between them that they'd find out and enjoy as well.

Within a very short time the dishwasher was loaded, the leftovers were stowed in the fridge and the kitchen clean. The big sunroom area of the back room at the end of the kitchen had been cleared when the kitchen table had gone outside and the Christmas tree was surrounded by lots of presents, as well as chairs and cushions so everyone had a niche to perch to watch the fun.

Simon had Tara on his lap, Mia and Angus were sitting with Louisa on the lounge they'd pulled in, and the girls were hopping and crawling around the tree as they shared out the presents one at a time.

Everyone sat except Rayne. He leant against the wall to the left of Maeve so he could watch her face, and he knew she wished he'd take the chair Simon had offered and sit down next to her. But he didn't. He didn't deserve to be a part of the circle. Felt more of an outsider than he ever had, despite the efforts of others. It was his fault he felt like that and he knew it. Just couldn't do anything about it.

He watched Simon take a present from the eldest child and hand it solemnly to Tara. When she opened it he saw her eyes flash to Simon's, saw the tremulous smile and the stroke of her finger down the painted face of the Russian doll. Those dolls that had other dolls inside. This looked like a very expensive version of those.

Cute. But a strange present to give. Though he had no idea about giving presents himself. He frowned, realising he should have thought about that on the way here. He didn't have any to give.

Tara didn't seem to know about the tinier dolls inside and Simon laughed and showed her how they came apart and another pretty painted doll was removed from the centre. And another and another. Until there was a dozen little painted dolls in a line along the arm of the chair. Simon's little sisters had eyes wide with wonder and he suspected there was a little moisture in Tara's eyes, and even Maeve's. He was missing something here.

Maeve shifted her body so she was closer to him and gestured for him to lean down.

'Tara's parents died when she was six. So she was in an orphanage until she grew up. Since then she's never owned a doll.'

Damn! No wonder she understood a little of his awkwardness on arrival. He wasn't the only one who'd had it hard. He'd always been grateful his mum had stayed straight long enough to keep him out of care. Even though he'd been the one doing the caring at home. At least it had been his home and he had had a mother.

The present-giving moved on and Maeve was given a little hand-made wheatpack, a drink bottle with a straw, and a pair of warm socks as comfort aids for labour, and they all laughed.

He watched Maeve smile and thank Tara, but the little twitch in her eyelid made him wonder just how calm the woman having his baby really was about the approaching birth.

His own uneasiness grew with the thought. It wasn't like neither of them didn't know a lot about birth. He'd been at many, but mostly he had been the paediatrician there for Caesarean babies or other newborns at risk.

And Maeve had done her midwifery so she was well versed in what would happen. But it was a bit different when it was this close to home. There were those other times when the unexpected happened.

He really needed to talk to her about that. He glanced at the clock. Fifteen minutes since last time he'd looked at it. Not too bad. And then it was over. The paper was collected, hugs were exchanged and everyone sat back. Louisa asked about fresh coffee or tea and Maeve shifted to the edge of her chair. He put out his hand and helped her up.

Her hand felt good in his. He tightened his grip.

'We're going for a drive.' She said it to the room in general and there was a little pause in the conversation. Then she looked at Louisa and smiled. 'I'll be back by two-thirty to make that brandy sauce.'

Simon groaned. 'Make sure you are. That sauce is to die for.' Everyone laughed again and Rayne wondered, with dry amusement, if he really was the only one who got the warning directed their way.

Louisa said, 'Hold on for a minute.'

And Maeve shrugged and said, 'I'll just go to the loo before we go.' He thought they'd never get away.

Then Louisa was back with a small basket. Quickest pack he'd ever seen. 'Just a Thermos of tea and a cold drink. Some Christmas cake and rum balls in case you get hungry.'

He looked at her. 'I'm pretty sure nobody could be hungry leaving this house.' Looked at her plump cheeks, pink from exertion. Her kind eyes crinkled with the pleasure of giving her food. 'Thank you.' He lowered his voice so that nobody else heard. 'I was going to take Maeve to the seats by the boatshed. This is perfect.'

She held up a finger. 'One more thing, then.' And within seconds was back with a small brown paper bag. 'Bread scraps for the ducks.'

He shook his head. He had never ever met anyone like her. 'You are my new favourite person.'

Then Maeve came back and he tucked the paper bag into his pocket so he could take her hand and carried the basket in the other.

CHAPTER FIVE

The lake

DRIVING AWAY FROM the house, he felt like a load fell from his shoulders. He never had done other people's family events well and the feeling of being an outcast had grown exponentially when he'd had to add the words 'ex-inmate' to his CV.

He realised Maeve was quiet too, not something he remembered about her, and he looked away from the road to see her face. Beautiful. She was watching him. He looked back at the road. Better not run over any kids on Christmas morning, riding their new bikes.

'So where are we going?'

'I saw a boathouse down on the lake. Thought we'd just sit on one of the park benches beside the water.' He looked at her again. 'That okay?' He could smell the scent of her hair from where he was sitting. He remembered that citrus smell from nine months ago.

'Sure.' She shrugged and glanced at the seat between them. 'What's in the basket?'

He had to smile at that. Smile at the memory of Louisa's need to give. 'Emergency food supplies Simon's grandmother worried we might need.'

Maeve peered under the lid and groaned. 'She put in rum balls. I love rum balls. And I can't have them.'

He frowned. She could have what she liked. He'd give her the world if he had the right. 'Why can't you have rum balls?'

She sighed with exasperation. 'Because I'm pregnant and foetuses don't drink alcohol.'

He looked at her face and for the first time in a long time he felt like laughing. But he wasn't sure he'd be game to.

Instead, he said, trying to keep his mouth serious, 'I hope our baby appreciates the sacrifices its mother has been through.'

Tartly. 'I hope its father does.'

That was a kick to the gut. He did. Very much. He turned into the parking area of the boatshed and parked. Turned off the engine. Turned to face her.

'Yes. I do. And I am sorry I haven't been here for you.'

She sighed. 'I'm sorry you didn't know. That I couldn't share the pregnancy with you.'

He thought of his state of mind in that prison if he'd known Maeve was pregnant and he couldn't get to her. God, no. 'I'm not.' He saw her flinch.

'Surely you don't mean that now. That's horrible.' She opened the car door and he could feel her agitation.

Regretted immensely he'd hurt her, but couldn't regret the words. Saw her struggle to get out of the low car with her centre of balance all haywire from the awkwardness of the belly poking out front.

Suddenly realised it sounded harsh from her perspective. He didn't know how to explain about the absolute hell of being locked up. About the prospect of staying locked up for years. About his guilt that his mother had died to get him out and he'd actually been glad. He still couldn't think about the load of guilt that carried. He opened his own door and walked swiftly round to help her out.

Finally Rayne said very quietly, 'I would have gone mad if I'd known you were pregnant and I couldn't get to you. There was a chance I wasn't coming out for years and years.'

She stopped struggling to get herself from the car. Wiped the tears on her cheek. Looked up at him. 'Oh. Is that why you didn't read the letters?'

'I lost access to everything, Maeve. I was a faceless perpetrator surrounded by men who hated the world. I'd never hated the world before but I hated it in there. The only way I could stay sane in that toxic environment was to seal myself off from it. Create a wall and not let anything in. The last thing I needed was sunshine that I couldn't touch and that's what your letters were to me. That way led to madness and I had to stay strong behind my wall.'

'I shouldn't have sent them, then?'

It certainly hadn't been her fault for sending them. She was an angel—especially now he'd read them. 'You couldn't have known. But they were something I looked forward to. I was going to open them when I got out. As soon as I got out. But then I got scared you would tell me not to come and I needed to see you and Simon one more time to explain. So I decided to open them after I saw you.' He rubbed the back of his neck. 'I'm so sorry I caused you pain.'

Maeve looked up at Rayne and saw what she'd seen nine months ago. Big shoulders under a black shirt, black hair cut shorter to the strong bones of his head, dark, dark eyes, even more difficult to read, but maybe they were only easy to read on the way to the bedroom. And that wicked mouth, lips that could work magic or drop words that made her go cold.

This was going to be tougher than she'd expected it to be. Something Tara had said to her a couple of days ago filtered back into her memory. Something about her knowing men who had been to prison and were harder, more distanced from others when they got out.

The problem was Rayne had already been distanced from people before he'd been wrongly convicted.

But when he'd said he was glad he hadn't opened her letters, and she'd responded emotionally with the hurt of it, she'd been thinking about herself. Not about why he would say something hurtful like that. Not about what he'd been through. She promised herself she would try to help heal the scars that experience had left him with—not make the whole transition more difficult.

Guess she'd have to learn to filter her reactions through his eyes. And that wasn't going to be easy because she liked looking at things her way.

But it should be easier with him here, not harder. The thought made her feel cross. 'For goodness' sake, help me out of this damn car.' Not what she'd intended to say but now she thought about it she'd be a whole lot more comfortable with him not standing over her.

The dirty rat laughed.

But at least he put his hand out and again she sailed upwards with ridiculous ease until she was standing beside him.

'You really are a princess, you know that?'

She glared at him as she adjusted her dress and straightened her shoulders. Re-establishing her personal space. 'You have a problem with that?'

He looked at her, and if she wasn't mistaken there could even be a little softening in that hard expression. 'Nope. I love it.'

Warmth expanded inside her. There was hope for the man yet.

Rayne shut the door behind her and picked up the basket. Tucked her hand under his other arm, and she liked that closeness as they sauntered across to the lake-side seats.

Like nothing was wrong. She let it go. She'd always been a 'temper fast and then forget it' person so that was lucky because she had the feeling they had a bit of getting used to each other to come.

Further down the shore, a young boy and his dad were launching an obviously new sailing boat into the lake and a small dog was barking at the ducks heading their way away from those other noisy intruders.

'I love ducks,' Maeve said. 'Always have. I used to have a baby one, it grew up to be an amazing pet. Used to waddle up and meet me when I came home from school.'

'What did you call it?'

She could feel a blush on her cheeks. He was going to laugh. Maybe she could make up a different name. A cool one.

He bumped her shoulder gently with his as if he'd read her mind. 'I want the real name.'

She glared at him. 'I was going to give you the real one.'

'Sure you were.'

Quietly. 'Cinderella.'

Yep, he laughed. But it was a good sound. And so did she. Especially for Christmas morning, from a man only a few weeks out of prison who'd recently lost his mother and found out he was going to be a father. Going to be a father very soon. It felt good she'd made him laugh.

'Imagine,' he said. Then he turned and studied her face. His eyes were unreadable but his voice was sombre. 'Thank you for even thinking of giving me a chance.' And when she saw the sincerity, and just a touch of trepidation, now she felt like crying.

Wasn't sure she should tell him about this morning—what if she scared him?—but couldn't resist the chance. 'You know, I woke up today and all I wanted for Christmas was to be able to talk to you.'

His eyes widened in shock. And something else—she wasn't sure but it could have been fear. Yep, she'd scared him. Fool.

She felt her anger rise. Anger because it shouldn't be this hard to connect with a guy she'd been powerless to resist and it wasn't like he'd been doing something he hadn't agreed to either that night they'd created this baby together. So there was a force greater than them that she believed in but she wasn't so sure it worked if only one of them was a convert. 'It's not that hard to understand. I'm having a baby and there is supposed to be two of us. And if you don't hate me, think about it.'

She turned away from him. Didn't want to see anything negative at this moment. She watched the little boy jumping up and down as his little sailing boat picked up the breeze and sailed out towards the middle of the lake.

Nope. She needed to say it all. Get it out there because if it wasn't going to happen she needed to know now. She turned back to him. 'So what I'm saying is thank you for coming, even though you didn't know I was pregnant, thank you for driving all this way on Christmas to see us.'

'That's nothing.'

'I haven't finished.'

He held up his hands. 'Go on, then.'

'If you want to do the right thing, do something for me.' She took a big breath. 'I'm asking you to stay. At least until after the birth. Be with me during the birth, because if you're there I will be able to look forward to this occasion as I should be—not dreading the emptiness and fear of being alone.'

Rayne got that. He also got how freaking brave this woman was. To lay herself out there to be knocked back—not that he would, but, sheesh, how much guts had it taken for her to actually put that request into words? He felt the rock in his heart that had cracked that morning shift and crack a little more.

Heck. 'Of course I'll stay. Just ask for anything.' Well, not anything. He didn't think he was the type of guy to move in with, play happy families with, but he could certainly see himself being a little involved with the baby. He was good with babies. Good with children. For the first time in a long time he remembered he had an amazing job helping children and their parents and maybe it was a job he should go back to some time.

But he had no experience about making a family. No idea how to be a father. No idea what a father even did, except for those he'd seen at work. Simon's father had just seemed to be 'there'. He didn't know how to do 'being there'.

He glanced around the peaceful scene. Another little

family were riding shiny pushbikes along the path. They all wore matching red helmets. The dad was riding at the back and he guessed he was making sure everyone was okay. That seemed reasonable. Maybe he could do that. The birds were chirping and hopping in the branches above his head like the thoughts in his brain.

This place had an amazing vibe to it. Or it could be the collective consciousness of celebrating Christmas with family and friends creating the goodwill. But he'd never felt anything like it. He looked at Maeve. Or seen anyone like her.

She was staring over the water into the distance but there was tension in her shoulders. Rigidity in her neck. And he'd put that there. He'd need to be a lot better at looking after her if he was going to be her support person in one of the most defining moments of her life. Of both their lives.

He stepped up behind her and pulled her back to lean into his body. Lifted his hands to her shoulders and dug gently into the firm muscles, kneaded with slowly increasing depth until she moaned and pushed her bottom back into him until her whole weight was sagged against him.

She moaned again and he could feel the stir of his body as it came awake. Down, boy. Not now. Definitely not now. He could barely get his head around any of this, let alone lose the lot in a fog of Maeve sex.

'That feels *so-o-o* good,' she said.

He just knew her eyes were closed. He smiled. 'I'd

need to get lots of practice to build up my stamina for the event.'

'Mmm-hmm,' she agreed sleepily.

He shifted his fingers so that they were circling the hard little knot in her neck and she drooped even more.

'You might need to sit down.' He could hear the smile in his voice. Drew her to the bench they were standing beside and steered her into a sitting position. Went back around the bench so he was standing behind her—which helped the libido problem as he wasn't touching her whole body now.

He began again. Slow circular rotations of his fingers, kneading and swirling and soothing the rigidity away, for her, anyway. His body was as stiff as a pole.

He'd never had this desire to comfort and heal a woman before. Plenty of times he'd wanted to carry one to bed with him, but this? This was different. His hand stilled.

'Don't stop.'

He stepped back. Created distance from something he knew he wasn't ready for. Might never be ready for. 'I remembered the bread.' Pulled the brown paper bag from his pocket and gave it to her. A heaven-sent distraction to stop her interrogation into why he'd stepped back.

'For the ducks,' he said.

'Oh.' He heard the disappointment fade from her voice. Watched her straighten her shoulders with new enthusiasm. She was like a child. And he envied her so much. He couldn't remember when he'd felt like a child.

Then she was into planning mode again. 'You'll have to stay at the manse so I can find you when I need you.'

Just like that. Room, please. 'I can't just gatecrash Simon's grandmother's house.'

She threw a knobby crust of bread at a duck, which wrestled with it in a splash of lake water. 'Sure you can. Locum doctors and agency midwives come all the time when one of the hospital staff goes away. That's where they stay. The manse has lots of rooms and Louisa loves looking after people.'

Unfortunately too easy. He'd said he'd be there for the birth. He said he'd be her support person. He'd said he'd do anything and the second thing she asked for he was thinking, No!

H pushed back the panic. It would be better than the hotel. And not as bad as just moving into a house with Maeve and having her there twenty-four seven as his responsibility not to let anything happen to her.

Now, that was a frightening thought.

He wasn't on a good statistical run with saving people, which would be why he was an orphan now, and he went cold. Couldn't imagine surviving if anything happened to Maeve on his watch.

He did not want to do this. 'Sure. If Simon's grandmother says it's fine.' He thought about his friend. 'If Simon doesn't think I'm pushing my way into his family.'

'Simon spends every available minute with Tara.

Which reminds me. Tara is my midwife. I might ask
her to run through some stuff with us for working together in labour. She's done a course and it works beautifully for couples.'

His neck tightened and he resisted the impulse to
rub it. Hard. Or turn and run away. Couple? Now they
were a couple? She must have sensed his withdrawal
because she made a little sound of distress and he threw
her a glance. Saw a pink flood of colour rise from her
cleavage. Was distracted for a moment at the truly glorious sight that was Meave's cleavage, and then looked
up at her face.

She mumbled, 'I meant a couple as in you are my
support person in labour.'

Hell. He nodded, dropped his hands back onto her
shoulders. Tried not to glance over the top of her so
he could see down her dress. He was an emotionally
stunted disgrace, and he had no idea what Maeve saw
in him or why she would want to continue seeing him.
He needed to be thankful she was willing to include
him at all.

But he couldn't come up with any words to fix it.
He watched her throw some more bread scraps to a flo-
tilla of black ducks that had made an armada towards
Maeve. They were floating back and forth, their little
propeller legs going nineteen to the dozen under the
water. A bit like he was feeling, with all these currents
pulling him every which way.

Across the lake the Christmas sailboat was almost

at the other side. He could see the father and the little boat boy walking around the path to meet it. That father knew what to do. He wasn't stressing to the max about letting his kid down. What training did he have? Maybe, if bad things didn't happen, if he didn't stuff up, if Maeve didn't realise she deserved way better than him, he'd do that one day with his own son.

Or kick a ball. Ride bikes with him and buy him a little red helmet.

Or maybe Maeve's baby would be a little miniature Maeve. That was really scary. Imagine having to keep her safe? The air around him seemed to have less oxygen that it had before, leaving him with a breathless feeling.

'Want to see what's in the basket?' Maeve was pulling it onto the seat beside her. 'We'd better eat something out of it before we go back.'

She handed him the rum balls. 'Eat these so I don't.' Began to put mugs and spoons out.

He took them. Battened down the surge of responsibility that was crowding in on him as Maeve began to make a little picnic. Like any other family at the side of the lake. He didn't know where the conversation should go or what he was supposed to do. She handed him a cup of tea and he almost dropped it.

He felt her eyes on him. 'Relax, Rayne.' Her voice was soft, understanding, and he wasn't sure he deserved that understanding but he did allow his shoulders to drop a little. 'It's all been a shock for you. Let's get through the next week and worry about long term later. I'm just glad you're here and that you've said you'll stay for the labour.'

She was right. He felt the stress leach away like the tea seemed to have soaked into the brown dirt. He sat down beside her.

She handed him the bag of crumbs. 'Bread-throwing is therapeutic.'

Like a child. 'You are therapeutic.' But he took the bag. Before he could throw more crumbs, a tiny, yapping black-curled poodle came bounding up to them, the red bow around his neck waving in the slight breeze. He raced at the ducks and stopped at the edge of the water, and the black ducks took off in a noisy burst of complaint because they'd just found another benefactor in Rayne and now they had to leave.

A little girl's tremulous cry called the dog from further down the street and the black dog turned, cocked an ear, and then bounded off towards his mistress.

'So much for duck therapy.'

'Poor Rayne. Come, snuggle up to me and I'll make you feel better.'

He smiled and was about to say something when they heard the quack of another duck from the bushes beside them. He frowned and they both looked.

'Is it a nest?'

'Could be tangled in something.' He was about to stand up and check the bush when the sound came again and the branches rustled with movement. He stilled in case he frightened whatever was caught in there and they watched the bushes part until a little brown bird appeared, not a duck at all, a slim bird with a long drooping tail that shook itself free of the undergrowth.

'Ohh…' Maeve whispered on a long sigh of delight. 'It's not a duck making that noise—it's a lyrebird.'

Rayne watched in amazement. 'A lyrebird mimic? As in Lyrebird Lake? I guess that figures.' But there was something so amazing about the pure fearlessness of a wild creature glaring at them as it moved a step closer and cocked his head to stare their way.

Then the little bird, no larger than a thin hen, straightened, spread his fan-shaped tail in a shimmer of movement and proceeded to dance at the edge of the lake for Maeve and Rayne.

A gift for Christmas.

Backward and forward, shimmering his harp-shaped tail as it swayed above his feathered head, and Rayne had never seen anything like it in his life as he clutched Maeve's hand in his and felt the tight knot in his chest mysteriously loosen the longer it went on. He glanced at Maeve and saw silver tears glistening.

He hugged her closer, drank in the magic without questioning why they were being gifted with it. All too soon it was over and the tail was lowered. One more stern look from the bird and he stepped nonchalantly back into the bush and with a crackle of foliage he disappeared.

They didn't speak for a moment as the moment sank into both of them.

'Wow,' whispered Maeve.

'Wow is right,' Rayne said, as he turned and wiped away the silver droplets from Maeve's face. Leant over and kissed her damp cheek. 'I feel like we've just been blessed.'

'Me, too.' And they sat there in silence for a few minutes longer, in an aura of peace between them that had been missing before, and slowly the real ducks came floating back.

CHAPTER SIX

Back at the manse

WHEN THEY GOT back Maeve disappeared into the kitchen to make her brandy sauce. Most of the family were out in the back yard—apparently the Christmas lunch table was set out there again—and the little girls were engrossed in their new possessions.

Simon waylaid Rayne and steered him back out the door away from the family. 'So what have you two decided?'

Rayne wasn't sure he'd decided anything. Maeve had done all the planning and now it was up to him to keep his end of the bargain. 'Maeve wants me to stay for the birth. I've said I will.' Simon looked mildly pleased. 'It's the least I can do.' There was that statement that had upset Maeve and it didn't do anything positive to Simon's frame of mind either if the frown across his friend's brow was an indication. He had no idea why it kept popping out.

'Is it that hard to commit to that? You slept with her.'
His friend was shaking his head.

He held up his hand. 'Simon, I'm sorry. The last
time I saw you it was an awful night. My world was
about to implode. I didn't intend to end up in bed with
Maeve.' He paused. Looked back in his mind and shook
his head. 'But you should have seen her. She was like
some peach vision and she poleaxed me.'

Simon glanced sardonically at him. 'And she dragged
you off to bed?'

'Nope.' He had to smile at that memory. 'I carried
her.' And she'd loved it.

Simon raised his brows. 'Up two flights of stairs?'
Then he put his hand up. 'Forget I asked that. Tara says
the sparks from you two light up the room. I get that. I
get being irresistibly drawn to someone. And I get that
you don't do commitment.'

Simon laughed dryly. 'But I thought I didn't do commitment until my Tara came along.'

Rayne looked at his friend's face. Had never seen it
so joyous. As if Simon had finally found his feet and the
whole world. Rayne couldn't imagine that. 'I meant to
say congratulations. Tara seems a wonderful woman.'

Simon's smile grew. 'She is. And she so tough and…'
He stopped, shook his head ruefully. 'Nice diversion.
But this is about you.' Simon searched his face and he
flinched a little under the scrutiny. 'Are you in for the
long haul?'

Freaking long haul. Geez. He didn't know if he would last a week. 'I'm in for the labour. I'm in for what I can do to help Maeve for the birth. But as soon as I cause problems in her life I'm out of here.'

'And if you don't cause problems in her life?' The inference was he had already let her down, and he guessed he had.

'I didn't know she was pregnant.' Thank God.

Simon shrugged. 'Tara said you didn't open the mail. And I know you wouldn't answer my calls. Why?'

It was his turn to shrug but his bitterness swelled despite his effort to control it. 'I didn't want to bring her into that place. Either of you. I had to keep the good things pure. And when I got out, I didn't want to read that she might refuse to see me. So I came here first.'

'Have you read the letters now?'

'Yes.' Could feel the long stare from Simon. Those letters just reiterated how much he was capable of stuffing up other people's lives.

Simon sighed long and heavily. 'I love you, man. I'm even getting used to the idea that you will be in Maeve's life now. In all our lives. But don't stuff this up.'

So he'd read his mind? Rayne almost laughed, even though it was far from funny. 'That's the friend I remember.'

'Yeah. Merry Christmas.' Simon punched his shoulder. 'Let's go ask Louisa if you can stay. She'll be over the moon. She likes you.'

'I get the feeling your grandmother likes everyone.'
Simon laughed. 'Pretty much.'

Maeve had already asked Louisa.

'Of course he can stay,' Louisa enthused. 'So he'll
be with you when you have the baby.' She sighed happily. 'Things have a way of working out.'

Maeve grimaced on the inside. *Things weren't 'working out' yet.*

There were a lot of things she and Rayne had to sort
yet, not the least his attitude of *It's the least I can do.
Grrr.* But, she reminded herself, this morning she'd
been on her own. And he was here!

The magnitude of that overwhelmed her for a moment and she paused in the rhythmic stirring of thick-
ening liquid in the bowl and just soaked that in. Rayne
was here. And he was staying. At least until after the
birth, and that was all she could ask for. Yet! She wondered if they would actually get much alone time.

Wondered if he was up for that. Wished she was
skinny and gorgeous and could drag him off to bed. Or
be carried there by her gorgeous sex object 'partner',
round belly and all.

Partner. She'd always been uncomfortable with that
sterile word. Not that Rayne was obviously sterile. And
he wasn't her boyfriend. He certainly wasn't her lover.

'You want me to do that?' Louisa's worried voice.
Maeve jumped and stirred again in the nick of time before she made lumps in the sauce.

'Wool-gathering.' Louisa's favourite saying and she'd picked it up. It described her state of mind perfectly. Little floating fibres of thought creating a mess of tangles in her brain. Mushing together to make a ball of confused emotions and wishes and fears and silly impossible dreams. Like the flotsam of leftover wool collected from the bushes where the sheep had walked past.

Well, Rayne was nobody's sheep. He'd never been a part of the flock, had never followed the rules of society except when he'd taken his incredibly intelligent brain to med school at Simon's insistence.

Men's voices drifted their way.

And here they came. Simon and Rayne. Two men she loved. The thought froze the smile on her face. She really loved Rayne. Did she? Fancied him, oh, yeah. The guy could light her fire from fifty paces away. But love?

Maybe brotherly love. She looked at her brother, smiling at something Louisa had said. Nope. She didn't feel the way she felt about Simon. And there was another bonus. She could stop fighting with Simon now that Rayne was back. Fait accompli.

Her mind eased back into the previous thought. The scary one. That she did really love Rayne. There was no 'might' about it. She really was in no better spot than she had been this morning because though Rayne was physically here she wasn't stupid enough to think he was in love with her. And he could leave and have any woman he wanted any time he wanted.

The sauce was ready and she poured it into the jug.

The beauty of this recipe, the reason she was the only one who made it in her family, was the secret ingredient that stopped the film forming on the top. So it didn't grow a skin.

That was a joke. She needed the opposite. She needed to grow ten skins so she could quietly peel away a new layer of herself to show Rayne so that she didn't dump it all on him at once. Because she knew it would require patience if she wanted to help him see he had a chance of a future he'd never dreamed about.

That he could be the kind of man any child would be proud to call his or her father. The kind of man any woman wanted to share her full life with—not just the bedroom.

What was with these pregnancy hormones? She needed to stop thinking about the bedroom. She ran her finger down the spoon handle on the way to the sink. Coated her finger in the rich golden sauce. Lifted it to her lips and closed her eyes. Mmm...

Rayne tried not to stare at Maeve as she parted her lips to admit a custard-covered fingertip. Watched her savour the thick swirl. Shut her eyes. Sigh blissfully as she put the spoon in the sink. Geez. Give a guy a break. If the day hadn't been enough without the almost overwhelming urge to pick her up from amidst all these people and ravish a heavily pregnant woman.

Louisa was talking to him. 'Sorry.' He blinked and turned to the little woman and he had the idea she wasn't blind to what had distracted him if the twinkle in her eyes was anything to go by.

'I said if you would like to follow me I'll show you your room. It's small but I think you'll like the position. And all the rooms open out onto a veranda and have their own chair and table setting outside the door.' She bustled out of the kitchen and he followed.

'That's the bathroom. It's shared with Maeve and Simon and Tara.'

He nodded and paid a bit more attention to the fact that this old country manse had to be at least a hundred years old. The ceilings were a good twelve feet high and the wood-panelled walls looked solid and well built.

Louisa gestured to a door. 'Maeve said she didn't mind there was a connecting door between the two. Do you?' She twinkled up at him.

'Um. No. That will be fine.'

'I thought it might be. Especially as she's getting near to her time and if she wanted to she could leave the door open between you.'

It was a good idea. That look of nervous anticipation he'd seen in Maeve's eyes this morning, he didn't like to call it fear, did need addressing. And it wasn't like he hadn't seen her without clothes. He brought his mind sternly back to the present.

If he could help by being close then that would give him purpose as he tried to come to grips with becoming an unexpected part of a large, noisy, hugging family— all that contact took a bit of getting used to.

He still couldn't believe they weren't all wishing him back to prison away from Maeve. But he knew for a fact Maeve was glad to see him. Maybe too glad, considering the prize she'd won.

Louisa opened the door next to Maeve's and, sure enough, it was a small room, but it did have a double bed against the wall and a chest of drawers. All he needed. 'Thanks, Louisa. It's great. Can I fix you up for it?'

'Lordy, no. I don't need money. I'm well looked after. But you may end up working every now and then for Angus at the hospital if he gets stuck. Everyone helps everyone in Lyrebird Lake.'

Well, not where he'd come from. He felt like he'd fallen into some religious sect and they were going to ask for his soul soon, except he knew that Simon was regular. And Maeve. And this sweet, generous older lady was obviously sincere. So it looked like he had a casual job as well as a place to lay his head. Though he couldn't see him being needed much at the hospital. 'Maybe I can help around the house. Or the garden? I wouldn't say no to be able to burn off some energy.'

She looked at him, a good once-over that had him wishing he'd tucked his shirt in and shaved, but she nodded. 'I have a pile of wood I need chopped before winter. The axe is in the wee shed under the tank stand. It's a bit early in the year but whenever you feel the need you just go right ahead and chop.'

He grinned. Couldn't help himself. Of all the things he'd thought might happen as he'd driven through the night to get here, getting a job as a woodcutter hadn't figured in the speculations.

He followed her out. 'Have I got time to nip back to the pub and let them know I won't be staying?'

'Have you left anything there?'

'No.' You didn't leave things in pub accommodation. Or maybe you did in Lyrebird Lake. Who knew?

'Well, that's fine. Denny Webb will be over visiting his wife at the hospital. Angus will pass the message on to the ward sister.'

Louisa waved to his car out in the street. 'You could bring your things in and then wash in the bathroom if you want.' She had noticed the bristles. 'And we'll see you back in a few minutes because it's nearly time for Christmas lunch.'

Obediently Rayne walked out to his car and brought in his overnight bag. The rest of his stuff—one small suitcase—was under the tarpaulin in the back of the truck. Not that he had much. He'd pretty well given everything else away. Had never been one for possessions. Wasn't quite sure what had influenced him to buy the old Chev. He'd passed it in a car yard on his way in from the airport and it had reminded him of his mother in happier times.

After his sleep in the motel for eight hours he'd walked back to the car yard an hour before closing time. Had told the guy if he could arrange a full mechanical check by a third party, transfers and insurance and tank of petrol in the time they had left, he'd pay the full price.

By the time he'd had a feed and returned, his car was waiting for him. So he did have one possession.

And an exit strategy. Both good things.

Walking back through the kitchen and outside, it seemed that Christmas lunch would be even noisier than breakfast.

Simon offered him a beer before they all sat down and, to hell with it, he took the glass and it was icy cold, and even though they were in the shade from the trees, it was pretty warm outside.

It was Christmas in Queensland and the beer tasted like Australia. Strong and dry and producing a sigh of momentary content. He noted some corny Christmas music on the CD player and Maeve was holding one hand over her left ear, pleading for it to stop. Tara was laughing and Louisa looked offended.

He leaned towards her. 'So you don't like carols?'

'Not twenty-four seven for the last month,' she whispered. 'Save me.'

He laughed. And gave her a quick squeeze as she went past with another jug of sauce to put on the end of the table. She glanced back and she looked at him like he'd given her a present. *Be careful there,* he thought to himself. Expectations and what he could actually deliver could differ.

Angus came up and stood beside him. Raised his glass. 'Lemonade. I'm on call.' He grimaced. 'But cheers. I hear you're staying.'

'Cheers.' He lifted his beer. 'Staying until after the baby at least.'

'Good.'

That was unexpected approval. 'Thank you.'

'It's for Maeve. And Simon. But I'm guessing it's not all easy on your side either. Not easy to get used to all this when you didn't expect it.'

Rayne glanced around. 'It's taking some.'

Angus nodded. 'Just chill. This place is good at helping the chill factor. Maeve has a lot of support so you won't be doing it on your own. And Tara is a good midwife.'

Change of subject. Great. 'Which reminds me. Congratulations on your new daughter-in-law-to-be. I haven't seen Simon look this happy, ever.'

Angus nodded. Glanced at his son, who had Tara's hand clasped firmly in his. Tara was laughing up at him. 'Best Christmas present I could wish for.' Then he glanced at his own wife and daughters. 'Finding the right woman is hard but incredibly worth it.'

'Okay, everyone,' the woman he was regarding said. 'Sit.' He inclined his head at her, gave Rayne a faint smile, and moved away to hold Louisa's chair, and then his wife's. He sat at the head of the table and Louisa sat on his left, with Mia on his right.

Simon sat at the other end with Tara next to him and Maeve on the other side. Rayne was in the middle opposite the two little girls, who were giggling at something Simon had said.

After this morning, he wasn't surprised when the elder of the two girls said grace, and for a fleeting moment he wondered with an inner smile whether, if he had a daughter, he would ever hear her piping little voice bless this table at Christmas. His throat thickened and he drew a quiet breath, and in a reflex he couldn't control he blocked it all out. Blocked out the tinny Christmas music, the laughing people, the beautiful woman expecting his baby beside him.

Maeve felt the distance grow between her and Rayne and wanted to cry. There had been moments there when he'd seemed to be settling into the day better than she'd expected. Especially when she'd noted his obvious rapport with Louisa, but, then, who didn't feel that? Louisa was a saint. Even when she'd first arrived and been at her most prickly and morose, Louisa's gentle, good-natured kindness had won her round before she'd known it.

She'd seen him talking to Angus. Well, since she'd arrived she'd decided Angus was a man's man, so that wasn't surprising. Rayne hadn't really spoken to the girls or Mia since they'd been introduced, but in fairness he hadn't had much chance. She couldn't help hoping he would exhibit some signs he was good with children. The guy was a paediatrician, for goodness' sake. And soon to be a father.

Tara leaned across the table and distracted her by offering the end of a Christmas cracker to pull. 'I'm not sure how many of these I'm supposed to pull,' she said in a quiet aside. 'I just did it with Simon and of course he won. And with Amber and she won. But I want a hat.'

Maeve smiled. 'You can pull any bon-bon offered. It's the bon-bon owner's choice who they want to pull them with. So take any you can.' Maeve had pulled a lot of bonbons in her time. The two young women had tested their strength against each other, and Tara had been a little more competitive than Maeve had expected, and that made her smile.

Maeve pulled harder and the bon-bon banged and split in half. Tara got the bigger half and the hat and prize. This time Tara crowed as she won. Simon clapped. He didn't miss much where Tara was concerned, Maeve thought with a pang. She glanced at Rayne. He was watching but his face was impassive and she got the feeling he wasn't really there.

Not so flattering when she was sitting beside him. 'Would you like to pull a bonbon with me?' Darn, did she have to sound so needy?

He blinked. 'Sorry?'

'A Christmas cracker.' She waved the one that was on her plate. 'See who wins.'

'Oh. Right. Sure.'

Such enthusiasm, she thought, and realised she was becoming a crotchety old woman by waiting for Rayne to behave like her fantasies.

'It's okay. Don't worry. I'll pull it with Tara. She loves them.' She meant it. No problem. Then he surprised her.

'Oi. I love them, too.'

That was the last thing Maeve had expected him to say. 'You love bon-bons?'

'Yeah. Why not?' His eyes crinkled and she sighed with relief that he was back with her. 'Not like I had that many family lunches over the years. That Christmas at your place was the first. You made me coconut ice.'

He remembered. The thought expanded in ridiculous warmth. 'I made everyone coconut ice at Christmas. For years. But it's very cool that you remembered.'

He held his hand out for the end of her Christmas cracker and she waved it around at him. 'I want to win.'

They pulled it and Rayne won. 'Oops,' he said. 'Try mine.' They realigned themselves to pull again and she could tell he tried hard to let her win but the cracker broke the larger end on his side. He got the prizes. Life sucked when you couldn't even win in a cracker-pull.

'Can I give it to you?'

'Not the same.' Shook her head. Pretended to be miffed.

He raised his brows. 'But I can't wear two hats.'

Then she said, 'Men just don't understand women.'

Rayne looked at the woman beside him, 'I'm hearing you.' He held out the folded hat. She took it reluctantly, opened it out and put it on. He'd given her the red one to match her dress and she looked amazing in a stupid little paper hat. How did she do that? He felt like an idiot in his.

He decided to eat. It seemed they were last to reach for the food again but, then, they'd made inroads into the basket Louisa had sent with them to the lake. He was starting to feel sleepy and he wasn't sure if it was the fact he'd driven all night, though he'd slept most of yesterday after the flight. Or maybe Louisa's rum balls were catching up with him. He stifled a yawn.

'I'm a bitch.'

The piece of roast turkey that was on the way to his mouth halted in mid-air. 'Sorry?'

'You're tired. I'd forgotten you haven't slept.'

He had to smile at her mood swings. The idea that life would not be boring around Maeve returned with full force.

They ate companionably for a while, he answered a question from Louisa on how the drive had been and gradually relaxed a little more with the company. 'I'll snooze later. Isn't that what everyone does after Christmas lunch? Wash up and then lie around groaning and doze off until teatime?'

'You're eating off a paper plate. The washing up's been done.' She smiled at him and his belly kicked because he was damned if there wasn't a hint of promise in that smile. More than a hint.

She bent her head and spoke softly into his ear. 'Not everyone sleeps.'

Geez. He wasn't making love with Maeve when Simon's room was two doors down. Imagine if she went into labour and everybody knew he'd been the one responsible for the induction. His neck felt hot and he couldn't look at anyone at the table.

'Rayne?' She laid her hand on his leg and it was all he could do not to flinch. Since when had he ever been at this much of a loss? The problem was his libido was jumping up and down like a charged icon on a computer.

She yawned ostentatiously and stood up. 'Happy Christmas, everyone. I think I'll go put my feet up.'

'Bye, Maeve.' From Simon and the girls.

'Don't go into labour, Maeve. I'm too full,' Tara said.

She turned back to Rayne. 'You coming? I think we need to talk some more.'

His ears felt hot. He needed to get himself back on an even footing here. It seemed she'd turned into a militant dominatrix and while the idea of submitting to sex wasn't too abhorrent, it didn't fit with the very late pregnancy visual effect. And he wasn't enamoured by the smothered smiles of his lunch companions.

'Sure. I'll just help Louisa clear the table first.'

She narrowed her eyes at him. 'Fine.'

Hell. She'd said, '*Fine.*' Which meant she was emotional and he might just have heard a tiny wobble in the word, which meant maybe he should go and comfort her.

Louisa shooed him away. 'You cleared at breakfast. Off you go and help that girl put her feet up.'

He caught Simon's perplexed glance at his grandmother and then at him. They both shrugged. How did you help someone put their feet up? Either way, he'd had his marching orders from two women. Maybe he should get his own place or they'd have him emasculated before New Year.

He stood up. Gave Simon a mocking smile and walked after Maeve.

CHAPTER SEVEN

Resting after lunch

MAEVE HAD GOT as far as slipping her shoes off, she'd been stupid, telling him to follow her, and she'd better learn from her mistakes pretty damn quick if she didn't want to drive him away.

She stewed on that thought for a minute until she heard Rayne's quiet footsteps coming down the hall and she didn't know whether to sit on the bed, stand at the window, looking decorative, or just freeze where she was looking at the closed door like a rabbit in head-lights.

Time took care of that because Rayne knocked, paused and then opened the door and put his head around. She didn't get time to do anything except feel her heart thumping like a bass drum.

It was the Rayne from nine months ago. Black brows slightly raised, eyes dark and dangerous, a tiny amused tilt to those wicked lips. 'Louisa said you needed a hand to get your feet up?'

She licked dry lips. 'You can come in.' But when he did push open the door and shut it again the room shrank to the size of a shoebox and they were two very close-together shoes. 'Um. I am a bit tired.'

He glanced at the queen-sized bed then back at her. Looked her over thoroughly. 'Want a hand getting your dress off?'

'Thanks.' She turned her back and once he'd worked out there was no zip and she only wanted him to help her lift it over her head, the task was accomplished in no time.

No real seduction in that swift removal. She tried not to sigh. While he was draping the dress carefully over the chair she was thinking as she sat on the bed, *Thank goodness I changed my stretchy granny undies for the cute lace pair.*

He seemed to be staring at her chest. 'Nice cleavage.' Well, at least he appreciated something.

He was so big and broad standing over her and she patted the quilt she was sitting on. She wished he'd take off *his* shirt. 'Are you staying?'

'Staying? As in coming to bed with you?'

'You did say everyone lies down after Christmas lunch?'

He sat on the bed beside her. Then he turned his head and looked her full in the face. 'I'm not going to have sex with you but I'm happy to lie beside you while you rest.'

She pulled a face at him. Her own desire to snuggle

up to him was withering like a dehydrating leaf. 'I wouldn't want to force you to do anything you didn't want to.'

He grinned at her but there was a definite flare in his dark eyes that left her in no doubt she was wrong. A flare that made all the saggy disappointment feelings sit up and take notice again. 'It's not that I don't want to get closer.' He was telling the truth and at least that made her feel a little bit better. 'But I think we need to talk a whole lot more before we fall into…' he hesitated, didn't even offer a word for what they were both thinking about '…first.'

Talk? When she was sitting here in her lacy bra and panties—admittedly with a huge shiny belly out in front—behind a closed door with all those pregnancy hormones saying ooh-ah. 'Talk?' She fought back another sigh. 'That sounds more like a girl thing than a guy thing.'

He shrugged, stood up again and then leaned down, slipped an arm behind her knees and the other under her shoulders and placed her in the middle of the bed. Oh, my, she loved the way he did that.

Then he bent, unlaced his shoes and removed them, loosened his belt and then sat back down on the bed in his jeans. Reached for the folded light sheet at the bottom of the bed she'd been resting under in the afternoons, swung his legs up and draped the sheet over both of them.

Then he slipped his arm around her shoulders so her head was resting on his chest and settled back.

She was still smarting from the 'not having sex with you' comment. 'Is this the pillow talk I missed out on last time?'

He didn't seem perturbed. 'You do have a nasty little bite when you don't get your own way, don't you?'

She hunched her shoulders. 'It comes with not knowing where I stand.'

'Well,' he said slowly, 'I see that. But I can't tell you what I don't know. And if you want me to make something up then you're resting your head on the wrong chest.'

It was not what she wanted to hear and yet it was. And this particular chest felt so good to lean on. She relaxed and snuggled in a little closer. 'So you're saying you won't lie to me.'

The sound of his heart beating in a slow, steady rhythm reverberated under her ear. God, she'd missed this. 'I won't lie to you.'

She lifted her other hand slowly and ran her fingertip down the strong bulge of his bicep. An unfairly sexy bicep. Her girl parts squirmed in remembered ecstasy. Conversation. Remember conversation. 'Not lying to me is a good start.'

'You're supposed to say you won't lie to me either.' She could tell he was dead serious. Fair enough.

She wriggled awkwardly, trying to shift her weight

until she'd managed to roll and could see his whole face. Said just as seriously, 'I will not lie to you.'

She couldn't read the expression in his eyes but his mouth was firm. 'So if you want me to go, you tell me. Not telling me is a lie too.'

She frowned at him. 'I'm not sure I want to hear about it if you want to go.' Then she sighed and lay back down again. 'But I guess that's fair.'

He was shaking his head. 'You don't understand and you need to get where I'm coming from. I may not be good at this whole father thing, Maeve. I'll try but I don't have a lot of family experience, and no paternal role model, to draw on.' She could hear the slight thread of panic in his voice. Had to remind herself that a few hours ago this guy had had no idea he would be having a child some time in the next few days.

She thought about his 'no family experience' statement. Well, she guessed he'd never had a father to learn from or even subconsciously copy. Maybe he was finding that pretty daunting. 'Did you know your father at all?'

'Nope. I asked. All my mother said was he was dead and didn't offer any clues. Not even his name. And my mum wasn't into men staying over so no "special" uncles. If she spent the night with a man, she usually stayed out.'

Maeve thought about that. 'So when you were young you stayed home alone? At night?'

Maeve squeezed his arm in sympathy and Rayne

could feel himself begin to freeze her out. Had to force himself to let her offer comfort because if he was going to try to make this work he had to at least attempt to learn to do these things too. Apparently it was what families did and he needed to at least give it a shot.

He dispelled the myth that he had been alone. 'We lived in a dingy block of flats. You were never alone. You could always hear people in the other units.'

She nodded against him. 'So you never got scared on your own at night?'

He nearly said no. But he'd said he wouldn't lie. 'When I was younger I got scared. Especially if someone was shouting or I could hear someone yelling on the footpath. The worst was if a woman screamed down on the street. I always worried it was my mum and I wasn't doing anything to help her.'

He'd never told anyone that. Didn't know why he'd told Maeve. He moved on and hoped she would forget he'd said it. 'Guess I'd make sure my kid was never left alone until they wanted to be left.'

She squeezed him again. 'Perhaps your mum thought the people she was with were more disturbing than the idea of you being alone.'

His mum had actually said something like that. He hadn't believed her. Had there been a grain of truth in it after all? And Maeve had picked up on it all these years later. 'You don't judge her, do you? My mother?'

Maeve shrugged on his chest. 'Who am I to judge? I know nothing about her. I just know I've always admired you and she must have had a part in that. She was your mother.'

That heavy carpenter's rasp was back down his throat. Sawing up and down and ripping the skin off his tonsils. Or at least that's what it felt like as his throat closed. He searched for some moisture in his mouth. 'Even when I said I'd been in prison because of her, you were sad for me that she was dead.'

He'd been thinking about that a lot. Couldn't get his head around the fact that Maeve saw the part of him he hadn't shown to many people. Except Simon. But he doubted her brother would have discussed it with his little sister.

She snuggled harder and his arm protested and began to cramp. He told it to shut up.

Then she said, 'Even though you didn't meet your father, I think you'll be a good dad. And you certainly tried to look after your mum from a very young age. You're probably better father material than many men who had dads.'

He grimaced at the fact that maybe he had become a little parental with his mum, but that didn't change the fact he hadn't been able to save her.

Maeve was like a dog with a bone. 'You'll be fine. You're a paediatrician so at least you're good with kids.' She settled back. The law according to Maeve.

'At least I'm that,' he said dryly. 'I'm good with sick kids.' And especially the ones who were left alone and needed company.

She went on, 'I was too young to understand about how you grew up. You always looked tough and capable when I saw you.'

Rayne listened to her voice, the husky tigress lilt tamed a little now, and thought about what she'd said. So he'd appeared tough and capable. He guessed he had been. By the time she'd been in her early teens he'd almost grown out of his, and his mum had begun to need a bit more care taken of her. A couple of dangerous overdoses. A problem with her supplier that had left her badly bruised. The way she'd forgotten to eat. She'd had two close shaves with the law and had told him if she ever got convicted she would die if she went to prison.

The last years had been a downward spiral and he'd tried most things to halt it. The number of rehab centres, fresh towns, health kicks they'd tried. Things would go well for a few months and he'd get tied up at work. Miss a couple of days dropping in then she'd start to use again.

The best she'd been had been in Santa Monica. She'd looked young for the first time in years. Had got a job as a doctor's receptionist at one of the clinics he worked from in the poorer area, a place where kids who needed care they normally couldn't afford could access a range of different doctors. And she'd been good at it.

She had connected well with the people who didn't need anyone to look down on them. He'd valued the once a week he'd donated his time there, away from the upmarket private hospital he'd worked in the rest of the time. And he'd cheered to see her making a life for herself. Fool.

Until the day she'd worked and gone home early. It had been his day as well and he'd finished late. Locked up. The investigation had been well in progress by the time he'd found out all the drugs had been stolen. Had known immediately who it had been. He hadn't been able to track her down anywhere until finally she'd rung him. Pleading. Promising she would never, ever, touch anything ever again, if he would say it was him. That this was her chance to go clean for life.

He'd hoped maybe it was true and that she would stop using. Then had begun to realise the fingers had been pointing to him anyway. So he'd made a conscious decision to try a last attempt at saving her.

He'd tried ringing Simon so he wouldn't find out from someone else that he would probably be going to prison. Hadn't been able to give the explanation on the phone and had had that ridiculous idea to fly out, explain and then fly back in twenty-four hours. He'd thought he should have just about that much time be-fore it all came crashing down. Before the police came for him!

'Hey,' Maeve whispered, but she wasn't talking to him. The belly beside him rolled and shifted and his eyes fixed on the movement, mesmerised. He glanced quickly at Maeve, who was watching him with a gentle smile on her face, lifted his hand and put his palm on the satin skin. And the creature below poked him with something bony.

Geez. He looked back at Maeve.

'Cool, isn't it?' she said softly. And put her hand over his. And he realised with a big shift of emotion that the three of them were together for the first time. 'He likes you.'

His eyes jerked to her face. 'It's a he?'

She laughed. 'I really don't know. Just find myself calling him he. Maybe because you weren't here.' He winced at that.

'Might be a girl.' She shrugged. 'I really don't care which.'

'I hope she looks like you.'

She looked at him as if she were peering over a pair of glasses at him. 'Why on earth would you want your son to look like me?'

'Okay. A boy could be like me but it would be very sweet to have a little girl who looks like you.' Then he spoilt it all by unexpectedly yawning.

She laughed. 'You need a nap more than I do. Why don't you take your jeans off? We can talk more later. Then you can roll over and I'll cuddle you.'

'Bossy little thing.' But suddenly he felt morbidly tired and he did what he was told, not least because his arm had gone totally to sleep now and his jeans were digging into him.

When he climbed back onto the bed and rolled to face the door, she snuggled up to him as close as her big tummy would allow. It actually felt amazing when his child wriggled against him. Geez.

Maeve listened to Rayne's breathing change and she lay there, staring at his dark T-shirt plastered against his strong shoulders as he went to sleep.

She tried to imagine Rayne as a little boy, from a time when his first memories had begun to stick. Dark, silky hair, strong little legs and arms, big, dark eyes wondering when Mummy would be home.

It hurt her heart. She wanted to hug that little boy and tell him she'd never leave him scared again. How old had he been when his mother had begun to leave him? She had a vague recollection of hearing Simon say to her parents that Rayne's mum hadn't started using drugs until after something bad had happened when Rayne had gone to school.

She wondered what had happened to Rayne's poor mum. Something that bad? It couldn't have been easy, bringing up a child alone with very little money.

Her childhood had been so blessed. Always her hero brother Simon and three older sisters to look after her, as well as both well-adjusted parents, although her mum was pretty definite on social niceties.

Her dad was a fair bit older than her mum, but he'd always been quietly there, and her mother had come from a wealthy family and always been a determined woman. She'd been spoilt by her dad, but had sometimes felt as if she wasn't quite enough of a star for her mother. Hence the try-hard attitude she really needed to lose.

She would be thankful for all her blessings of family and now having this gorgeous, damaged man appear just when she needed him. He hadn't run. He'd promised to stay at least until after the birth. Had tried to fit into a strange family's Christmas Day, which must be pretty damn hard when he was still reeling from being in prison and adjusting to society again, and he'd just found out he'd fathered a child.

She stared again at the powerful neck and short hair in front of her eyes and the way the thick strands clung to his skull like heavy silk. Resisted the urge to move her hand from around his chest to touch it as she didn't want to wake him, but her fingers curled.

She could imagine her baby having hair just that colour, though, of course, hers was black like her dad's as well, so the kid didn't have much choice. But she would think of it as his father's hair. Would he have Rayne's eyes and mouth too?

Imagine.

A long slow pulling sensation surged in her belly from under her breasts down to her pubic bone, growing tighter and then after a while easing off. Just one.

Braxton-Hicks. Practice contractions. Not painful. Just weird, as if the baby was stretching out straight. But she knew it wasn't. Soon they would come more frequently. Maybe for a couple of hours at a time and then stop. For a few days probably. She'd told other women this so many times, but it was strange when it was yourself you were reassuring.

This time she'd welcomed it without the accompanying flare of nervousness she'd been fighting for weeks. Giving birth was a job that needed to be done and now that Rayne was here the time was right. Whatever happened, whatever her birth journey was meant to be, Rayne would be there to share it all. The best Christmas present of all.

Rayne woke an hour later, straight from dreaming about Maeve. Like he'd woken nearly every day for the last nine months. Except this time he really had her in his arms, his hands really were cupping her glorious breasts, her taut backside really was snuggled into his erection, which was growing exponentially with confirmation of the contact.

They must have rolled in their sleep.

She murmured drowsily, not yet awake, and languidly backed into him a little more. Unconsciously, his hands slid over her belly, pulling her closer.

The little person inside that belly nudged him and he recoiled in startled appreciation of where his actions were leading. 'Sorry,' he murmured, and slid his hands down to the sides of Maeve's abdomen, but Maeve was having none of it. Took his hands and placed them back on her breasts. Wriggled into him.

'Have mercy, Maeve,' he whispered in her ear, but he couldn't help the smile that grew on his face. She wriggled against him again and he groaned. Slid his rear end across the bed to make room for her to shift and turned her to face him. 'You are a menace.'

'And you feel so good against me,' she whispered back drowsily. Then tilted her face for a kiss, and there was no way he could resist those lips, that mouth, or keep it to one kiss. And the gentle salute turned into a banquet of sliding salutations and memories that re-surfaced from all those months ago. How they matched each other for movements, timing, a connection be-tween them that had him pulling her closer, but the big belly in the middle made everything awkward, yet erotic, and he must be the most debauched man on earth to want to make love to this woman who was so close to giving birth.

As if she'd read his mind, she said, 'If we don't make love now, you'll have to wait for ages.'

He really hadn't thought of that. 'Maybe we should wait.' But he seriously didn't want to. And she obviously didn't. Nine months of fantasy and the woman of his dreams was demanding he make love to her.

No-brainer really.

In the Maeve fog that was clouding his mind he wasn't really sure what he'd been thinking to knock her back before.

Still in the fog, he slid from the bed, ripped his T-shirt off his head in one movement and kicked off his briefs. Knelt back down and dropped a big kiss right between Maeve's awesome assets. Geez, he loved her breasts.

He slid his hands around her back and unclasped her bra. Sighed as the two gorgeous spheres eased out of the restraining material like big, soft plump peaches. The circular areolas surrounding her nipples were dark peach, highlighted for a tiny baby to find easily, and he skimmed his fingers across in awe while she watched him with a womanly smile as old as the ages.

He swallowed to ease the dryness in his throat. 'They say pregnant women in the third trimester of pregnancy have erotic dreams and surges of erotic desires.'

'That's very true,' she whispered, pulling him closer and tilting her mouth for him to kiss again. When they paused for breath there was no concept of stopping. But he was doing this right, and gently, and he wanted to show her just how beautiful she was in his mind and in his heart. 'Then we'd better take our time.'

CHAPTER EIGHT

Labour and birth

WHEN MAEVE WOKE up Rayne was gone. But the contraction tightenings weren't gone. That darned love hormone.

She did not want to have this baby on Christmas Day. It was okay for baby Jesus. He'd never been materialistic, but Maeve knew how she'd feel about the one day of the year that belonged to everyone, in her corner of her world anyway. But it was her own fault.

Still, she could not regret this afternoon in Rayne's arms. She smiled a long, slow, satisfied smile. Regret definitely wasn't the word that sprang to mind.

Revel, ravish, rolling around with… Scraping the bottom of the barrel there, but *reaaaalllyyy* amazing just about covered it. Her skin flushed at the thought of how wonderful he'd been, so unhurried, showing her a world of gentleness that had brought tears to her eyes. He had paid homage to her body, coveted her belly, and just plain loved her, something she'd missed so badly as her body had changed, and he had banished for ever the idea he wasn't the man for her.

Which was an excellent thing if she was about to have his baby.

Another contraction followed on the thought. That love hormone again.

She glanced at the clock. It was seven-thirty in the evening. Almost sunset. Less than five hours until midnight. 'Hang in there, baby.'

She climbed awkwardly out of bed. Pulled on a robe and gathered something light to wear for the evening. Something comfortable like a sarong. They'd probably sit out the back or go for a leisurely walk along the lake. Another contraction tightened her belly, this time with a little bit of discomfort.

They were still not lasting long but she guessed she wasn't going to go too far from home. At least there was no car journey involved, like there would have been if she lived in the city. Here, they'd just pick up Tara from the room down the hall—she grinned at that, same house—then walk across the road to the birth centre. It was all pretty streamlined, actually. Almost a home birth without the organising of equipment involved.

Rayne would be stressed. Simon would worry. But she would be calm. Could be calm now because she deputised other people to do the worrying and from this moment on she would have faith in her body, in a natural process she was designed to achieve. It was exciting really. And Tara would be there. She giggled. She hoped Tara had digested her lunch by now.

She thought about giggles. That's right. In early labour you apparently felt like giggling. The fact labour had finally arrived after all the waiting. Happy hormones. She grinned in the mirror. Actually, she did feel like giggling. Even the fact that she knew this would pass onto harder and stronger contractions was funny. At the moment, anyway. No doubt she'd change her mind later.

She slipped out of the bedroom door and into the bathroom with a smile on her face. She could hear the rumble of Simon and Rayne's voices coming from the kitchen. The thought made her feel warm. She would not have believed the change in her world in the last day. It was like she'd been released from her own prison. That thought put her feet back on the ground. She shouldn't joke about it. Rayne really had been released from prison.

She hung the robe on the hook at the back of the door, climbed into the shower and relaxed again as she revelled—there was that word again—in the hot water that soothed any tension away from her shoulders. Another contraction started its slow rise in intensity and consciously she sent all the negative thoughts down the drain with the soapy water, and breathed out.

Still ten minutes apart, plenty of time to tell people. She just wanted to hug the excitement and her baby to herself. This was the last day that she and her baby would be together so intimately. A miracle in itself.

She stayed in the shower for a long time.

Until Rayne knocked on the door. 'You okay in there?' A hint of concern in his voice.

She had to wait for the contraction to stop before she could answer. They were getting stronger but that was a good thing. More powerful, not more painful, she reminded herself. A tiny voice inside muttered about that not being true but she ignored it. The pain eased.

'I'm fine.' Wow. Her voice sounded kind of spacy. Endorphins.

'Can I come in?'

'Sure,' she breathed. Then had to repeat it a bit louder. 'Come in.'

Rayne pushed open the door and a cloud of steam billowed out past his head. He waved it away and stepped into the bathroom. 'You've been in here for ages.' He crossed the tiles to the corner shower. Stood outside the curtain. 'Is there something I should know?'

He waited. She didn't answer and he could hear her breathing. Eventually he pulled back the curtain so he could see her. She smiled at him and he thought she looked almost half-asleep. Looked again. Now, that was something you didn't see every day. A glistening wet, very rounded, amazingly breasted, porcelain pregnant lady naked in the shower, with her black hair curling on her shoulders.

She said, 'If we ever live together, you'll need a very large hot-water system.'

He had to smile at that. He assumed Louisa did own one of those if this house could sleep twelve. 'I'm getting that.'

'And also,' she went on in the same distant voice, 'my contractions are about seven minutes apart.'

His heart rate doubled and then he slumped against the wall. Sex fiend. He'd done that. Come on. Pull yourself together. You're a doctor, for crikey's sake.

'Is that a good thing?' he asked cautiously. Who knew what Maeve was thinking? He was trying to be supportive because that was his job, and he'd agreed without coercion when, in fact, he wanted to run screaming to Simon.

'As long as baby waits till after midnight, that's fine.'

Rayne glanced at his watch. Eight o'clock. Four hours until midnight. Of course she'd have her own way and the baby would wait. Four hours of stress.

'Shall I go and tell Simon? Or Tara?'

'No hurry.'

It was all very well to say that, along with some heavy breathing, and he observed, as if from a long way away, that his fingers were white where he was clutching the handrail. 'You sure?'

'Mmm-hmm…' Loud exhalation.

Geez. Rayne prised his fingers off the towel rail and

straightened off the wall. 'Um. Might just mention it to them in case they want to go out.' Though where they would go on Christmas night was a mystery.

Quietly, on an out breath, an answer came from the shower. 'Okay.'

Rayne left and he wasn't quite jogging. He skidded into the kitchen but it was empty. Typical. This house had crawled with people all day and now he couldn't find anyone when he needed them. Even Louisa was missing but he guessed she, out of all of them, deserved a rest.

Poked his head out the back door but the darkening yard, a space that had seen so many Campbells, was deserted.

He went back inside, walked down the hallway, but both Simon and Tara's doors were ajar and he guessed if they were in there they'd have closed the doors. He went out to the front veranda in case they were sitting on that bench, looking at the nodding animals, and he was distracted for a minute by the fairy-lights that had come on with the sunset. Nobody there. He glared at the manger. Mary and Joseph had had their baby in a manger, with animals and wise men, so what was his problem?

He ran his hand distractedly through his hair. Took a deep breath. It was okay. Maeve was calm. Happy even. The hospital was across the road for pity's sake. He could see the porch lights. All he had to do was be a support person.

It would have been nice to have that 'couples' discussion with Tara that he'd had a knee-jerk reaction about today before Maeve had gone into labour. But, *no-o-o*, Maeve had had to have nookie.

What was it he'd learnt in med school? A first-time mum, after a slow start while the contractions got sorted out, dilated about a centimetre an hour. To get to ten centimetres was ten hours. Right? Or maybe she was already six centimetres then it would be four hours. Or less if she'd got there this quickly. His mind was spinning faster than the wheels of the new Christmas push-bike some happy, oblivious-to-the-drama-inside kid was pedalling past too late to be out.

He forced himself to take another breath. Yesterday he would not have believed all this was going to happen. Yesterday he had been wondering if she would see him. Today she was his responsibility.

Well, he'd been in at the beginning so he had to stay for the hard part.

'Rayne?' He spun round and Maeve was leaning on the door to the front veranda. She looked like she'd just stepped off a plane from Fiji, with a hibiscus sarong wrapped around her and not much else. He could see her cleavage from here.

'Why are you staring at the manger?'

He wasn't looking at the manger now. Cleavage. 'Umm. Looking for Tara and Simon.'

She leant her head on the doorframe. 'They're on

the side veranda outside their rooms, watching the stars come out.'

He strode back across the lawn and up the steps to her side. 'Okay. You okay?'

'I'm fine. But I'd sort of like you to stay with me.'

'Yep. Of course.' He was obviously really bad at this support-person caper. Where was the midwife? 'So did you tell Tara?'

'I wanted to find you first.'

Not the choice he would have made. 'Fine. Let's do it now.'

'You said *fine*…'

She leant against his arm and smiled up at him and as if she'd pressed a button he leant down and kissed her lips in an automatic response. Just one day and they had an automatic response?

He stepped back. Must have picked up on some of her endorphins because he could feel his panic settle a little. *Fine.* Yep, he had been feeling freaked out, inse-cure, neurotic and emotional.

His voice softened, lowered, and he gently turned her back towards the house. 'How can you be so calm?'

'I've had nine months to think about this happening. You've had twelve hours.'

Had it only been twelve hours? It felt like twelve days. But, then, that's how things seemed to happen around Maeve and him. Acceleration with the pedal pressed and they were driving off into the future at a hundred miles an hour.

'Do you do anything slowly?' he said as they walked down the hall. He grinned at her. 'Apart from the way you're walking up the hallway now.'

'I put my make-up on slowly.'

'Does that mean if I took you out I'd be one of those guys hanging around waiting for his woman to get ready?'

'I might speed up for you.' Then her face changed and she stopped, closed her eyes as she leant against him. He lifted his hand and rested it on her arm and her shoulder dropped its tension beneath his fingers as if he'd told her to relax, and it startled him.

She sighed out, 'Boy, I can tell these contractions are doing the job.'

That was good. Wasn't it? 'We still waiting for midnight?'

'No choice now. It's all up to baby. You just have to hold my hand for the ride.'

He could do that. Glanced down at her hand, thin and suddenly fragile looking, as they set off again. 'It would be an honour,' he said very quietly. And it would be. She was blowing him away with her strength and serenity.

Simon and Tara, also holding hands again—spare me, he thought—appeared in the hallway and Maeve had a contraction before he could say anything.

Tara let go of Simon's fingers with a smile and went towards them. No need to say anything. So he didn't. Wasn't really his place anyway.

And they didn't ask. Their restraint was amazing and he could only follow their lead.

When the contraction was over, Tara murmured, 'Good job. When did they start?'

'About an hour ago.'

'So what do you feel like doing?' Tara was walking beside Maeve as they drifted down the hallway to the kitchen. Simon smiled at Rayne.

'You should see your face.'

'Shut up.' But there was relief and he felt the smile cross his own face. 'Geez, mate. Yesterday none of this was happening.'

'I know. In that context you're actually doing well. But open your letters next time.'

Rayne gave him a hard look. 'Try being where I was and you might not feel so sure about that.'

The smile fell from Simon's face. 'You're right. But I would never do something as stupidly noble as that. But I should have known you would. I'm sorry I was so quick to believe in your guilt.'

Rayne heard Maeve laugh at something Tara had said and looked at Simon and dropped the whole subject. This wasn't about him. Or Simon. 'How can she laugh?'

They both walked towards the kitchen. 'See, that's why I chose obstetrics over paediatrics.'

Rayne thought about the stress he'd been under already. 'You think giving birth is funny? It's a wonder you haven't been killed.'

Simon laughed again and it felt good to loosen the tension between them. The dynamics were certainly tricky. Especially if he didn't make the grade to stay around for the long haul. But he would worry about that later.

'Rayne?' Maeve's voice.

He quickened his pace and left Simon behind. 'I'm here.'

'I want to go in the bath and Tara thinks it might be easier if I don't have to move from this bath here to the one in the birth centre. So maybe we should go over there fairly soon.'

'Sounds sensible to me.' Sounded amazingly sensible. A hospital, or a birth centre at least with a hospital next door.

Louisa appeared. Caught on very quickly what was happening. 'I'll pack a hamper.'

He looked at her. Felt more tension ease from his shoulders. 'You have a feeding fetish.'

'Must have.' She winked at him. 'I'm too old for any other kind of fetish.'

Simon and the two girls looked at her in comical surprise but Louisa was off to do her stuff.

'I'll see you over there,' Tara said. 'I'll go ahead and run the bath and then come back. We can check baby out when you get there. Take your time, unless you feel you have to hurry.'

What sort of advice was that? Rayne thought with a little flutter of his nervousness coming back. He for one felt like they had to hurry. But Maeve was nodding and doing a go-slow. She didn't even look like making a move.

Simon said he'd leave them to it. Maybe go and see his dad and let him know what was going on.

Rayne watched him go and thought, So the obstetrician leaves? He looked towards Maeve's bedroom. 'Do you have a bag packed?'

'Yep.' She was just standing there with a strange little smile on her face, looking out the window at the Christmas fairy-lights in the back yard. The clock on the wall ticked over a minute. And then another. He felt like ants were crawling all over him.

'Um. You want me to go and get the bag?'

She turned her head and smiled vaguely at him. 'You could.'

So how was he supposed to find it? This must be the kind of stuff normal people talked about when they were planning to have a baby. People who had more than twelve hours' notice they were going to be a support person in a labour. The woman would say, "My bag is in my wardrobe if we need it. My slippers are under the bed." Bathroom kits and baby clothes would have all been discussed. Baby names!

He tamped down his panic again. 'Where is the bag?'

'Behind the door.'

At last. He could do something. He looked at Maeve as if she might explode if he left, and then turned and strode up the hallway for the bag. Was back within seconds.

'Do you need anything else?'

She blinked. Smiled. 'Are you trying to organise me?'

Sprung. 'Uh. Just making sure everything is ready when you want to go.'

'It's really important—' she was speaking slowly as if to a child who wasn't listening '—that the birthing woman is the one who decides when to go to the birth centre. She has to feel like she *needs* to be somewhere else before she leaves the place she feels safe in *now*.'

'So this is what you tell women in antenatal classes? About when they go to the hospital?'

'And the men,' she said with a patronising smile.

They went across to the birthing centre at nine o'clock. Walked across the road, slowly, because Maeve had to stop every few minutes. The stars were out. Christmas night. The air was still warm and Maeve was wearing the sarong.

He had her overnight bag over his shoulder, the hamper from Louisa in one hand and Maeve's elbow in the other.

'It's a beautiful night,' Maeve said after a very long drawn-out breath.

Yes. Yes, beautiful, he thought. *Come on.* 'Yep. You okay?'

She had another contraction and they stopped again.

Tara met them at the door. Nobody else was in labour so they had the place to themselves.

The midwife on duty was over at the hospital but would come across for the birth.

Angus was the doctor on call for obstetrics and would wait outside the door in case they needed him. All these things he found out in the first three minutes because he had requests, too! He really didn't know if he could handle a lifetime of responsibility for Maeve. What if something went wrong?

Tara sent him to make tea because Maeve needed to go to the ladies and he was pacing outside the door.

He was back too quickly.

He could feel Tara's eyes on him and he looked at her.

'Maeve is low risk, Rayne,' Tara said. 'It's her first baby. She's here on the day before the baby is due. Her waters haven't broken. She has no infections. Her blood pressure is normal. She's only been in labour for two hours at the most.' A sympathetic look. 'Why are you worried?'

'It's my first baby too?'

'Sure. I get that.'

He didn't think she did. 'I'm a paediatrician. They only called me for the babies that might need help and I've seen a lot of very sick babies. I guess my idea of normal birth is a bit skewed.' Or more than a bit, and in any case he'd only found out about this baby today.

'I get that too. But Maeve's baby will be fine.'

He wanted to believe that. 'What if it isn't?'

'Then we will manage. It's what we do.' She glanced around the homey birthing room for inspiration, or at least something that would reassure him. 'Why don't you check the equipment? And the resuscitation trolley? All the drugs on the trolley? Check the suckers and oxygen.'

He couldn't help his horror showing in his face. 'You haven't checked those?'

She actually laughed. 'Yes, Dr Walters, I have checked those. But I'm trying to distract you!'

'Oh.' Now he felt dumb. 'Sorry.' He put his finger under the collar of his T-shirt because suddenly it felt tight.

Tara's voice was gentle. 'Maybe doing those things would be helpful if Angus called you in an emergency in the next few weeks.'

He sighed. Get a grip. Thank goodness Tara did have a sense of humour. 'Sorry. It's just been pretty sudden. I'm not normally such a panic merchant.'

She looked at him. 'I have no doubt that's true. I think you've done exceptionally well, considering the scenario you've fallen into. But here's the thing.' Her voice dropped and her face was kind but serious and she glanced at the closed bathroom door. He started to wonder if Maeve and Tara had cooked up this pep talk for him between them.

He guessed he'd never know.

'I need you to be calm. I need you to be Maeve's rock. You don't need to say much—just be here. Agree with her. She really wanted you to be here. And hold her hand when she wants you to. Rub her back when she wants you to. Okay?'

He took a big calming breath. 'Okay.'

'No more panic vibes, please. And in the meantime you can familiarise yourself with the equipment only if you need distraction.'

Okay. He got that. The bathroom door opened and Maeve came out. He sat quietly in the corner of the room while Tara felt Maeve's abdomen, discussed the lie of the baby, which was apparently pointing in exactly the direction and attitude they wanted, and listened to his baby's heartbeat.

Geez. That was his baby's heartbeat. Cloppety, cloppety, clop. It was fast. He knew foetal hearts were fast. But was that too fast?

Calm. He needed to be calm. Dissociate. That was the answer. Pretend it wasn't his baby. Okay. He felt calmer. In fact, he felt in total control. It was cool. Normal heart rate.

'Rayne?'

'Yes, Maeve.'

'Can you hear our baby's heartbeat?'

'Yes, I can. It seems very fast!'

Tara looked at him with eyebrows raised.

He racked his brains. 'Baby must be as excited as we are.'

Maeve laughed. 'That is so cute.'

Cute. Geez. He stood up. Might go check the equipment.

* * *

The next hour was traumatic.

Then Maeve decided to get out of the bath and the hour after that was even worse.

But baby was fine. Heart rate perfect, with no slowing after contractions. Rayne's heart rate slowed after the contractions because during the contraction it doubled. And not just because he was rubbing Maeve's back non-stop.

Between contractions Maeve was calm. Rational. Gathering her strength for the next wave. During contractions it was hell.

Noisy. Intense. Painful when she had his hand in hers and dug her nails in.

Tara was the rock. Quiet. Steady. Unflappable. Like the calm in the storm. He'd look across at her when a contraction was at its height and she would be smiling. Gentle and calm. This was Maeve's profession as well. How did these women do this day in, day out?

'I am so going to be at your birth, Tara,' Maeve ground out as the contraction finally eased.

'Good. We'll swap places.'

Rayne shook his head. How could they carry on a normal conversation when two minutes ago she was ready to rip all their heads off?

And then it was time to push. Eleven forty-five p.m. He looked at Maeve. It had been incredibly hard work. Perspiration beaded her brow, and he leant across and wiped it.

'Hey, Rayne,' she said softly. 'You okay?'

How could she possibly care about him when she was going through hell? 'As long as you're okay, I'm okay.'

'I'm fine.'

He smiled. 'I'm *fine* too.'

She smiled back wearily. 'Home straight now.'

There had been a bit of a lull in the contractions after a series of torrid strong ones. 'So why has it stopped?'

'Nature's way of giving us a break before the last stretch.' Then her face changed. 'Oh.'

The next twenty minutes would be forever etched in his mind. Angus was outside the door in case he was needed. He'd checked, but they didn't see him. Simon had arrived as well but was waiting to be invited in afterwards. He'd bet there was some pacing happening out there. As much as he was suffering in here, it would have been a hundred times worse imagining outside the door. Especially with the Maeve soundtrack they had playing.

With each pushing contraction a little more of the baby shifted down. The excitement was building and Maeve was much more focused now she could use the contractions to make things happen. If there was one thing his Maeve could do, it was make things happen.

Maeve was impatient. No surprise there. She moved position several times, kneeling, leaning on a ball, leaning on Rayne. Even sitting on the toilet, but that stressed him out until Tara smiled and put a towel over the toilet seat so he could stop envisaging his baby falling into the toilet bowl. But eventually they were standing beside the bed, and he could actually see the hair on his baby's head.

'You're doing well,' Tara said.

Well? Doing well? She was freaking amazing, incredible. 'Come on, Maeve. You're nearly there, babe.' He saw her glance at the clock and register it was a few minutes after midnight. She'd got what she wanted, and she looked at him.

Triumph, thankfulness and new determination, and he realised it would never be the same between them again. But that was okay. He could admit she was stronger than him. In some ways, anyway. Maeve turned to face him. 'I want to sit back on the bed against the pillows.'

So he lifted her and put her back on the pillows. 'Love that,' she panted, and even in that moment their eyes met and she tempted him. Then she relaxed back against the pillows, hugging her knees, and gave one long outward sigh. And suddenly the crown appeared then a head of black hair, stretched into a face, one shoulder and then the other.

'Want to take it from here, Rayne?' Tara murmured, and he got it instantly. He stepped in and put his hands under his baby's armpits and, gently eased with the pressure Maeve was exerting, his baby entered the world with his own hands around him in a rush of belly, thighs, long legs and feet and a tangle of cord and water—and suddenly in a huge internal shift and crack through the wall of years of keeping emotion at bay, tears were streaming down his face.

Maeve was staring down with surprise and he lifted the squirming buddle of...? He glanced between the legs, grinned. 'It's a boy!' His eyes met hers and for that moment, when she looked at the baby, and then him and then the baby again, he didn't see how anything could ever stand between them.

His son cried. Loudly and lustily, and Maeve gathered him and snuggled him up against her breasts, and the baby's cries quieted instantly.

Boob man. Chip off the old block. He experienced such a swell of emotion his heart felt like it was going to burst.

In shock he saw the second midwife—where had she come from?—lean in to dry the little legs and arms and belly and rub the damp hair before she stepped back and replaced the damp towel with a warm bunny rug over them both until the baby was in a Maeve skin and bunny-rug sandwich.

Tara delivered the placenta and then a big warm hospital blanket covered Maeve's legs and belly and arms until finally her baby was tucked snugly with just his downy cheek against his mother, turned sideways toward Rayne, with big dark eyes and little squashed nose, and deep pink rosebud lips and a gorgeous mouth like Maeve's. And it was done.

His chest felt tight. 'Hello, there, buddy,' Rayne said softly.

He glanced at the clock. Ten past twelve. Boxing Day baby. Eighteen hours after arriving in Lyrebird Lake here he was—a father. New responsibility swamped him.

CHAPTER NINE

Emergency

MAEVE LAY THERE with the weight of her son on her chest, feeling the little wriggles on the outside of her body instead of the inside as he shifted. Could smell the unmistakable scent of new babies, and blood, and almost taste the relief in the room.

Why were they all worried? She had this. She looked at Rayne, who was sinking into the chair beside the bed that Tara had pulled up for him, unnaturally pale. His hand was halfway to the baby and hung suspended in the air as if he didn't know whether to touch or not.

'He's your son,' she whispered. Wishing he would kiss her. As if he'd heard her, he half stood and leaned across and kissed her lips. His hand drifted down and he touched the downy cheek of their child.

'Thank you. He's amazing. You were incredible.' He blinked a couple of times. 'Are you okay?'

'Buzzing,' she said, and grinned at him, and he shook his head and sank back in the chair. Looked like Rayne had aged ten years, she thought to herself. Still, the years sat well on him.

She glanced at Tara, who was taking her blood pressure. Waited until she was finished and then caught her hand. 'Thanks, Tara.'

Tara smiled mistily. 'I'm going to hold you to that promise.'

'Why? Because you know you'll be much quieter than me?'

Tara laughed. 'You always will be more outspoken than I am. You tell it like it is. Fabulous birth. I loved it.'

She glanced back at Rayne, who was looking at them both as if they were mad.

Tara said, 'Can Simon and Angus come in now? Then everyone will go away so you three can get to know each other.'

Maeve looked at Rayne, who left it up to her, so Simon and Angus came in.

After congratulations Tara took Angus aside, and Maeve could distantly hear that they were discussing the labour and birth, the blood loss, which had been a little more than usual but had settled now, and she saw Simon pump Rayne's hand.

'You look ten years younger, Simon.' Maeve teased him, as he leaned in to kiss her.

'I gave them to Rayne. You, sister, dear, are a worry that thankfully is not mine any more.' He slapped Rayne on the back. 'Welcome to parenthood, Rayne. It's never going to be the same again.'

Rayne still looked in shock. For a tough guy that was pretty funny. 'I get that premonition.'

'You look pale,' Simon said.

'I feel pale.' Rayne glanced across at the new baby, a baby with his own huge dark eyes and maybe it was his mouth.

Maeve remembered a new mother telling her once that when her baby had been first born she could see all the familial likenesses but after a couple of hours she'd only been able to see her baby as whole. Maeve tried to imprint the separate features before that happened. She could see his father's stamp as plainly as if there was a big arrow pointing to it. The brows and nose were from her side.

Rayne shook his head and smiled at her and she soaked up like a hungry sponge the amazed awe he was exuding in bucketloads. She must look a mess but for once she didn't care.

Maeve relaxed back in the bed, letting the euphoria wash over her. She'd always loved watching the way new mums seemed to have this sudden surge of energy, and now she was feeling it herself. She did feel that if she needed to, she could pick up her baby and run and save them both. Probably needed a few more clothes on for that, though, or she'd be scaring people.

She'd discarded the sarong hours ago. Clothes had seemed too much of an annoying distraction in the maelstrom of labour. Her baby wriggled and began to suck his fingers on her chest. His head lay between her breasts with his cheek over her heart, and she smiled mistily down at him. Next he would dribble on his fingers then he would start to poke and rub her with his wet hands as his instincts began to take over.

Yep, he was doing that now, she was careful not to distract him as his little head lifted and he glanced around.

Simon and Angus left and she barely noticed as she saw her baby look and sniff for the dark areolas and the nipple he would find a way to arrive at.

'Watch him,' she whispered to Rayne, who leaned closer. 'He'll bob his head and wriggle and find his own way to where he needs to go.'

The baby's hands were kneading the softness of her breast under his tiny fingers, and his pink knees had drawn up under his belly as if he was going to crawl. 'Can't you just move him there?' Rayne said quietly.

'I could, but he needs to do a sequence. He needs to learn to poke out his tongue before he attaches, and he'll get there under his own steam at just the right moment.'

'He's only half an hour old.'

'That's why a baby stays skin to skin on his mother's chest for that first hour. Shouldn't get nursed by anyone else or have needles or get weighed or anything. It gives them the chance to do all this and the breast-feeding rates go through the roof if the baby attaches by himself. You watch.'

Baby was bobbing his head up and down like a little

jack-in-the-box, and Maeve saw him narrow his gaze on the left nipple and lean towards it. Tiny jerking movements, and shoulder leans, and hand scrunching, and slowly his body changed angle, his neck stretched, and incredibly he was almost there. Another wriggle and head bob and stretch, a series of little tongue peeps as he began to edge closer.

'Come on, little guy,' his father whispered, and she had a sudden vision of Rayne on the sideline of a tiny tots soccer game, being the dad yelling, 'Go, son!'

'Do you like Connor as his name?'

Rayne looked at her. Grinned. 'Spelt with two ns.'

'Lord, yes. As much as I like the Irish version of Conor, this child will not go through life having to spell his name, like I did.'

'Or have people say "Rain, as in wet?"'

'I was teasing.'

'Beautifully.' He leaned across and kissed her and in that moment her world was complete. 'I think he looks very much like a Connor.'

'You can choose the second name.' She saw his face shutter. Felt the withdrawal.

'I didn't do enough to warrant that privilege.'

She felt the slap of reality right when she didn't want to. Acknowledged he was feeling inadequate, and maybe even vulnerable at the moment but, hey, she was the one with no clothes and had exposed herself to the world. She narrowed her eyes at him. 'Then try harder.'

She searched in her mind for a way to make him see

that unless he wanted to, they would never lose him. 'Besides, he's going to cost you a fortune.'

He grinned and she saw the tension fall from his shoulders. Saw his look at her and the comprehension of how adroitly she'd manoeuvred him. Given him something he really could do, regardless of his parenting skills. His smile had a touch of the old bad-boy Rayne who'd been missing for the last few hours. 'In that case, how about the middle name of Sunshine?'

She knew he was kidding. She hoped he was kidding. 'Is that Sunshine from Rayne?'

Just then Connor found the nipple, poked out his tongue, opened his mouth wide and swooped. On! And didn't let go. Maeve gasped and smiled. 'That feels really weird.'

Rayne sat back in wonder. Tara leaned in from passing by and nodded. 'Good work, young man.'

'Connor.'

'Nice name. Welcome, Connor.' And she smiled at them both.

'Connor Sunshine.'

'Really?' She grinned at Maeve, who glared briefly at Rayne before looking back at her son. 'Awesome.' Then Tara had a brief feel of Maeve's belly, to check her uterus was contracting, gave it a little rub, then went back to sorting the room and writing the notes.

'You should've seen your face.'

But Maeve had moved on. Was gazing down at her son, whose jaw was working peacefully, his hands each side of his mouth, fingers digging into her breast every now and then. And all the while his big dark eyes stared up into her face. A swell of love came out of nowhere. Like a rush of heat. Her baby. She would protect this tiny scrap of humanity with her last breath.

'He's incredible,' she whispered, and all joking disappeared as they both watched him.

The next fifteen minutes were very peaceful. They didn't talk much, mostly just stared, bemused at the new person who had entered their lives and would change them as people for ever.

Until Maeve felt the first wave of dizziness and realised the wetness beneath her was spreading and she was beginning to feel faint.

Rayne watched the downy jaw go up and down on Maeve's breast and marvelled at the dark eyes watching his mother. He could feel his heart thawing and it wasn't comfortable. Maeve had had his baby.

He thought about the last twenty-four hours. Driving to Lyrebird Lake, not knowing if she would see him. Or knowing if that powerful current between them from the night so long ago had been real or instigated by the events that he'd known would follow.

Then seeing her this morning, pregnant, catching her as she'd fallen, daring to calculate on the slightest chance it could possibly be his child when Maeve should never have conceived. His fierce exultation that had drowned out his shock.

The swell of emotion was almost a physical pain in his chest as he went over the last tumultuous few hours of labour and finally the birth. Now here he was. A father with his son. A helpless newborn with him as a father. At least Connor had a father.

'Take him, Rayne.'

'He's still drinking.' Rayne was glued to the spectacle but something in her voice arrested him.

'Started bleeding,' she said faintly. 'Get Tara.' Her eyes rolled back, and she fainted like she had when he'd first seen her, only this time he caught his son.

Rayne's heart rate doubled. 'Tara!' Hell. He scooped Connor off his mother's chest as Maeve's arms fell slack, wrapped him in the bunny rug that had covered them both under the big blanket and hugged him to his chest as he leaned over Maeve.

Connor bellowed his displeasure at being lifted off his mother and automatically he patted his bottom through the rug.

Tara scooted back to the bed from her little writing table in the corner, lifted the sheet and sucked in a breath at the spreading stain on the sheets that just then flowed down the sides of the bed. 'Hit that red button over there for help and grab the IV trolley. We'll need to insert cannulas.' He saw her slide her hand over Maeve's soft belly, cup the top of her uterus through the abdominal wall and begin to rub strongly in a circular motion as he forced himself to turn away and do what needed to be done.

Once he'd pushed the emergency bell, he strode into

the treatment room he'd cased earlier and grabbed the IV trolley and pushed it back towards the bed, not as fast as he'd have liked because it was awkward with his son tucked like a little football against his chest. Connor had stopped crying and when Rayne glanced down at him his dark eyes were wide and staring.

Put the cannulas in. That he could do. He glanced around for somewhere to put Connor. Saw the little crib and tucked him in quickly. Connor started to cry.

'Sorry, mate.' He could find and secure veins on tiny infants so he should be able to do it on someone bigger. Someone he couldn't afford to lose.

'What size cannulas do you want?'

'Sixteen gauge. Two.'

Right. Found the size, the tourniquet, the antiseptic. Saw the tubes for blood tests. 'Which bloods?'

Another midwife hurried in after him and Tara glanced up and spoke to her. 'Get Angus back here first, then lower the bedhead so she's tipped down, give her oxygen, then draw me up a repeat ten units of syntocinon. Obs we'll get when we get a chance.'

Tara hadn't taken her hand off the uterus and the flow had slowed to a trickle but the loss from just those few minutes of a relaxed uterus had astounded Rayne with its ferocity. At least two litres had pooled in the bed.

She turned to him. 'Purple times two, one orange and one blue. Coags, full blood count, four units cross-match.'

'Angus is on his way,' the other midwife said, as she lowered the bed and slipped the oxygen mask onto

Maeve's white face. 'Just some oxygen, Maeve.' The girl spoke loudly and as he withdrew the blood for the tests he realised Maeve might be able to hear.

'Hang in there, Maeve. Don't be scared. We'll get it sorted.' Incredibly his voice sounded confident and calm. Not how he was feeling on the inside. He wondered if Tara was as calm as she seemed.

Angus hurried in. Took over from Tara down the business end, checking swiftly to see if there was any damage they'd missed, but the sheer volume and speed of the loss indicated a uterus that wasn't clamping down on those powerful arteries that had sustained the pregnancy. Tara began assembling IV lines and drugs. She gave one bag of plain fluids to him and he connected and secured it. Rayne turned the flow rate to full-bore volume replacement until they could get blood.

An orderly arrived and the nursing supervisor who carried the emergency record started writing down times and drugs as she listened to Tara who spoke as she sorted the emergency kit.

The second midwife was writing Maeve's name on the blood-test tubes. When she was finished she wrote out a request form and sent the samples on their way. Then she hooked Maeve up to the monitor and they all glanced across at the rapid heartbeats shooting across the screen in frantic blips. Her blood pressure wasn't too bad yet but he knew birthing women could sustain that until it fell in a sudden plunge. His neck prickled in the first premonition of disaster.

Angus looked up at the second orderly. 'Bring back two units of O-neg blood. We'll give those until we can cross-match.'

'I'm O-neg if you need more.' Blood. She needed blood, Rayne thought, and wondered how often this happened for them all to be so smooth at the procedures. He glanced at Maeve's face as she moaned and began to stir with the increase in blood flowing to her brain from the head-down position change.

He wanted to go to her but Tara handed him the second flask loaded with the drugs to contract the uterus. 'Run it at two hundred and fifty mils an hour,' she murmured, and he nodded, connected it and set the rate. Then stood back out of the way. The whole scene was surreal. One moment he had been soaking in magic and the next terror had been gripping his throat as Maeve's life force had been seeping away.

'Given ergot yet?' Angus was calm.

'No. But it's coming.' Tara was drawing up more drugs. Rayne's legs felt weak and he glanced across at Connor roaring in his cot. He picked him up and the little boy immediately settled. He hugged his son to him.

'You okay?' Angus looked at him.

No, he wasn't, but it wasn't about him. He crossed to sit back in the chair beside Maeve's head so he could talk to her as she stirred. They didn't need him staring like a fool and fainting, with his son in his arms. Couldn't imagine how frightening this would be for her. 'It's okay, sweetheart. Just rest. Angus is here.'

Her eyelids flickered and for a brief moment she looked at him before her eyelids fell again. 'Okay,' she breathed.

He looked at Angus. 'Why is she still bleeding?'

'Might be an extra lobe of placenta she grew that we missed.' Angus was massaging the uterus through Maeve's belly like Tara had been doing. 'Or could just be a lazy uterus. Or could be a tear somewhere. We'll try the drugs but if it doesn't settle, because of the amount of loss, we'll have to take her to Theatre.'

Angus glanced at the nursing supervisor. 'Call Ben and Andy, clue them in, and have operating staff standing by. We can always send them home.'

Nobody mentioned it was early Boxing Day morning. The supervisor nodded and picked up the phone. 'And phone Simon,' Angus said, with a quick glance at Rayne. 'We'll need his consent.'

Consent for what? Operating theatres? He could give that consent. No, he couldn't. He had no legal claim on Maeve or his son. He had nothing except Maeve's permission to be here. He was no one. Shook himself with contempt. It wasn't about him.

And what would they do? But he knew. They would do what they needed to do to save her life. And if Maeve could never have children again? He thought of the powerful woman who had majestically navigated the birth process with gusto. Imagined her distress if the chance would never be hers again.

He imagined Maeve dying and reared back from

the thought. They would get through it. She had to get through it.

'She's started to bleed again,' Angus said to Tara. 'Get me the F2 alpha and I'll inject it into her uterus.' To the other midwife, he said, 'Check the catheter isn't blocked and I'll compress the uterus with my hands until we can get to the OR.'

The next two hours were the worst in Rayne's life. Worse than when they'd come for him in Simon's house and he'd seen Maeve's distress, worse than when he'd been sentenced to prison, worse than when he'd found out his mother had died.

Maeve went in and for a long time nobody came out. Simon sat beside him in the homey little waiting room that was like no other waiting room he'd ever seen.

It had a big stone water cooler and real glasses to drink from. A kettle and little fridge to put real milk in your tea and a big jar of home-made oatmeal biscuits. And a comfortable lounge that he couldn't sit on.

He paced. Connor didn't seem to mind because he slept through it in his bunny rug. Rayne couldn't put him down. Not because Connor cried but because Rayne couldn't bear to have empty arms while he waited for Maeve to come through those doors.

'Do you want me to take Connor?'

'No!' He didn't even think about it. Looked down at his son asleep against his chest. Doing at least something that he knew Maeve would like while he waited. 'What's taking them so long?'

'She'll go to Recovery when they've sorted everything. Then Dad will come through and talk to us. Or maybe Ben or Andy.'

'Are they good?'

'Superb.'

'I feel so useless. I worried about being a good enough father. That's nothing in the big picture.'

'It's not a nothing. But this is bigger. But you'll be fine. She'll be fine.'

Rayne heard the thread of doubt in Simon's voice and stopped. Looked at the man who would become his brother-in-law. Because he would marry Maeve. If she'd have him. He didn't deserve her. Would never have presumed to think she'd have him. But after this fear of losing her he'd take her faith in him and hold it and be the best dad a man could be. And the best husband.

Surely that would be the start of good enough?

He had a sudden vision of waking up in bed beside Maeve for every morning to come for the rest of his life. How the hell would he get out of bed?

But Simon. He'd forgotten that Maeve was the sister Simon was most protective about. How could he forget that in the circumstances? Because he needed to think of other people in his life now. He wasn't alone. He had Maeve, and Connor, and apparently a whole family or two. He glanced down at his son again and then at Simon.

He stopped where Simon was sitting. 'Can you hold him for a sec? My arm's gone to sleep.' It hadn't but he could see Simon needed something to hold as well. Tara was in the operating theatre with Maeve and she couldn't help him.

He watched his friend's face soften as he took the sleeping infant. Saw the tension loosen in the rigid shoulders. He missed the weight of Connor but was glad that Simon had him for the moment. Funny how a tiny helpless baby could help both of them to be stronger.

And then the doors opened and Angus came out. He looked at Simon first and then at Rayne.

'She had a spontaneous tear in her uterus. Probably a weakness in the muscle she was born with. It took a while to find it and she lost a lot of blood. But she's stable now.'

Rayne felt his body sag. Was actually glad that Simon held Connor.

'No more normal births for her. And a Caesarean in a bigger centre next time in case it does it again.'

So they had saved her uterus. Not bad for a tiny country hospital. 'So more blood transfusions?'

'And fresh frozen plasma and cryo. They'll need some of your blood over at the blood bank because we've used nearly all of theirs.'

It was the least he could do.

'Do we need to ship her out to a bigger hospital?' Simon had stood and his father was smiling at him with his nephew in his arms.

'I don't think so. And I would if I thought she needed to go. Would have spirited her there half an hour ago if I could have, but the crisis is past.' He grinned at Simon, who was swaying with the baby. 'Can't you men put that baby down?'

Rayne glanced at his friend. The relief was soaking in slowly. 'We're sharing the comfort. So she'll be fine?'

'She'll have to spend a few more days in hospital than she expected but she'll be spoiled rotten in Maternity.'

Rayne thought of going back to the manse without Maeve and Connor. 'Can I stay there, too? In the room with her and Connor? Help her with the baby?'

Angus raised his brows. 'Can't see any reason why not. Might mean that Tara will hand her over because she's not budging and I think she's nearly out on her feet.' He glanced at his son with a tired smile. 'Tara did a great job, Simon.'

So many amazing people here. So many he had to thank. Rayne stepped up to Angus and shook his hand. How could he ever repay them? 'Thank you. Thank the other guys.'

'We'll call in a favour if we need it.' Angus smiled.

Rayne looked at him. Saw a man who would be ruthless if he needed something for his little country hospital, and understood that. Smiled at it. Got the idea that resources could be hard to come by here when life threw a curve ball but those who had chosen to live here had saved his Maeve. They could have him any time they wanted.

He saw that he'd been accepted and was therefore fair game. He could deal with that. Thought for the first time about where Maeve might want to live and that, for the moment, if it was here he could cope with that.

Ten minutes later Simon took Tara home and Rayne carried Connor back to the room that would be Maeve's. The night midwife, Misty, took him through to the nursery and they finally got around to weighing Connor and giving him his needles, then she ran her hands all over him, checking that everything was fine.

She listened to his heart and handed the stethoscope to Rayne with a smile. 'Tara said you were a paed.'

Rayne listened. His son's heart sounded perfect. No valve murmurs. No clicks. He ran his own hands over him as if he were a baby he had been asked to check. But this wasn't a baby of some other lucky couple. This was his son. His hands stilled. This child depended on him for all the things his own father hadn't given him and he would deliver.

Misty handed him clothes and he looked at the tiny singlet. Thought of Maeve.

'Maeve's missing this. Wish she was here to share it.'

'Have you got your phone?'

He looked at her blankly. It wasn't like he could ring her. It must have shown on is face.

Misty laughed. 'You are tired. I can take photos of you dressing Connor and you can show her later.'

He shook his head. He should have thought of that. Handed her the phone in his pocket and Misty started snapping.

Rayne glanced at the sink as he lifted the singlet to stretch it widely over Connor's head. 'So when do we bath him?'

Misty shook her head. 'Not for twenty-four hours. He still smells like Mum and it helps him bond and feel secure and remember what to do when he goes for his next feed.'

Rayne vaguely remembered that from something Maeve had said, along with the skin to skin with Mum in the first hour.

Connor stared sleepily up at him as he dressed him. 'And what if he gets hungry before Maeve comes back?'

'He'll be fine. Tara said he fed well at birth. That's great. He could sleep up to twelve hours before he wakes up enough to feed again this first day. It's made such a difference letting them have that one long sleep after birth. Breastfed babies feed at least six to ten times a day and he'll catch up later.'

'I should know this stuff.' He shook his head. 'I've been out of it for nearly a year and in the States the doctors don't really discuss breastfeeding issues.'

She laughed. 'Everyone does everything here.'

He captured and pulled Connor's long fingers gently through the sleeve of the sleeping gown. All the experience came back as he turned the little boy over onto his front and tied the cords of his nightgown. Made him feel not so useless. He could do this for Maeve. He folded the gown back carefully so it wouldn't get damp if he wet his nappy. 'Don't you use disposable nappies here?'

'Not until after they do their first wee. Those new disposables are too efficient and it's hard to tell sometimes.'

'Fair enough.' He clicked the pin with satisfaction and tugged the secure nappy. Good job.

Misty nodded approvingly. 'You can even do a cloth and pin nappy without help. Not many dads could do that the first day.' The phone rang and she handed him a clean bunny rug. 'Excuse me.'

She poked her head back into the nursery. 'They're bringing Maeve back now.'

Rayne felt relief sweep over him as he wrapped Connor and put him snugly back into his little wheeled cot. Tucked him under the sheets so he didn't feel abandoned. His eyes were shut. Misty had put nappies and wipes and assorted linen under there in case he needed it in the room overnight and Rayne trundled the cot out the door and down the hallway, where two men were pushing a wheeled bed into the room.

His first sight of Maeve made him draw in his breath. She looked like Snow White, icily beautiful, but deeply asleep and as white as the sheets she lay on with her eyes shut. Her black hair made her look even paler and his heart clutched in shock. Unconsciously his hand went down until he was resting it on Connor's soft hair, as if he needed the touch of his son to stay calm.

She stirred as the bed stopped against the wall of the room. Blinked slowly and then she opened her eyes, focused and saw him. Licked her dry lips. Then softly, barely perceptibly, she murmured, 'Hi, there, Rayne.'

'Hi, there, Princess Maeve.' He pulled the cot up to the side of the bed. 'Your son is beautiful.'

'Our son,' she whispered.

'I love him already.' He didn't know where the words had come from but he realised it was somewhere so deep and definite in him that it resonated with truth and the smile on Maeve's face as she closed her eyes assured him it was the thing she most wanted to hear.

'Then I can leave him to you while I sleep.'

'I'm here. I'm not going anywhere.'

'Thank you.' And she breathed more deeply as she drifted back to sleep.

He watched her chest slowly rise and fall. Glanced at the blood running into a vein in her left arm and mentally thanked the donor who had provided it. Checked the drugs running into a right-arm vein. Watched Misty as she straightened the IV lines, the monitor leads and the automatic blood-pressure machine, set to record every half an hour, until they were all in a position she could glance at every time she came into the room.

Rayne shifted his intended chair slightly so he could see too. Frowned over the fact that Maeve's heart rate was still elevated, her blood pressure still low. But respirations were normal. And even as she slept just a tinge of colour was returning to her face.

He pushed Connor's cot quietly towards the big chair beside the bed and sank back into it. Then pulled the cot halfway between the bed and the chair so that either of them could stretch out their arm and could touch their son. Then he settled down to watch Maeve.

CHAPTER TEN

MAEVE WOKE AND the room was quiet. It was still dark through the windows outside and her belly felt like it was on fire. At first she thought Rayne was asleep but he shifted and sat straighter when he saw she was awake and she wondered vaguely if he'd been awake all this time. Watching over her. It was an incredible thought.

'Hi.' She couldn't keep a frown off her face.

'Pain not good?'

She decided shaking her head would be too much movement. 'Eight out of ten.'

He stood up. 'I'll get Misty.' Left the room in a few long strides and she tried to lessen the tension in her body. What the heck happened to her beautiful natural birth? And how had she ended up being sore both ends? Now, that sucked. Closed her eyes and decided to worry about it tomorrow.

Misty came back in with Rayne and brought some tablets and a bottle of water with a straw.

Rayne slid his arm under her shoulders and eased

her up so slowly and gently that it barely hurt to move. She swallowed the pills and savoured the water as it ran down her throat as he laid her down again.

Misty checked all her observations then Connor's, without rousing him, and then lifted the sheets and checked her wound and her bleeding and nodded with satisfaction at both. 'Looking beautiful.'

She heard Rayne, say, 'You midwives are weird.'

It would hurt to laugh. Misty laughed and left the room and Maeve smiled. She turned her head carefully and looked at Connor. Sleeping like a baby. Hugged that thought to herself then looked at Rayne, who was watching her. There was something different about him.

'You okay?'

He smiled and there was so much caring in the look he gave her that she felt herself become warm. 'I'm okay, as long as you are,' he said.

Meaning? 'Been a pretty torrid day?'

He stood up. Smiled down at her. Took her hand in his and turned it over. Careful of the IV lines, she thought. It was just a hand. Then he kissed her palm and it became a magic hand.

Then he said, 'A first for me as well. You scared the daylights out of me.'

Funnily, she hadn't been scared. 'I wasn't scared. You said not to be. Thank you for being there.'

He shook his head. 'Connor is amazing.' He looked towards the door. 'These people are amazing.' He glanced at her. 'You are beyond amazing.' Then he leaned down. Kissed her dry lips and tucked her in. 'Go back to sleep.'

When she woke in the morning Rayne was still there. His eyes were closed but for some reason she didn't think he was asleep. The drips had stopped feeding blood and had changed to clear fluid, so she guessed that was a good thing.

Connor was still sleeping. She reminded herself that babies could sleep up to ten or twelve hours after the first feed to get over the birth and she didn't need to feel guilty she hadn't fed him again. Remembered he'd probably make her pay for it later by feeding every time she wanted to put him back in his cot. Though she couldn't imagine wanting to put him back in his cot. It felt so long since she'd held him in her arms.

'Good morning.' Rayne's eyes were open. 'How do you feel?'

'I must look like a dishrag.'

'You look beautiful. A little pale and interesting as well.'

'At least I'm interesting.' She winced as she smiled too hard.

'I'll get Misty.' He left and came back with Misty, who was almost ready to hand her over to the morning staff.

So they repeated the whole Rayne lifting her, tablet taking, observation thing, and this time she didn't want to go back to sleep afterwards. She wanted to change out of her horrible gown and get into her nightie. Get up and shower, but she didn't think she'd be able to do it.

Could feel herself getting cross. 'Why don't you go back to the manse and have a sleep?'

Rayne lifted his brows and looked at her. Smiled. 'Later. When you have a wash, and get into your nightie, and have Connor's next feed. I don't know you well but I know you enough to see you want to be fresh, and hold your son, soon.'

He looked at her and shrugged. 'I want to help you, and help the midwife helping you, and I can be the muscle so you don't have to hurt yourself trying to do all those things.'

She looked at him. Flabbergasted. Was this guy for real? 'Aren't you tired?'

'No more than you. I'll sleep later.'

'I can't let you do that.'

Another enigmatic smile. 'You're not running this show, Princess Maeve. I am.'

Ooh. Bossy. She was too weak, and it was hard not to sort of like it. 'Then maybe later, if you're good, you can put me in the shower,' she said with a tired smile.

'I don't think you'll be up to a shower but we'll see.'

But she dug her heels in. 'I'm not being washed in bed like a baby.' They all looked at Rayne for help.

'Fine,' he said.

So they agreed on a compromise before Misty went off. Once Maeve's pain tablets had kicked in and she wasn't too sore, they disconnected her IVs for the few minutes it would take, and Rayne lifted her to the edge of the bed then carried her to the shower chair and the hand-held shower nozzle, and gently hosed her all over, washed her back and her legs, until she began to feel human again. Amazing what some hot water and a change of position could do.

Misty made her bed up with fresh sheets and plumped up her pillows so that when Rayne had helped her dry and dress again she could sink back and relax.

'I'm walking back to the bed under my own steam.' She glared at him. He held up his hands.

'Your call. I'm happy to watch.'

So she eased herself into a standing position, and it wasn't too bad now that she'd loosened up. She tentatively took a few steps, knowing there was no way he would let her fall because his arms were right behind her. Not a bad feeling to have.

She straightened up more and she felt tender, but okay. She could do this. She looked up at Rayne to poke out her tongue, but then a wave of faintness caught up with her.

He must have seen the colour drain from her face because he said, 'No, you don't.' Before it could get too disastrous she found herself back in her bed, with Misty pulling up the sheets and saying, 'Someone needs to tell you about the blood you lost last night.'

When the world stopped turning she looked up to see Rayne frowning darkly at her. She thought vaguely that he was still too damn good looking even when he frowned. 'You're a stubborn woman.'

But Misty smiled at her as she tucked the sheets in. 'Stubborn women are the best kind because they never give in.'

Rayne rolled his eyes. 'Another mad midwife saying.'

Five minutes later Connor made a little snorting noise, and they both turned their heads to see, watched him shift in his cot, blink and then open his eyes.

'He's awake.'

Rayne saw the longing on Maeve's face and was so glad he'd stayed for this.

'Good morning, young man. Your mother has been through a lot while she waited for you to wake up.' He reached down and untucked the sheets and opened the bunny rug. A black tar train wreck lay inside. Was even glad he'd stayed for this. He'd cleaned up enough dirty nappies in his time to make short work of even the biggest mess and it seemed his son had quite a capacity. Go you, son.

Connor grumbled but didn't cry, as if confident of the handling he was receiving.

Rayne looked across at the bed and Maeve was holding her stomach to stop herself laughing, and they grinned at each other in mutual parental pride. Then he pinned up the new nappy efficiently and lifted Connor away from his bunny rug in his hospital clothes so

Maeve could see his long legs and feet as he tucked him carefully in her arms.

Rayne watched her face soften and her mouth curve into such a smile, and the ball in his chest tightened and squeezed. This stuff had turned him into a wimp but he wouldn't have missed it for the world. He tucked a pillow under Maeve's arm so she didn't have to hold Connor's weight and watched as she loosened her neckline to lift out a breast.

Now, there was a sight he'd never tire of as Connor turned his head and poked out his tongue. Rayne put his hand under Connor's shoulders to help Maeve manoeuvre him closer until Connor opened his mouth, had a few practise attempts and then a big wide mouth and onto the breast. Just like that.

Maeve sighed and rested more comfortably back on the pillows, and Rayne sat back with wonder filling him until he thought he would burst.

My God.

How had this happened? Yesterday he had been lost, without purpose or future, a social misfit and almost-pariah, following his instinct towards a woman who so easily could have turned him away.

Now he had a family, Maeve and Connor and him—his family. And this morning he knew there would be battles of will, adjustments to make, discoveries and habits and ideas that might clash, but he could never doubt he had love for this incredible woman he had almost lost as soon as he'd found her, and that love would only grow bigger—probably daily. The future that was theirs stretched before them like a miracle. A Christmas miracle.

Rayne looked with wonder at the big country-style clock on the wall and watched the hand click over to six-thirty a.m. Exactly twenty-four hours since his car had rolled down the street and swerved towards the woman he'd been searching for as she'd walked towards him.

'Rayne?' Maeve's voice was softly concerned. 'You okay?'

He shook his head. The room was blurry. Stood up and stepped in close to the bed, leant down and slid his arm around the two of them and gently rested his cheek on Maeve's hair. He'd just discovered that she made him feel brand new. That he could do anything. And he most certainly was the only man for this job of looking after his family. 'I need to hug the most important two people in my life.'

She rested back into his arms with a contented sigh. 'Feel free any time.'

Over the next day there were a lot of firsts.

Connor's first bath, a joyous occasion where Maeve sat like a princess packed up in pillows and watched while Rayne deftly floated and massaged and swirled his son around like he'd been doing it for years.

'You're so good at that,' Maeve said approvingly. 'Still, I always tell the mums it's nice to shower with your baby. One of the parents undresses and hands baby in to go skin to skin with the person in the shower and the other—that will be you Rayne.' She grinned up at him. 'You lost. You just get to take him back and dry and dress him while I have the fun part.'

Rayne grinned. 'Poor me. I have to watch the naked lady with the awesome breasts in the shower with my baby.' Maeve held her tummy and tried not to laugh.

Then came the visitors with hugs and kisses of relief.

Also along came things for Connor. His first knitted set of bonnet, booties, cardigan and shawl all lovingly created by his step-great-grandmother, Louisa, who also brought food just in case the hospital ran out.

His first pair of tiny jeans and black T-shirt to match his dad's, from Uncle Simon and Tara.

Goodness knew where he'd got it from, because he'd barely left her side, but Rayne produced a bright yellow rubber duck for Connor's bath because his mother loved ducks.

Tiny booties shaped like soccer boots with knitted bumps for spikes from Mia and the girls at morning teatime and a welcome-baby card that had a three-dimensional baby actually swinging in a seat from a tree that the girls had fallen in love with.

But the excitement all took its toll.

'You look exhausted. Enough. I'll go back to the manse and you sleep.' Rayne stood up.

It was lunchtime, and Maeve was ready for a sleep.

Rayne kissed her. 'I'll come back any time you need me. If you want to get out of bed or Connor is unsettled and you want someone to nurse him, I'm the man. Ring me.' He looked at her. 'Promise.'

'Bossy.'

'Please.'

'Okay.' Not a bad back-up plan. She watched him go with a prickle of weak tears in her eyes and sighed into the bed.

'He did well,' Tara said, as she closed the blinds of the room.

'He did amazingly.'

'You did amazingly. But I agree with you and with him. It's time for sleep.' She checked Connor was fast asleep after his feed and quietly backed out.

As the door shut Maeve relaxed back into the bed and glanced at her downy-cheeked son. It had happened. She couldn't tell if he looked like either of them because now he looked like her darling baby Connor.

The whole labour and birth were over. And the next stage was just beginning.

The beginning of shared parenthood with a man she knew she loved. She didn't know if Rayne felt the same, but she was too tired and tender to worry about that now. That he was here was enough.

Rayne's solid support had been a thousand times stronger than she'd dared to hope for, his pre-birth nerves were a precious memory to keep and maybe occasionally tease him about, and she could see that Rayne would take his responsibilities to Connor and to her very seriously.

Lying in Rayne's arms yesterday seemed so far away in time with what had happened since then but as she drifted off to sleep she knew there was so much they could build on. She just needed to be patient, she thought with sleepy smile on her face, and trust in Rayne.

CHAPTER ELEVEN

FOUR DAYS LATER Maeve went home with Connor and Rayne—her family. Home being to the manse and the fabulous cooking of Louisa, who had decided the new mother needed feeding up.

Rayne, being fed three meals a day at least, was chopping wood at an alarming rate to try and keep his weight down from Louisa's cooking.

Simon went back to Sydney for work and planned to return each alternate weekend, and Tara was going to fly down to Sydney on the other weekends until their wedding in four weeks' time.

Selfishly, Maeve was glad that Tara had stayed with them, instead of following Simon to Sydney, and with Rayne booked to do the occasional shift over in the hospital on call, she had ample back-up help with Tara and, of course, Louisa, who was in seventh heaven with a baby in the house.

They'd shifted Connor into Rayne's room with the connecting door open and Rayne bounced out of their bed to change and bring Connor to her through the night.

Life took on a rosy glow of contentment as she and Rayne and Connor grew to be a family. The joy of waking in the morning in Rayne's tender arms, the wonder on his face when he looked at her with Connor, the gradual healing of her body, the steady increase of confidence in breastfeeding, managing Connor's moods and signs of tiredness, and the ability to hand him to his father's outstretched hands all gelled. Life was wonderful.

Her brother's wedding approached and their mother was coming. It was four weeks after the birth of Connor and Maeve was suddenly nervous.

Rayne decided Maeve had been twitchy all morning. Her mother was due to arrive along with Maeve's three older sisters. He'd seen her change her clothes four times and Connor's jumpsuit twice before the expected event.

On arrival her mother kissed Maeve's cheek and an awkward few moments had passed right at the beginning when she looked Rayne over with a sigh and then stepped forward and shook his hand.

'Hello, Rayne. Maeve said you were very good when Connor was born.'

So this was what Maeve would look like when she was older. Stunning, sophisticated and polished, though Desiree was blonde, perhaps not naturally because she had dark eyebrows, but a very successful-looking blonde.

He glanced at Maeve and the woman holding his

son had it all over her mum for warmth. 'It was Maeve who was amazing.'

A cool smile. 'I'm glad she's happy.'

'So am I.' Which left what either of them really meant open to interpretation.

Maeve broke into the conversation. 'You remember my sisters, Ellen, Claire and Stephanie.'

'Ladies.' He smiled at the three women, who were cooing at Connor.

Maeve hung onto his hand and Connor was unusually unsettled, probably receptive to the vibes his mother was giving off.

Luckily Desiree was swept up into the final wedding preparations and they all managed to ease back on the tension for the rest of the afternoon.

The next day Simon and Tara's wedding was held in the little local church and most of the town had come to celebrate with them.

It was a simple and incredibly romantic celebration. The church ladies had excelled themselves with floral decorations. Tara looked like the fairy on top of the cake, thanks to the absolute delight Mia, Simon's stepmother, had taken in spoiling her, and beside him, Simon nearly cried in the church when she entered.

A big lump had come to Rayne's throat when he thought about his friend finding such happiness and he couldn't help his glance past the bride and groom to the chief bridesmaid, his Maeve, who looked incredible in the simple blue gown Tara had chosen for her attendants.

Except for the divine cleavage, nobody would suspect Maeve had recently given birth, because she'd returned to her pre-pregnancy size almost immediately.

As Rayne listened to the words of the priest the certainty inside him grew that he could answer yes to all of it.

By the time Simon and Tara were married all he wanted to do was hold Maeve in his arms and tell her he loved her.

But he would have to wait.

The reception was a huge outdoor picnic, all the speeches a success, and the ecstatically happy couple finally left for their honeymoon in Hawaii and would then fly on to Boston, where Maeve's father waited to meet his stepson's new wife.

Back at the manse after the wedding Rayne needed a beer and a bloke to drink with, because the only sane woman was Louisa, who kept feeding him.

Maeve still hadn't settled, though she seemed to stress more than anything about Connor being even a little upset, which was strange when before she'd sailed along blithely and just enjoyed him. The help from her mother wasn't doing its job.

Rayne decided he would survive until Maeve's mother left. He'd lived with worse people and his lips twitched. Could just imagine Maeve's mother's downturned mouth if she knew he was comparing her to a cellmate.

'There you are, Rayne.' The object of his thoughts appeared and he plastered a smile on his face.

'Connor is crying and Maeve asked for you. Though I can't see what you can do that I can't.'

'Thank you.' Excellent reason to escape. 'The wedding was great but I think everyone is tired now. I'd better go and see.'

When he gently opened the door to their room he found Maeve with tears trickling down her face as Connor screamed and kicked and fought the breast.

'Hey, Connor, what are you doing to your poor mum?'

Maeve looked up tragically and he crossed the room to sit beside her on the bed. He dropped a kiss on her head. 'He won't feed. And Mum keeps telling me to put him on the bottle.'

'Bless her,' Rayne said, tongue-in-cheek and Maeve's eyes flew to his, ready to hotly dispute that, until she saw his smile.

Her own smile, while still watery, gradually appeared. 'She makes me crazy.'

'Really? I hadn't noticed.' He leaned forward, kissed her, remembered again how each day he felt more blessed, and took the unsettled Connor from her. Tucked him over his shoulder and patted his bottom. 'It's been a big day. And you've been busy making sure Tara had a fabulous time so you've run yourself into the ground. Why don't I take Connor for a drive and you can have a rest before tea?'

'No, thanks.'

Maeve looked even sadder and he frowned. 'What?'

'Can't I come with you both?'

He grinned. 'You mean escape? And leave your mother here without us?'

Maeve looked guilty at the disloyal idea. 'She means well.'

'I know. Maybe we could get Louisa to look after her. Your mum's probably tired too. It's a long flight and she only got here yesterday.' He had a vision. One that he'd been building up to for days now but had wanted to leave until after the wedding. 'I'd really like to take Connor to the duck pond. Would you like to come with us for an hour until sunset?'

Maeve nodded, looked brighter already, so he left her to get ready, and sought out Louisa first, begged a favour he promised to repay, then found Maeve's mother.

Gently does it, he warned himself. 'What do you think if I take Connor for a little drive. Just to get him asleep in the car?'

A judicious nod from the dragon. 'That's an excellent idea.'

Now for the smooth part. 'Maeve wants to come but she feels bad about leaving you on your own.' Desiree opened her mouth but before she could invite herself he said, 'But I see Louisa had just made you a lovely afternoon tea and is dying to have a good chat with you. What would you like to do?' Opened his eyes wide.

Desiree slid gracefully into the trap and relief ex-

panded in his gut. 'Oh. Poor Louisa. It would be rude
not to stay for that. Of course.' She looked pleased.
'How thoughtful. She really is a lovely woman.'

'One of my favourite people.' And wasn't that true.
Then he escaped to his family and bundled them into
the car.

Ten minutes later Maeve sat on the bench in front of
the lake, holding Connor in the crook of her arm. Their
son had decided he preferred to feed alfresco and was
very happily feeding. Every now and then Maeve would
throw breadcrumbs to the ducks with her free hand.

Rayne stood behind her, gently rubbing her shoulders. They both had smiles on their faces.

Maeve said, 'I don't think I could bear to lose a man
who rubs my shoulders like you do.'

Rayne felt the happiness expand inside him. 'Does
this mean you want me to stay?'

She twisted her neck to look at him and pretended
to consider it judiciously. 'Yes, I think so.'

Rayne had waited for just this opening and unfortunately in the euphoria of successful strategies he rushed
it. 'Only if you'll marry me.' The words were out before he could stop them and he cursed his inability to
be smooth and romantic when she deserved it all. He'd
done everything the wrong way around here.

She opened her mouth to reply and quickly he moved
around to face her and held up his finger. 'Wait.'

'So bossy,' she murmured, and he smiled as he went

down on one knee beside her—right there in front of the ducks.

'Please. Wait for me to do it properly.' He took her free hand in his, brushed the crumbs off it and kissed her fingers. Maeve leant back against the bench and Connor ignored them both as he continued with his afternoon tea.

Rayne drew a deep breath and let it go. Let everything go, let the past, the mistakes and the pain and uncertainty all go so they could start fresh and new and perfect. Because the three of them deserved it. 'My darling, gorgeous, sexy...' he paused, smiled at her '...impossible Maeve—'

Before he could finish she'd interrupted. 'Impossible?'

'Shh.' He frowned at her and she closed her mouth. 'Darling Maeve—' and he couldn't keep the smile off his face '—will you do me the honour, please, of becoming my wife and share with me the rest of my life?'

Her face glowed at him, a trace of pink dusting the high cheekbones that were still far too pale. 'Now, that, as a proposal of marriage, was worth waiting for.'

'An answer would be good. Come on.'

She teased him. 'My darling, strong, sexy as all get out Rayne.' Leaned forward and kissed him while he knelt before her. Connor still ignored them both. 'Yes. Please. Pretty please. I would love to be your wife and share your life.'

His relief expanded and he squeezed her hand. 'You won't regret it.'

Her face softened. 'I know I won't. But my mother wants a big wedding.'

He smiled. He could do that. It was a small price to pay for the world he now had. 'I thought she might. As long as Connor is pageboy and you are my bride, I will agree to anything.' He stood up and hugged her gently again and smiled into her hair. 'It's not going to be dull.'

A month later Maeve woke on the morning of her wedding in her parents' house huge in Boston. Down the hall Tara was sleeping without her new husband because Simon had gone to support Rayne on the night before his wedding. She wished she'd been able to stay with Rayne but they would never have got that past her mother.

Connor stirred beside her and she sat up with a warm feeling of relief in her stomach and reached for him. Rayne would be missing Connor and her as much as they missed him.

How could life change so dramatically in just two months? The answer was simple. Rayne loved her. Which was lucky because her mother had put them all through hoops as she married the first of her daughters off in the grand fashion.

There had been family dinners at exclusive restaurants, wedding breakfasts under the marquee in the back garden, and bridal teas with all the local ladies, as well as bridal showers and multiple rehearsals and today, finally, the wedding of the year.

Maeve had always wanted a big wedding, the chance to be the big star, but funnily enough now that it was here she knew she would have been happy with a two-line agreement in front of a celebrant as long as she was married to Rayne.

Her mother wouldn't have been happy, though, and it was good to see Desiree finally pleased with her. But today she would marry Rayne, they would pack up and leave on their honeymoon then head back to Lyrebird Lake, and Maeve couldn't wait.

Her husband-to-be had been amazing. Patient. Comforting when she'd become stressed, loving when she'd least expected it but had secretly needed that reassurance, and always so brilliantly patient and capable with Connor—and her mother.

When she thought about it, Rayne had learnt to be patient with mothers very early in his life and he was showing his skills now.

Her over-achieving sisters were here and she realised she'd finally grown out of worrying that about a hundred relatives were scattered in nearby hotels. She and Rayne and Connor were united in the birth of their family and their future and she couldn't wait.

Eight hours later Rayne stood beside Simon, this time as the groom and Simon the best man, and Rayne's hands were just slightly shaking.

In Boston, their bigger than *Ben Hur* wedding that Maeve's mother had organised had seemed to never get any closer.

But finally, today, it would happen. Their family would officially be joined forever. Maeve was putting so much trust in him he felt humbled, and before God, and before the ceremony even started, he silently vowed he would never let her down.

The music started, the congregation stood, and then she was there. A heartbeat, a shaft of divine light, and she appeared. Standing at the end of that very long, very floral-bouqueted aisle, with her father beside her and a huge church full of people to witness them being bound together.

Maeve's next older sister, the first bridesmaid, was almost up to them, coming closer with stately precision, Connor in her arms in his tiny suit, because that was the only thing Rayne had insisted on.

Then the second sister, and then the third, and then... Maeve. Sweeping down the aisle towards him, way too fast. To hell with the slow walk, he didn't bother to look for her mother's frown at the break in protocol, just grinned at her and held out his hand. He loved this woman so much.

The mass began and he missed most of it as he stared at the vision beside him. Remembered the last two months, the joy he'd found, the deep well of love he hadn't realised he'd had to give.

'Do you take this woman...?'

Hell, yes! He remembered to let the reverend finish. More waiting until finally he could say, 'I will.'

'Do you, Maeve, take this man…?'

The words drifted as he stared again into her eyes. Those eloquent eyes that said he was her hero, always would be, that she believed in him so much and loved him. What more could a man want?

Then she said, 'I will.' That was what he wanted!

'With the power vested in me and before this congregation I now declare you man and wife…' And it was done. Rayne lifted the veil, stared into her tear-filled eyes and kissed his wife with all the love in his heart in the salute.

Maeve clutched her husband's hand and couldn't help the huge smile on her face. The cameras were flashing, she was moving and signing and smiling, and all the time Rayne was beside her. Protecting her, loving her, and finally reaching out to take Connor from her sister so that he carried their son and it was time for the three of them to walk back up the aisle as a family.

Maeve met Rayne's eyes, saw the love and knew this was the start of an incredible life with the man she had always loved. She couldn't wait.

* * * * *

WAKING UP TO
DR. GORGEOUS

EMILY FORBES

For anyone who has ever fallen in love when they didn't intend to—it's never the wrong time!

CHAPTER ONE

'OMG, FLICK, I wish you'd been able to see this place.'

Luci had spoken to her best friend several times already today but she couldn't resist calling her again to update her on her good fortune.

'It's nice, then?' She could hear the smile in Flick's voice.

'Nice! It's amazing.' Luci wandered around the apartment while she chatted. 'It's right on the harbour. The beach is just across the road. I'm looking at the sea as we speak.' She could hear the waves washing onto the shore and smell the salt in the air. 'I don't know how Callum is going to manage in my little house.'

It was a bit odd to be walking around a stranger's apartment. Luci had spent her whole life surrounded by people she knew so to travel halfway across the country to swap houses with a stranger was odd on so many levels. It had all happened so quickly she hadn't had time to consider how it would feel. Callum Hollingsworth's apartment on the shores of Sydney Harbour was modern and masculine. While her house wasn't particularly feminine it was old and decorated in what she guessed people would call country style. No surprises there, it was definitely a country house. It was clear that her house-swap partner's taste in decorating was quite different from hers. She felt self-conscious, wondering what he would think of her place, before she realised it didn't matter. She didn't plan on meeting the guy.

She heard the whistle of the Indian Pacific through the phone. The two friends had spent the past few days chilling on Bondi Beach, a girls' getaway that Flick had suggested before Luci settled into her house swap and study course in Sydney, and Flick returned to South Australia on the iconic trans-continental train.

'Are you on the train?' Luci asked.

'Not yet,' Flick replied. 'I'm just grabbing a coffee and waiting to board.'

'Make sure you call me when you get home,' she told her.

'Of course I will. What are you going to do with the rest of your day?'

'I think I'll take a stroll around my new neighbourhood. The hospital is a half-hour walk away so I might head in that direction. Work out where I have to be tomorrow. I don't want to be late.' Luci was enrolled in an eight-week course in child and family health being run through the North Sydney Hospital and she needed to get her bearings. 'Look after my mum and dad for me.'

That was her one big concern. As an only child of elderly parents—her mother called her their 'change of life' baby—Luci was nervous about being so far away from them, but Flick had promised to keep an eye on them. It wasn't hard for her to do as Luci's dad was the local doctor and Flick worked for him as a practice nurse.

'I will. Enjoy yourself.'

Luci ended the call and had another wander around.

It wasn't a massive apartment—there was an open-plan kitchen, living and dining room with a large balcony that looked out to the beach across the road. Two bedrooms, two bathrooms and a small laundry finished it off, but it had everything she would need. She dumped her bags in the spare bedroom. Having the two bedrooms was a bonus because she didn't feel comfortable about taking over Callum's room. That felt too familiar.

The sun shone on the water of Sydney Harbour, white boats bobbed and the houses peeked out between eucalyptus trees. Luci couldn't believe how perfect it looked. She'd grown up in country South Australia, born and bred in Vickers Hill in the Clare Valley, and she'd never travelled far. Her father very rarely took holidays and when he did they spent them on the coast, but the coast she was familiar with was the Gulf of St Vincent with its calm waters, like a mill pond. It never felt like the real ocean.

Then, when she'd married her high-school sweetheart at the age of twenty-one, they'd had no money for holidays. She'd married young, as had most of her friends, but she hadn't found the happy-ever-after she'd wanted. Like so many other marriages, hers hadn't lasted and she found herself divorced and heartbroken at twenty-five.

But now, perhaps, it was time to travel. To see something of the world. She couldn't change what had happened, the past was the past. She had grieved for a year, grieved for the things she had lost—her marriage, her best friend and her dream of motherhood—but she was recovering now and she refused to believe that her life was over. Far from it. She had a chance now to reinvent herself. Her teenage dream needed some remodelling and this was her opportunity to figure out a new direction, if that's what she decided she wanted. She was finally appreciating the freedom she had been given; she was no longer defined by her status as daughter, girlfriend or wife. No one in Sydney knew anything about her. She was just Luci.

It was time to start again.

Luci turned off the shower and wrapped herself in one of the fluffy towels that she'd found in the guest bathroom. She pulled the elastic band from her hair, undoing the messy bun that had kept her shoulder-length bobbed blonde hair dry, then dried herself off. She was exhausted and she was looking forward to climbing into bed. She was far more tired than she'd expected to be. She'd spent the past three days sitting in lectures. She'd thought that would be easier than the shift work on the wards that she was used to, but it was mentally tiring.

Still, it was almost the end of her first week. Only two more days to go before the weekend. Perhaps then she'd have a chance to see something of this side of Sydney. She and Flick had walked from Bondi to Bronte and back and had spent the rest of their time relaxing. Sightseeing hadn't been high on their agenda but Luci had never visited Sydney before and she wanted to get a feel for the city.

She was familiar with the route from Callum's apartment in Fairlight to the hospital on the opposite side of the Manly peninsula as she was walking that route every day. She was getting to know the local shopkeepers and was exchanging 'good mornings' with a couple of regular dog walkers. It was a far cry from Vickers

Hill, where she couldn't take two steps down the main street without bumping into someone she knew, but she was starting to feel a little more at home here. She kept herself busy, not wanting to give herself a chance to be homesick. Being somewhere new was exciting, she told herself, and she had limited time so she needed to make the most of her opportunities.

The people in her course were getting friendlier by the day. It seemed city folk took a little longer to warm up to strangers but Luci had gone out to dinner tonight with a few of them, just a burger in Manly, but it was a start and Luci knew she'd feel even more at home after another week.

She knew where to catch the ferry to the city and she'd walked on the beach but she hadn't yet had time to test the water in the tidal swimming pool that was built into the rocks. That would be added to her list of things to do. She hadn't done nearly as much exploring as she had planned to, and if all the weeks were this busy, her two months in Sydney would fly past. She'd have to make time to see the sights, but first she needed some sleep.

She hung the towel on the rail in the bathroom, went through to her bedroom and slid naked between her bedsheets. She kept the window blinds up and the window slightly open. From the bed she could see the stars in the sky and the sound of the ocean carried to her on the warm spring air. The ocean murmured to itself as it lapped the shore. It was gentle tonight and she could imagine the waves kissing the sand, teasing gently before retreating, only to come back for more.

She dozed off to the sound of the sea.

* * *

It felt like only moments later that she woke to an unfamiliar sound. A slamming door.

She was still getting used to the different sounds and rhythms of the city. She could sleep through the early morning crowing of a rooster and the deep rumble of a tractor but the slightest noise in the middle of suburbia disturbed her. Rubbish trucks, the tooting of ferry horns, slamming of car doors and the loud conversations of late-night commuters or drinking buddies on their way home from the pub all intruded on her dreams, but this noise was louder than all of those. This noise was close.

She heard footsteps on the wooden floorboards and saw light streaming under her bedroom door as the passage light flicked on.

Shit. There was someone in the house.

She put her hand on her chest. Her heart was racing.

What should she do?

Call out?

No, that would only draw attention to herself.

Find a weapon of some sort? She'd seen a set of golf clubs but they were in a cupboard near the front door. She couldn't get to them and there was nothing in the bedroom. Maybe a shot of hair spray to the face would work—if only she used hairspray.

Should she call the police? But how quickly would they get here? Not fast enough, she assumed.

She had no idea what to do. She'd never had to fend for herself.

She sat up in bed, and scrabbled for her phone in the dark. She was too afraid to turn on the light, worried it would draw the attention of the intruder. She clutched the sheet to her chest to cover her nakedness. Perhaps she should find some clothes first. She didn't want to confront a burglar while naked.

She could hear him crossing the living room. The tread of the steps were heavy. Man heavy. She could hear boots. The steps weren't light and delicate. He wasn't making any attempt to be quiet. There was a loud thump as something soft but weighty hit the floor. It didn't sound like a person. A bag maybe? A bag of stolen goods?

Her heart was still racing and the frantic pounding almost drowned out the sound of the footsteps. That made her pause. This had to be the world's noisiest burglar. She hadn't had much experience with burglars but surely they would generally try to be quiet? This one was making absolutely no attempt to be silent. Plus he had turned the lights on. Definitely not stealthy.

He was a terrible burglar, possibly one of the worst ever.

But maybe he thought the house was empty? Perhaps she should make some noise? Enough noise for two people.

She heard the soft pop as the seal on the fridge door was broken. She frowned. Now he was looking in the fridge? Making himself at home. She was positive it wasn't Callum. Luci had spoken to Flick earlier in the day. Callum had well and truly arrived in Vickers Hill and according to her friend he was creating a bit of a stir. Luci hoped he wasn't going to prove difficult—he was supposed to be making things easier for her dad, not harder, but she couldn't do much about it. All it meant to her was that it wasn't Callum in the apartment.

And she was pretty sure by now that it wasn't a burglar either, but that still meant a stranger was in the house.

She needed to get dressed.

She switched on the bedside light and was halfway out of bed when she heard the footsteps moving along the passage. While she was debating her options she saw the bedroom door handle moving.

OMG, they were coming in.

'You'd better get out of here. I've called the police,' she yelled, not knowing what else to do.

The door handle continued to turn and a voice said, 'You've done what?'

When it became obvious that the person who belonged to the voice was intent on entering her room she jumped back into bed and pulled the covers up to her chin, grabbing her phone just in case she did need to call the cops.

'I'll scream,' she added for good measure.

But the door continued to open and a vision appeared. Luci wondered briefly if she was dreaming. Her heart was racing at a million miles an hour but now she had no clue whether it was due to nerves, fear, panic or simple lust. This intruder might just be the most gorgeous man she'd ever laid eyes on. Surely someone this gorgeous couldn't be evil?

But then Ted Bundy sprang to mind. He was a good-looking, charming, educated man who just happened to be a serial killer. 'Don't come any closer,' she said.

He stopped and held his hands out to his sides. 'I'm not going to hurt you, but who the hell are you and what are you doing in my room?' he said.

'*Your* room?'

Was this Callum? She was certain she'd chosen the

guest bedroom but, anyway, what was he doing here?
He couldn't have got back to Sydney that quickly. He
was supposed to be a thousand miles away, staying in
her house. That was how a house swap worked. 'Why
aren't you in Vickers Hill?'

'What the heck is Vickers Hill?'

Luci frowned. 'Who are you?'

He couldn't be Callum. So whose room was she in
exactly?

'Seb. Seb Hollingsworth.'

Seb.

'You're not Callum?'

A crease appeared between his superb blue eyes as
he frowned. 'No. I'm his brother.'

Luci almost missed his answer, distracted as she was
by the thick, dark eyelashes that framed his eyes.

'Brother!' Why hadn't Callum warned her? She sat
up in the bed, taking care to make sure the sheets prevented any sort of indecent exposure. 'Callum didn't
mention you.'

'So you do know Cal, then?'

'Sort of.'

He lifted one eyebrow but said nothing.

Luci could play that game too. And she used the silent seconds to examine the vision a little more closely.

He truly was gorgeous. Tall, really tall, with thick
dark hair, chestnut she'd call it. He had eyebrows to
match that shaded piercing blue eyes and a nose that
may or may not have been broken once upon a time.
His lips were full and pink, and a two-day growth of
beard darkened his jaw.

His torso was bare but he held what appeared to
be a black T-shirt in his hand. Just what had he been

planning on doing? she wondered, before she was distracted again by his broad shoulders and smooth chest. He reminded her of someone, she thought as her eyes roamed over his body.

The statue of David, she thought, brought to life. He was made of warm flesh instead of cool marble but had the same, startling level of perfection.

Her heart was still beating a rapid tattoo. Adrenaline was still coursing through her system but not out of fear. Now it was a simple chemical, or maybe hormonal, reaction.

'I think you have some explaining to do,' said the living, breathing statue.

In Luci's opinion so did Callum, Seb's absent brother, and she was blowed if she was going to explain herself while she lay in bed naked. She clutched the sheet a little more tightly across her breasts. 'Let me get dressed and then we can talk.'

The corner of Seb's mouth lifted in a wry smile and there was a wicked gleam in his blue eyes. Luci felt a burst of heat explode in her belly and she knew that the heat would taint her body with a blush of pink. She could feel the warmth spreading up over her chest and neck as Seb continued to stand in the doorway. Did he know the effect he was having on her? She had to get rid of him.

'Can you give me a minute?' she asked.

'Sure, sorry,' he replied, looking anything but sorry. 'And while you're at it,' he added, glancing at the phone that was still clutched in her hand along with the sheet, 'do you think you could ring the police and tell them it was just a misunderstanding? I don't want the neighbours getting the wrong idea.'

'I didn't actually ring the police,' Luci admitted.

He turned and left the room, pulling the door closed behind him, and she could hear him laughing, a deep, cheerful sound that lifted her spirits.

Luci waited to hear his footsteps retreat before she was brave enough to throw off the sheets once more. She climbed out of bed on shaky legs and pulled on a T-shirt and a pair of shorts. She padded down the hallway to the open-plan lounge and kitchen to find Seb with his head in the fridge, giving her a very nice view of a tidy rear covered in denim. His bare feet poked out of the bottom of his jeans.

She stepped around a pile of luggage that had been dumped beside the couch. A brown leather jacket was draped over a duffel bag and a motorbike helmet sat on the floor beside a pair of sturdy boots, the boots that had been stomping down the passage. There was a thick layer of reddish-brown dust covering everything.

She ducked through the kitchen and into the dining area, where she stood on the far side of the table, putting some distance between them. Despite the fact that he looked like something created by Michelangelo and appeared to be related to the owner of the house, she wasn't prepared to take his word for it just yet. Until she'd decided he wasn't a serial killer she wasn't taking any chances.

He stood up and turned to face her. His chest was now covered by his black T-shirt—that was a pity—and he had two small bottles of beer in his hand.

'Beer?' he asked as he raised his hand.

Luci shook her head.

He put one bottle back in the fridge, closed the door and then twisted the top off the other bottle and took a swig. He watched her as she watched him but he didn't seem as nervous as her. Not nearly.

He stepped over to the table, pulled out a chair and sat down. He pushed the chair back and stretched his legs out. He was tall. His legs were long. He was fiddling with the beer bottle and she couldn't help but notice that his fingers were long and slender too.

He lifted his eyes up to meet her gaze. 'So, sleeping beauty, do you have a name?'

'Luci.'

'Luci,' he repeated, stretching out the two syllables, and the way the 'u' rolled off his tongue did funny things to her insides.

'So where's my big brother? And why are you in my bed?'

Luci swallowed nervously. His bed? Of course, his room, his bed. That warmth in her belly spread lower now, threatening to melt her already wobbly legs just a little bit more.

'I didn't know it was your bed. I didn't know anyone else lived here.'

Callum hadn't said anything but she'd never actually spoken to Callum. Not that she was about to divulge that bit of information. That would just come across as odd. Her dad's practice manager had organised the whole house-swap thing. Luci had exchanged emails with Callum and had been intending on meeting to swap keys but he had messaged her to say his plans had changed. He'd left Sydney a day earlier than they had discussed so he'd left a key under a flowerpot for her, but she was certain he hadn't mentioned a brother. Not at any stage.

So what did this mean for her house-sitting plans? Would Seb ask her to leave? Would Callum?

'So where is he?' Seb wanted to know. 'Should I be checking the rest of the house? You haven't done away with him, have you? Did he treat you badly and you've sneaked in here to have your revenge?'

Luci laughed and wondered about the type of women Seb associated with if that was the direction his thoughts took him. 'He's in Vickers Hill.'

'Ah, Vickers Hill. You mentioned it before. Where is that exactly?' Seb arched his right eyebrow again and Luci found herself wondering if he could also do that with the left one. The idea distracted her and she almost forgot his question.

'In South Australia. In the Clare Valley,' she explained as she stepped into the kitchen. She needed to put some distance between them. To give herself something to do, she switched the kettle on, taking a mug and a green tea bag from the cupboard.

Seb took another pull of his beer. 'What is he doing there?'

'He's gone to work in a general practice. It's part of his studies.' She didn't mention that he was working with her father. If Callum wanted his brother to know what he was up to, he could tell him the finer details. But Seb not knowing Callum's movements only led to more questions. Where had Seb been? Why didn't he know what was happening? His room certainly didn't look inhabited. It had looked exactly like a guest room, which was what Luci had expected. There had been no sign of his presence other than a few clothes in the wardrobe, which she had assumed was the overflow from Callum's room. But perhaps those clothes belonged to Seb.

'So, if Cal's in Vickers Hill, what are you doing here?'

'We've done a house swap,' she replied as she poured boiled water into her mug.

'A house swap?' he repeated. 'How long are you staying?'

'Eight weeks. Until Christmas.' *Please, don't ask me to leave tonight*, she thought. She was half-resigned to the fact that her plans were about to change but she really didn't want to pack her bags and find somewhere else to stay in the middle of the night. This was her first trip to Sydney. 'If that's all right,' she added, pleading desperately. She had no idea where she'd go if he asked her to leave. Back to Bondi, she supposed, but the prospect of doing that at this late hour was not at all appealing.

Seb shrugged. 'It's Cal's house, whatever plans you've made with him stick. I just crash here when I'm in town. I called it my room but, I guess, technically it's not.'

Luci wondered where he'd been. Where he'd come from. But she was too tired to think about that now.

'I'll stay in Callum's room,' he added.

'Thank you.' She threw her tea bag in the bin and picked up her mug. 'I guess I'll see you in the morning, then.'

She took her tea and retreated. Seb looked interesting and she was certainly intrigued. He was giving her more questions than answers and she needed, wanted, to find out more, but it would have to wait. She had to get some sleep.

But sleep eluded her. She tossed and turned and wondered about Seb. Maybe she should have just stayed up and got all the answers tonight. Instead she lay in bed and made up stories in her head, filling in all the blank spaces about the handsome stranger with imagined details.

It wasn't often she got to meet a stranger. And a gorgeous, fascinating one to boot. In Vickers Hill everyone knew everyone else and their business. Meeting someone new was quite thrilling compared to what she was used to. Excitement bubbled in her chest. A whole new world of possibilities might open up to her.

She smiled to herself as she rolled over.

Things had just become interesting.

CHAPTER TWO

SEB PUT HIS empty beer bottle down on the kitchen table and stared out at the dark ocean through the branches of the eucalyptus. He could hear the waves lapping on the shore and could see the lights of the yachts rising and falling on the water. He'd missed the sound of the ocean but he wasn't thinking about the water or the boats or the lights now. He was thinking about the woman he'd found in his bed. The absolutely stunning, and very naked, woman.

It had been a surprise, to put it mildly. He detested surprises normally—experience had taught him that they were generally unpleasant—but he couldn't complain about this one. He'd found women in his bed unexpectedly before but he couldn't recall any of them being quite as attractive as Luci.

He closed his eyes but his mind was restless and he couldn't settle. He should be exhausted. He'd had a long and dusty eight-hour ride from Deniliquin and he'd been looking forward to a shower, something to eat and then bed. In that order. That had been his plan until he'd discovered Luci in his bed. His plan had been delightfully disrupted by a gorgeous naked woman.

He wasn't sure that he really understood why she

was here. Or why Cal wasn't. He hadn't spoken to his brother for several weeks. They didn't have that sort of relationship. Seb wasn't even in the habit of calling ahead to let Callum know he would be in town. They were close but unless there was a reason for a call neither of them picked up the phone. And when they did their conversations were brief, borne out of necessity only and usually avoided if possible.

Seb had tried to talk to Cal after Cal had been injured in a cricketing accident, an accident that had almost cost him his left eye, but even then they had never got to the heart of the problem. Neither of them were much good at discussing their feelings.

But despite their lack of communication they still shared a brotherly bond. They had relied on each other growing up. The sons of high-achieving surgeons, they had spent a lot of time by themselves, supervised only by nannies. Perhaps that was why they had never learned to discuss their feelings—the nannies certainly hadn't encouraged it and Seb couldn't remember many family dinners or even much support in times of crisis. Not that there had been many crises, just one big one for each of them in their adult lives. They'd been lucky really.

But their childhood bonds had remained strong and Cal had always had a bed for him. Until now. Which brought him back to the question of what Luci was really doing here. And what did it mean for him?

He ran his hands through his hair. It was thick with dust and sweat from hours encased in a helmet. He still needed a shower. The sea breeze wafted through the balcony doors, carrying with it the fresh scent of salt. Perhaps he should go for a swim instead. The cool water of Sydney Harbour might be just what he needed to stop his brain from turning in circles.

There was no light coming from under Luci's door so he stripped off his jeans in the living room and pulled a pair of swimming shorts from his duffel bag. He left his house key under the flowerpot on the back balcony and jogged barefooted down the stairs and crossed the road to the beach. The sand was cool and damp under his feet and the water was fresh.

He didn't hesitate. He took three steps into the sea and dived under the water. He surfaced several metres offshore but the water was shallow enough that he could still stand. The sea was calm and gentle and refreshing but it wasn't enough to stop his head from spinning with unanswered questions.

Vickers Hill, South Australia. He'd never heard of Vickers Hill. How the hell had Callum ever found it? But if the girls there looked like Luci, he couldn't blame him for wanting to visit.

He turned and looked back across the beach to the apartment block. It was a small complex, only three floors, and Callum's apartment took up the top floor, but there was nothing to see as it was all in darkness. But he could imagine Luci, sleeping in his bed. The image of her, at the moment he'd first seen her, filled his mind.

In his bed with the sheets pulled up to her chin, her blue-grey eyes huge with apprehension. He'd got just as much of a shock as she had but at least he'd been semi-clothed. He'd been unable to see anything but he'd known that beneath those sheets, his sheets, she had been as naked as the day she was born.

As she had sat up in bed the covers had slipped

down, exposing the swell of her breasts, before she'd clutched the sheet tightly, pulling it firmly across her chest. He'd had his T-shirt in his hand, halfway to the shower when he'd discovered her, and he'd had to surreptitiously move his hand so the T-shirt had covered his groin and his reaction. It had been pure and primal. Lust, desire.

He knew he'd let his eyes linger on her for a few seconds too long to be considered polite. Had she noticed?

Her eyes had watched him carefully. Her face was round with a heart-shaped chin and she had lips like a ripe peach. She was thin but not skinny and she had firm, round breasts that it was impossible not to notice. He'd seen them rise and fall under the sheet as she'd panicked. He could have happily watched her breathing all night.

His eyes had been drawn to four small, dark freckles that made a diamond shape against the pale skin on her chest. One sat about an inch below her collarbone, another on the swell of her right breast with a matching one on the left, and the fourth one, the one that formed the bottom of the diamond, was tucked into her cleavage. The pattern was stamped on his memory.

He should have given her some privacy, backed out of the room, but he'd been transfixed.

He closed his eyes now and floated on his back but he could still see Luci's pale skin decorated with the perfect diamond imprinted on the backs of his eyelids. It was late and he was physically exhausted but he knew there was no way he'd be able to sleep. Not yet.

He flipped onto his front and swam further into the harbour. In the pale starlight he could see the outline of his boat tied to its mooring. With long, fluid strokes he passed several other boats floating on the water as he swam out to his cabin cruiser.

His hands gripped the ladder at the stern and he pulled himself up onto the small ledge at the rear. He ran his hand over the smooth, sleek lines of the cabin as he made his way round to the large, flat bow. He stretched, resting his back against the windscreen. This boat was his sanctuary. He'd bought it almost three years ago as a project. It had good lines and plenty of potential and had been advertised as needing some TLC or a handyman's touch. He was no builder but he was good with his hands and he'd figured the learning curve would keep his mind occupied, which was just what he'd needed at the time. He had needed a project, a focus, something to keep him busy, so he could avoid dealing with his alternate reality.

Three years down the track he had made good progress emotionally but he couldn't say the same about the boat. It was still far from finished, although he had managed to get it to the stage where he could enjoy a day out. The engine worked, as did the toilet, but the kitchen and sleeping berths still needed serious attention. That was his current project, one he intended to finish while he was back in Sydney this time. He had an appointment scheduled for tomorrow evening to meet a cabinet-maker who was, hopefully, going to make new cupboards for the kitchen. While it was far from perfect, it didn't matter. It was perfect for him.

The boat represented freedom.

Seb didn't want to be tied down and the boat gave him a sense of having a place in the world without commitment. Eventually, when the renovation was completed, he planned to live aboard. Having a boat as his place of residence appealed immensely as he could close it up and leave or take it with him. It would be a fluid living arrangement, transient enough that he didn't have to think of living aboard as settling down. It wasn't a big commitment.

He wasn't ready for commitment. He'd tried it once, with disastrous results.

Luckily for him Callum didn't show any signs of settling down either, which meant he always had a place to crash. It was reassuring to know that he had a place to stay that didn't require any commitment from him. Was that immature behaviour? Perhaps. Irresponsible? Maybe. He hadn't thought about what he'd do if Callum ever did settle down. At least he hadn't until tonight.

Seeing someone else in his room—he always thought of it as his, even though he was an infrequent visitor—seeing Luci in his bed, made him wonder what he would do if Callum ever wanted to make changes. What if he wanted to rent out that room or live with a girlfriend? Either one would put *him* out on the street.

Was he being selfish? Taking advantage of Callum's generosity? Was it time he grew up and stopped relying on his big brother?

But no matter what Cal's intentions were, being tossed out onto the street by Luci was still a possibility if she was uncomfortable about having him share her space. He'd told her he would stick with Callum's plan but what if she decided she didn't want him there?

One thing at a time, he decided. He'd only been back for five minutes. It wasn't worth wasting time worrying about things that might not happen. It was far more enjoyable to spend his time thinking about a pretty blonde who was curled up in his bed.

Seb laced his fingers together and rested his hands behind his head as he looked up at the sky. There were no clouds, the sky was dark and clear, the stars bright against the inky blackness. He picked out the Southern Cross, its familiar diamond shape marking the sky reminding him of the other diamond he'd seen earlier.

Things were about to become interesting.

Luci was up early. She showered and grabbed a piece of fruit for breakfast, trying to keep the noise to a minimum. There was no sound from Seb's room and she didn't want to disturb him. She hadn't heard him come back in last night but his motorbike helmet, jacket and boots were still piled on the living room floor so she assumed he was sleeping. She stuffed her laptop into her bag and slung it across her body, biting into her apple as she walked out the front door.

Today was her last full day of lectures. Tomorrow she and the other nineteen registered and enrolled nurses would have orientation at whichever child and family health centre they had been assigned to for their placements, and the course would then become a mixture of theory and practice. Luci was looking forward to getting out of the lecture room and dipping her toe into the world of family and community health.

The lectures had been interesting but she wasn't used to sitting down all day. The training room was an internal one in the hospital. It was small and windowless and by the end of the day Luci was itching to get outside into the fresh air. She was planning on taking a walk along Manly beach to clear the cobwebs from her mind. She stretched her arms and back and rolled her shoulders as the group waited for the final lecturer of the day. The topic for the last session was indigenous health, which had the potential to be interesting, but Luci didn't envy the lecturer their four o'clock times-lot. She doubted she was the only one who was think-ing ahead to the end of the day.

Luci heard the sound of the door click open and swing shut. It was followed by a murmur from the back of the room that intensified in volume as it swept down the stairs. The room had half a dozen rows of tiered seating and she was sitting near the front. The room was buzzing and Luci turned her head to see what had got everyone so excited.

Seb was at the end of her row, about to step down to the front of the room. What on earth was he doing here?

He shrugged out of his leather jacket and dropped his motorbike helmet on a chair. He was dressed casually in sand-coloured cotton trousers and a chambray blue shirt that brought out the colour of his eyes.

He looked seriously hot.

He pulled a USB stick from his shirt pocket and plugged it into the computer. *He was the lecturer?*

He looked up, ready to address the room, and his eyes scanned the group, running over the twenty or so attendees. Luci's stomach was churning with nerves and her palms were sweaty as she waited for him to pick her out in the room. It didn't take long.

He spotted her in the front row and smiled. His blue eyes were intensely bright in his ridiculously handsome face and Luci swore the entire room, including the two male nurses, caught their collective breath. Her knees wobbled and she was glad she was already sitting down.

'Hello.' He was looking straight at her and everything around her dissolved in a haze as she melted into his gaze. 'I am Dr Seb Hollingsworth.'

Dr! Did he just say Dr? The motorbike-riding, leather-jacketed, living, breathing marble statue was a doctor? Somehow he'd let that little piece of information slide.

Luci missed the rest of his introduction as she tried to remember if she'd told him what she did. She'd talked about the house swap but perhaps she hadn't told him she was a nurse, which might explain why he hadn't mentioned he was a doctor. It was hard to remember anything when he was standing right in front of her, looking at her a bit too often with his bright blue eyes.

His voice was strong and deep and confident and Luci could feel it roll through her like waves rolling onto the shore. His voice caressed her and she was tempted to close her eyes as she listened. Maybe then she would be able to concentrate.

He was talking confidently about the cultural differences between the indigenous communities and those families with European backgrounds and the impact that had on the health of the children.

'Indigenous families are often reluctant to bring their children to the health clinics because of the lessons history has taught them. Many are fearful but we know that early intervention and health checks save lives. Education is the key, not only by the health professionals but also by the schools. We know that educated people have a better standard of living and better health. We have been running playgroups and early learning sessions to encourage the families to come to the clinics and the hope is that the parents will then feel comfortable enough to enrol their kids in school. Our current focus from a health perspective is on nutrition and family support so for any of you who will spend time working with these communities during your placements you'll need to be aware of the cultural sensitivities.'

Luci knew she should be taking notes but she was too busy watching and listening. She hadn't been able to keep her eyes closed. It was too tempting to watch him. And she knew where to find him if she had any questions.

'Funding is an issue—nothing new there,' he was saying, 'but the health department will continue to lobby for that. Our stats show there are benefits with these early intervention health programmes.'

There were lots of questions as Seb tried to wrap up his session. Luci guessed they all wanted to prolong the time that he spent in the room and even when he dismissed the class several of them crowded around him like kids around the ice-cream truck.

Luci gathered her notebook and laptop and shoved them into her bag. She wasn't going to hang around. If he was finished by the time she was packed up she'd stop and talk to him, otherwise she'd leave. She picked up her bag and started up the steps.

'Luci! Can you wait a moment?' Seb's voice stopped her in her tracks.

She hesitated. She had nowhere she had to rush off to. She had no reason not to wait. She dumped her bag on a chair and sat down, aware that some of the other girls were looking at her curiously. That was okay. She was used to being stared at and talked about.

Seb finished his discussions with the other students and came over to her.

'*Dr* Hollingsworth?' Luci was determined to get the first words in but that didn't seem to faze Seb.

'Nurse Luci.' He was smiling at her, making her insides turn somersaults. Again. 'Have you got time for a drink?'

'Why?'

'It seems we have some things to discuss, I thought it might be nice to share our secrets over a drink.'

'I don't have any secrets,' she fibbed.

His grin widened. 'Everyone has secrets,' he said. He had his jacket and helmet tucked under one arm and he picked up Luci's bag with his other hand. 'Come on, I'll give you a lift.'

'Where are we going?'

Seb smirked, obviously sensing victory, and replied, 'The Sandman, it's about halfway down the beach.'

The bar was on North Steyne Street, a little over a kilometre away. Luci had walked past it before. 'I'll meet you there,' she said. The walk would give her a chance to clear her head and hopefully time to get over her jitters. She wasn't sure if this was a good idea but she couldn't think of an excuse on the spot. She couldn't think of anything much when Seb looked at her and smiled.

Luci took her bag from Seb and slung it over her shoulder. When she reached the beach she rolled up the legs of her khaki pants and slid her canvas sneakers off her feet and walked along the sand. The late-afternoon sun bounced off the waves, turning the water silver. Kids with surfboards ran in and out of the ocean, their shouts drowning out the screeching of the seagulls. The beach was busy. She didn't know a soul but she was fine with that. Back home she couldn't walk down the street without bumping into half a dozen people she knew and it was a pleasant change to have anonymity, especially after the past six months. It wasn't always so great having everyone know your business.

She stepped off the beach opposite the bar. She walked on the grass to brush the sand from her feet then slipped her shoes back on. Seb had beaten her there and he lifted a hand in greeting as she crossed the street. As if she wouldn't have noticed him—the bar was busy but he was easily the most noticeable person there.

Somehow, despite the crowd, he'd managed to grab a table with a view of the beach. He stood up as she approached and offered her a stool, his motorbike helmet on a third stool, like a chaperone.

'What can I get you to drink?'

'What are you going to have?'

'A beer.'

'That sounds great, thank you.'

Sturdy Norfolk pines lined the foreshore, guarding the beach, and Luci watched the ocean through the frame of the trees. She took her phone out of her bag as Seb went to the bar and snapped a photo of the view. She sent it to Flick captioned, After-work drinks, could get used to this! But she resisted saying anything about the company she was keeping. There was no way to describe how he made her feel. Nervous, excited, expectant. She was silly to feel those things, she knew nothing about him, and she knew she couldn't share her thoughts, Flick would think she'd gone crazy.

She slipped her phone into her bag as Seb came back to the table.

He handed her a glass. 'So, you're a nurse?'

'And you're a doctor.'

'I am. Is that how you met Callum? Through the hospital? How come I've never met you?'

Luci laughed. 'Which question do you want me to answer first?'

'Your choice.'

He was looking at her intently and her heart pounded in her chest. He made her feel nervous—a gorgeous man paying her attention. It was such an unfamiliar situation but she would have to admit she rather liked it. She didn't even mind the nerves. It was exciting.

She took a sip of her beer as she thought about which answer to give him.

'I've never actually met your brother. And I've never been to Sydney before, which would be why we've never met. Callum needed a place to stay and so did I. The house swap was convenient for both of us. Nothing more than that.'

Luci had been restless since her divorce and Flick had been pushing her to get out of Vickers Hill, but she'd needed more than a push. She was buying her ex's share of their house and she couldn't afford to pay her mortgage and rent elsewhere so it wasn't until the house-swap idea had been suggested that she'd been brave enough to actually put a plan in motion. Having the opportunity to study *and* have free accommodation had been a big deciding factor for her. Which brought her back to the matter at hand. Where was she going to be able to stay now? It would be extremely inconvenient if she had to change her plans.

'Callum didn't tell me that he had any other tenants,' she said. 'I suppose I could look into nurses' accommodation through the hospital if you want me to move out. Do you know if the hospital has any student accommodation? I'm afraid I don't know anyone in Sydney to stay with.'

Seb shook his head. 'You have more right to be there than I do. I told you, whatever plans you made with him stick. It's his place and I'm not even technically a tenant. I only crash there when I come to town. I can ask one of my mates to put me up.'

'When you come to town?' Luci queried. 'You're not employed at North Sydney?' She had assumed he was a staff doctor. 'Are you just a guest lecturer?'

'Not exactly.' Seb picked up his glass and Luci's eyes followed the path of his drink from the table to his lips. She watched as he took a long sip. She could scarcely believe she was sitting at a bar, having a drink with a stranger. She'd never been out with a man she'd just met. Not one on one. For as long as she could remember she had been part of a couple.

Seb made her feel nervous. But it was a good kind of nervous. An exciting kind.

He swallowed his beer and continued, 'I'm employed by the state health department and I'm based out of North Sydney Hospital but I spend most of my time in rural areas. There doesn't seem to be much point paying rent in the city, especially not at Sydney prices, for the few nights a month that I'm in town so I crash at Cal's.'

Disappointment washed over her. He was only in town a few nights a month. Did that mean he'd be gone again soon?

'If you're only here for a few days then I'm sure we can manage to share the space,' she suggested, hoping she sounded friendly and hospitable rather than desperate, but the truth was she'd quite like the company. While she was enjoying her anonymity she'd never lived on her own before—she'd left home and moved into university accommodation and then married Ben. She was finding Callum's apartment a bit too quiet. She liked the idea of having company and she had a feeling she could do a lot worse than Seb's.

'I need to be honest,' he replied. 'I'm here for longer than a few days this time, it'll be closer to six weeks, and in the interests of full disclosure I'll be working out of the community health centre attached to the hospital. Where will you be doing your placement?'

'There.' Because Luci was from interstate she'd been given the most convenient placement.

'So we'll be working together too,' Seb added, 'but if you're happy to share Cal's space for a few days, we could give it a trial and see how we go.' He smiled at her and Luci's heart flipped in her chest. 'If it doesn't work out, I'll find somewhere else to stay. How's that sound?'

It sounded all right to her but she paused while she pretended to give it some thought. She nodded. 'Okay.'

'That's settled, then.' He tapped his drink against hers. 'House mates it is.' He sipped his beer and asked, 'So tell me about Vickers Hill. Your family is there?'

Luci nodded. 'My parents. I work at the local hospital.'

'Is it a big town?'

'Big enough to need a hospital. Your typical country hospital. We have obstetrics and some aged-care beds and we do some minor surgery as well.'

'So why the change to family and community health?'

'I needed to get out.'

'Of the hospital?'

Luci shook her head. 'Of Vickers Hill.'

'Why?'

Luci sighed quietly. There was no point keeping everything a secret as she figured he'd find out most of it eventually anyway. His brother was in Vickers Hill, working with her father. There would be no secrets. Not that her father would talk about her but Luci knew there were patients who couldn't resist gossip. And if Callum looked anything like Seb did, Luci knew there'd be no shortage of patients booking appointments with the new doctor. 'I got divorced six months ago and I just felt I needed to get out of town for a while.'

'Has it been messy?'

'Not messy so much as awkward. My dad is the local doctor—Callum has gone to work in his clinic,' she explained, 'so everyone, and I mean everyone, knows me. My ex-husband and I grew up together, we dated since high school, got married at twenty-one and divorced at twenty-five.'

'You were together, what, ten years?'

'About that.'

'That's a long time. This must be tough for you.'

No one else, other than Flick and her parents, had really understood how her divorce had impacted on her but Seb had hit the nail on the head immediately.

Her divorce had turned her world upside down. Every day of her life had included Ben. He was part of her history. Their friendship and relationship had shaped her into the person she was today and it had been difficult to separate herself into her own person. Ben was wrapped up in her identity and she was having to shape a new one for herself. It had been tough. Really tough.

Perhaps it was the distance lending Seb perspective.

Everyone at home seemed to be having just as much difficulty adjusting to Luci being single as she was, which was partly why she had decided, or agreed with Flick's suggestion, to leave. The locals weren't moving on as quickly as she would like, which had made things even more difficult for her. It had taken her a lot of adjusting but she was finally coming to terms with the end of her marriage, and she felt the process would be faster if she didn't have to contend with local opinion as well.

'It has been rough,' she admitted. 'I reckon a divorce is sad and stressful enough, without having an entire town involved. Because everyone knew us, had seen us grow up, they all seemed to think that our divorce was somehow their business. I was tired of everyone either feeling sorry for me because I couldn't keep my husband or offering to set me up with their nephew, grandson or best friend's boy.'

'So you ran away?'

He was watching her closely and Luci could feel herself starting to blush. She wasn't used to such close attention. She turned away, breaking eye contact. 'It was time for a change.'

Feeling sorry for herself was self-indulgent. She needed to move on but in a town where everyone knew her business that was hard to do. The truth was she hadn't coped well at all but that was none of their business. That's why Flick had been able to talk her into this crazy idea to take a study break in Sydney, and looking around her now she had to admit that it hadn't been such a mad idea after all. She was actually feeling like she was able to put her marriage behind her. But the demise of her marriage had also cost her the chance of motherhood and that wasn't so easy to come to terms with.

But she preferred to think she was running towards her future rather than away from her past. She didn't want to get pigeonholed, which was the danger if she'd stayed put, but there was no need to explain everything. Seb didn't need to know it all. Unlike at home, she could choose to keep her secrets. This was her opportunity to tell people only what she wanted them to know and she intended to make the most of it.

'Well, I reckon there's plenty in Sydney to keep you so busy that you won't have time to think. And I promise not to introduce you to any eligible men. Unless you ask me to,' he added. He finished his beer, pushed back the cuff of his shirt and looked at his watch. 'I have a meeting to get to but can I give you a lift home first?' he asked as he picked up his helmet.

'That would be great,' she said, but she should have said no.

Seb offered her his leather jacket to wear for protection, just in case something untoward happened. His hands brushed hers as he slid the jacket over her arms and when his fingers brushed her neck as he fastened the strap of his spare helmet under her chin Luci thought she might melt on the spot. And she still had to get on the bike and sit behind him and wrap her arms around his waist. She wasn't sure her brain could be trusted to convey all those messages.

She should have declined his offer, she'd remember that next time.

But it was too late now. She'd been on a motorbike before. It was probably no different from cycling—it would all come back to her once she got on. Her ex had a trail bike that he'd used to ride around his parents' property and to school. He would pick her up every morning and give her a lift, but they'd been seventeen then. She couldn't remember the last time she'd ridden on the back of his bike, and as she wrapped her arms around Seb's waist and felt his body heat radiating into her she thought she certainly didn't remember feeling like this.

The bike vibrated between her thighs. She pressed her legs into the seat as she held on tight. Her face was tucked against his shoulder blade and she could smell him. He smelt fresh and tangy; there was a trace of citrus in his aftershave, lime perhaps.

She probably should have walked home but she was glad she hadn't. She was quite happy right where she was.

CHAPTER THREE

LUCI'S MORNING STARTED with orientation at the family and community health clinic attached to North Sydney Hospital. She spent the morning getting her ID, setting up her email and running through the safety policies and procedures for the site. Once the administration side of things had been dealt with, she would start work. The course participants would be given a case load as the service tried to get through their waiting list. The system was under the pump, there were always more people who needed the service.

Her diary showed her running an immunisation clinic. It was an easy, straightforward introduction that didn't require her to have detailed backgrounds or rapport with the clients. She worked steadily through the hours after lunch. She had bumped into Seb once but it seemed that the staff worked autonomously and she was almost able to forget that he was there. Almost.

But all that changed when her two-thirty client didn't keep her appointment. Melanie Parsons had booked her son, Milo, in for his six-month check and immunisations. When she failed to arrive Luci pulled up her file on the computer. There were numerous entries and lots of red flags.

This woman was a victim of domestic violence. Her past medical history included three full-term pregnancies, one miscarriage and a long list of broken bones and medical treatment for bruising and lacerations. And they were only the things she'd consulted a doctor about. Luci would bet her house that there were more incidents that had gone unreported.

Luci picked up the phone and dialled the client's number. The community health centre's policy stated that all no-shows had to be followed up with a phone call. She checked the file again. It was possible that Melanie had just forgotten her appointment or was catching up on some sleep; it couldn't be easy having three children under the age of five.

But the phone went unanswered.

Luci needed to be able to record a reason for the non-attendance. In instances where that wasn't possible she had been told to let the co-ordinator know. She went to discuss the situation with Gayle, the health centre co-ordinator, to find out what the next step in the process was.

Gayle brought Melanie's notes up in her system.

'Can you discuss this with Dr Hollingsworth?' she suggested. 'He knows Melanie, he's treated her before.'

Luci heard the unspoken words and she'd seen the supporting evidence in Melanie's file. Seb had treated her for injuries sustained at the hands of someone else.

She knocked on Seb's open door.

'Have you got a minute?' she asked. He was entering notes into the computer system. He looked up and smiled. His blue eyes sparkled and Luci felt herself start to blush.

'Sure.'

She stepped inside and closed his door. She didn't want anyone else to overhear the conversation. 'Melanie Parsons. Do you know her?'

Seb nodded. 'Is she here?'

'No. She had an appointment to get her baby's six-month immunisations but she hasn't shown up. Gayle suggested I talk to you about her.'

'Have you called her?'

'Yes. There was no answer.'

'Do you know her history?'

Luci nodded. 'I've read her file.'

'Someone will need to call past her house and check on her. What time do you finish?'

'I don't think I should be the one to do a home visit,' Luci objected. 'She doesn't know me from a bar of soap.' She was not the right person for that particular job. Someone who had already established some rapport with Melanie would be far more suitable.

'I agree. But if our timing is right we can go together. You can immunise the baby and I'll see what's up with Melanie,' Seb replied. He clicked his mouse and opened his diary. 'I should be finished by three-thirty. Let me know if that works for you.'

Seb was waiting at Reception for her when she finished her clinic. 'Do you want me to drive or navigate?' he asked her as he signed out one of the work cars and collected the keys.

'I don't think I'm game to drive on your roads,' Luci replied. The streets of Sydney were narrow, winding and steep, not at all like the wide, straight roads she was used to. 'But I should warn you, my navigating skills might not be much good either as I'm not familiar with Sydney.'

'No worries. I'll get the map up on my phone.' Seb handed her his phone and she followed him out to the car.

It wasn't long before Seb pulled to a stop in front of a squat red-brick house. It had a low wire fence and a front lawn that needed mowing. There was an old station wagon parked under a carport at the side of the house and a couple of kids' bikes were lying abandoned behind the car in the driveway. The house could do with a coat of paint but it looked lived in rather than neglected. Luci had seen plenty of houses just like it in country towns in her district.

The driveway gate squeaked as Seb pushed it open, announcing their arrival. He closed it behind Luci before leading the way up the concrete path to the veranda. He knocked but there was no answer. The screen door was locked but the front door was ajar. Someone was home. Luci could hear the sound of children playing.

'Melanie?' Seb called out. 'It's Dr Hollingsworth. You missed Milo's appointment at the clinic. I need to know that you are okay.'

Through the screen door Luci could see movement in the dark passage. A woman came to the door but didn't unlatch it. She stood, half-hidden behind the door with her face turned away from them to her left.

'Hello, Melanie.' Seb struck up a conversation as if it was perfectly normal to talk through a door. 'Milo was due for his six-month check-up and vaccinations today. This is Luci Dawson.' He lifted a hand and gestured towards Luci. 'She's a nurse at the health centre.

Seeing as we're here and you're home, can we come in and see the kids?'

Melanie nodded. She unlocked the door and stepped aside. She was thin. Luci knew they were the same age but Melanie looked older. Her shoulder-length brown hair was lank but her skin was clear. However, Luci didn't really take any of that in. She couldn't when all she could see was Melanie's black eye. Her left eye was slightly swollen and coloured purple with just a hint of green. The bruise looked to be a day or two old.

'Thank you,' Seb said, as he stepped into the hall and reached for Melanie's chin. Luci expected her to flinch or pull away but she didn't. She must trust Seb.

Luci knew Seb had looked after her before. He'd filled her in on his involvement on the drive over here but Luci hadn't anticipated that she would see the evidence of Melanie's husband's abuse for herself. She hadn't been expecting that.

Seb turned Melanie's face to the right.

'You're hurt.'

'I knocked into the corner of the car boot.' Melanie's eyes were downcast.

'I haven't heard that one before.'

'It's nothing. I've had worse. You know I have,' she said, as she turned away and led them into the house. They followed her into a tired-looking sitting room. The arms of the couch were ripped and stained but Melanie had put a sheet over the cushions in an attempt to brighten the room or maybe disguise the state of the furniture. Everything looked well worn and tired. A bit like Melanie.

She collapsed onto the couch and Seb pulled an upright dining chair closer to the couch and sat on it, facing Melanie. 'What was it this time?'

'It's not his fault, Dr Hollingsworth. I'm pregnant again.'

'And how is that not his fault?' Seb's voice was quiet. He wasn't judging her but Luci could tell he was frustrated.

'He says we can't afford more kids.'

'It takes two, Melanie. He can't blame you.'

Melanie kept her eyes downcast. She had her hands in her lap, clenched together, and Luci knew she was close to tears. Luci wanted to tell Seb to let it go but she knew he couldn't. They couldn't ignore what was going on here. She knew from Melanie's file that she already had three kids—Milo, who was six months old, a two-and-a-half-year-old toddler and a four-year-old. That was a handful for anyone, let alone a woman with an abusive partner.

Seb had told her that he had advised Melanie to take her kids and leave. She had left once but had then gone back, making the usual excuses about him being the kids' father and saying that she loved him. Luci knew it was a difficult decision and something that was hard to understand unless you'd been in that position yourself or had worked with victims of domestic violence. The women were often trapped by their circumstances and Luci suspected that would be the case for Melanie. With three kids under five it was unlikely she had time to work, which meant she had no source of income if she left. And potentially no roof over her head either.

Even while Luci realised it wouldn't be easy, she couldn't stop the twinge of jealousy that she felt when she heard that Melanie was pregnant again. Luci would give her right arm for a family.

But she knew she had to put her own issues aside. Her job, their job, was to help Melanie. Luci wanted to jump in, she had suggestions on how to assist Melanie to change her situation, but Seb must have sensed her desire to offer her opinion and he put a stop to it by asking her to do Milo's health check. Did he think Melanie would open up more if she wasn't in the room? He was probably right. Melanie was unlikely to want to discuss her problems in front of a stranger.

'Milo hasn't had a cold or been unwell?' Luci clarified with Melanie. 'Any concerns at all?' she asked, figuring that as Melanie had three children she would know what to look out for by now.

Melanie shook her head. 'He's been fine. He's on baby formula now and some solids. He's in the room across the hall.'

'No ear infections, colds or reaction to any other immunisations?'

'No.'

Luci picked up her nursing bag and crossed the hall and found herself in a child's bedroom. A bunk bed stood against one wall and Milo's cot was in the opposite corner. He was lying in his cot but he was awake. His eyes followed her as she came towards him.

There was a change mat leaning against the cot and she put it on the bottom bunk. She chatted softly to Milo as she lifted him out of the cot. She could smell a dirty nappy. She laid him down and undressed him, removing his nappy and singlet. She needed to check his hips and testes and it would also give her a chance to check for any bruises or other signs of maltreatment. She was relieved to find nothing. His soft baby skin was unmarked and besides his dirty nappy he was perfectly clean and seemingly well cared for. She found a clean nappy and his blue health-care book on a shelf. She changed his nappy and listened to his chest then recorded his length and weight. He was in the average range for both. He seemed like a happy, healthy little boy.

She gave him his oral polio vaccine and then his immunisation injection and then she couldn't resist a cuddle. She took a deep breath, getting her fill of tiny baby smell. He smelt like talcum powder and baby lotion and the smell made her heart ache. She closed her eyes and wondered if coming to Sydney to study family and community health had been the right decision. She'd been so keen to escape Vickers Hill that she hadn't really considered the ramifications of taking the course. She was going to be exposed to plenty of babies and pregnant mothers. Perhaps she should have enrolled in an aged-care course instead.

Milo was grizzling a little after his injection so Luci took him back with her and handed him to his mum. She recorded the details of the vaccinations in the little blue book while she listened to Seb's conversation with Melanie.

'It's worse when he's been drinking,' she was saying.

'Today is Friday. I suppose he'll be going to the pub after work tonight?' Seb asked. When Melanie nodded he continued, 'Is there someone you could ask to come over? A friend, your mum or a sister? If you are going to stay here then I think it would be wise to have someone else here with you for support when he gets home.'

Melanie wouldn't maintain eye contact and Luci knew she had no intention of following Seb's suggestion.

'Your decision, Melanie,' Seb said as he stood up. Perhaps he realised he was getting nowhere. 'But I will be checking to make sure you keep the appointment that I'll make for you with the counsellor, okay?'

He gathered his things and Luci went with him out to the car.

'We can't just leave her there,' Luci exploded as she clicked her seat belt into position. She'd been fighting to keep her temper under control and had just managed to hold it together until they had some privacy.

'What else do you suggest we do?' Seb asked. 'She doesn't want to leave and when she has left in the past it's never been for long. She always goes back. We have to pick our battles.'

'But she should be thinking about the children.'

'Melanie says he's never hurt them. Did you see anything to indicate otherwise?'

'No.' Luci shook her head. 'Milo was perfectly healthy and happy but still it's no way for those children to grow up. They shouldn't have to see that, plus it perpetuates the cycle of abuse.'

'I know that. Trust me, we're working on it. I will make an appointment for her to see a counsellor. For us to be able to make any real difference we need to support Melanie to find a way out of this. She will need somewhere to live and she will need money. There is new legislation that can force the perpetrator to leave the premises so that the victim can stay in their home, but I'm not convinced that is a workable solution. It makes it far too easy for the abusive party to find the victim. Court orders ordering them to stay away are violated on a regular basis. This is a problem that can't be fixed overnight and it can't be fixed unless Melanie wants it to change, but I promise I will be doing everything I can.'

Luci nodded. 'I'm sorry,' she apologised. She should have guessed Seb would do what he thought was best. 'I jumped down your throat.'

'It's okay. I know it's hard to understand when you're strong and independent how someone else can put up with circumstances that you would never dream of tolerating. But try to see it from Melanie's point of view. She feels she doesn't have any other option. Again it's about education and support. But these things take time. Not everyone can just up and leave. If you want to work in community health you're going to need to have patience and empathy. Don't stop wanting better things for people but don't expect them all to be like you.'

Luci got off her high horse. She knew all that. She didn't have to look too hard to find the similarities between her situation and Melanie's. She understood how much effort and energy and strength it took to leave the familiar. She hadn't left Vickers Hill without a push from Flick, and her circumstances were far better than Melanie's. She'd only had to leave behind an ex-husband—one who had never beaten her, just one who'd decided he wanted a different life. She knew she couldn't be critical of Melanie or Seb.

'Now, let's talk about something else,' Seb said as he turned onto the main road. 'Something happier. What are your plans for the weekend?'

'I should be studying,' she replied, as she tried to put Melanie and her circumstances out of her mind. Seb had said he would monitor the situation and she had to trust him to do that. 'I have an assignment due Monday.'

'How long do you need?'

'I'm not sure. Why?'

Seb shrugged. 'You said you've never been to Sydney before. I have a free day tomorrow. If you like, I could show you around.'

She should get started on her assignment but when faced with a choice between spending her day with a gorgeous tourist guide or her laptop it was a no brainer. If she got started on her assignment tonight she should be able to finish it on Sunday. She'd get it done on time even if it meant staying up all night. She wasn't about to knock back Seb's invitation.

'I'd love that, thank you.'

There was a sticky note from Seb stuck on the kettle. In two days he'd figured out that the first thing she did every morning was switch the kettle on. She smiled as she read the note and waited for the water to boil.

Meet me on the beach at ten a.m. Bring togs, a hat and sunglasses.

Excitement swirled in her belly. She knew she needed to get her assignment finished but she'd just work all day tomorrow. She wasn't going to miss this opportunity for sightseeing or spending time with Seb. In just a couple of days she could already feel herself changing, becoming the person she thought she could be. She was leaving the old Luci behind. Leaving behind the doubts and the failures. This was her time to start again, to step through the doorway and into her future, and it felt like Seb could help open the door.

She slipped a white cotton sundress over her black bikini, sunglasses over her eyes and a soft, straw hat onto her head. Figuring she'd need a towel if she needed her bathers, she stuffed one and some sunscreen into a bag and headed to the beach across the road.

The beach was small, really only a cove, and apart from a couple and their dog it was empty. Luci scanned up and down along the sand but she couldn't see any sign of Seb. Assuming he wouldn't be far, she sat on the sand and looked out to sea. Little boats bobbed on the water at their moorings, but there were a lot fewer than normal. People must have headed out for the day. The weather was perfect for boating, the sky bright blue and cloudless, the water relatively calm, and the sun was already warm.

Movement to her right caught her eye and she watched as a man rowed a dinghy towards the shore. He had his back to her and was bare to the waist, and she watched the muscles in his back flex and relax as he pulled the oars through the water. As the boat got closer she realised the oarsman was Seb. She barely knew him and it wasn't like she could recognise his movement patterns or even the shape of his shoulders and torso yet, but she recognised the funny fluttery feeling in her stomach that she got when he was nearby.

The boat ran aground and he stowed the oars and jumped out in one fluid and graceful movement. He turned and smiled when he saw her waiting there. His hair was wet, it looked darker than his normal chestnut, and his bare chest was lightly tanned and perfectly sculpted. His swimming trunks were damp and clung to his thighs. She swallowed as the fluttery feeling in her stomach intensified.

'Good morning,' he greeted her.

'Good morning,' she replied, hoping the sun was hiding the blush that she could feel stealing over her cheeks.

He reached out a hand and helped her to her feet. His hand was warm and strong but his grip was gentle. The butterflies in her stomach went crazy.

'You're ready?' he asked her.

'Where are we going?'

'Out on the harbour.'

Luci looked doubtfully at the boat at the water's edge. 'In that?'

Was he kidding? The boat was barely ten feet long and had no motor.

'At first.' He was laughing at her discomfort. 'You're not a sailor?'

'I grew up in the country. This looks a little small,' she said, as she stood and surveyed the little vessel.

'It's okay. I have a bigger boat.' He smiled at her and Luci noticed that his eyes were the same bright blue as the sky. 'This is just the tender to get us out there. Hop in.'

He took her bag and held her hand as he helped her into the dinghy. Her body came to life with his touch. The butterflies took flight and swarmed out of her stomach and lodged in her throat. She didn't think she could breathe. But he had to let go of her to push the boat off the beach and then she was able to inhale a lungful of salty sea air.

He spun the boat around and jumped in, sitting on the seat opposite her. Their knees were almost touching.

He gripped the oars and pulled through the water. She could see his muscles straining. His biceps and triceps alternately tensed and relaxed. His pectoral muscles flexed in his chest. His abdominal muscles were taut. She could feel a blush deepening on her cheeks. She looked out at the harbour as she tried to get herself under control.

'What is your boat called?' she asked, as she scanned the yachts, reading the names painted on the hulls.

'She doesn't have a name yet. She needs a bit of work and once she's finished I'll work out what to call her. It will depend on how she feels.'

'She?'

'All boats are female.'

'Why is that?'

'I'm not sure.' He grinned and she suspected he was about to spin her a story. 'Probably because no matter how much money you spend on them, it's never enough.'

'Hey, that's not fair,' she argued, as he laughed. 'We're not all high maintenance.'

'Well, I hope *you're* not because you might be disappointed by today if you are.'

Luci doubted that. In her opinion the day was already off to a very good start.

Seb pulled the dinghy to a stop beside a sleek white cabin cruiser, then secured the tender before stepping on board and reaching for her hand. Luci was prepared for her reaction to his touch this time and managed to take a deep breath before she took his hand. He helped her on board and then picked up a boathook and dragged a mooring rope closer and tied off the tender.

'Come, I'll give you a tour before we take off.'

'A tour?' Of what? she wondered. Surely there wasn't much to see?

He opened a small gate at the rear of the boat and Luci stepped off the back ledge. There was a steering wheel with a driver's seat and a small bench seat ran perpendicular to that along the left-hand side of the boat. Luci knew that left and right weren't called that on a boat but she didn't know much else.

Seb put her bag on the seat. 'Follow me,' he said as he ducked his head and made his way down three small steps into the front of the boat.

Luci hadn't noticed the steps until Seb showed her but she did as she was told, finding herself in a compact cabin. A kitchen bench complete with a sink ran along the wall to her right and a small table surrounded by a bench seat sat to her left. In front of her, at waist height, raised above a bank of cupboards, was a large flat wooden surface. But all of that barely registered. Seb was still shirtless and the small confines of the cabin meant he was standing only inches from her. She realised that he must have swum out to the boat to retrieve the tender before rowing back to shore to collect her. His chest was smooth and almost hairless and she could see the white spots where the salt had dried on his skin.

'This is it.' Seb's head was almost brushing the ceiling and his left hand almost brushed against her as he gestured to the space around them. 'I have to install new kitchen cabinets and appliances, these have seen better days, and...' he slapped his palm a couple of times on the flat wooden platform '...get a decent mattress for my nautical futon and then I'll be able to take her out for more than just day trips.'

'You'll be able to sleep on the boat?'

'I already have but only in my swag. But if I'm going to live on her I want something a little more comfortable and permanent than that.'

'Live on it?'

'That's my plan. There's a bathroom in here, the toilet is working,' he said as he opened a narrow door next to the bed, 'and once the shower is operational and the new kitchen is installed I'm good to go.'

'But it's so small!' Luci looked around. It possibly had everything a man might need but there was no getting away from the fact that it was at the compact end of the scale spectrum.

'Haven't you ever had a holiday in a caravan?'

Luci laughed. 'A holiday, yes, but I'm not sure I'd want to live in a caravan.' *Or on a boat.*

'I've spent plenty of nights in my swag under the stars with just my bike and a camp fire for company. This will be five-star compared to that. And whenever I get tired of one place I can just haul up the anchor and be off.'

Luci didn't want to rain on his parade. It wasn't her place to comment on his choice of accommodation and she supposed it did sound romantic—for a while.

She wondered what it would be like to be so free. She was busy trying to pay off the mortgage on her house and it would be years until she was free of that commitment. But while she could see the appeal of being debt-free, she knew that deep down she would still want a home. She needed that security.

'It sounds like fun,' she said, determined not to be a naysayer.

She looked around. It didn't take long. The boat

was only big enough for one person to live on—just. It looked like Seb wasn't planning on sharing it with anyone on a permanent basis and she wondered why. He was a smart, attractive man; he must have women lining up at his door. Why would he choose to hide away on a boat built for one? A boat that for all intents and purposes seemed very much like a bachelor pad?

The tour over, she followed him back up the steps.

'Have a seat,' Seb said, indicating the bench seat to the left of the wheel. 'There are cold drinks in the ice box and life jackets and a bucket under your seat. Fire extinguisher here.' He pointed to a small red cylinder attached to the side of the steering mechanism. 'And that concludes the safety briefing.'

'You're making me nervous.'

'I may not have finished the cosmetic side of things but I promise she's seaworthy,' he said as he pushed a button and the engine roared to life. He released the boat from her mooring, put it into gear and headed out of the cove.

The boat's engine rumbled under her feet and the noise made conversation difficult but Luci didn't care. She stowed her bag beneath her seat and stretched out, enamoured with the view of both scenery and the driver. North Head and South Head jutted out into the ocean to their left. Luci could see a lighthouse on top of South Head and whitecaps on the water of the Pacific Ocean through the rocky outcrops, but Seb veered to the right, staying within the harbour, and followed the Manly ferry on its way to Circular Quay.

Seb pointed out the Prime Minister's house and Taronga Park Zoo as they motored further into the harbour. It was incredibly beautiful. And busy. It seemed like half of Sydney must be out on the harbour but that didn't detract from the experience.

The Opera House blossomed on the foreshore to their left and Seb slowed the boat down as they approached the iconic building. The drop in speed was accompanied by a decrease in engine noise, allowing them to talk normally.

'This is just brilliant. Thank you so much,' she said as Seb took them under the Harbour Bridge. She looked up at the massive steel structure that spanned the harbour. 'Have you walked across it?' she asked.

Seb laughed. 'You know you can drive across it? Or catch a train? Walking across is the sort of thing tourists do.'

'Well, I'm a tourist.'

'Add it to your list. But you might prefer to climb it or the south pylon. You get a pretty good view of the harbour from up there.'

She was disappointed. It didn't sound like Seb would offer to keep her company if she did want to walk across the bridge.

She rummaged in her bag for her phone to take some pictures. She might not get this view again.

'What, no selfie?'

She turned to find he was grinning at her.

'I'm not that photogenic,' she said, but she suspected that he was. It was a good excuse to capture a picture of him. She stepped beside him and held the phone at arm's length. He put his arm around her and she leaned in and snapped a photo of the two of them.

She checked the photo. Still shirtless, Seb was lean, muscular, gorgeous and definitely highly photogenic. She'd managed to capture the bridge in the background but she doubted anyone could look past Seb. Not that she planned on showing that photo to anybody, it was strictly for her eyes only.

He circled the boat, turning in front of Luna Park and the clown over the entrance gate grinned manically at them as they passed the jetty. Luci could hear kids screaming on the roller-coasters and she hoped he wasn't planning on taking her to the sideshows. She wasn't keen to spend the afternoon surrounded by a bunch of kids. She needed something less stressful than that but thankfully Seb kept going, steering the boat back towards the Opera House.

'Hand me your phone and I'll take a photo of you,' he said as he put the boat into neutral and idled in front of the Opera House.

Luci passed him her phone and Seb looked at the screen. The tiles that covered the sails of the building sparkled and shimmered in the sunlight, blindingly white against the brilliant blue of the sky. Luci shone just as brightly in the foreground.

She was sublime. She'd taken her hat off for the photo and her golden hair glowed. The sun was on her face, the tip of her nose was going slightly pink and her cheeks were flushed from the breeze. Her eyes were hidden behind sunglasses but she was laughing as he pressed the shutter. Her sundress framed her diamond-shaped freckles. He checked the photo, wishing he'd thought to take it on his phone. That way he would have had a copy to keep.

He tried to ignore the stirrings of lust as he put the boat into gear and cruised between Mrs Macquarie's Chair and Fort Denison and headed for Milk Beach. Luci was like a breath of fresh air in his stale world but his world was no place for her. She was gorgeous but she seemed far too delightful and pure for someone as jaded and disillusioned as he was. Too innocent. The women he'd chosen of late had been just as disheartened by life as he was. There had been no agenda other than short-term, mutual satisfaction, no danger of him damaging anyone's fragile psyche. Girls like Luci were not for him. Or, more specifically, he was no good for girls like her.

He cut through the wake of dozens of other boats, powering through the churned-up water that crisscrossed the blue of the ocean with white foam. The harbour looked magnificent and as they rounded Shark Island the mansions of Point Piper and Rose Bay clung to the hills on their right, adding to the picture-perfect view they had from his boat.

Milk Beach came into sight ahead of them and he pulled back on the throttle as he eased the cabin cruiser into the bay. He cut the engine and dropped anchor a hundred metres off the beach. From this spot they could look back towards the Sydney skyline and, as the boat swung around so her bow faced the city, he heard Luci's intake of breath.

'Wow!' She turned to him and smiled. 'Did you park here deliberately?'

The Harbour Bridge rose majestically across their bow.

'I did.' He was pleased with the reaction he'd elicited, it was just what he'd hoped for. 'The view's pretty good, isn't it?'

'It's incredible.'

It was, he thought. Luci was looking across the water to the bridge but he was watching her. 'I thought we could stop here for lunch and a swim,' he said. The small beach was busy with day trippers but he had been careful to anchor his boat away from the few others that were also enjoying a day out, in order to give them some privacy.

He grabbed the ice box and some cushions from the bench seat and took Luci around to the bow of the boat, where there was room to stretch out. He dropped the cushions on the deck, they would need some padding as the fibreglass hull of the boat could get a little uncomfortable after a while.

Luci spread her towel over the cushions and pulled her sundress over her head, revealing a very tiny bikini. Four triangles of black fabric tied together with black ties. His eyes were drawn to the diamond freckles that nestled between the swell of her breasts.

She pulled a tube of sunscreen from her bag and rubbed it into her shoulders and chest. Seb's brain pounded in his head and his heart raced, sending blood rushing through his body into all five of his extremities. He squatted down and took the lid off the ice box, giving himself a minute to regain his composure. He breathed deeply. He could smell the sea air and sunscreen. He thought he could also smell Luci. Fresh and floral. This girl was doing his head in. She was quite unselfconscious, apparently quite comfortable stripping off in front of him. He guessed there was no reason why she should worry. She had no reason to think he wouldn't be able to keep his eyes off her and people showed just as much flesh on Bondi Beach. But seeing her in a tiny bikini was sending his hormones wild. Not that it was her fault.

He was worried now, worried that she might prove

irresistible, worried that he could find himself in hot water. She was down to earth, gorgeous, funny and she smelt sensational. And now she was stretched out beside him wearing nothing but a string bikini. He wasn't sure how he was going to be able to keep his hands to himself.

He wasn't sure he wanted to.

Actually, he knew he definitely *didn't* want to but he had no idea what she thought. Maybe she was looking for some fun, maybe she was disillusioned after her divorce and was looking for some short-term satisfaction, but he suspected it was just wishful thinking on his part. He didn't even know how long she'd been divorced. It could be five minutes or five months. She could have sworn off men altogether.

He offered to rub sunscreen onto her back. That was a legitimate way of not keeping his hands to himself and was possibly the best idea he'd had in a long time, along with inviting her out for the day. Her skin was soft and velvety smooth under his fingers. She lifted her hair away from the nape of her neck, getting it out of his way, and he was sorely tempted to press his lips to the knobbly bone at the base of her neck where it met her shoulders.

Instead, he stepped back, opened the ice box and offered her a drink. God knew, he needed something to help him cool off. He passed her a bottle of water. She sipped her water and then lay back, lifting her face to the sun and closing her eyes.

Seb turned back to the ice box and began to assemble a small plate of cheese, crackers and fruit. He was trying to keep busy, to keep his mind on mundane things and off the fact that a very attractive and semi-naked woman was lying inches away from him. He was unaccustomed to feeling this nervous, and to make matters worse Luci appeared completely at ease and unaware of the effect she was having on him. Which was probably just as well.

He could probably learn a thing or two from her. She was relaxed, easygoing and she didn't appear to have let her failed marriage stop her from having fun. She certainly hadn't shut herself off from others, like he had. He knew he had laughed more often and smiled more frequently in the past three days than he had in the past three years. And the only thing that had changed was that Luci had come into his life. He had separated himself socially, his focus had been on his work and his boat for the past three years, and he had kept any interaction with others to a minimum. His chosen response to any invitation was to decline it politely and yet Luci hadn't hesitated to say yes to all three of his invitations—an after-work drink, a lift home on his bike and now a day on his boat.

For a man who had knocked back most opportunities to spend time with other people over the past three years he didn't want to think about why he was suddenly inviting someone into his life. He must be crazy. Maybe his solitary lifestyle was slowly driving him mad.

What was it about Luci that made him feel the need to spend time with her?

He knew what it was. It was the way she made him feel.

Three years ago he'd lost everything, including a large chunk of his heart and soul, but Luci was waking him up again. He'd been holding his breath, marking time, treading water, and now he felt like he could breathe again.

He put the fruit platter into the shade and ran his eyes over her still figure. Her skin was already turning golden in the sun, her breasts were round and firm, her stomach flat, her legs were toned and athletic, and her toenails were painted pale pink.

Luci sat up. Had she felt him staring at her? Maybe, but she didn't seem perturbed.

'This is much more fun than studying,' she said as she sliced a piece of cheese and popped it onto a biscuit. 'I have never spent a day like this before. All the boat trips I've ever been on involved fishing with my dad in the Gulf of St Vincent in a little tinny, much like the one you rowed before. Nothing nearly as fancy as this.'

'Wait until I finish her. Then we'll be talking fancy.'

'Really?'

Seb laughed. 'No. I don't need fancy. She just has to be comfortable. A decent bed and a fridge and I'll be happy.'

Luci stretched her arms over her head and her breasts lifted. They were barely contained in her minuscule bikini and Seb couldn't help but notice. He was finding it extremely difficult to ignore her. He really was in trouble.

'Poor Callum,' she said with a half sigh as she surveyed their surroundings. 'I wonder what he's up to this weekend. I think he might have drawn the short straw in the house-swap stakes.'

Seb smiled. 'I'm sure he'll be okay.'

'Have you spoken to him?' she asked.

'No. I sent him a text, saying I was in town and that

I was crashing at his place—after discussion with you. He replied saying he's not fussed.'

'I hope he's settling in.'

'You said he's working with your dad?'

'Yes. And with my friend Flick.' Luci laughed, a warm, rich sound. 'God, I hope he survives. There'll be plenty of patients inventing illnesses in order to get a look at the new doctor. I hope he's made of stern stuff.'

'You don't need to worry about us Hollingsworths. We're tough.' They were definitely the strong, silent type, masters of putting on a brave face and keeping their own counsel. Sometimes he wasn't sure how they had managed to get through the couple of traumatic events they had faced in their lives but he didn't want to think about those days now. Today was about Luci and he was keen to find out more.

'You haven't spoken to your dad?'

'No, I've spoken briefly to Mum but not Dad. He works such ridiculous hours, I don't like to interrupt unless it's something really important. He's supposed to be retiring this year. I know Mum is looking forward to that. Perhaps they'll finally be able to do some of the things they've been putting off. But, of course, that depends on Dad finding someone to take over the practice. Even though Vickers Hill is only a couple of hours from Adelaide, not everyone wants to work in the country and he won't leave his patients in the lurch.'

'Vickers Hill is north of Adelaide?' Seb asked, even though he knew the answer. He'd looked it up, intrigued to know where Luci had come from.

Luci nodded. 'Known for its wine. Dad has bought a small acreage and he and Mum are going to grow grapes and have chickens and ducks. That's the plan anyway. I think they should move further away otherwise Dad will find it hard to retire completely. Old patients will still come to him with their troubles if they see him around town but I guess that's for him to sort out.'

'Can you see them leaving?'

'Not really.'

'And what about you? Are you missing home?'

'Not one bit. How can I be missing home when I'm surrounded by this? So far I don't have any regrets about coming to Sydney. I'm going to make the most of my time here.' She looked up at Seb and he wondered if spending time with him qualified as making the most of things. He hoped so. 'I jumped at the chance to come to Sydney. Well, not so much jumped, Flick pushed me, but now that I'm here it seems like it was a really good decision.'

She rolled over onto her stomach and Seb struggled to keep his eyes off her very shapely behind.

'You have no idea how nice it is to just relax and do my own thing, without everyone telling me what they think is best for me. I'm old enough to work that out for myself.'

He did have some idea what it was like to have everyone interfering in his life in what they thought was a helpful way. That's why he loved having the boat. It had been his escape route and he was convinced it had saved his sanity. He'd been able to disappear and avoid talking to anyone.

Luci might profess that she had chosen to take Flick's advice to study interstate but he still thought a large part of her motivation stemmed from having a reason, an excuse, to leave. He still thought she was running away. She might deny it but he recognised the signs. He had seen those same signs in himself. He knew exactly what it was like—he'd been running for three years. He recognised the need to get away from all the people who knew you and your past and your story.

But even though he thought Luci was running away from Vickers Hill he knew he was in no position to judge her for it. He'd shut himself off from the world completely. At least she was still living.

He knew that was the difference between them. For the past three years he hadn't been living. He hadn't thought he was allowed to enjoy life. It hadn't felt right but was it okay? Was it allowed? Did he have to continue to ignore the world?

Possibly. It was the only way to ensure it didn't hurt him again.

But he knew it was going to be hard to ignore Luci.

'And what is it you should be doing?' he asked, continuing the conversation she had started.

'I don't know yet.' She laughed. 'That's a little ironic, isn't it, but it's early days still. I'll figure it out. On my own. My life is different from how I pictured it. I just have to figure out what I want it to be like from now on. And one benefit of being divorced is that I can figure it out for myself. It's up to me.

'What did you think your life would be like?'

She shrugged and averted her eyes. 'Married with kids.'

He supposed that was quite different from being divorced with no kids. 'Your husband didn't want kids?' he asked. Maybe that was why they'd got divorced.

'No, he did. We both did.' Luci was restless. She rolled back over so she was sitting up now. 'But he decided he didn't want them with me.' She stood up and dropped her hat and sunglasses onto her towel. 'I think I might go for a swim.'

It was clear she wanted to avoid this particular conversation. There was obviously more to the story but he wasn't going to push her. It was none of his business. He would listen if she wanted to talk but from what she had already said she was tired of interference. He decided he would just let her be but he wondered about her ex-husband. What sort of man was he? Luci had told him they had been together for almost ten years. What sort of man took that long to decide that he didn't want to be with someone? What sort of man married a girl like Luci and talked about raising a family together, only to leave her right when they should have been starting that future?

Seb felt a sudden surge of anger towards Luci's ex. He wasn't normally a violent man but he could see the hurt in her eyes and hear it in her voice and something within him made him wish he could fix it. But that reaction was out of character for him. He expected other people to leave him alone, not to interfere in his life, and he had learnt to do the same. But he wanted to help her and had no idea what to do.

He suspected she was not over the divorce and not over the loss of her dreams for the future but he had no idea what she needed. He could almost feel steam coming out of his ears and knew he needed to cool down. Calm down.

Luci was treading water a few metres from the boat, looking towards the shore. He dived in after her. He would keep quiet. He was good at that, it was easy not to speak about his thoughts and feelings or anything emotional. He floated on his back and waited to see what Luci would do. After a few minutes she drifted over to him.

'If you weren't messing about in boats when you were growing up, what did you do on weekends?' he asked.

'Chased the boys,' she replied.

Her mood had shifted, she was happy again. He thought that by nature she was a sunny person and that drew him to her even more. She balanced out his sombre side. He hadn't always been dark but the events of three years ago made him more reserved, less carefree and more sceptical about the good things in life.

'I thought the boys would have been chasing you.'

'There wasn't much chasing going on, if I'm honest. The girls played netball in winter and tennis in summer. The boys played footy and cricket. Our parents tried to keep us busy. We'd ride around town on our bikes and during harvest we'd often lend a hand if we had friends who had vineyards or farms. There was plenty to keep us out of trouble.'

Her stomach rumbled.

'Time for lunch?'

She nodded. 'Swimming always makes me hungry.'

Sex always made him hungry and Luci made him think of sex. Therefore he was hungry too but he didn't mention that.

Luci was looking back at the boat. 'I didn't think that through when I went for a swim.'

'What?'

'How I was going to get back on.'

'Swim to the back, and I'll help you up the ladder.' The ladder was short but it required substantial upper-body strength to haul yourself out of the water. 'I'll go first and give you a hand.'

They swam side by side and when they reached the boat Seb stretched up for the top rung of the ladder and pulled himself up onto the deck.

'Reach up and give me your hand.' He leaned down and grasped her hand in his. 'Grab the ladder with your other hand,' he said as he pulled her up into the boat and into his arms. Luci might not have thought about the logistics of getting back on the boat but Seb hadn't thought about the logistics of helping her. There wasn't much room at the back, just the small ledge. His back was to the gate and to open it he had to turn round and let her go. He didn't want to do that. They were squashed into a space less than a metre square. Her body was soft against his, slick with water. Her skin was cool and he could feel her heart beating in her chest, beating against his.

She looked up at him.

They stared at each other in silence until he could stand it no longer.

He didn't stop to think about what he was doing. He couldn't think. All he could do was see and smell and feel.

He saw her blue-grey eyes looking at him, the freckles dusted across the bridge of her nose, the tip of it turning red with the sun. Saw the pink rosebud of her lips and wanted to taste her.

He couldn't ignore her and he couldn't resist. He bent his head, making his intention clear, waiting for her to tell him to stop. But she remained quiet. He couldn't hear the sound of the ocean or the other bathers. All he could hear was the sound of their breathing, heavy in the stillness. He could see her eyes watching his and then they flicked down to his lips. He knew she understood his intention but she didn't protest and that was all the invitation Seb needed.

CHAPTER FOUR

HE BENT HIS HEAD.

Luci lifted her chin, offering her lips to him, and he claimed them. Claimed her.

He kissed her firmly, just like he'd been wanting to.

He pressed his lips to hers. She tasted of salt and she smelt of sunshine.

She parted her lips, opening her mouth to him. His tongue darted inside, tasting her, touching her. He couldn't control his desire. She was irresistible. But while his own lack of control surprised him she surprised him more when she kissed him back. His hands slid down her back and over the bow of her bikini top. With one flick of his fingers he could untie that bow and he would be able to feel the swell of her breasts pressed against him, skin to skin. But this time he did resist. He moved his hands lower until they cupped her buttocks instead. Firm and round, they fitted perfectly into his palms.

He pulled her into him, pressing her against him as he deepened the kiss. Her mouth was warm, soft and inviting. Her body was cool and soft under his hands.

His body was hard and firm and he held himself back. He didn't want to overpower her.

He felt her hands on his chest. They were cool over his racing heart.

She pushed gently against him, pulling away.

She looked up at him. Her blue-grey eyes were enormous, her pupils dilated. She was panting softly. She was out of breath, they both were.

They stood in silence, looking at each other, waiting for someone to say something. He wasn't going to apologise for kissing her. It had been the right time and the right place and she certainly hadn't resisted. But now she looked unsure. Albeit thoroughly kissed.

Her lips were dark pink now, almost red. She didn't look upset. Just uncertain.

He didn't think she wanted an apology. She hadn't objected but now she looked wary.

'Should I stop?' he asked.

She didn't reply immediately. She just stood, wrapped in his arms, staring up at him, and he could almost see her thoughts spinning in her brain, swirling behind her eyes.

'I don't know what you should do. I don't know what *I* should do,' she replied. 'I can't think.'

'Did I make you uncomfortable?' He wasn't going to apologise for kissing her. He wasn't sorry and he didn't think she was either.

'It's not that.' She paused and stepped away. 'But I wasn't expecting it.'

'The kiss?' he asked. He was pretty sure she'd seen it coming.

She shook her head. 'No. How it felt.'

He thought it had been amazing but his heart stopped for a second as he wondered if perhaps she hadn't been quite so astounded. 'And how was that?' he couldn't stop himself from asking. He had to know.

'Different.'

'Good different?' He had never fished for compliments before but he had to know if the kiss had rocked her world in the same way it had his.

'Good *and* different. I don't know if there's such a thing as "good different". I'm not used to different. I think that's the unexpected thing. I'm not used to kissing a man I've just met. I'm not used to kissing anyone except my ex-husband.'

'Really?' That was it? She'd had one relationship?

'Ben and I were together since I was fifteen. I've only been divorced six months.'

In that sentence lay the answers to several of his questions, the first being how long she had been divorced, but the second answer was even more telling. If she'd been ready to move on from her marriage then six months was a reasonable length of time, but if the end of her marriage hadn't been something she'd chosen then a period of readjustment was only normal. She'd said her husband had met someone else. Seb guessed she wasn't ready to do the same. But that didn't preclude them from having some fun. Not if she wanted to. It was all up to her.

'I get it. You need time.'

'Don't get me wrong. It felt good but I don't know if it felt right. I'm not sure what I should be doing. I don't know if I need more time but part of me feels like I should be a bit cautious and the other part is saying just close your eyes and jump.'

'Only you can make that decision,' he said. He wanted her to jump, he desperately wanted her to jump, but he knew that wasn't his call. 'Let me know what you decide. I'm not going to put any pressure on you but I will say this—you're only here for a few weeks. We can enjoy each other's company, no strings attached, no commitment, and then say goodbye. But it's up to you. Think about it. You know where to find me.'

He dropped his arms from around her waist and leaned back to open the gate, allowing them to step into the boat.

They spent the rest of the afternoon talking. Conversation flowed easily, there were no awkward pauses, but the awareness was always there. He could feel the tension in the air around them, crackling and sparking, but they both ignored it. They talked about work, about places he'd visited and her home town; they talked about everything but the kiss they'd shared and where they were going to go from there.

He was serious about his suggestion, though. He was pretty sure she wasn't the one for him long term, it was obvious she wanted to settle down and have a family, something that was definitely not on his agenda, but she was only in town for eight weeks and he was only committed to Sydney for six weeks. There was no reason they couldn't have some fun together. They could enjoy each other's company and then say goodbye. But he would give her space. For now. This had to be her decision.

Luci towelled herself dry and slipped her sundress over her head. She'd had enough time in the sun but the extra layer wasn't to prevent sunburn, it was to provide her with a bit of a barrier. Not that it afforded much protection but she needed all help she could get to ensure she didn't just throw herself back into Seb's arms.

She should be having doubts and reservations. She had known him for less than three days and she had *never* kissed a man she barely knew before. She'd never properly kissed anyone other than her ex-husband.

She should be having doubts and reservations about kissing him, full stop, but that wasn't the issue. It wasn't Seb who was making her nervous but the consequences of her actions.

She didn't want to make a mistake or do anything that might jeopardise her time in Sydney. There were more important things than kissing a handsome stranger. They had to live together and work together. There were a whole lot of reasons why she should keep her distance and only one thing, her hormones, was telling her differently.

She was a single adult, there was no rule saying she couldn't take this further, but she really wasn't sure if she was ready. She needed some ground rules. She'd never done 'no strings attached' and she wasn't sure if she could. Until she had processed the idea she felt it would be wise to keep her distance.

The kiss had been amazing. She'd seen it coming and she hadn't stopped him. She hadn't wanted to. She'd wanted to touch him, to taste him, but she hadn't realised how hard it would make it to deny herself more. It was going to be difficult. She would have to find other ways of keeping busy. If she was busy she wouldn't have time to think about him.

Seb had pulled some more food out of the ice box and assembled a picnic lunch. Luci was starving and she was more than happy to sample the selection. While she was eating she couldn't talk but when they did talk Seb kept the conversation neutral. They talked about inconsequential things, a polite conversation between two virtual strangers, skirting around the issue that she couldn't stop thinking about.

But not talking about the kiss didn't stop her from thinking about it.

Seb shoved the crowbar behind the last of the kitchen cabinets in the galley of his boat. He had spent most of his spare time for the past week hunkered down, removing the shower and the kitchen cabinetry. The carpenter had told him not to expect the new fittings to be ready for installation for another fortnight but he needed to dismantle the old fixtures and he needed to keep himself occupied.

The demolition work was achieving three things— he was progressing nicely with his renovations, he was keeping his mind occupied, to a point, and he was keeping his distance from Luci. He had promised to give her time and space but over the past couple of days he'd found that if he spent too much time in the same space as her it was becoming increasingly difficult to resist the pull of attraction. It was difficult to be around her and not touch her. All he wanted to do when she was around him was to explore their attraction but he had promised not to push her.

Once again his boat was his sanctuary but this time he didn't need it to help him over his heartbreak. This time it was to keep his mind off his desire rather than his despair. The physical work was a good antidote for the desire. He was so knackered by the end of the day that he would fall straight to sleep when he went to bed. That was a fourth benefit of the demolition work.

He'd had several brief affairs over the past three years but he had been very careful to avoid meaningful relationships. If Luci was willing there was nothing stopping them from having some fun, as her time in Sydney was limited anyway, but he realised she might still be working through her own issues. It would probably be wise to spend some time working out whether her issues were major or minor. He wasn't prepared to get involved in anything too emotional—a physical relationship was fine but he didn't want anything more serious than that.

There were all sorts of reasons why he should avoid Luci and he knew them all, he'd been running over them constantly.

She had led a sheltered life. A *very* sheltered life.

They had to work together.

They had to *live* together.

It was all a little bit too close.

But that didn't alter the fact that he was excited by Luci and it had been a long time since he'd been excited by anything.

Although he knew it still might be better to avoid her he couldn't avoid her completely. They had to work together and on Friday afternoon she knocked on his consulting-room door. He could smell her before he saw her. She smelt of frangipani.

'Hi,' he said as he looked up. 'How's it going?'

'Good.'

She smiled at him and her blue-grey eyes sparkled. She looked happy. She glowed and he had the sense that she was filled with light that then spilled out to brighten everyone else's day. At least, that's how he felt when she was around.

'Melanie Parsons is in the clinic today,' Luci told him. 'She has an appointment with the psychologist and then I'm going to do the health check on her four-year-old. I wasn't sure if you wanted to see her.'

'Good idea. What time is she booked in with you?' he asked as he looked at his diary.

'She's next. I'm just going to grab a coffee and by then she should be done with the psych consult. Give me ten minutes to get started on the toddler check and then come in.'

Luci was just helping Harper down from the exam table when Seb knocked on the door. She took Harper out of the room to the play area where Harper's two-year-old brother was busy with the building blocks while Seb caught up with Melanie. When she returned Seb had been given the update on the two psychologist appointments Melanie had already had.

'We are working on my responses so that I can try to manage the situation,' Melanie told him. 'And then we're going to tackle the best way to get Brad in for a session as well.'

Milo was strapped into his pram in the corner of the room. He started to grizzle.

'Sorry,' Melanie apologised, 'He's due for a feed.'

Seb thought it was interesting that Melanie felt she needed to apologise for something that was perfectly understandable. She started to get out of her chair to attend to the baby when Luci offered her help.

'Don't worry about him. I'll see if I can settle him for a bit, let you finish with Dr Hollingsworth.' Luci lifted Milo out of the stroller. She blew a raspberry on his foot and his grizzles stopped, becoming happy chortling instead. She laid him on the exam table and distracted him with a mirror and a game of peek-a-boo, allowing Melanie to continue.

The young mother was watching Luci play with Milo while she spoke to Seb. 'And I think I need to make an appointment to discuss a more reliable form of contraception. After this next one I reckon I'm done. Some days I feel like I'm not even managing with the three I already have.'

Seb's antennae went up. 'I'll speak to the psychologist and recommend that you continue with regular visits until a few months after this next baby is born.' He didn't want to let Melanie slip through the cracks in the system. If she needed help and support he wanted to make sure she got it. For her sake and for her children's sake.

'Thank you,' she replied with a nod as she stood up, preparing to leave. She picked Milo up from the exam table to put him back into his stroller. 'Do you have kids, Luci?' she asked.

Melanie was bending over, strapping Milo into his pram, and she missed Luci's expression. But Seb didn't. She looked like someone had slapped her.

'No, I don't,' Luci replied.

'You should. You're a natural.'

'Mmm-hmm.' Luci turned away and Seb wasn't able to see her face. He couldn't tell if her expression had changed or not.

'I don't seem to have the energy,' Melanie remarked.

'I imagine managing them twenty-four-seven is very different from seeing them for ten minutes at a time,' Luci said. 'I'm not surprised you're tired.'

'Exhausted is the word, I think. But I'll get through it. What other choice do I have?' she remarked as she pushed the pram towards the door.

'Are you okay?' Seb asked Luci the moment Melanie left the room.

'I'm fine.'

She didn't look fine.

'I'm concerned about Melanie, though,' she said, changing the subject. 'Do you still think the kids are safe?'

'How was Harper's health check?' he asked, letting her change of topic go—for now. 'Were there any red flags with her weight or teeth or any unexplained bruises?'

Luci shook her head. 'Everything was within normal ranges.'

'I've never seen any signs of neglect or abuse. The kids are clean and well fed. I think she's coping. Maybe just, at times, but I don't think the kids are in any danger.' If he thought the children were in any danger he wouldn't sit on his hands. 'Her kids' welfare comes before her own, which is part of the problem, but also why I'll insist that she continue with regular psych reviews. If anything changes, hopefully we'll pick up on it.'

Luci was nodding but she still looked upset. He felt that he'd learned to read her expressions in just a few days and he was still worried about her. He wanted to find out why she'd looked so shocked. He ignored his self-imposed ban. He wanted to spend time with her. 'Have you got plans tonight?' he asked.

'Only to cook up a stir-fry.'

'Would there be enough for two?'

'You'll be home?'

So she'd noticed that he'd been MIA. He wondered if she had missed him. He nodded and offered, 'I'll bring wine.'

'Sure.'

'Dinner smells good.'

Seb's voice startled her and made Luci jump. She had her head over the wok and the sizzle as she fried the garlic and crushed chilli had blocked out all other sounds.

'It's just chicken and noodles,' she said as she scraped the marinated chicken strips into the pan. The aroma of fried garlic always smelt good but she hadn't really thought about the practicalities of serving up a dish laden with garlic. Oh, well, she supposed it was one way to make sure Seb didn't kiss her again.

She glanced over her shoulder when she heard the familiar snap as Seb broke the seal on the screw top on the bottle of wine he held. He poured two glasses and handed one to her before leaning back on the kitchen bench.

Was he planning on hanging around in the kitchen while she cooked?

She'd been surprised that he was free tonight. He'd barely been home all week. She'd heard him come in late at night but he definitely hadn't been home for a meal and she'd expected he would have other plans. She'd wondered if he had been deliberately avoiding her and had thought about shooing him out of the kitchen now, but dinner would only take five minutes so she may as well enjoy his company. Sitting home alone was no fun.

The house had been far too quiet this week without Seb. She still wasn't used to being on her own. After her divorce she'd formed a habit of eating at her parents' house a couple of times a week or sharing a meal with Flick. But being in Sydney, where she didn't have a large network of friends, had made her nights long and lonely. She'd never really been on her own before and she'd discovered she didn't like it. But that didn't mean she was going to fall for the first guy to cross her path. She needed to develop some resistance along with her independence.

She sipped her wine, hoping it would calm her nerves. It felt like they were on a date. Not that she really knew how that felt. She and Ben had been together since high school and she couldn't even remember their first date, but she guessed it would have been at a school friend's birthday party. They had probably played silly party games and drunk some wine they'd pinched from a parent's cellar.

She wished she was cooking something a bit more complicated than a stir-fry, something that required more attention. Something that would require her focus but, as it was, she could whip up a stir-fry blindfolded and that meant she had plenty of time to think about Seb.

Even though she hadn't seen much of him that week she could always tell when he'd been to the apartment. She could smell him. The air was different and even now, despite the aroma of garlic and chilli, she could still smell him. He had showered after work—that must have been while she'd been at the supermarket—and she could smell soap and aftershave. He'd changed into a pair of stone-coloured shorts with a fresh navy T-shirt. His feet were bare and he looked relaxed and comfortable. He certainly didn't look nervous or like he was dressed for a date.

Luci took another sip of wine and concentrated on copying Seb's calm approach as she served up the stir-fry and sat at the table opposite him.

He tucked into the bowl of noodles, scooping up several forkfuls before he paused to take a breath.

'This tastes great, thank you,' he said, as he topped up their wine glasses.

Luci had intended to do some studying after dinner but she could fast see that plan disappearing if she had too much wine but she didn't refuse the top-up. After a week of lonely nights it made a pleasant change to share a meal with someone. And it was even more pleasant when that someone was Seb.

'Two weeks down, how's it been going?' he asked her as he sipped his wine. 'Have you recovered from Melanie's visit?'

'What do you mean?'

'Something she said upset you.'

'You noticed that?'

'I did. What was it?'

'I know she didn't mean any harm but if I had a dollar for every time someone asked me if I had kids I'd have paid off my mortgage. I just don't understand why so many clients feel they have a right to ask personal questions.'

'I think she thought you were a natural with kids. She meant it as a compliment.'

'I realise that but I didn't expect that every second person would ask me if I have children. I bet they don't ask you the same thing, do they?'

'Some do,' he admitted, 'but I guess it probably is more of a question between women.'

'They all seem to assume that if a woman is working in family health or paediatrics or obstetrics she would either have kids or want them.'

'But you do want them.'

'Yes, but I don't want to think about it all the time. Obviously my divorce has changed my plans somewhat. I'm not exactly in a position to start a family but I don't want to tell clients my life story.'

'Fair enough.'

'I guess I hadn't anticipated that the subject of children would be raised so often. I need to find an answer to the most popular question, which is, "So, Luci, do you have children?"'

'Why don't you just tell them that you're only young? You've got plenty of time.'

It wasn't a bad suggestion. It wasn't Seb's fault that time wasn't on her side but he didn't know that.

'A lot of these mothers are younger than me. I don't want them to feel I'm judging them. If I had my way I *would* have had children by now. All I've wanted, all my life, was to have kids and to be a young mum. My parents are old. Dad is almost seventy and Mum is a couple of years younger. They are wonderful parents but growing up I really noticed their age. Especially in my town where so many people start their families young, my parents could have been my grandparents and I didn't want to be like that. I also want more than one child. I was an only child and I didn't want that for my kids. Having a family has been my dream since I was a teenager.'

'Why don't you tell them you're waiting for the right

man, then?' He scooped up the last mouthful of his dinner and didn't speak again until he'd finished it. 'Or do you think you had the right one in Ben?'

'Obviously I did when I married him.' She had thought that was it for her. As far as she'd been concerned, her life had been sorted when she'd walked down the aisle and become a wife. Until she'd found that it could easily be unsorted.

Ben couldn't have been the right man for her. If he had been, surely they'd still be together? Or perhaps she just wasn't the right woman for him. But when they'd got married she hadn't known what else was out there. Neither of them had. Ben had found someone he felt suited him better and Luci had to hope that there was someone else out there for her too.

What would her perfect man be like?

She looked across the table. She suspected he would be a lot like Seb. That was dangerous territory. She needed a change of topic. A safer direction. 'How was your week?' she asked. 'I barely saw you. Have you changed your mind about sharing the house?'

'No. I wanted to give you some space. Being around you was testing my limits. It's been difficult to put you in the "friend" zone so I thought it would be best if I stayed out of the way. I've been working on my boat.'

Hearing Seb put their situation like that made her wonder if she wanted to be in the 'friend' zone. She didn't think she did but she was still confused about what she should be doing. It was still safer not to do anything. He hadn't apologised for kissing her. She was glad about that. The kiss had been good, she didn't want an apology, but she wasn't ready to revisit it either.

He was looking at her so directly but she couldn't

respond. It was safer not to reply to his comment. To break eye contact, she stood and picked up their empty bowls, clearing the table. She took the bowls to the sink and rinsed them, keeping her back to Seb.

'You don't need to stay out of the house, that doesn't seem fair.' She found her voice once she wasn't looking at him.

'I thought it was easiest for both of us. I promised I wouldn't make you uncomfortable.'

'I'm not uncomfortable. I just can't jump into another relationship.' Even though she was tempted. 'I know I should spread my wings but jumping into something with the first man who crosses my path doesn't really fit that. I think I need to test the water. I've never even been on a proper first date. Maybe I should be the one who spends more time out of the house. Maybe I should meet some more people.'

Seb had been hoping to hear Luci say she'd made a decision. His ego had let him believe that if he gave her time and space she'd miss him. But perhaps she had a point. Perhaps she *did* need to meet other people. Perhaps then she would see that he could be the perfect person with whom to test the water.

But maybe he had a solution to this dilemma.

'I've been invited to a dinner party tomorrow night. If you'd like to come with me it would give you a chance to meet some other people.'

He hadn't actually thought about going until just now. The whole premise of the evening hadn't appealed to him but now, with Luci's provisos, it was suddenly more attractive.

When Ginny had invited him he'd declined the invitation. That had become his habit over the past three years but he knew Ginny wouldn't mind a last-minute change of mind. They had been friends since high school and she had made a lot of effort to keep in contact, especially recently. Even when Seb had been difficult and unsociable, Ginny had kept him in the loop, inviting him to parties and functions. He'd declined almost all of her invitations but he appreciated the fact that she hadn't given up on him. Perhaps it was time he said yes.

'Like a date?' Luci queried.

CHAPTER FIVE

'NOT EXACTLY.' HE wished he could offer to take her on a proper first date but if she was going to insist on meeting other people then tomorrow night's party would be a good compromise. If everything went according to his plan he could organise a first date after that. 'A friend of mine is hosting a "dates with mates" party. It's for singles. Each guest is expected to bring a partner who they are not romantically involved with—it's a way of meeting new people, of broadening your set of acquaintances and potentially meeting someone who you could date. So it fits within your rules. We'd be going as friends and you'll get to meet new people. What do you think?'

She nodded. 'Sure. I'd like that.'

He was surprised by her immediate reaction. There was no hesitation, no further questions. She was far more adventurous and sociable than he was.

Luci pulled her hair into a sleek ponytail and applied a coat of pale pink lipstick before zipping herself into the strapless black jumpsuit she'd bought that day. She'd seen it in a shop window that she passed on her way to work and had loved it but had had no reason to buy it.

Until today. She'd told herself she hadn't bought anything new in ages so it was a justified purchase. She told herself a lot of things. That she wasn't looking forward to the date, that it wasn't really a date and that she was keen to meet other people when, in fact, she was nervous about pretty much all of it. She was nervous about whether or not she looked okay, whether she'd fit in to the crowd, whether Seb would like her outfit, and what he would be thinking about their 'non-date'.

Seb looked her up and down when she joined him in the lounge room. 'Wow. You look sensational.' Luci relaxed. At least now she knew what he was thinking. 'I was going to suggest we take my bike but perhaps we should call a cab.'

'The bike is fine,' she replied. She enjoyed going on the bike. It gave her a chance to wrap her arms around him and hold on tight. What wasn't to like about that? 'Just let me grab my boots.' She swapped her gladiator sandals for her old work boots and carried her sandals down the stairs to put on when they reached the party. Seb unlocked the compartment under the seat of his motorbike and pulled out his spare helmet, exchanging the helmet for Luci's sandals and the wine. He had his spare jacket tucked under his arm and he held it for her while she slipped her arms in before helping her to fasten her helmet.

He started the bike and Luci straddled the seat behind him. She wrapped her arms around his waist and held on tightly as he rode through the streets of the North Shore to Cremorne Point. He parked his bike on the road behind the house and helped Luci off. She changed her shoes and checked her hair in the mirror, then took a deep breath. She'd come up with the idea of meeting new people but the reality of walking into a party where she knew just one person was more daunting than she would have thought. It was another new situation for her. Something else she'd never done.

Seb took her hand and squeezed it. He must have known she was nervous but having him hold her hand only intensified the feeling. At the same time it felt so good that she didn't want to object.

The party was already under way and music filled the night air. Seb opened the back gate and led her along a narrow path that followed the side of the house. When they emerged into the front garden Luci caught her breath. The house sat right on the harbour and the view was incredible. A white, open-sided marquee had been erected in the centre of the lawn with a dining table positioned beneath it, and closer to the water's edge Luci could see a long bar, loaded with glasses and drinks, that framed the view across the harbour to the Opera House and the bridge.

The garden was lit with hundreds of lights—fairy-lights, up-lights and down-lights—and the Opera House glowed as the sun set. It looked spectacular.

Ginny came to greet them and Seb introduced her.

'Welcome,' Ginny said, and she kissed Luci on both cheeks. 'I'm so glad you agreed to come. It's been ages since I've seen Seb and I was afraid he was going to turn down this invitation too.'

'Thank you for including me,' Luci said as she gestured to the garden. 'This looks amazing.'

'Thanks but I can't take all the credit. The decorating is my work. I'm a food stylist by trade, but the house belongs to another friend of mine—Michael. Come with me, I'll introduce you.'

Seb and Luci followed Ginny across the lawn to the bar where the other guests had gathered and Luci tried to keep track of who was who during a whirlwind introduction. First up was Paulo, a Spanish chef, who Ginny had met on an assignment. She introduced him with the comment, 'I can make food look pretty but I can't cook so I invited Paulo.' Then there was Michael, who owned the house, and he was followed by a model, a footballer, a massage therapist, Ginny's brother, who worked in finance, a lawyer he knew, an actor and a food blogger. Luci was unsure what a food blogger actually did but the woman was extraordinarily thin so Luci assumed it didn't actually involve eating. It was an interesting assortment of people and Luci thought the evening would either be a lot of fun or a huge disaster.

Ginny had a seating plan arranged and they were told it would change between each course. Luci started the night between Paulo, the Spanish chef, and Michael, her host.

Michael was smooth, dark and good-looking, with a European heritage, Luci suspected. Besides this gorgeous house, he also owned three restaurants. A fact he successfully mentioned within the first few minutes and several times thereafter. He seemed to think Luci should be suitably impressed. She was, but not by him. He was obviously wealthy but that wasn't high on Luci's list of priorities. He also had a very high opinion of himself but no sense of humour. Luci preferred someone who could make her laugh and would let her be herself. She suspected Michael was not that sort of man. She wasn't interested in material objects. She wanted a family and she would give up everything else if she could have that. Nothing else was that important.

Paulo, to her left, was outrageously handsome and quite charming but he wasn't her type of man either. He didn't make her heart race or her breath catch in her throat. He didn't give her the fluttery feeling she got in her stomach whenever Seb was near. If nothing else, this dinner party was helping her to narrow down her type of man.

Somehow she managed to survive the first course and conversations that she wasn't particularly interested in. For the main course she found herself sitting between the actor and the footballer, a rugby league player. He had limited conversation, appearing to be restricted to the topics of rugby and golf, neither of which Luci knew anything about. Her mind drifted to the opposite side of the table where Seb was now seated. She never seemed to have any difficulty talking to him. They had discussed all manner of topics.

She turned her attention to the actor on her other side, leaving the rugby player to try to strike up a conversation with the girl on his right. The actor turned out to be 'between jobs' and working as a barista and he was pleasant enough, although she was pretty sure he was gay. Not that it mattered as she wasn't interested in him anyway, but she wondered who had invited him.

Somehow, through all the various seat changes and movements, she managed to keep one eye on Seb and hoped no one noticed. She thought she was being subtle but it was hard to know. She did her best to concentrate on what the other guests were talking about but as the evening wore on she found it increasingly difficult. All she wanted to do was to swap seats and plonk herself next to Seb.

Even though he made her feel nervous, Luci knew it

was the right kind of nervous. The exciting kind. The possibility that something could happen if she was willing. She wondered what the rules were if you decided that the mate you came with was the same one you wanted to go home with. So far, in her opinion, no one could compare to Seb. He didn't need to be the perfect man, it didn't even matter if he was the first one to cross her path, she just knew that she wasn't going to get him out of her system without exploring the possibilities.

If she was honest she'd admit—to him and to herself—that she'd thought about little else for the last week. She didn't want to live in the past. Her marriage was over and at some point she was going to have to try again. And she was more than happy to try again with Seb.

She looked across the table and found him watching her. She blushed and hoped he couldn't read her thoughts. No. It was time to share those thoughts. If she wanted to be a grown-up she had to take the leap. She wanted to stretch her wings and she hoped Seb would give her the opportunity to do just that.

She smiled at him and stood up as dessert was cleared away. Guests gathered in smaller clusters as coffee was served in the garden but before Luci could make her way to Seb she was cornered by Michael. At the beginning of the evening she had thought the evening would either be interesting or a disaster. It looked like it was heading down the path of complete disaster.

She stood patiently for another few minutes as Michael talked some more about himself. She searched the crowd for Seb as she waited for a polite time to escape. Seb was on the other side of the garden, talking to the model who was Ginny's brother's date. Their eyes locked and Michael and his conversation receded into the background. Why was she wasting time with him?

'Would you excuse me?' she said.

She saw Seb break away from the model at the same time. He was coming for her. Luci waited and fell into step beside him, following him in silence down to a wooden garden seat that sat at the harbour's edge.

Finally it was just the two of them.

As she sat next to him her thigh brushed his leg and she wondered if she should move, if he needed some space. But she didn't want to move, so she stayed put. The now familiar butterflies careened around in her stomach. She wanted to touch Seb. Wanted to feel him.

A light breeze blew off the harbour, sending a shiver through Luci.

'Would you like my jacket?' Seb offered.

'No, I'm okay.'

He put his arm around her shoulders and pulled her into his side. He was warm and solid and Luci wanted to close her eyes and soak up the feeling of being in his arms again.

'Are you having fun?' he asked her.

'Not really,' she replied. 'The rugby player is boring, Michael is only interested in himself and Paulo was nice but a bit too smooth for me.'

'Too smooth? I wouldn't have thought that was a thing.'

'It most certainly is, and I think the barista-slash-actor is gay.'

'Really?'

'Yep.'

Seb laughed.

'Why is that funny?' Luci asked.

'It means there's one less bloke in the running.'

'In the running for what?'

'For your attention.'

Luci hesitated for a fraction of a second, wondering if she should tell him what she thought. She decided she should. 'It doesn't matter. I've found the one.'

'Ginny's brother?'

'No. Not him.'

'There isn't anyone else.'

'Yes, there is, but I'm not sure if it's within the rules of the night. Are you allowed to go home with the same person you came with?'

'Go home with? As in together?'

She nodded.

'Are you serious?'

She nodded again. 'As long as it's not against the rules.'

'I don't give a damn about the rules,' Seb said as he stood and reached for her hand. 'Let's get out of here.'

They barely stopped to say thank you and goodnight to Ginny before making a beeline for Seb's bike. Luci ignored Ginny's knowing smile. She didn't care what anyone thought. What happened between her and Seb was their business, no one else's. Luci was going to do exactly what she wanted for a change and if anyone tried to tell her it was a bad idea she wasn't going to listen.

She slid her hand under Seb's shirt as she sat behind him on the bike. She rested her hand against his chest and imagined what the rest of the night would be like.

They barely made it up the stairs and into the apartment before their clothes started coming off.

Seb kicked off his boots and Luci did the same with hers. He tossed his leather jacket on the floor and pulled his shirt over his head, discarding items of clothing on the passage floor. Luci's jacket followed.

He lifted her up and she wrapped her legs around his waist as he pushed her against the passage wall. He bent his head and kissed her. She opened her mouth and kissed him back.

Her hands were pressed into his shoulder blades. His skin was firm and smooth. He looked as though he'd been carved from marble but he was warm and pulsing with life. He carried her further into the apartment and she could feel his erection pressing between her thighs.

'Your room or mine?' he asked.

'Yours. It's closer.' Luci didn't think she could wait much longer.

He put her down and reached behind her to unzip her jumpsuit.

'The zip is on the side.'

His hands found the zip and he bent his head as her jumpsuit fell away and pressed his lips against the diamond-shaped freckles on her chest.

'I've wanted to do that since the first time I saw you.'

His fingers brushed over her breasts as he released her bra. He cupped one breast in his hand as he took the other into his mouth, making Luci think she might burst into flames.

She reached for his waistband and unzipped his trousers, discarding them on the floor along with her outfit.

Seb scooped her up and laid her on the bed. His boxer shorts joined his trousers as Luci admired him.

The marble angel in all his glory. His chest was broad and tanned from hours on his boat. Her eyes followed the line of his sternum where it divided his pecs, down to the ridges of his abdominals. Below his belly button a light trail of hair led her eyes further to where his erection was proudly displayed. He was absolutely gorgeous. Perfectly sculpted and ready and waiting for her.

She swallowed feeling moisture pooling between her thighs. She hooked her fingers under the elastic of her knickers, wanting to discard them, but Seb leaned forward and moved her hands. He lifted her hips and gently tugged her underwear down. His fingers brushed the backs of her legs and she felt like she might explode right now. He slid her knickers down over her calves and dropped them on the floor.

Now they were both naked but Luci didn't have time to feel self-conscious. She wasn't thinking about how she looked, she could only focus on how Seb made her feel.

He knelt at the foot of the bed and spread her legs, pushing her knees gently apart. He ran his tongue along the inside of her thigh, starting at her knee. He kept moving up and Luci lifted her hips as his tongue delved and flicked and tasted her.

She reached for him and pulled him up onto the bed. He knelt between her thighs and she circled his erection with her hand, running her thumb over the tip of his shaft. Felt him quiver.

He bent his head and took her breast in his mouth. His tongue was hard and wet as it flicked over her nipple. Luci moaned and arched her back. It had been months since she had felt this way, and couldn't wait any longer.

'Take me now, Seb,' she begged. The tension of the last few days made her impatient. There would be time later to explore, but right now she needed release.

He reached into the bedside drawer and handed her

a condom. Luci tore the packet open and rolled it onto him before guiding him into her. She lifted her hips and let him fill her.

She met his thrusts, timing them with her own. She had to learn a new rhythm, faster and harder. He consumed her and she let him.

CHAPTER SIX

SHE CRIED OUT as she came and felt him shudder as he joined her.

It was different.

But good.

There was such a thing as good different after all.

They had made love fast and impatiently, unable to restrain themselves, and then they made love slowly, getting to know every inch of each other. Luci was adventurous and brave as she discovered the joys of sex with Seb. There was no routine, there was no expectation or pressure. It was all new and exciting.

Luci could remember when sex had been like that—when she and Ben hadn't been able to get enough of each other. When they had been young and first married they had grabbed every opportunity and then again when they'd decided it was time to start a family. She'd had plenty of sex but somewhere along the line it had lost the fun and become a chore. At some point it had become another thing on the list of jobs that had to be done.

She knew when that had happened. When, month after month, her dreams of falling pregnant hadn't eventuated. She'd started worrying, constantly taking her temperature, changing her diet, insisting on sex on certain days of the month, certain times of the day—and it had taken the fun out of it. Was it any wonder Ben had started looking elsewhere? She'd blamed him for destroying their marriage single-handedly when the reality was that she'd played her part too.

Remembering how much fun sex could be cheered her up immensely. She still knew how to enjoy life.

She smiled as Seb tucked her in to his side and trailed his finger down her arm. The night hadn't been a complete disaster after all.

'So how was the water?' Seb asked, as his fingers ran over her hip bone and down to the top of her thigh.

Luci's brain had turned to mush. 'Pardon?'

'The water?' Seb repeated. 'You wanted to dip your toe in. I want to know if it was to your liking.'

Luci grinned. 'Very much so. I've decided there is such a thing as good different. But this is all new to me. I need some guidelines.'

'What do you mean?'

'I need to know if we are dating or just having sex.'

'What do you want?'

'I need to have some fun but I also want to see what dating is like in the modern day. When I leave Sydney I need to know what to expect. I need some practice.'

'I think you'll find you'll be fine. Trust me,' he said. 'But I'm happy to be of service for the next four weeks while I'm still here. We can have fun until I leave or until you get sick of me.'

Luci appreciated the fact that he didn't suggest he'd get tired of her first.

'But I do have one condition,' Seb added.

'What's that?'

'We are exclusive while it lasts. No dating anyone else.'

Luci nodded. She had no intention of looking else-where. She couldn't imagine needing to.

'So when Michael calls and asks you out, you'd bet-ter have an excuse ready.'

'Really? Michael? I thought I made it perfectly clear that I wasn't interested.'

'For some men that only makes you more appeal-ing. For some it's all about the chase. I can see I have a lot to teach you,' he said, as he kissed her shoulder. 'So much to do and so little time.'

'Where do you want to start?' Luci replied with a smile.

'How about we start with this?' he said, flipping her onto her back and ducking his head under the covers.

Luci closed her eyes and gave herself up to him. There was no room in her head for thoughts of anything other than the waves of pleasure that consumed her.

Seb knew exactly what he was doing. This might just be the best decision she had ever made.

Seb woke her in the morning in the same way he'd said goodnight, then got up to make her a cup of tea.

'We might be going about this a little backwards but I have a first date planned,' he said as she sat up in bed and took the tea.

'Now?'

'You might have time for a shower.' He grinned.

The shower took a little longer than normal. Having Seb in there with her, offering to wash her back, wasn't necessarily the timesaver one might expect.

She dressed in jeans, canvas sneakers, a T-shirt and Seb's spare leather jacket and climbed on the back of his bike. Her thighs complained as she stretched them over the seat but she wasn't complaining. She might be a bit stiff and sore but it was an ache she was more than happy to put up with.

'Where are we going?' she asked.

'I'm taking you out for breakfast.'

That sounded good. She was starving.

Seb rode to Milson's Point on the north shore and pulled into a parking spot beside the harbour bridge. There were numerous cafés along the opposite side of the street and Luci wondered which one he had chosen, but Seb didn't cross the street. Instead, he took her hand and led her along the ramparts of the bridge and up a flight of stairs.

'You're going to walk across the bridge with me?' Luci asked as they reached the top and she found herself on the pedestrian walkway that ran along the eastern side of the bridge. 'I thought this was the sort of thing only tourists did?' she teased.

'I figured you're worth making an exception for. But if I'm going to do this then this is the best time of day. It's quiet enough on a Sunday morning to still be relatively peaceful. We can take our time and we'll have breakfast at the other end.'

The view was spectacular, better than Luci had imagined. The Opera House, the botanic gardens and the city skyline were laid out before them as they headed south across the bridge. The sun was still low in the sky to their left and the Opera House sparkled like a sugar-coated meringue on the edge of the harbour. She'd seen it from the water, in daylight and at night-time and now from a higher vantage point. It didn't disappoint, no matter what. She thought it was an incredible building and she knew it would always remind her of Seb.

There was a light breeze blowing, just enough to get the flag on top of the bridge moving but not enough to be unpleasant. They stopped numerous times to watch the ferries crisscross the harbour and the tiny yachts dart across the water. By the time they descended onto Cumberland Street in The Rocks Luci was famished. The combination of sex and walking had certainly fired her appetite. Seb ordered a big breakfast—bacon, eggs, tomato, spinach, mushrooms, hash browns. Luci had smashed avocado on toast with bacon on the side. She needed an energy boost.

'Can I ask you something?' she said as she cut into her bacon.

'Sure.'

'Why don't you have a girlfriend?'

'You mean, what's wrong with me that you haven't noticed yet?'

'No. Maybe.' Seb was teasing her but she was serious. 'Why *is* a guy like you single?'

'A guy like me? What *am* I like, exactly?'

'Oh, no, don't go fishing for compliments. Just answer the question.'

'Well, as long as you were thinking complimentary things, I'll explain,' he said. 'I want the freedom to do the things I want to do, to go where I want to go. Last year I spent about forty weeks in the country in four different towns. I don't see the point in long-distance relationships. I don't have a girlfriend because I don't want a serious relationship.'

'Have you *never* had a serious relationship?'

'Only one but that ended three years ago and I'm used to doing things my way now. I can't really see the need to commit to one person, not when so many relationships end badly.' He speared a mushroom with his fork before he looked up at her. 'Would you go through it all again?'

Luci nodded. 'I would. I liked being married,' she said honestly. 'I didn't like how my marriage *ended* but I'm not going to let that dictate how I spend the rest of my life. I liked being part of a couple, sharing my life.' It would be a long, lonely existence if she vowed never to go down that path again and if she was going to achieve her dream of motherhood she needed to be in a committed relationship. It wouldn't work any other way. Not for her at least, who had always dreamed of the whole package. 'You don't want that? Someone to share your life with? A family of your own?'

'No.' Seb drained the last of his coffee and pushed his chair back. 'I don't,' he said as he stood up.

Clearly that conversation was over. Luci would remember not to raise that topic again. She didn't want to rock the boat. There was no need to. They didn't need to have in-depth, detailed discussions about their hopes and dreams. This was all temporary, she reminded herself. It was supposed to be just a bit of fun.

They spent the next hour wandering through the markets in The Rocks before Seb took her to climb the south pylon of the bridge on their way back across the harbour. Their conversation stayed neutral, away from anything that could be considered remotely emotional, but Luci wasn't going to let it ruin her day. There was no rule that said he had to open up to her, and besides that he was the ideal date. He was attentive, funny, thoughtful and gorgeous. It had been a perfect first date.

* * *

Over the next ten days Seb took her on several dates that were almost as good. They visited the zoo and shopped in Paddington. They ate dinner in Chinatown, oysters beside the Opera House, burgers in Manly and fish and chips in Watson's Bay. But her favourite date was the day they'd hired a kayak and paddled to Store Beach. Just thinking about it now made her smile. She had been surprised by how many secluded coves there were around the harbour and she loved being able to escape the city so easily.

Store Beach was only accessible by boat, which meant it was quiet. She preferred the quieter beaches to the bustle of Bondi and Manly. Perhaps it was the country girl in her or perhaps it had something to do with the fact that when they had a beach to themselves they took advantage of that. They had made love in the water that day, something she was positive they wouldn't have been able to do at Bondi, and she knew she was going to file these memories away and revisit them when Seb was gone from her life. This might be temporary but she would always have the memories.

Spending time with Seb was therapeutic, mentally as well as physically. She felt happier than she had in a long time and she no longer thought about babies and failed marriages or Ben and his new wife, Catriona, every day. She had other things on her mind. She was becoming the person for the next stage of her life and she was starting to feel that she would be okay. She still wasn't sure that she'd be okay on her own but Seb was showing her how to put herself out there again. She knew that if she had been able to do it with him she'd be able to do it with the next guy. And maybe the next guy would be the one.

Her life was far from over. She would take her second chance. She would achieve her dreams, one way or another. Seb was right, she had time on her side and she wasn't going to let Ben take it all away from her. She would go after her dream and she would make it happen. She would learn as much as she could about herself while Seb was giving her that chance so she could grow and move forward.

Luci's time in Sydney was almost half-gone. The time was flying past; her days were busy and so were her nights. She wasn't sure how she was going to manage back in Vickers Hill. She couldn't remember how she used to fill her days. Work, housework, dinner with her parents and a game of netball once a week didn't seem like much now compared to what she was packing into her days in Sydney. So she'd better make the most of it.

She was feeling more confident and comfortable at work. She'd decided not to be so precious about comments and questions from clients as to whether or not she had children. They didn't know her circumstances so she replied with, 'Not yet,' and left it at that. She wasn't wearing a wedding ring so at least she was spared from those expectations that she and Ben had had. From the moment they'd got married that had been the next question. She'd initially used the excuses of 'We've only just got married' or 'We're saving for a house' but the questions hadn't really bothered her until she'd been trying to fall pregnant. She had needed to develop a tougher skin.

Spending time with Seb was definitely helping. He

kept her mind and body busy and she no longer thought about having kids every hour of every day. She had relaxed. She had a little over four weeks remaining and she was determined to enjoy every second. The rest of her life could start after that. She had time.

But she very quickly got used to spending her days and nights with Seb and when he told her he needed to go away for a few days for work she found the prospect of being alone again quite daunting.

'I have been asked to go to Budgee to work in their community health clinic for a few days later this week. The doctor's wife and daughter have been injured in a car accident and the doctor has flown down to Sydney to be with them. There's no hospital there any more so there's no other cover.'

'Why have they asked you?'

He shrugged. 'I was there about eighteen months ago for six weeks so they figure I'll be more familiar with the work than others. And, besides, it's what I do.'

She knew that. He'd told her he spent a lot of time travelling to different parts of country New South Wales.

'You could come with me if you like.'

'How do you figure that?'

'The doctor's wife is a nurse so with her out of action the town has lost their nurse and doctor. I could arrange a few days there for you as part of your course.'

Luci didn't care if people accused Seb of favouritism. Going with him was preferable to being left alone in Sydney, even if it was only for three days, which was how she found herself being driven down the main street of Budgee two days later.

It was a pretty town three hours west of Sydney

over the Blue Mountains, with a small-town feel. The main street was wide, not dissimilar to main streets in most country towns across Australia, and this one was planted with oak trees and lined with beautiful old public buildings. A wide, grassy strip ran down the centre of the road. A military memorial stood at one end near the pub; a majestic building with wraparound balconies and elaborate wrought-iron railings. The two-storey red-brick post office stood in the middle of town opposite the limestone town hall. Further down the street, past the police station, the Catholic church faced off across the road from the Presbyterian one, standing sentinel at the end of town.

They had left Sydney early and arrived at the clinic by ten. They were going to spend the morning working there before visiting an aboriginal settlement in the afternoon.

'Budgee used to have a small hospital,' Seb explained as he turned off the main street, 'but the services gradually dwindled as the community decreased in size and as the roads and transport improved, making it unnecessary for each country town to have its own facilities. The government "consolidated"—their word—the services, which was all well and good in most cases except for emergencies. Budgee lost its hospital but retained a community health centre, which was moved into the old hospital ironically, and the local doctor spends two days a week here and three days a week in surrounding towns.'

Seb pulled into the car park of the old hospital and Luci followed him inside. She spent what was left of the morning doing health checks, just like she would have done in Sydney, along with fielding the same personal questions interspersed with questions about the health of the local nurse and her daughter.

For lunch she and Seb grabbed a meat pie from the local bakery and ate in the car as Seb drove them to the aboriginal settlement thirty minutes out of town. Budgee was in the centre of a wine-growing region and the town was surrounded by vineyards. It reminded Luci of Vickers Hill, having the same look and feel of home. Did Vickers Hill still feel like home? She wasn't sure. She'd changed since she'd been in Sydney. She was different now and she wasn't sure if she would be able to settle back into her old life.

Was it living in a big city that had changed her or was it Seb?

She didn't know the answer to that either, although she suspected the latter.

As they drove through the countryside she almost felt as though they were on a date. Seb was dressed casually in an open-necked, short-sleeved shirt that showed off his muscular forearms. His long fingers were wrapped around the steering wheel. Last night they'd been caressing her breasts and bringing her to another orgasm, and she could still feel some tenderness between her thighs after another night of lovemaking, but it was definitely not an unpleasant sensation.

Seb was tapping his index finger and humming along in time to the song that was playing on the radio. She looked at his face, at his perfect profile as the scenery flashed past. They were still driving past rows and rows of vines, dense with green foliage, and she was tempted to tell him to pull over. She wondered if they had time for a quick make-out session in the car. She hadn't behaved like that for years but something about him made her feel like a teenager again, a reckless, rebellious teenager with only one thing on her mind.

He turned his head to look at her; he must have felt her scrutiny. He took one look at her expression and winked, and she knew he could tell what she was thinking.

She blushed and he laughed, rich and throaty, as he turned his attention back to the road.

'Hold that thought,' he said. 'There'll be time for fooling around later but we can't turn up at the settlement looking like we've just tumbled out of bed. Or out of the bushes.' He grinned and his eyes flicked briefly back to her.

A quick glance at her chest and Luci could feel the heat rising from her. The only thing stopping the windows from fogging up was the fact that it was almost as warm outside the car as inside.

If he looked at her like that once more she was going to have to pull on the handbrake and have her way with him.

'Pity,' she said as she reached across the console, ignoring the handbrake, and rested her hand at the very top of his thigh. She slid her hand between his thighs so her fingers rested against his groin. If he was going to make her sweat she was going to make sure he joined her. Two could play at that game. 'We could pull over and sneak down between the rows of grapes and make love on the ground between the vines.'

'You'll get covered in dirt.'

'I was planning to go on top,' she responded.

'Luci,' he groaned. 'That's not playing fair. I need to concentrate.'

'Are you sure we haven't got time for a quick stop?'

'Positive,' he said, removing her hand from his groin and putting it back in her lap. 'But we will have all night and I promise I'll make the wait worth your while,' he said as he drove past the signpost that welcomed them to the settlement of Frog Hollow.

She sighed and looked around as Seb drove down the main street. She needed to get her mind back on the job.

'So tell me again what I'll be doing here,' she said, trying to focus less on Seb and more on her duties.

'It does depend on who turns up but general health checks are the norm. BP, cholesterol tests, with referral for any high readings, plus counselling will take up most of your time. Just keep in mind there are different issues facing this population. Diabetes, eye disease, cardiovascular conditions, kidney disease and ear infections all tend to be more prevalent in the indigenous community and a lot of the problems arise because they don't have access to health care.'

'I remember what you told us when you gave the lecture.'

'Well, you're about to see it first-hand, although because the community of Frog Hollow made a decision to be a dry settlement we do see fewer issues here than elsewhere. There won't be scheduled appointments as such, we just see whoever turns up in whatever order they turn up, but expect to be busy as these remote clinics are only run once a month.'

Seb turned off the main street onto a side road that was made of dirt. Apparently only the main road in and out of town was tarred but the buildings were modern. Luci could see plenty of free-roaming chickens and dogs, as well as a number of kids riding bikes and playing in the street. There seem to be an awful lot of children not in school.

'There's no school in the settlement,' Seb explained, when Luci commented. 'The kids need to go into Budgee on the school bus but a lot don't make it in time. Today quite a few parents would have chosen not to send their kids to town because we were coming,' he said as he parked the car and switched off the engine.

Luci could see several people waiting, sitting on the veranda of the hall. She helped Seb to unload the medical kits from the car and take them into the hall. A temporary clinic had been set up at one end near the kitchen. There were two stations, one for her and one for him, basic and identical save for the fact that Seb's had an examination bed tucked against the wall, sectioned off behind a privacy screen.

They worked their way steadily through the locals who seemed quite content to sit and wait. They didn't seem impatient. They didn't seem to be watching the clock, like the clients in the city who always seemed to have somewhere else they needed to be. The pace suited Luci. It was nice to have time to stop and take a breath occasionally.

There were some things about home she hadn't missed—the lack of privacy, for example—but she hadn't realised just what a whirlwind life in Sydney was. The pace was frenetic, with everyone constantly on the go, but it wasn't until she had a chance to slow down that she realised how rushed she'd been.

From her station she could watch Seb working. He seemed to be primarily checking ears and eyes as frequently as she was checking blood pressures.

He looked up and smiled at her and she felt a warm

glow suffuse her. They worked well together. They did other things well together too and she hugged that thought to herself. She was looking forward to the end of the day, looking forward to tonight.

She stripped off her gloves as she finished with her patient and went out to the veranda to call the next one, only to find there was no one else waiting. She wondered if their day was done, if they could return to Budgee and finish what she'd started.

She went back inside the hall and was preparing to pack away her things when she saw Seb incline his head at her and nod at his patient, and she knew he wanted her to join them.

Seb was looking into the ears of a little boy who looked about three or four years of age. The boy's mother sat beside him. She was heavily pregnant and the fabric of her summer dress strained across her belly.

'Nadine, this is Luci Dawson, one of the community health nurses,' Seb said as he switched sides to look into the little boy's left ear. 'Luci, would you mind checking Nadine's blood pressure for me while I finish up with Byron? This is Nadine's fifth pregnancy and she hasn't had any problems, but she hasn't had any antenatal care either and she's not sure of her dates. She thinks she might be about seven months but seeing as we're here I thought we'd do a bit of a check.'

'Sure.' Luci smiled at Nadine.

The woman looked much further along than seven months. Luci couldn't imagine not having any antenatal care herself but Seb had warned her that things were different out here. Nadine looked relaxed but Luci knew Seb was worried.

It was hard to pinpoint her age. Her brown skin was

smooth and glowed but her eyes looked tired. She could be anywhere from twenty-five to thirty-five. Even so, a fifth pregnancy was a lot.

Luci wrapped the blood-pressure cuff around Nadine's arm and pumped it up. She popped the stethoscope in her ears and listened for the heartbeat followed by silence as the cuff deflated. Her blood pressure was fine.

'All normal,' she told Seb.

'Good.' Seb nodded. 'Byron seems to have another slight middle-ear infection, swimmer's ear most likely. I'll give him a course of antibiotics but no swimming for a week, okay? And before you go I'd like to listen to the baby's heart and take a couple of measurements, if that's all right. Can you just hop up on the bed behind the screen for me?'

Seb rifled through one of the medical bags and found the medication he wanted. He wrote Byron's name and the instructions on a label and attached it to the bottle.

Luci took the bottle and handed him the stethoscope. She picked Byron up and popped him on her hip and followed Seb around the screen. Protocol dictated that she needed to be present for the exam.

Nadine had already hoisted her dress up to expose her belly, which was as tight as a drum. Luci felt a familiar pull of longing and jealousy when she saw the woman's heavily pregnant frame but she tried her best to ignore it. She was a professional, she could do this.

Seb placed the bulb of the scope on Nadine's tummy and moved it around, listening for the baby's heartbeat. Luci watched him. She saw him frown and reposition the stethoscope. She could see Nadine hold her breath but then Seb smiled and Nadine relaxed and exhaled.

Seb pulled the stethoscope out of his ears and looped it around his neck. Luci handed him a tape measure, which he took but didn't immediately use.

'Well, that explains a few things,' he said as he smiled at Nadine. 'You're having twins.'

'Twins?' Nadine and Luci said in unison.

Seb nodded and his blue eyes sparkled. 'Now I know you've done all this before but this is the first set of twins you've had. I want you to have some antenatal care. I want you to make an appointment at the hospital in Dubbo—actually, I'll make it for you,' he said as he helped Nadine to sit up on the edge of the bed.

He pulled his mobile phone out of his pocket and scrolled through the address book, looking for the number. Nadine stood up and slipped her feet back into her flip-flops before taking Byron from Luci.

Seb had been put through to the right department and covered the speaker with his hand as he spoke to Nadine. 'Can you make it to Dubbo tomorrow afternoon?'

Nadine nodded and Seb confirmed the time.

'They will do an ultrasound scan,' he said as he ended the call. 'It's important that they try to confirm your dates and check that everything is on track. Any dramas, make sure you call the Budgee clinic. I'll still be there tomorrow and I'll phone Dubbo for an update,' he added, wanting to make sure that she understood he'd be around to keep an eye on her. He handed Nadine a card with the Budgee clinic number on it and added the number for the Dubbo hospital, along with the appointment time.

'Do you think she'll keep the appointment?' Luci asked as they hit the road a little later for the return trip to Budgee. Flocks of galahs and sulphur-crested cockatoos were feeding at the side of the road. The cockatoos rose up in a squawking mass as the car passed them but the little pink and grey galahs seemed oblivious. They kept their heads down, pecking away at the gum-nut seeds that were strewn on the ground.

'I hope so. Twins are obviously trickier to deal with, and gestational diabetes is high in the indigenous population so I'd like her to have the proper care. It'll be another month before anyone is back out at Frog Hollow. Anything could happen in that time.'

Luci's muscles groaned in protest as she lowered herself onto a child-sized kindergarten chair. Muscles she'd forgotten she had ached and every time she moved she was reminded of the night before. She'd been stretched, bent and contorted into all sorts of positions last night but she wasn't complaining even if her muscles were. She and Seb had barely made it back to the motel before tearing each other's clothes off. Their desire had been building all afternoon until it had reached fever pitch and they had almost sprinted to her room and spent the rest of the evening making love, stopping only briefly to shower and grab some food before they'd gone back to her room. Luci knew they must have looked like they had been having frenzied sex but she hadn't cared any more. It hadn't been like home. She could behave as she pleased out here and it pleased her to misbehave with Seb.

She smiled to herself as she thought about what they'd got up to, until she realised that the preschoolers sitting at the table with her weren't going to give her time to daydream.

She was spending the afternoon in the child-care

centre and kindergarten attached to the community health clinic. The work was pretty much the same, assessing the development of the children, but the approach was different. Instead of a formal appointment, Luci played with the children in the kindergarten environment, doing surreptitious development checks. Sitting with the kids while they drew pictures or constructed masterpieces out of cardboard rolls, boxes, egg cartons and metres of sticky tape gave her a chance to assess their hearing, speech and fine motor skills. Later she'd play outside with them in the sandpit and on the climbing equipment, observing their balance, co-ordination and gross motor skills.

If she noticed any issues she could then make referrals to the visiting therapists but, again, making appointments didn't necessarily work. Appointment times were not generally considered fixed and Luci had been told that a lot of the time the health-care staff just had to hope that some of the kids were in attendance at playgroup when the visiting therapists were in town.

Luci was writing a child's name on the cardboard robot that he'd made when she noticed Nadine and Byron coming into the centre.

Nadine looked tired today, definitely not as fresh as yesterday. The circles under her eyes had darkened and Luci thought her face looked a little pinched and drawn, as if she was in pain. Luci stood up. 'Nadine, hello. Are you on your way to Dubbo?'

Nadine nodded. 'I thought I'd drop Byron here while I went for my appointment, if that's okay. He knows this kindy.'

Budgee was about halfway between Frog Hollow

and Dubbo. Nadine had had to pass through town in order to reach Dubbo.

'Sure,' Luci replied as Byron ran off to play. 'Are you feeling all right?'

'I didn't sleep well and my back is a bit sore. I think I might have pulled a muscle when I picked Byron up this morning.'

'Have you got time for a cup of tea or water? Why don't you sit down and I'll get you something to drink?' Luci offered. But before she could usher her to a chair Nadine clutched her stomach and looked as if she was about to burst into tears.

'What is it?' Luci asked.

But Nadine didn't answer, she just looked down at the floor. Luci followed her gaze.

Nadine was standing in a pool of water.

CHAPTER SEVEN

'THAT'S NOT GOOD,' Nadine said.

Luci agreed but at least Nadine was in town, and Seb was only metres away in the building next door.

But before Luci had a chance to say anything further Nadine gasped and doubled over.

'Contraction?' Luci asked.

She looked up at Luci and her dark brown eyes were filled with fear. She nodded and said, 'It's too early.'

Luci knew that Nadine was unsure of her dates and today's appointment had been an opportunity to narrow them down, but there was the distinct possibility that it was far too early. In some cases labour could be delayed, even if the membranes had ruptured, but that was a clinical decision and once the contractions had started Luci knew there was very little they could do.

'Dr Hollingsworth is just next door,' Luci said, trying to sound calm and reassuring even as she fought back her own concerns. 'Do you think you can walk or shall I fetch a wheelchair?'

'I can walk if I can lean on you.'

Jenny, the child-care director, had seen what was happening and she came across the room, carrying an armful of old towels. Being a centre filled with preschoolers, they were well equipped for dealing with accidents similar to this.

'Jenny, we need to leave Byron here,' Luci said as Jenny dropped the towels on the floor.

'Of course.' She squatted down to mop up the mess. 'What about your older children?' she asked Nadine.

'They'll go home on the school bus,' Nadine managed to say, before another contraction swamped her. She gripped tightly onto Luci's arm. The contractions were close together and strong. Luci didn't like the look of this at all. She needed to get Nadine next door to Seb. And quickly.

Byron was engrossed with a big box of building blocks and trucks and didn't look up as Luci ushered his mother out of the centre.

'Heather, can you call Seb, please?' Luci started speaking to the receptionist in the community health clinic as soon as she and Nadine walked through the clinic doors. 'And an ambulance. Nadine is in labour.'

Heather stood up from behind the desk. 'Take her through here,' she said, directing Luci into one of the old hospital rooms. She wheeled a trolley over to the bed and handed Luci a hospital gown. 'There are gloves, scissors and basic clinical supplies on here. I'll call Seb and the ambulance and then check back to see if there's anything else you need. We're not fully equipped any more but I'll do my best.'

Luci nodded her thanks. 'You'd better phone ahead to Dubbo and warn them too. Nadine was on her way there for an antenatal appointment,' she added as Heather left the room. She turned back to Nadine, who was still clinging to her arm. 'Let's get you into this gown so that Dr Hollingsworth can examine you when he gets here.'

'Can you stop the labour? It's too early.'

Luci shook her head. 'Once your waters have broken there's nothing much we can do. These babies are on their way.' The best they could hope for was that the ambulance arrived before the babies did.

Seb hurried in just as Luci had finished helping Nadine to change.

'Nadine! I wasn't expecting to see you today. What's going on?' He sounded cool, calm and collected but there was no doubt he'd come at a run.

Luci handed him a paper hospital gown and he slipped his arms into the sleeves and waited as Luci tied the strings before he repeated the process for her. He washed his hands and pulled on a pair of surgical gloves as Luci wrapped a BP cuff around Nadine's arm.

'Let's see what's happening,' he said, as he positioned himself at the foot of the bed and got Nadine to lie back and bend her knees. 'Eight centimetres dilated,' he said.

There wasn't going to be much time to spare. But just as Luci was praying that the ambulance was close by Heather came into the room and dashed her hopes.

'The ambulance is forty-five minutes out of town at the scene of a car accident. They'll get here as quickly as they can but expect them to be a while,' she informed them.

Nadine was in the middle of another contraction and Luci didn't think she'd heard a word Heather had said, which was probably just as well. It wasn't great news but it didn't appear to faze Seb.

'It looks like your babies are going to be born in Budgee,' Seb told Nadine once her contraction had passed. 'Luckily for you, we've done this before.' There wasn't a trace of panic in his voice and he even had Luci believing it would all be all right.

'You okay?' He looked at Luci and mouthed the question. Nadine wouldn't be able to see his lips as her belly was blocking her view.

Luci wasn't sure. She didn't want to deal with a woman in labour. She'd managed to cope with Nadine's pregnancy yesterday, but actually delivering babies was a different thing altogether. But Seb didn't need to hear about her issues now. He needed her help. Somehow she'd get through this. She would focus on one thing at a time.

She nodded. Seb needed her. She would do her best to keep it together and wouldn't think about things that were out of her control.

'How quick were your other labours?' Seb asked Nadine. 'Have you been caught off guard before or have you been able to get to the hospital?'

'My third one was fast. She was born out at Frog Hollow.'

'But other than that it all went fine?'

Nadine nodded, unable to speak as another contraction gripped her. She was covered in a sheen of sweat and Luci wiped her forehead with a flannel.

'Were there any complications with your other deliveries?'

'No,' she puffed.

Seb picked a stethoscope up from the trolley and listened to the babies' heartbeats. They were both around one hundred and forty beats per minute—perfectly normal. Everyone else might be stressed but at least the babies weren't.

Heather returned and this time she was wheeling two

small cots side by side. She parked these in the corner of the room and lifted out a pile of blankets and a set of scales. She wiped out the cots and folded some of the blankets, putting them back into the cots to act as makeshift mattresses before covering them with clean sheets. 'We had these in storage but there's not much else,' she said. 'There's pethidine if you need it but that's about it.'

Seb got the message. He doubted he had time for pethidine to work to provide any pain relief for Nadine—these babies were in a hurry and Heather's underlying message was that there was nothing else on hand to help him manage premature infants medically. There were no drugs, no Vitamin K injections, no heat lamps and no emergency team standing by.

Babies had been born for thousands of years without all the modern interference but Seb knew the survival rate of premature twins had been low in those days. He would do his best and hope that the ambulance arrived soon. He prayed silently that everything would go right.

His gaze swept the room, looking for anything at all that might come in handy. There was an oxygen tank attached to the wall. He looked at Luci and then back at the cylinder. 'Can you see if that works?' he asked her.

Luci put down the flannel and crossed the room. She had been very quiet and he hoped she was coping okay with the drama, he wasn't really sure how much experience she had with this sort of situation. But her movements were practised and efficient. She knew the basic procedures and he just had to hope that he could prevent an emergency.

Luci opened the valve on the oxygen tank. She nodded.

That was one thing he had up his sleeve if needed, he thought as he turned back to Nadine.

Her labour was progressing quickly. That wasn't surprising given that it was her fifth pregnancy and delivery, but Seb wished it wasn't so. He would much prefer it if she could hold on until the ambulance reached them but that was looking highly unlikely because he could see the first baby's head crowning.

'I want to push,' Nadine told him.

He'd barely had time to check the position of the babies but there was no going back now. 'Okay. We're ready to go.'

Nadine's knees were bent. Luci stood beside her, holding her hand.

'Push,' he instructed.

He reached between her thighs and eased the baby's head out.

'Okay, relax now. Wait for the next contraction.'

Nadine panted swiftly between contractions and with the following one Seb delivered the baby's shoulders. The little girl slid out swiftly and he hoped it was because Nadine's body was familiar with the process and not because the other baby had kicked it out. He didn't want to deal with a breech presentation as well as the premature delivery of twins.

'It's a girl,' he told Nadine. She came out yelling and Seb placed her on Nadine's chest. Luci had loosened the hospital gown at Nadine's neck so the baby could lie skin to skin on her mother but Seb couldn't leave her there for long. She needed to be checked and kept warm and he needed to get ready to deliver the second baby.

'Can you do the Apgar test?' he asked Luci as he cut the cord.

Luci nodded and reached for the baby. 'I'll just check her out,' she explained to Nadine. 'You've still got some work to do.'

Seb briefly watched Luci holding the baby. It suited her. She had an expression of contentment and he hoped for her sake that she had a child of her own one day. He knew that was what she wanted.

'One minute Apgar eight out of ten. Pulse ninety-six, tinge of blue in the fingers,' Luci said as she put the baby on the scales. He was aware of her weighing the baby as she updated him. 'Two point four kilograms,' she said as she wrapped the baby. There was no time to clean her up as she needed to be kept warm and Luci needed to be ready to help with the second delivery.

Nadine's contractions were continuing strongly. The second twin was on its way. He checked what was happening and breathed a sigh of relief when he felt Twin B moving down into the pelvis.

Seb had to rupture the membrane for Twin B and the next thing he saw was the baby's head crowning. Thank God it wasn't breech.

'Five-minute Apgar nine out of ten,' Luci said, updating him on Twin A. 'Colour is good, heart rate ninety-eight.'

He nodded in acknowledgement to Luci but spoke to Nadine. 'Okay, time for number two. You can push with the next contraction.'

The second twin was slightly bigger but was delivered just as easily. He handed the little boy to Nadine then checked the cord before clamping and cutting it. Nadine had a quick cuddle before Luci took him to assess.

'Six out of ten. Pulse ninety-four. Sluggish reflexes, blue extremities, resp. rate thirty-five.'

The little boy was bigger, but not as healthy as his sister.

'He needs oxygen,' Luci said, and Seb knew she was looking to him to fix the problem. They had oxygen but how was he going to get it into a premature infant?

He looked around the room for inspiration as he prayed that the ambulance would hurry.

His gaze rested on the acrylic bassinettes.

'Can you connect some tubing to the oxygen cylinder?' he asked Luci as he covered Nadine with a blanket. The little boy was his priority now and there was nothing else he could do for Nadine until the ambulance arrived. If he could manage to hold the two bassinettes together he would be able to fashion a makeshift oxygen tent, which would be better than nothing in the short term. Taking the little boy from Lucy he placed him in a bassinette alongside his sister. He emptied the second bassinette and inverted it over the first. He grabbed a roll of medical tape and ran it around the edges of the cribs, taping them together. There was an opening where the sides had been cut down that would allow the carbon monoxide to escape. The 'tent' would be less efficient than he would like but it would be good enough.

Luci had connected the tubing to the oxygen cylinder. She passed the end to him and he slid it into the bassinette, taping it in place too.

'Run it at eight litres per minute,' he said as Heather came back into the room.

'The ambulance is five minutes away,' she told them, and Seb thought that was the best sentence he'd ever heard. He could handle five more minutes.

He left Luci to keep an eye on the babies as he spoke to Nadine. 'Your babies are okay. Your daughter is doing well, your little boy is having a little bit of difficulty breathing so we need to give him some oxygen, but the ambulance is almost here and will transfer them to Dubbo hospital.'

'What about me?'

'You'll go too.'

'Byron?'

'I've put him on the school bus with your other kids,' Heather said as she returned to the room with the ambulance officers in tow. 'Will there be someone home in Frog Hollow to take care of them?'

Nadine nodded. 'My husband is there and my sister will give him a hand.'

The next fifteen minutes passed in a flurry of activity as the ambos stabilised the babies and Seb gave Nadine an oxytocin injection and delivered the placentas.

Somehow they got the whole family into the back of the ambulance and Seb breathed a sigh of relief as he closed the back doors and watched the ambulance take off.

When he went back into the community health clinic Heather was rescheduling the rest of the day's appointments. She was proving to be worth her weight in gold today.

He left her to it and went to help Luci tidy up the makeshift delivery suite.

She was stripping the bed and had her back to him but he saw her lift her arm and wipe her hand across her face and he realised she was crying. Were they happy or sad tears? Her shoulders were shaking and as he got closer he could hear her sobs. It sounded like her heart was breaking.

He put a hand on her shoulder. 'Luci, what's the matter?'

She turned around but she was crying so hard she couldn't talk. He wrapped her in his arms and held her tightly until her tears eased but didn't stop completely. He brushed her hair from her forehead and kissed her gently. 'What is it, Luce? Tell me what's wrong.'

'I can't do this any more,' she sobbed.

'Can't do what?'

'Deliver babies. It's one of the reasons I left Vickers Hill, seeing other women holding their newborn babies. I can't do it.'

He frowned. 'You'll get your turn,' he told her. 'We've talked about this.'

But Luci was shaking her head. 'You don't understand.'

'Explain it to me, then.'

'Not here. I need to go home.'

'Home?' he asked. 'To Vickers Hill?'

She shook her head and gulped air as she tried to get her emotions under control. 'No. Back to the motel.'

He was happy to call it quits. It was almost the end of the day and hopefully Heather had managed to reschedule the remaining appointments. Rarely was anything so urgent with community health that it couldn't be pushed back. He would start earlier tomorrow if necessary, before they headed back to Sydney. Right now Luci was his priority.

He had bundled her into the car and driven her back to the motel and now she was sitting on the edge of the bed. Her face was blotchy and her eyes were red but she had stopped crying. He boiled the kettle to make tea, wondering if he should call room service for something stronger, but decided to wait.

He handed her a cup of green tea. 'What's going on?' he asked.

'I don't like delivering babies.'

He frowned. 'What's not to like? I agree, sometimes things can get a bit difficult but we had a really good outcome today, all things considered.'

'I know and I'm happy for Nadine but I find it soul destroying. It just reminds me that the thing I want most in my life isn't a possibility.'

'What are you talking about? We've had this conversation…you're young, you've got time.'

'It's not time I need,' she said with a shake of her head. 'There are some things I love about small country towns and there are things I can live without. Like delivering babies. That's part of the reason I wanted to get out of there. I don't want to deliver other people's babies. Not when I can't have my own.'

'What do you mean?'

'I can't have kids.'

He wasn't sure if he was following the conversation properly. 'But you told me you and your ex-husband were planning on starting a family.'

'We were trying to get pregnant. It didn't happen.'

'But that doesn't mean you can't have them. It just means it hadn't happened yet.'

'We tried for eighteen months. Nothing.'

'It still doesn't mean the problem lies with you.'

'I'm pretty sure it does. Ben has remarried and is expecting a baby with his new wife.'

Wow. He hadn't seen that coming.

'Why haven't you told me this before?' he asked.

'Because it was irrelevant to you.'

He was momentarily affronted until he realised she was right. Their relationship had no strings attached.

But that didn't change the fact that Luci was upset and his natural instinct was to try to fix things. Although this could be a slight problem. He might be out of his depth.

'I guess it's not,' he agreed. 'You've spoken about wanting to have kids but you never mentioned you couldn't.' He was surprised at how hurt he felt that she hadn't confided in him but he wasn't stupid enough not to realise that he hadn't confided in her either. There was plenty of information he had kept to himself so why should he be upset to find she was no different? He didn't normally have double standards. 'Do you know what the problem is?'

Luci shook her head. 'No.'

'You haven't been tested?'

'It's a long story.'

'I'm not going anywhere.' Never had a truer word been spoken. They were in the middle of New South Wales. They had nowhere to go, nothing else to do. He had all the time in the world.

Luci sipped her tea. 'The doctors said the same thing as you did initially. They told us we were young and healthy and there was no reason to worry. They said we should try to relax, try to just enjoy it, and if, after a year, we weren't pregnant then they'd do tests. So we listened and decided to keep trying. I had no idea how hard it would be to "relax" in that situation. We kept working. We thought we'd pay off some more of our mortgage and Ben wanted to expand the family business and suddenly eighteen months had passed. So we went back to the doctor and tests were suggested.

'We started the process but by now we were worried. We started discussing what we would do if the tests showed a problem. Would we go down the IVF path? That's expensive and we weren't sure how we would afford it. We were already stressed and things just got worse, and then Ben met Catriona. When Ben left me there didn't seem any point in continuing the testing process and when I heard that Catriona was expecting a baby I figured I had my answer.' She shrugged. 'It didn't matter what the tests showed. The problem was with me.'

Seb could understand her devastation and her logic but that didn't mean she was right. 'But it could have been any number of things.'

'Well, until I find someone who I want to try again with it doesn't matter. What matters is trying to get on with my life. Ben took away my marriage and I've recovered from that, but he also took away my dream of having a family. Even if the problem lay with me as a couple we could have adopted or fostered kids, we could have made something work, but now I either have to give up on my dream or start again. I decided to start again. I will do it. I want this more than anything but it still hurts when I see pregnant women or women with their babies. It reminds me of what I might never have and it's part of the reason I wanted to move away from working in a country hospital. I had to assist with deliveries and I'd want to be happy for the parents but every time it just felt like my heart was breaking.'

'Working in family and community health might be just as difficult.'

'I know. I'm coming to realise that,' she sighed. 'But it's still an area that interests me. It's a double-edged sword in a way. I want to work with kids but I didn't think about the fact that so many women with young children would be pregnant with another one. But I'm hoping that eventually I'll feel better about it. It will either wreck me or help me but I don't expect it to happen overnight. One thing at a time.

'I've got over the end of my marriage, perhaps one day I'll accept that I can't have a family, but for the moment I just prefer not to talk about it. Not talking about it means I can try to ignore it. It's obvious the problem lies with me, but I'm not ready to think about what it means.'

All along Seb had had the feeling that she'd been running away and now he knew why. He couldn't blame her for not wanting to be around when her ex's new partner had the child she'd been longing for.

And now it was Seb's turn to feel as though his heart was breaking. In sympathy with Luci. *I'm so sorry.* What else could he say?

But he couldn't help her. There was nothing he could do. As much as he wanted to, he couldn't fix this. He couldn't give her what she wanted but he could take care of her. At least for now.

He lay on the bed with her and wrapped her in his arms and waited until she fell into an exhausted sleep.

But sleep eluded him. He lay in the dark and thought about Luci.

It had been a long time since anything, or anyone, had affected him this strongly. Since anyone had made his heart ache.

This was exactly what he'd been trying to avoid. He

didn't want to feel. He didn't want to hurt for someone else. And he didn't want to think about what that meant.

In the space of three weeks he had seen her ecstatic, nervous, passionate, playful, flirty and full of despair. Unlike him, she wore her heart on her sleeve. He felt he had known her for much longer and he knew he would miss her when they parted ways, but their time was limited. He would be leaving Sydney in a little over a fortnight. This wasn't a long-term proposition and her problem was not his to solve. As much as he'd like to, he couldn't fix things for her and she hadn't asked him to.

He would enjoy the next few weeks, distract her and hopefully take her mind off her problems. He would give her time to heal and then he'd let her go.

Luci picked up her wine glass and followed Seb up the steps of his boat and around to the forward deck.

The carpenter had finished installing the new kitchen while she and Seb had been in Budgee. The boat was finished, still unnamed but finished, and to celebrate Seb had invited her to spend the weekend on board. Seb had cooked a simple meal of steak and salad, the new kitchen had been tested and the new bed christened. So far the weekend was fabulous.

The boat bobbed gently on the calm waters of the Hawkesbury River. It was a beautiful warm night. There were thick clouds on the horizon and rain had been forecast. The air was heavy with humidity but so far the rain held off. The sunset had been incredible and, for now, the sky was clear and black.

Luci sat beside Seb and he slipped his arm around her shoulders, tucking her in against him. She was naked under her cotton dress and Seb wore only a pair of shorts. His body heat radiated out to her. She leaned back against the windshield of the boat and looked up at the sky. It was sprinkled with tiny stars that looked like diamonds on black velvet.

There were no other lights, on the water or on the shore. She felt like they had the world to themselves. Luci sighed. Seb was constantly surprising her with their dates and this one was particularly romantic. Lying on the deck of the boat, feeling like they were the only two people in existence, she could see the attraction of having somewhere to escape to. It was quite possibly a necessity in order to maintain your sanity if you lived in a city like Sydney, but she still couldn't imagine making this her life. As romantic as the night was, she imagined it would be a very isolated existence with no one to share it with.

'Do you think you'll ever get lonely out here on your own?'

'Maybe,' Seb replied. 'But that's a chance I'm willing to take. I've never been lonely before.'

'You've never had anyone else stay?'

He shook his head. 'No.'

'Why is that?' Luci was curious and also flattered to think she was the first, but realised there could just as easily be another explanation that had nothing to do with her. 'Was it because the boat wasn't ready?'

'No. I've stayed the night many times but I've never felt the need to share this with anyone else before.'

'Why did you ask me?'

'I thought you might like it,' he said simply.

'Not to keep you company?'

'I'm happy with my own company.'

That had been a question that had been bothering her

since the first time she'd set foot on his boat. His desire to have an escape, to keep a bachelor pad of sorts had seemed at odds with someone who was so vital and charismatic.

'Have you never thought about sharing your life with someone?' She knew he'd had at least one lengthy relationship but she still wondered why it hadn't developed into something more serious. He was only thirty-one. Far too young to have decided to spend his life alone. What had happened that had made him so solitary?

Despite her divorce Luci hadn't given up on finding love again. She wasn't assuming Seb would want to share his life with her but she wondered what had happened to make him so against the idea of sharing his life with anyone.

'Once upon a time I assumed I would marry and have kids, that it was something that was in my future. But it was just that. In the future. I assumed it would happen one day but I had no real plans that it had to happen by a certain point in my life. I guess I thought I would finish my studies, get married, eventually have a couple of kids, but it hasn't turned out that way. And I'm okay with that. I'm okay on my own.'

She had shared so much of herself with him—her hopes and dreams, her failures and disappointments. She knew him intimately yet she still knew very little about what had made him into the man he was today.

What had shaped him? What had led him to the decisions he had made? What were his hopes and dreams? Surely no one really hoped to spend their life alone, did they? Something must have happened to bring him to that conclusion.

'Yet now you've decided that you don't want that future. What has happened that has made you think you'd be better off alone?'

'I lost someone unexpectedly.'

'Your girlfriend?'

She felt his answering nod.

'What happened?'

'She was killed in a hit-and-run accident.'

'Oh, Seb.' Luci felt awful now. She'd forced the admission out of him and perhaps it wasn't something he'd wanted to share. She didn't know what she could say to make things better but before she could say anything Seb continued.

'It happened right outside our house. It was the day we were moving in together. Emma had parked opposite the house and she was carrying boxes inside. A car came round the corner and ran her over. I don't know whether she couldn't see where she was going, she might have stepped into the path of the car, but she hit her head when she fell. I guess she didn't have time to put her arms out. When I got home there was an ambulance in the middle of the street but it was too late. *I* was too late.

'She died from head injuries. I like to think she never knew what had happened but I don't think that's true. She didn't die instantly. It messed me up for a long time. Thinking about what she went through. How she suffered. And I don't want to experience anything like that again. That's why I've chosen to live my life the way I am.'

Finally Luci was able to understand. She couldn't imagine going through that experience. The trauma, the guilt, the despair. She knew he would have felt all those things, especially guilt. He would blame himself for not getting there sooner, not being there to help his girlfriend with the boxes. He would think he could have made the difference. Luci knew him well enough to know that he would struggle to forgive himself. She finally understood.

'Did they ever find the driver of the car?' she asked.

'No.'

He'd lost everything that day. He'd thought losing Emma had been the worst thing that could happen but things had got worse from there, much worse. But Seb wasn't sure if Luci could handle hearing about what had happened next. He lapsed into silence as he fought his demons. Fought with the guilt that still haunted him. He had never forgiven himself for not being there earlier. He had been held up at work, agreeing to see an extra patient. If he hadn't he would have been there. *He* would have been carrying those boxes and he wouldn't have lost everything.

'Seb?' Luci interrupted his thoughts.

Maybe if he explained everything to her she would understand why he was so different from her. Why he was the darkness and she was the light. Why he struggled to see the beauty in the world.

He continued. 'The coroner ordered a post-mortem. The cause of death had to be officially determined in case Emma hadn't died from injuries sustained in the accident. They had to determine whether it had been natural causes or manslaughter. Not that it mattered in the end as the driver was never found,' he said, and he could hear the bitterness in his voice, 'but the post-mortem found that Emma was pregnant. I was going to be a father.'

CHAPTER EIGHT

HE FELT LUCI squeeze his hand in the darkness and heard her little intake of breath but she didn't speak, allowing him to continue.

'Emma had told her sister about the baby and apparently she was planning on telling me that night. She wanted it to be a surprise on what would have been our first night in the house. I've hated surprises ever since.'

He had lost everything. Not just his girlfriend but his future. He hadn't really ever thought seriously about being a father, he'd just assumed it would happen one day, but to be given that news and then have it taken away from him immediately had devastated him.

'Losing something I never had and never knew I wanted; I didn't understand how that could hurt so much.' It had destroyed his belief that good things could happen and he had only seen darkness for a long time after that. Mostly that was still all he saw.

'I imagine the feeling is similar to knowing that the thing you want most in the world is never going to happen for you.'

Luci's voice was thick with tears and he realised she did understand how he felt. She would have had the same feeling over and over again, every month, when she had been desperate to fall pregnant and it hadn't happened. Month after month. But she'd got through it.

Had his confession been hard on her?

'I didn't mean to upset you,' he told her. He'd wanted her to understand. He wasn't sure why but it seemed important that he share his past with her but he hadn't meant to upset her.

'I'm okay. I'm upset for you.'

'My whole life changed in the space of a few minutes. I took a new direction after that. I never moved into the house. I couldn't bring myself to do it. I sold the house and bought my motorbike and this boat instead. I couldn't settle, I was restless, I still am. That was my attempt at domesticity, at living a normal life, and it didn't turn out as I'd planned. I lost everything at once, things I didn't even know I had, and it took me a long time to feel like my life was back under control. I think it's enough now to be responsible just for my own life. I don't ever want to go through that pain again.'

Over the past three years he had slowly recovered from Emma's death but he hadn't forgotten how he'd felt and he wasn't sure that he wanted to put himself out there again for love. 'I don't want to put myself in that position again.' He didn't ever want to be vulnerable again. He had worked hard to get back on top of things and he didn't ever want to lose his way again. He was determined to be the master of his own destiny but that made it very difficult to let someone else in.

He had moved on, to a degree, but he knew the events of that day had changed him and he never again wanted to feel that pain of loss that he felt was inevitable if he opened up his heart. So he had lived a solitary existence. He didn't want to have a home. He didn't want to put down roots. Becoming invested in something, attached to something, scared him. He knew how easily it could be ripped away. 'When you love someone it isn't for ever. It can't be. Life doesn't work like that.'

'No one is meant to live a whole lifetime alone,' Luci argued. 'There are highs and lows, disappointments and tragedies, as well as happiness and joy in life, and *I* think it's better to share those times with someone else. Sharing those feelings can soften the lows and enhance the highs. Joy and sadness are both better shared. Let me show you.'

She stood on the deck and lifted her dress over her head. She wore nothing underneath the thin cotton shift. She stood before him, naked and gorgeous, and offered him solace.

His reaction was immediate. He knew how the pleasures of the flesh could wipe out the traumas of the past, even if only temporarily. He'd had plenty of experience in that method of recovery over the past three years but never had he felt the satisfaction that he felt when he was with Luci. He got a sense of peacefulness with her and that was something that had never lasted before. Along with the physical release Luci was somehow able to provide emotional release too.

He pushed his shorts down and over his feet so he too was naked and knelt before her. His erection stood to attention, stiff and strong, but he ignored it.

He ran his hands up the insides of her thighs, parting them.

She opened her legs wider for him as his fingers reached the junction of her thighs. He slid his fingers inside her. She was warm and moist.

She moaned and pushed against him as he ran his

thumb over the bud at her core. He replaced his thumb with his tongue and all his troubles were forgotten as he licked and sucked until she shivered with his touch. He cupped her buttocks with his hands and held her against him, burying himself in her, losing himself in the sweet saltiness of her.

She gasped and held his head with her hands. She moaned again, a little louder. Spread her legs a little wider. Let him in a little deeper.

He felt her legs start to shake. He rose and lifted her off her feet and she wrapped her legs around him. He was vaguely aware of thunder rumbling in the distance as he turned and pushed her against the windshield. The storm was on its way.

He locked her between his body and the slope of the glass. Bent his head and licked her breasts as he drove himself deep inside her.

Her skin glowed ghostly pale in the moonlight and he could see the four freckles, dark against her skin, on the swell of her breast. Over her right shoulder he could see the Southern Cross, the diamonds in the sky that would always remind him of her.

He ignored the storm and the stars and the memories as he focused on feeling, touching and tasting. He rode the waves of pleasure with Luci.

He didn't miss Emma any more. He hadn't missed her for a long time. He'd taught himself to be alone but as he lost himself in Luci he realised all the other things he'd been missing. All the things that not feeling had deprived him of. The pleasure of sharing not just physically but emotionally.

He had shut himself off and Luci was helping him to open up again. She saw the good in the world. The brightness and the light. He had blocked that all out. Not wanting to risk being hurt, he had shut out all the beauty as well.

Her arms were around his neck and he felt her legs tighten around his waist as she met his thrusts, urging him to go faster. She was warm and wet as she clung to him. She was brightness and light. Even after what she'd been through she hadn't given up on the idea of love.

'Now, Seb. Now!'

She arched her back as she came, trembling in his arms.

He shuddered with the release as a fork of lightning split the sky, followed by a clap of thunder booming overhead just as they came together, sharing the pleasure.

He could smell her. She was warm and sweet. He pressed his lips against her shoulder as he tasted her. She was salty and sweet.

Clouds drifted overhead, obscuring the stars, and he smelt the rain just before it began to fall. Fat, warm drops fell on their bare skin.

Luci was still in his arms and he carried her downstairs to his bed, their clothes abandoned on the deck as the storm raged overhead.

It passed quickly but he didn't notice. They lay in peaceful, contented silence. He wasn't thinking about love and loss. He wasn't thinking about anything other than the satisfaction and pleasure of having someone to hold.

Perhaps Luci was right. Maybe having someone to share things with could sometimes make things better.

He fell asleep with Luci in his arms as the storm rolled to the east.

* * *

Luci stowed her suitcase in the luggage compartment under the bus that was going to take her back to Vickers Hill. She climbed on board with mixed emotions. Her uncle had died three days ago so the trip home was tinged with sadness but while she was looking forward to seeing her family she wasn't sure if she was quite ready to be back in Vickers Hill. She didn't feel as if she'd been gone long enough to erase people's perceptions of her. Would they still think of her as 'poor Luci', the girl who couldn't keep her husband? Or would they have moved on to something else?

She was also wary about seeing Ben but she knew there would be no avoiding it. Her uncle had been married to his great-aunt. There weren't enough degrees of separation in country towns. She would have to see both Ben and his new wife, Catriona, and just to complicate things further Luci knew Catriona would be heavily pregnant. She was due to give birth any day now.

She could use Seb's cool head and rational thinking but he was hundreds of miles away. She knew he'd been worried about how she was going to cope with all the different stresses but she'd assured him she'd be fine. She didn't want him to worry, even though she was worried herself. She was a big girl. She'd have to cope. She couldn't expect Seb to fight her battles, he wouldn't always be there for her, but she admitted to herself it would have been nice.

Despite the fact that it had only been a few hours since he had dropped her at Sydney airport to catch the flight to Adelaide she was missing him already. But she was only planning on being gone for two days. She could last that long.

She had got used to his company very quickly. He made her laugh. He listened when she talked. He made her feel happy and positive. Plus he was gorgeous and smart and good in bed. What wasn't to like?

The only problem was that he didn't want to settle down.

So ultimately he wasn't the man for her. She knew that but it didn't stop her from wishing things were different.

She wanted to find the person she was supposed to spend the rest of her life with. There must be someone out there for her. It wasn't Ben and it wasn't Seb, not unless she could change his mind—an unlikely event— and she was running out of time.

She'd known from the very beginning that his time in Sydney was limited, as was hers, but his holidays started in eight days and she knew he was planning on leaving then. He was heading off on his boat, leaving her to finish her stint in Sydney. She would have another fortnight in Sydney on her own after Seb left and she was already dreading it, not looking forward to being on her own again. She wasn't looking forward to being without Seb, but there wasn't anything she could do about it.

Things were out of her control. She couldn't control his plans and she couldn't conjure up a man. She would just have to be patient.

At least she knew now that she could open her heart. Finding love shouldn't be impossible if she was open to it.

She closed her eyes and rested her head on the window as the bus chugged through the northern suburbs of the city. She fell asleep dreaming of Seb and woke as the bus slowed on its approach into Vickers Hill.

She'd forgotten how dry and brown the countryside could get, even when it was only the beginning of summer. In five weeks she'd already grown used to being surrounded by water, by the ocean, and the blue and sometimes rainy grey of Sydney was very different from the brown and pale, washed-out grey of the Clare Valley.

The scenery was unfamiliar but the smell was the same. She could smell the dust in the air. It smelt like home but did it feel like home? She wouldn't know until she got off the bus.

The bus pulled up in the main street of Vickers Hill. She wanted to go and see Flick, there was so much to tell her, but she needed to see her parents first. She checked her watch. They would be having lunch. Her father would have taken the day off to bury his brother, Callum would have him covered, but even when he was working her parents had a tradition where her father would break for lunch and go home and eat with her mother. Luci would join them and then attend the funeral. There would be time to see Flick later.

The funeral had gone as well as could be expected. A death was always sad but her uncle had been old and it had been his time. Luci couldn't help thinking that her father might be next, though. She would feel so differently if it had been her father's funeral. He was younger than his brother, but not by many years, and she wanted him to live long enough to see his grandchildren. She wanted to give him that gift. Her parents had nieces and nephews and great-nieces and great-nephews but Luci knew it wasn't the same thing as grandchildren.

Ben along with several of Luci's cousins and nephews had been the pallbearers for her uncle's coffin. She had watched Ben as he had helped to carry her uncle out of the church and into the graveyard beside it. Her parents supported her uncle's wife, her aunt by marriage and Ben's great-aunt, as they buried her husband.

Luci chatted to her cousins as everyone made their way from the church to the wake, which was being held in the beer garden at the back of the local pub. She spent the next half-hour talking to familiar faces but she felt out of place. Having changed in the past few weeks, she wasn't sure she belonged here any more.

She was thinking about leaving, about excusing herself to get some breathing space, when she saw Ben approaching. She looked for Catriona but couldn't see her. She hadn't noticed her in the church either. It was too late to escape now as he was heading right for her, so she waited; she couldn't avoid him for ever.

He greeted her with a kiss and Luci waited to see what effect that had but she felt nothing. No regret. No desire. It was like greeting an old friend and she supposed that's now what they were. They had been friends for too long to cut him out of her life altogether. She could do platonic kisses.

'Hi, Luce, you're looking well.'

In contrast, she thought he looked tired. He was a little greyer at the temples. Perhaps a little bit heavier. It had only been a few months since she'd last seen him so how much could he have changed? Or was she just comparing him to Seb?

She pushed Seb out of her mind.

'Hello, Ben. How are you? How's Catriona? *Where's* Catriona?' Luci wondered if Catriona was too pregnant, too uncomfortable to stand at the funeral.

'She's in hospital. Our baby was born yesterday.'

'Oh.' Luci was taken by surprise. Why hadn't her mother told her? Warned her? Was everyone still trying to protect her?

Or perhaps with everything else going on in her family this week it had slipped her parents' minds. Her mother had a habit of telling her things twice or not at all, getting confused between what she'd told Luci's father and what she'd told Luci. Luci supposed she couldn't blame her for forgetting in the scheme of things. Ben and Catriona's baby didn't really matter to Luci, and why should it matter to her mother?

She didn't need protecting. She was sad for herself, but she didn't begrudge Ben his happiness.

She really had moved on, she realised. She'd been talking the talk but without really knowing. This was the test and it was good to find she could be happy for Ben.

'Congratulations,' she said.

Ben was watching her closely. 'I'm sorry. I didn't realise you didn't know. I thought someone would have said something. I wasn't planning on being the one to tell you.'

'It's okay. I would have found out sooner or later. What did you have?'

'A daughter.'

A baby girl. 'Details?' she asked, pleased to know she could remember the niceties.

'Seven pounds three ounces and we've named her Mia.'

Luci breathed a silent sigh of relief. She'd been worried that Ben might choose one of the names they had picked out and she was glad he hadn't. It was highly unlikely that she would get to use the names she'd chosen, Eve for a girl or Joe for a boy, but even so she didn't want Ben to use 'their' names.

'I'm happy for you,' she told him truthfully. She knew he wanted children just as much as she did. She couldn't begrudge him that happiness, but it didn't negate the sadness she felt that she was still childless.

She should go and find Ben's parents, her ex-in-laws, and congratulate them. She knew that by doing that, it would help to stop any unwanted smalltown gossip. She would be doing herself a favour. And it would give her a reason to say goodbye to Ben. She was ready for that. She didn't want him back but she couldn't deny that she was jealous of his new life. He had everything she wanted.

She excused herself and was relieved to see Flick making her way through the pub and into the garden. Luci forgot about seeking out her ex-in-laws and made a beeline for her friend, wrapping her in a big hug.

'God, it's so good to see you,' she said.

'Sorry I couldn't come to the funeral,' Flick replied as she hugged her back. 'Callum was covering the clinic for your dad so he needed me to help him.'

Flick had a sparkle in her eye. She looked well. Happy. But Luci was too preoccupied to pay any more attention than that.

'Why didn't you tell me Ben and Catriona had the baby?'

Flick shrugged. 'She was only born yesterday. I figured your mum would tell you and we'd talk about it today. Who did tell you?'

'Ben.'

'Oh, hell. Are you okay?'

Luci nodded. 'I think so. Sad for me, if I'm honest, but otherwise okay. I'll hold it together. I'm not going to give anyone here the satisfaction of seeing me fall apart. I'm tired of being the one everyone talks about.'

'Well, don't get your hopes up.' Flick laughed. 'No doubt they'll be talking about you again now that you're back and everyone has seen you talking to Ben.'

'I'm not back for good,' Luci responded, and wondered whether that was really how she felt. Could she come back permanently?

She wasn't sure.

But where else would she go?

She had no idea.

'You're not thinking of staying in Sydney, are you?' Flick asked. 'Are you enjoying it that much?'

Luci kept quiet, which was a mistake.

Flick jumped straight to a conclusion. 'OMG, is it Seb?'

She'd told Flick a little bit about him. Not everything. She wanted to keep some of what they'd shared to herself but it had been obvious in her conversations that they'd been spending a lot of time together and Luci hadn't been able to keep the happiness from spilling into her voice.

'I'd stay in a heartbeat if he asked me to but I can't see that happening.'

When Luci saw the expression on Flick's face—eyes wide open, jaw dropping—she realised she'd said the words out loud and remembered that Flick was working with Seb's brother. 'Promise me you won't say anything to Callum!' she hissed.

'Why would I? But does Seb know how you feel?'

Luci shook her head. 'Of course not. It's just a bit of fun.'

'Seriously? That doesn't sound like you.'

'What do you mean by that?'

'Well, you have to admit that even for around here you settled down early. You were always the one who was going to have the serious relationships.'

'Seb is only in Sydney for another week. I can't afford to get serious.'

'So you're just using him for sex.'

'Shh!'

'Well, you are doing the deed, aren't you?'

'Yes.' Luci blushed, thinking about the sex. Where and when and how good it had been. 'And often,' she added, wanting to see Flick's reaction.

Flick laughed. 'You go, girl! So why is it just a bit of fun? Why can't it be more serious than that? It doesn't matter if he's leaving Sydney. You could go with him.'

'No.' Luci shook her head again, knowing she was trying to convince herself as much as Flick. 'It's not a long-term proposition. Not at all. We want different things out of life. He's great but he doesn't want to settle down. I can't afford to waste time on someone who doesn't want the same things as me.'

It was a pity. Such a pity. Luci understood why he felt that way but it was still a shame. He didn't know what he was missing.

But did she? Why was it that she was so desperate to have kids? Could she be content without them?

She didn't know what she was missing either but she just knew that something was. There was a yearning in her heart. Not only for a partner but for a family.

She knew what she needed to make herself complete. A man wouldn't be enough. And if she knew that she needed to be a mother without ever having been one, who was to say that Seb couldn't know he didn't want to be a father? That wasn't for her to judge.

Flick opened her mouth and Luci had the suspicion that she was about to tell her something important but right at that moment the crowd went silent. All at once.

Heads turned as the noise ceased and all eyes were focused on the door that led from the pub out to the garden.

Standing in the doorway was Seb.

CHAPTER NINE

IT WAS IMMEDIATELY obvious that he wasn't from around here and it had nothing to do with the fact that he was a tall, dark, handsome stranger. You could always expect a few strangers at a funeral but Seb wasn't wearing the country uniform. All the male mourners were wearing smart jeans, their polished boots and a shirt that was obviously kept for best. Seb was wearing neatly ironed chino pants, a black T-shirt and his leather jacket. The other men all had suntanned faces with white foreheads where their hats sat, and despite the hours Seb spent on the water he didn't have the same weathered look of years spent outdoors.

The stunned silence was followed by a swell of murmuring as everyone tried to figure out who this man was. Luci could hear people asking each other if they knew him.

'OMG, what is he doing here?' she muttered.

She could feel Flick looking from her back to Seb and back to her and she knew Flick's jaw had dropped open again.

'Is that him?'

Luci nodded. She couldn't speak.

'Holy…' Flick said under her breath. 'He looks like

more than just a *bit* of fun. He looks like a whole *lot* of fun.'

'Shush,' Luci said, whacking Flick on the arm before making a beeline for Seb. She had to get him out of the pub. People had only just moved on from discussing her and Ben and she knew there was no way they'd be able to resist talking about her again now that they'd laid eyes on Seb and realised he was here for her.

Was he here for her? she wondered as she was halfway across the room. Maybe he was here to see Callum? Although that made no sense whatsoever. She knew that the two brothers didn't even talk that often, so why would he have travelled halfway across the country to see him?

He was grinning widely by the time she reached his side. His blue eyes sparkled and to keep herself from jumping into his arms she grabbed his elbow and pulled him back through the doorway, out of the garden and into the pub. She would have kept walking too, wanting to get him right out of the building and into the street, away from flapping ears and prying eyes, but Seb planted his feet and once he did that she had about as much chance of moving him as a mosquito had in a cyclone.

'What are you doing here?'

They were in a short, narrow corridor between the pub kitchen and the rest rooms and it was only a matter of time before they were interrupted, but Seb didn't seem to mind. He leaned against the wall and pulled her into him. She could see he was about to kiss her and she wasn't going to let him do that. Not in front of her family and the rest of the town.

She put her hands on his chest, keeping them separated by a few inches of air, but the gesture hardly afforded her any protection. His chest was firm and solid under her fingers and his thighs were strong and powerful against her legs. She could feel herself melting into him as her resistance weakened. She might as well have let him kiss her, the effect would have been the same.

'I thought you might be finding things difficult,' he said. 'I wanted to be here for you.'

She was touched that he had even thought that, let alone jumped on a plane and somehow made it to Vickers Hill just hours after she had. He was gorgeous. She couldn't believe he was standing in front of her, in her home town, looking at her with his blue eyes and ridiculously long, dark eyelashes. She'd been wishing he was here and somehow her wish had come true. She wasn't going to deny that it was good to see him.

'I love it that you're here,' she told him. And she did, except for the fact that the gossip mill was going to go into overdrive again, but that wasn't his fault. She couldn't expect him to understand how her home town worked. She'd just have to deal with the questions later. 'But my uncle was old so while a funeral is never the best situation it's okay. I think my dad is going to find it hard but I'm all right.'

'I wasn't thinking about your uncle. I was thinking that you would be seeing Ben and Catriona. I thought that would be hard on you. I wanted to be here to support you.'

'Oh.' He really was incredible. She couldn't believe he had come all this way for her. 'Catriona had the baby yesterday.'

'Did you know?'

Luci shook her head.

'How are you feeling?'

'Mixed emotions, if I'm totally honest. I'm actually pleased for Ben that he's found happiness and I'm not sorry that he's had a child, but I am sorry that it might not happen for me.' She didn't want Ben, there was no sense of longing, of wishing they were still a couple. The spark was well and truly extinguished, but she did want what he had.

'I'm here for you. Just tell me what you need me to do. Do you want to get out of here?' he asked.

She did. Desperately. She wanted Seb to take her away from all this. Now that he was here she knew he would be all she could think about. But he'd asked her what she needed, not what she wanted. And she needed to have dinner with her parents.

She shook her head. 'I'm supposed to be having dinner with my family.' She didn't want to introduce him to anyone, she wasn't ready for that. She didn't want to explain or start any rumours. It wasn't worth it when it would all be over in a week. These considerate gestures that Seb insisted on making—turning up here to offer support, walking with her across the harbour bridge, bringing her a cup of tea every morning in bed—not to mention being simply gorgeous, were going to make it hard to walk away, but there was no other option. That was the agreement they had made. She wasn't ready for the end yet. But it wasn't her choice.

'Why don't you do that, then, and I'll see if I can catch up with Cal and meet you later. After dinner.'

He didn't push her for an invite. He seemed to know what she needed before she did. She wanted to go with him now but knowing he would be waiting for her at the end of the day was enough. She was glad he was here.

She nodded. 'Okay. Where are you staying?' she asked, hoping he wasn't staying at Callum's. That was her house. That would be weird.

'I booked a room at the hotel.'

She didn't need to hear any more. That was perfect.

'Room eleven,' he added with a wink and a grin, and Luci nearly gave in right then. She was sorely tempted to ditch the family dinner in favour of jumping into bed with Seb.

But instead she had to be content with grabbing a fistful of his shirt and pulling him towards her. She kissed him hard, not caring who saw them. She didn't care any more. He had come all this way for her and she didn't want to waste a minute of the time they had left together.

She'd be gone again tomorrow. Let them talk.

'I'll see you later,' she said as she pushed him out of the pub.

Luci sneaked into her parents' house just before sunrise, avoiding the fourth and ninth floorboards in the hall because she knew they creaked. She felt like a teenager again, even though she knew she shouldn't have to worry. After all, she'd been married and divorced, but old habits died hard.

She hoped they were asleep. She didn't want to explain where she'd been, what she'd been doing. She had spent the night in Seb's bed and after saying goodbye he'd headed off early in order to make it back to Adelaide in time for his return flight.

Luci climbed into her old bed but she couldn't sleep. Her mind was turning in circles.

She needed to start planning her next move. To work

out how she was going to fulfil her dreams. Seb wasn't going to be a part of that. She knew he didn't want a proper relationship and she was determined to fulfil her dreams of motherhood one way or another. She assumed it would have to be through adoption and she wanted to find a partner who would support her in that. She couldn't afford to waste time on Seb. They had eight more days together and then it would be over. They would go back to their own lives. She couldn't focus on Seb, there were more important things for her to worry about.

The decisions were hers to make and hers alone.

Luci disembarked from the plane in Sydney and switched on her phone. As expected, there was a message from Seb asking her to text when she arrived safely, but there was also one from her GP, asking her to call back. Luci waited until she got back to the apartment to return the call.

'Could you come in for a chat?' her GP asked. 'There's something I need to discuss with you.'

Her GP was in the neighbouring town to Vickers Hill. Luci hadn't wanted to see anyone with ties to her dad's clinic so ever since she'd got her driver's licence she'd made the fifteen-minute drive along the highway.

'Actually, I can't,' she said. 'I'm in Sydney. Is there a problem? I'll be here for another three weeks.' Luci couldn't imagine what it was about. She was perfectly healthy and so was everyone else, as far as she knew.

'Can you talk now?'

'Yes,' she said, sitting on the couch.

'I received a letter today from the lab that did your fertility tests. The letter contains your test results.

Apparently they were upgrading their computer system at the same time that you went for testing and some of the results were mistakenly filed as "sent" when they were actually pending. The lab has only just realised their mistake. I'm sorry, I never realised that these weren't forwarded to you. You haven't been in for an appointment.'

'It doesn't matter,' Luci replied. 'It turns out the results were irrelevant.'

'What do you mean?'

'It was obvious that the problem was with me. Ben had no trouble getting Catriona pregnant. The results don't matter, it's not like I'm in a situation to have a baby now. I'm divorced and single, I'm not trying to get pregnant any more.'

'I still think you should know the results. It's not quite as simple as you think. The tests indicated that the problem wasn't solely with you.'

'What does that mean? Ben's reproductive system seems to work fine.'

'The problem was with the two of you together.' Luci frowned as Veronica continued. 'Your body was producing antibodies against Ben's sperm. It's very uncommon and especially rare to see in women, but it meant that your body was having a kind of allergic reaction to the sperm. The antibodies attach to the sperm and impair motility, making it harder for the sperm to penetrate the cervical mucus and therefore fertilise the egg. IVF would have been a relatively simple procedure for you. In your situation there would have been a high chance of success for the two of you.'

'What?' Luci couldn't believe what she was hearing.

'We could have had children?' They could have had the family she'd dreamed of?

'With IVF assistance, almost certainly,' Veronica agreed.

'How?'

'The sperm would be injected directly into the harvested egg. If the sperm aren't swimming freely there would have been no opportunity for your body to attack. The antibodies wouldn't have had a chance to attach to the sperm. With IVF a viable embryo would have been created and it would then have been implanted.'

'So I can have kids?' Luci still wasn't absolutely sure that she was getting the right message. Was that what Veronica was telling her? She held her breath as she waited for the final confirmation.

'Yes. Either with the right partner or with IVF.'

Luci breathed out as tears welled in her eyes.

'It's rare for a woman to produce anti-sperm antibodies so it's quite likely that with a different partner you wouldn't have the same issues,' Veronica went on, but Luci was only half listening. She was still processing the idea that she could have children.

'But don't forget, this condition is very successfully overcome with IVF assistance. Identifying this is a good thing.' Veronica was still speaking. 'You and Ben may have been incompatible but that doesn't mean all men will be. And there's more good news. Your eggs were healthy. You're young and fertile. You have time. It will happen for you, I'm sure of it.'

'Thank you.'

Tears spilled out of Luci's eyes and rolled down her cheeks as she ended the call. Mixed emotions engulfed her. The news was incredible but it was tinged with anger and regret. Just when she felt she had come to terms with the demise of her marriage to find out that Ben's betrayal had robbed her of her dream of motherhood was almost too much to bear. When she had thought she couldn't fall pregnant she'd been able to forgive him for leaving her. She had blamed herself as much as him. But now?

If he had stayed they could have worked this out. With IVF *she* could have been the one who had just had a baby. She could be a mother now.

She needed to think. She needed a walk to help focus her mind. She changed into a pair of shorts and her sneakers and headed for the beach.

As she walked she realised it was unlikely that her marriage would have survived regardless. They had broken up because of the stress of infertility but Ben had very quickly moved on. If she'd been unable to rely on him to stick by her through that situation she knew she wouldn't have been able to rely on him for anything else. Quite possibly he would have run for the hills the moment the going had got tough. Quite possibly she would have ended up divorced with a baby.

Would she want to be a single mother?

Yes.

If she could have a baby without a partner she knew she would take that opportunity. She had never imagined herself as a single mother but she knew that if that was her only option she wouldn't hesitate any more. She still wanted a baby more than anything.

More than she wanted Seb?

Yes. Her heart ached with longing and her womb ached with emptiness. A baby was very much her priority.

She had fallen in love with Seb but planning a future

with him had never been realistic and especially not now. He was her second ever boyfriend and she wasn't even sure she could call him that. They weren't thinking about the future and he didn't want commitment. He didn't want to settle down and she was pretty sure he wasn't going to want kids.

She would have to break up with him. It was her only option.

She wanted it all but if she couldn't have it all she was going to choose motherhood, or the possibility of it at least, and if her dream was to become a reality she needed to find the man who could help her to make that happen.

Which meant she needed to break up with Seb.

He was starting his holidays at the end of the week. He was heading off in his boat so their relationship wasn't going to last any longer than that anyway, no matter what she wished for, so the best thing to do would be to end it now. Quickly and swiftly. Waiting a couple more days wasn't going to make it any easier. She needed to move on to the rest of her life.

The decision was made. Now all she had to do was tell him.

Telling him would give him the chance to change his mind if he wanted to and she knew she was still hopeful that he would make that choice. Perhaps he would decide that she was worth it.

The sun was low in the sky as she returned to the apartment. Her phone buzzed in her pocket. She pulled it out and looked at the caller ID. Seb.

'Where are you? Is everything okay?'

He sounded worried but she didn't think she could

put his mind at ease so she opted for a simple reply. 'I'm almost home. I'll see you in a minute.'

But Callum's apartment wasn't home. And Vickers Hill hadn't felt like home either.

Luci knew she wouldn't be going back to Vickers Hill. She'd felt like a fish out of water there. Everyone was settled or, worse, if they weren't she had known them all her life and she knew she wasn't going to find the man she was looking for amongst them. She needed new faces. New places. She had no idea where she would go but she knew she wouldn't go back.

She would need to find somewhere that felt right.

Also, she needed a man, or his sperm at the very least, and a place to live. But one thing at a time. Her first priority was to speak to Seb. She needed to tell him her decision. There was no point delaying. She needed to get on with things. She was a girl with a mission.

The door to the apartment was open. Seb was waiting for her. He still looked worried. There was a little crease between his eyebrows and his blue eyes were dark with concern. But she almost didn't notice. It was a hot night and he was dressed only in a pair of shorts. Shirtless and bare-chested, she found it hard to notice anything else.

He looked incredible. She'd almost forgotten how gorgeous he was. She should ask him to put a shirt on, she wasn't going to be able to concentrate when he was semi-naked, but she resisted. Why deprive herself of her last chance to see him like this? She could use the memory.

He greeted her with a hug. God, that felt good. His arms were strong, his embrace warm, and Luci could have stayed there quite happily for the rest of her life.

'I've missed you,' he said as he let her go. 'Is anything wrong?' He ran a thumb under her eye and Luci's knees buckled slightly at his touch. 'Have you been crying?'

Her tears had dried long ago but she knew her eyes would still be puffy and red. She wiped a hand across them. 'Yes. But they were happy tears, I think.'

'You think? What's going on?'

'I need to sit down.'

Seb ushered her to the couch. 'Can I get you anything?'

She shook her head. 'No. But I need to talk to you.' Luci launched into her news. She knew if she waited she'd chicken out. She was sorely tempted to spend one last night with Seb and tell him tomorrow but it wouldn't be any easier then. She needed to do this now. 'I had a phone call from my GP today. She was calling about some test results. Results that I should have got ages ago but the lab made a mistake. I didn't really notice that the results hadn't come back because of everything else that was going on at the time between Ben and me.'

'Are you okay?'

'Yes. I'm perfectly okay. That was what she was ringing me about. Apparently I am perfectly healthy and fertile. I can have children. The problem wasn't with me. It was with *Ben* and me. But even so we could have had a family together if we'd stuck it out. IVF would have fixed it.'

'Wow.' Seb sat back and ran his hands through his hair. The muscles in his arms and chest flexed and Luci averted her gaze so she wasn't tempted to throw herself into his arms. 'Does Ben know?'

She shook her head. 'No.'

'Are you going to tell him?'

'I hadn't thought about it. Probably not. It doesn't matter to him any more. He's moved on. I have too. My marriage is over but now I have a chance to fulfil my dream of having a family. I *am* going to chase that dream. Which means I need to find the man who wants to follow that same dream, the man who wants to share my future. I know that's not what you want so I need to say goodbye.'

'Now?'

Luci nodded. She knew it would be hard. It was so tempting to spend their last remaining nights together but she knew the longer she waited the harder it would get. If her heart was going to break she wanted to get it over and done with.

'You'll be gone in a few days anyway. We both knew it was only a bit of fun, just a temporary arrangement. It was always a matter of when, not if, and I need to move on to the next phase of my life. I appreciate every minute, everything we have shared, you have helped me more than you'll ever know. I know I'm ready to let someone else into my life now.'

'What are you going to do?'

'I'm not sure yet. Finish off my last two weeks here while I try to work out what this all means and then I don't know what. But I'm not going back to Vickers Hill. I doubt the man for me is there and I'm not sure that a big city is for me either.'

'So that's it? This is goodbye?'

She nodded, forcing herself to stay strong. 'We don't want the same things, Seb. We've both been honest about that. I was always going to want to find a way to have a family. You've always said that isn't on your agenda. I need to go.'

Now was his chance to tell her he'd changed his mind. That he couldn't live without her. She held her breath, waiting to see what he would do.

'Okay.' Seb sat forward, resting his elbows on his knees, and sighed. Luci stretched out one hand, wanting to run it over his back, but she hesitated just inches from his skin then pulled her hand away. She didn't know if he wanted or needed comfort.

Seb pushed himself to his feet and turned to face her. His blue eyes were still troubled but his voice was strong. He nodded his head. 'I respect the fact it's your decision to make. I'll just grab a few things and I'll sleep on the boat.'

Disappointment flooded Luci's chest and surged through her belly. She'd pinned her hopes on him changing his mind, even though she'd known it was a long shot, and it was devastating to know that he wasn't going to argue with her. That he wasn't going to change his mind. But neither was she.

She wanted to tell him that he didn't need to leave tonight but then realised it was probably better if he did. He wasn't the man for her future. He had been a perfect interlude but she couldn't let emotion derail her dreams.

But saying goodbye to Seb took some of the gloss off her dream. Gaining the knowledge that she could have kids meant she was losing him. She needed to remember he had never really been hers in the first place.

This was goodbye.

She loved him but that was irrelevant. She had said she would give her right arm to have a chance at motherhood; giving up Seb was much harder.

She wasn't going to let the chance to have a baby feel like a consolation prize. She wanted a child more than anything. She had to remember that. But that didn't stop the tears from flowing again as she watched him walk out the door with his duffel bag and bike helmet. He travelled light, leaving only with what he'd come with, and taking her heart with him.

CHAPTER TEN

SEB HAD FINISHED his stint at the family and community health clinic. He was gone and Luci was doing her best to focus on her job. She had two days left before she went back to Vickers Hill for Christmas. She still hadn't decided what she would do after that. She'd make a final decision after the Christmas break. Hopefully by then her head would have cleared and she'd be able to think straight. She was having difficulty focusing, her thoughts turning constantly to Seb, and her heart was hurting so badly it was making her feel nauseous. She knew she had done the right thing, saying goodbye to him, but that wasn't making it any less painful.

The nausea was so bad today that she'd actually vomited up her breakfast and hadn't been able to keep anything down since. She felt like she might have contracted a virus. She had five minutes before her next appointment so she quickly took her temperature while she checked her emails. There was one from the doctor's wife in Budgee and Luci noticed it had been copied to Seb. She scanned the message. The doctor's wife had forwarded it from Nadine. She had wanted to send photos of her twins to Seb and Luci.

Luci opened the attachment. The twins appeared to

be thriving. It was amazing to see how much they had developed in four weeks. They were both starting to fill out and their chocolate-brown eyes were shining. Luci felt a pang of envy but she had hope now and the knowledge that one day she might be holding a baby of her own in her arms was making it easier to cope with all the pregnant clients and newborn babies she seemed to have on her list.

After an uncertain start in community health she was now enjoying getting to know her patients and being able to give continuity of care was rewarding. It was very different from working in a hospital and she had managed to establish good relationships with several of the regular clients, which was extremely satisfying. Melanie Parsons was a good example. She and her kids had been in to see her several times and Melanie appeared to be coping much better. She and her husband were both attending counselling and her husband had also joined AA. Luci was pleased that she had been able to witness what she hoped would be the start of something better for their family. Seeing the change in Melanie and getting emails from patients like Nadine made her feel that she was making a difference and doing something worthwhile, even if her heart was breaking.

The thermometer beeped and Luci closed her emails and read the display as her diary flashed to indicate that her next client had arrived. Her temperature was slightly elevated—she'd take something for that after she'd finished her next consult.

'What can I help you with today, Shauna?' she asked as her client sat and settled her toddler on her knee.

'I think I might be pregnant again.'

Luci waited for the usual stab of jealousy but it didn't

come. She didn't need to feel jealous any more, she was
certain pregnancy would happen for her one day. 'Have
you done a test?'

'I've done a couple,' Shauna said. 'One came back
positive and one was negative but I've got all the usual
symptoms. I feel sick, my boobs hurt and I need to go
to the toilet constantly. I thought maybe you could do
another test.'

Luci took a jar for a urine sample from the cupboard
and handed it to Shauna.

She tested it when Shauna returned. 'It's negative.
When was your last period?'

'Three weeks ago.'

'It might just be too early.'

The conversation made Luci think of her own situation. When had her last period been? she wondered.
She did a quick mental calculation. It had been almost
six weeks ago.

She and Seb had practised safe sex most of the time
but that night on Seb's boat, during the thunderstorm
and in the heat of the moment, protection had been the
last thing on her mind. She hadn't thought anything of
it then. Sex that night had been spontaneous, contraception hadn't been an issue for her then, and she hadn't
given it a moment's thought.

Maybe she was pregnant?

But that eventuality was more than likely just wishful thinking. Mind over matter. She was probably putting two and two together and getting five, she thought.
But the minute Shauna left the consulting room she took
a standard pregnancy test from the cupboard for herself.

She took it into the bathroom. She knew what she

was looking for. She'd done dozens of these. She was looking for two pink lines.

She waited. She'd never seen the two pink lines before.

Until today.

She double-checked the window. She leaned over the basin and triple-checked but the lines still remained.

Her knees buckled and she sat back on the toilet seat.

That explained the nausea and her slightly elevated temperature.

Her hand went to her stomach.

She was pregnant.

Seb was into his second week of holidays. He should be somewhere far away from Sydney. His plan had been to take his boat and travel but he hadn't been able to bring himself to leave. Not while Luci was still in town.

He'd realised too late that he should never have left so hurriedly the night Luci had said goodbye. He should have stayed and argued his case, only he hadn't known he'd had a case. Not then.

His knee-jerk reaction had been to leave. He didn't want to settle down, to commit—at least, that was what he'd been telling himself for three years—and it had taken him a while to realise he'd changed his mind. That *Luci* had made him change his mind. She had brought the light back into his life and her absence had taken it away again.

They had said goodbye but he hadn't been able to sever the ties so he sat on his boat, alone, in Fairlight Bay, watching the lights go on and off in Callum's apartment and wondering what Luci was up to. How she was doing. If she was missing him.

For the past three years he had been working toward fixing his boat, making it habitable on a permanent basis, but now he felt trapped. It was supposed to be his sanctuary but instead it felt like a prison cell. He escaped its confines every day, taking his bike from the garage he'd rented and cruising the highways, but the feeling of freedom never lasted. He didn't want to be free. He didn't want to be able to come and go as he pleased. He didn't want to be alone. He wanted to be with Luci.

He shouldn't miss her and he knew he should be pleased for her. She had an opportunity to be a mother, had a chance to get what she'd always wanted. But he wanted that to be him.

He had spent the last three years convincing himself, and everyone else, that he was fine, that he was happy to be alone, but he hadn't stopped to see if he actually was and now that Luci was gone from his life and he was alone again he realised that he wasn't okay. He needed her in his life.

He needed her.

He loved her.

And he didn't want to think about Luci finding another man. He didn't want to give someone else the chance he'd thrown away.

Once again he hadn't realised how badly he wanted something until it was gone but, unlike last time, it wasn't too late. He wanted Luci in his life and he would do what he could to keep her.

She wanted a family and he wanted her. Could he give her what she wanted?

He was going to have to because he couldn't imagine his life without her in it.

All he needed to know was whether or not she wanted him.

He knew she was due to leave Sydney tomorrow but he didn't know where she was headed. What were her plans? What was she going to do?

He only had a few hours to find out. It was two days until Christmas and Luci was due to leave Sydney on Christmas Eve.

He had one last chance to see her.

Luci had finished cleaning the apartment. She was leaving tomorrow. She would be back in Vickers Hill for Christmas.

She went into Callum's bedroom, just for one final check to make sure it was clean and tidy, although she knew it was. Seb had changed the sheets and tidied up. She knew because she was in here every day, thinking about him. She sat on the bed and ran her hands over the covers. They were tucked tight, not a stray crease in sight. Almost as if Seb had never been there.

She thought about the first night they'd made love. It had been in this bed. They'd been in too much of a hurry to get any further; they'd barely made it to here. But the bed showed no sign of their intimacy. It was almost as if it never happened.

But she had proof that it wasn't a dream.

Her hand went to her stomach.

There was the proof of what they had shared. She had all the proof she needed.

She had two things left to do—pack her bags and then see if she could get hold of Seb.

She had debated about when she should speak to him, when she should give him the news. She had thought about waiting until thirteen weeks, or maybe even eighteen, after her first scan, until she knew everything was all right, but she had decided it would be better to tell him face-to-face while she was still in Sydney, and she knew part of her wanted an excuse to see him one last time before she left.

There would be no easy way to share her news and she knew he didn't like surprises but he had the right to know about the baby. Their baby.

He had the right to have the opportunity to choose to be involved. Or not. She had no idea what he would choose to do but that was his prerogative.

Luci hadn't really ever expected to end up a single mother. Before the phone call from her GP she had assumed she would have to adopt in order to have a family and adopting in South Australia meant she needed a partner. She had assumed she would need to find a man.

But now she had the opportunity she'd been wanting—the chance to be a mother. A month ago she would have leapt at the chance, any chance, to hold a baby of her own in her arms, so why did she now want more? She knew she could manage on her own. She knew she didn't need a partner. The trouble was, this wasn't about what she needed. It was about what she wanted.

So she was getting what she'd always wanted, except now she wanted more. She wanted Seb too.

Although she knew she should be content with what was in store for her, it was hard when her heart ached constantly for what was missing from her life. She had traded one heartache for another. Why couldn't she have it all?

She stood up. She needed to get moving. Procrastination never solved anything.

She was staring at the clothes in her wardrobe, wondering where to start, when she was interrupted by a knock on the door.

She opened the door and burst into tears.

Seb was standing on the other side.

'Luci, what on earth's the matter?' he asked as he stepped across the threshold. He opened his arms and gathered her up, holding her close.

She let him comfort her. She was right where she wanted to be. If only she could just stay here, maybe everything would turn out as she hoped.

She cried into his shoulder and sniffed as she said, 'Nothing, I'm just tired. I haven't been sleeping well.' *Plus I'm an emotional wreck and I'm carrying your baby.* But that was *not* the way to deliver her news.

'Are you unwell?'

He stepped back, releasing her from his arms but not letting go completely. It felt good to have her in his arms again but he'd needed to see her. He'd needed to make sure she was okay. She looked like she had lost weight and her blue-grey eyes were filled with tears, but otherwise she looked fantastic. Her skin glowed and she looked perfectly healthy.

'No,' she said. 'I'm fine. I'm glad you're here.'

'Are you sure? You don't look happy to see me.'

She laughed and Seb breathed a sigh of relief. She sounded like the Luci he loved, full of laughter and happiness even if she had just been sobbing in his arms.

'Of course I am. I've missed you.'

Good. That cheered him up. Perhaps things would turn out in his favour. 'I've missed you too.'

She was looking up at him. Her eyes were shining and her pink lips were slightly parted, like an opening rosebud. He had come here to talk to her, to beg her for another chance, but he couldn't resist. He bent his head and kissed her.

She sighed gently and leaned into him and he felt her arms loop around his neck as she kissed him back. Soft and supple in his arms, he could feel his soul being restored as he held her. She tasted like heaven and he wished he could stay like this for eternity.

But he needed to find out if that was possible.

'Luci,' he sighed as he pulled away. He kept a finger under her chin, keeping her face tilted up at him. 'I need to talk to you.'

'Oh.' Something flashed behind her eyes. Was it disappointment?

He took her hand and led her to the couch. The place was spotless and its tidiness served to remind him that his time was limited. If he didn't get this problem resolved tonight, it would be too late. She would be gone.

He kept hold of her hand as they sat, making her sit close to him.

'What is it?' she asked. 'Is something wrong?'

Seb nodded. 'Yes. I've made a mistake. A big one. But I'm hoping it's not too late to fix it. I've discovered a pattern.'

'A pattern?'

'It's a problem I have,' he told her, 'where I can't seem to work out I want something until it's gone. But I'm hoping this time I haven't left it too late.'

'I'm not following you. Left what too late?'

'Us. I don't want to lose you. I don't want to let you go.' He picked up her other hand, holding them both, keeping her close. 'You have brought light back into my life. A purpose. An energy. A reason to look forward to the day. I didn't know what my life was lacking until you came into it. I thought I was okay on my own. Happy even. But I was kidding myself. I was surviving. I wasn't living and I definitely wasn't happy.

'I've missed you,' he said honestly. 'I look for you, I listen for you. I want to hear your laugh, I want to see your smile. I want to be the one who *makes* you smile. I don't want you to leave. I came here tonight to ask if you would consider staying in Sydney. With me. I want to see if we can make something of this thing between us. Before it's too late.'

He very rarely spoke about his feelings and he certainly hadn't bared as much of his soul in the past three years but it didn't seem to make any difference. Luci was shaking her head. 'It *is* too late. I'm going home.'

'Back to Vickers Hill?'

She nodded.

Seb's heart plummeted like a stone and settled heavily and morosely in his abdomen. He was losing her. 'I thought you'd decided that wasn't the place for you.'

'My circumstances have changed.'

How much could have changed in two weeks? Did she feel nothing for him?

'Have you met someone else?' Surely she couldn't have moved on that quickly? He didn't want to think of her with other men. He didn't want to imagine her searching for someone else to share her dream. What was wrong with him? Why couldn't she choose him?

'No, of course not. This is a practical decision. A financial one. I can't afford to start again.'

Despite the flicker of hope that had come to life as soon as Seb had started talking, Luci had other things to consider now. Another *person* to consider. She couldn't allow herself to get carried away until she was sure of Seb's feelings. Vickers Hill had been good enough for her growing up, it was a good place to raise a family and she would have support there. All the things she had hated at times about a small country town were now the reasons she was moving back. She knew people would rally around her. If she was going to be a single mother she wanted to do it somewhere familiar. Somewhere safe. 'This is the next stage of my journey.'

'Can you take that next stage with me?'

She shook her head, still determined not to jump head first too soon. 'You know I can't. You know what I want. Being a mother is something I've always wanted. If I have to choose between having a family and having you, I will choose children. I'm sorry. I wish I could have both but that's up to you.'

Luci had dreamed of Seb choosing to be with her but he had to choose everything. He had to choose her dream as well as her. This was her chance to see how he felt without telling him about the baby. She didn't want to force his hand, she didn't want him to feel that he had to make promises he wouldn't be able to keep, but she had nothing to lose now. If he didn't want a family she could still walk away.

'Luci, I love you and I want a future with you.'

'You love me?'

'I do. I know you want a family and I'm asking you to give me a chance. Let's see if we can have that future together.'

'I can't afford to wait. I haven't got time to see if it all works out. I can't.' She took a deep breath. It was now or never. She was either going to get what she wished for or not but either way the time had come to share her news. 'I'm already pregnant.'

'What? When? How?'

'The usual way, I suppose. Ironic, isn't it? I didn't think it could happen for me the usual way but it must have been that night on the boat.'

'In the storm?'

Luci nodded. 'I'm sorry. I know you hate surprises but you need to know.'

'Don't be sorry.' Seb shook his head and his eyes filled with tears. 'I'm going to be a father?'

Luci nodded. She took his hand and put it on her stomach as her nerves escalated another notch. Her dream was so close she could almost taste it and she couldn't stand the thought that it might all slip away. She tried one last time to convince him that things could work out. 'I know loving someone scares you and I understand that this is a big step for you, but you have to have faith that things will be okay. Bad things can happen but they don't always happen. You can't close yourself off just in case you get hurt. I intend to live my life and I want you to live yours. But I would like us to live our lives together, I'd like us to share our dreams. I love you and I think we can make this work but it's up to you. I know this will be a shock, it's a lot to take in and I don't expect you to decide what you want to do tonight, but you should know that I am going to have the baby.'

'Of course you are. And I'm going to be there with you. Every step of the way.'

'Are you sure?'

'Positive. I'm ready for this. I know you didn't want to fall for the first guy who crossed your path and I wanted to give you a chance to decide if you wanted me. That was why I thought we could take our time and see what happened but I know I want you. I know I want a future with you. And a family. I have thought about nothing else for the past two weeks.'

Seb reached for her. Brushing her hair from her face, he bent his head and kissed her and Luci could feel herself blossoming under his touch.

'I love you, Luci, and I promise that will never change.' He smiled at her and his blue eyes sparkled as he added, 'And now you need to invite me home with you for Christmas.'

'You want to come with me?'

'Where else would I be? I want to spend the rest of my life with you and that starts now. Plus I think it's time I met your parents. I need to ask your father for your hand in marriage.'

'You want to get married?'

'I do.'

'My father won't expect you to ask his permission.'

'I think he will and I'd like to do things properly. I need to at least tell him I intend to make an honest woman out of his only daughter before I tell him I knocked her up.'

Luci laughed. 'They probably wouldn't believe you. It's incredible, isn't it?'

Seb nodded. 'It's amazing.' He got off the couch and went down on one knee. He slid his hands under the hem of her shirt, exposing her belly. He kissed it gently and the touch of his lips sent flames of desire racing through her. His hands were on her knees and she felt her thighs fall apart under the caress of his fingers as she waited for him to slide his hands up her legs, but his fingers went no further. He knelt between her thighs but his focus was on her face.

'I came here to see if I could convince you to give me a chance to prove my love. I want to share your dreams with you. I want to share your life. Will you let me love you and our children for the rest of our lives? Will you marry me? Will you be my wife?'

Luci pulled Seb to his feet and wrapped herself in his arms. She kissed him deeply, fighting back tears. Her dreams were coming true but it was not the time for tears. She was getting everything she'd wanted since the moment she'd first laid eyes on Seb. This glorious, gorgeous man wanted to make a life with her and she wasn't going to refuse him.

'I will.'

EPILOGUE

LUCI SAT ON the front veranda and watched the sun rise over the ocean as she nursed her baby. This was one of her favourite times of day.

She and Seb had the best of both worlds. They had moved to the coastal town of Shellharbour after their wedding but were still only a two-hour drive from Manly. They could have a day in the city if they wanted and return to the relative peace and quiet of a large country town. They both had jobs at the local hospital in family and community health, and Luci was considering studying midwifery, but she had time to make that decision. Their daughter, Eve, was only four months old, she still had a couple of months of maternity leave and would only be going back to work part time. They had jobs they enjoyed, a lifestyle they loved, but most importantly they had their family.

Sometimes Luci could hardly breathe when she thought about how wonderful her life was and how much it had changed. Blessed with a daughter, a gorgeous husband and a new life in Shellharbour, she still sometimes wanted to pinch herself.

She lifted her daughter from her breast and held her

up against her shoulder, inhaling her scent of talcum powder, baby lotion and love.

She looked up as she heard soft footsteps on the wooden floorboards. Their house was full of visitors but she'd recognise that rhythm anywhere.

Seb stepped out onto the balcony, followed by the two-year-old Labrador they had somehow inherited with their house. She smiled as she thought about the man she had first met—the motorcycle-riding man who'd been adamant that he was going to live a bachelor life on his boat. Now he was a husband, a father, a home owner and a pet owner who had swapped regular trips to the country with a permanent job in a country town. He had traded his motorbike for a family car but he still had his boat, which he'd named *Diamond Sky*, which was moored in the marina five minutes from home. Their lives had changed dramatically in the course of a year but she knew he was happy and content.

'Merry Christmas, my love.'

Luci lifted her face for a kiss as Seb put a mug of green tea beside her and plucked Eve from her arms.

'Come here, my gorgeous girl.'

Eve gurgled and laughed and reached for her father with chubby little hands. She was a real daddy's girl but Luci didn't mind. She was living her dream.

'You're up early,' Seb said.

He was bare-chested and Luci felt the familiar stirring of longing as she looked at him. Even the sleepless nights associated with a new baby hadn't been able to diminish her desire for her husband.

'You know I love it out here and I didn't want to wake everyone else.'

Seb's parents were staying with them for Christmas. Seb's dad in particular was smitten with Eve and Luci knew that her in-laws saw this time as an opportunity to enjoy the things they'd missed out on with their own boys. Luci's own parents, not wanting to be separated from their first grandchild, had decided to retire to Shellharbour and lived just down the road, and Callum and Flick were also under their roof. Eve was being christened tomorrow and Cal and Flick were to be her godparents.

'We haven't taken on too much, have we? Hosting Christmas and then having Eve's christening?' Seb asked.

Luci shook her head. She was surrounded by family and she couldn't be happier. 'No. This is just what I wanted. Having everyone here with us is perfect.' She stood up and wrapped her arms around Seb and their daughter. 'Life is perfect,' she said as she raised herself onto her toes and kissed her husband. 'I love you. I love you both.'

* * * * *

LET'S TALK

Romance

For exclusive extracts, competitions
and special offers, find us online:

Get in touch on 01413 063232

For all the latest titles coming soon, visit
millsandboon.co.uk/nextmonth

MILLS & BOON

THE HEART OF ROMANCE

A ROMANCE FOR EVERY KIND OF READER

MODERN

Prepare to be swept off your feet by sophisticated, sexy and seductive heroes, in some of the world's most glamourous and romantic locations, where power and passion collide.
8 stories per month.

HISTORICAL

Escape with historical heroes from time gone by. Whether your passion is for wicked Regency Rakes, muscled Vikings or rugged Highlanders, awaken the romance of the past.
6 stories per month.

MEDICAL

Set your pulse racing with dedicated, delectable doctors in the high-pressure world of medicine, where emotions run high, passion, comfort and love are the best medicine.
6 stories per month.

Celebrate true love with tender stories of heartfelt romance, from the rush of falling in love to the joy a new baby can bring, and focus on the emotional heart of a relationship.
8 stories per month.

Indulge in secrets and scandal, intense drama and plenty of hot action with powerful and passionate heroes who have it all: wealth, status, good looks…everything but the right woman.
6 stories per month.

HEROES

Experience all the excitement of a gripping thriller, with a sizzling romance at its heart. Resourceful, true-to-life women and strong, fearless men face danger and desire - a killer combination!
8 stories per month.

DARE

Sensual love stories featuring smart, sassy heroines you'd want as a best friend, and compelling intense heroes who are worthy of them.
4 stories per month.

To see which titles are coming soon, please visit

millsandboon.co.uk/nextmonth

JOIN US ON SOCIAL MEDIA!

Stay up to date with our latest releases, author news and gossip, special offers and discounts, and all the behind-the-scenes action from Mills & Boon...

 millsandboon

 millsandboonuk

millsandboon

might just be true love...

MILLS & BOON
MEDICAL
Pulse-Racing Passion

Set your pulse racing with dedicated, delectable doctors in the high-pressure world of medicine, where emotions run high and passion, comfort and love are the best medicine.

MILLS & BOON
True Love
Romance from the Heart

Celebrate true love with tender stories of
heartfelt romance, from the rush of falling
in love to the joy a new baby can bring,
and a focus on the emotional
heart of a relationship.